PEERLESS DETECTIVE

MICHAEL RALEIGH

DIVERSIONBOOKS

Also by Michael Raleigh

Paul Whelan Mysteries
Death in Uptown
A Body in Belmont Harbor
The Maxwell Street Blues
Killer on Argyle Street
The Riverview Murders

Diversion Books
A Division of Diversion Publishing Corp.
443 Park Avenue South, Suite 1008
New York, New York 10016
www.DiversionBooks.com

For more information, email info@diversionbooks.com

First Diversion Books edition August 2015.
Print ISBN: 978-1-62681-780-7
eBook ISBN: 978-1-62681-242-0

PROLOGUE

The Much-Travelled Billy Fox

Lansing, Michigan, 1977

"See, you'll go home," the sergeant with the pock-marked face had once told Billy Fox, "and the place'll still be there, yeah, sure, but the whole thing will have changed. It won't be what you remembered. It won't be what you hoped."

I've lowered my expectations, Sarge.

In truth, Billy already understood many of the ways in which Lansing had changed for him. He had been gone five years and no longer hoped old fantasies might come true. Once, early on, he had imagined returning to Lansing as a war hero, a decorated veteran. But he'd managed to miss Vietnam. The closest he'd come to combat had been a bar fight in Texas which left him with a scar on the left side of his face and an understanding that in taverns there were limits to freedom of speech.

For Billy, his old life was captured in a photograph he carried in his bag. It wasn't much of a photograph—a battered Polaroid drained of its life by the years and hard use. Faded, cracked, patched crudely by tape across a corner, it was Billy's only picture of himself with Rita. It had been taken that summer, the one he thought of as the summer the old days ended. In the photo, half a dozen bored teenagers posed and mugged on somebody's front stairs. In the center stood Rita and Billy. There wasn't much detail to it, you couldn't even really see Rita's small features. But she was there for him to see, dark-haired and pretty—a contrast to the boy beside her, a gangly fair-skinned boy with a mop of light brown hair and improbable sideburns.

And there was something else, as well, something Billy could still make out in Rita's face—she was tough and streetwise in ways that the boy beside her had not yet fully understood. She came from a hard place and an abusive father, and she took nothing from anyone. An odds maker might have told Billy his chances with this girl were slim. And Billy would not have listened. So it was that she was able to shock him. Just once, but it was all that was needed. Two weeks after the picture was taken, Rita broke up with Billy, saying she would make changes in her life, that she was no longer a child. She said a person could just slip out of her life and into a new one. Billy had no idea what she was talking about, but it was clear that she meant what she said. Just a month later Billy's mother died, and in a gesture of melodrama that even at the time seemed stupid, Billy made his own change—he enlisted. He would serve, see action in Vietnam, prove himself.

And now, more than five years after he'd left, he was returning home to Lansing, Michigan, where he expected to find nothing of his past. He peered out the bus window, and the glass clouded from his breath. He rubbed at it to make his home town appear.

Lansing was dark and wet almost exactly the way it had been the night he'd left home, as though time had stopped and the city had frozen in place. A thick mist hung over it like cobwebbing, and Billy told himself his town was trying to hide from him. The Trailways bus made its last turn coming in, and the nervous man on the seat beside him lurched into him.

"I'm sorry."

"It's all right."

The man's gaze went to Billy's scar. Billy smiled at this jittery middle-aged man. He pulled his carry-on bag up onto his lap. Emboldened, the nervous man asked if Billy lived here.

How to explain his return to his hometown?

I'm here to settle old scores. I'm trying to find out where my life went. I'm here killing time while I try to think of something else to do.

There was a girl.

"No. I used to."

Yeah, this nervous man might understand that one, every guy would.

"So, this is homecoming after the service?"

"Yeah."

Yeah, this is homecoming.

It felt nothing like a homecoming. But he no longer thought of Lansing as home. In truth, he thought of no place as home. It struck him now that he had not felt a part of anything or any place for much of his life.

Indeed, for a brief, horrific time in Denver after his discharge, Billy Fox had been without a home in the purest sense, living on the street in downtown Denver, sleeping in one doorway after another until a worker from a rescue mission turned him onto a series of day labor jobs.

"So you're from Lansing?"

Billy looked at the gray-haired man. "I used to be. I grew up here."

And, Billy wanted to add, *I thought I owned the world.*

To the other man he added, "When I thought I had all the answers." He smiled.

The older man nodded. "We're all like that when we're young. And you still are. You've got your, you know, your prospects, you've got all your life ahead of you."

Prospects. Billy looked out the window. *Right.*

The Army had taught him things, it was true—some basic carpentry skills, car maintenance, a bit of boxing, how to drink, how to decide when to fight and when to walk. And of course, how to fire an M1 rifle. Yeah, that would come in handy. He tried to imagine his resume. Or, better yet, a job interview.

"What else can you do, young man, that will help our firm?"

"I can shoot your employees for you, sir, if they act up."

Billy looked out the window. The bus was late, Lansing hadn't waited up for him.

"Myself, I'm heading on to Chicago," the man said.

Billy wanted to laugh.

Small world. That's where I'll be heading next. That's where they say she went.

To his seat companion he said, "Nice town from what I hear."

"It's not bad." The man peered past Billy and squinted. He was a long-faced man with bags under his eyes, a tired-looking man. His hair was combed straight back, and it reminded Billy of the Old Man's hair, slick with Brylcreem. "I'm gonna be looking for work there," he added. "Good place to look for work," he said, but Billy caught the doubtful note in his voice. He didn't know what to say but it seemed there should be something to say.

"That's what somebody told me," Billy said. "You'll probably do okay there."

The man gave him a shy smile. "Hope so. I'm a little bit long in the tooth to be looking for work in a strange town, but I want to make a fresh start."

Billy nodded but had nothing to add to that. He had a sudden disturbing image of this older man walking the streets of a place where he knew no one. But he understood the need for a fresh start.

Outside, the mist grew thicker and Lansing looked comatose. Somewhere, he knew, the bars were busy, especially the ones frequented by the Oldsmobile plant workers, but it had begun to rain now, coming down in sheets and pelting the life from the streets. He recognized it all, but it was no longer home to him. He would not be staying. He was here to tend to personal matters. Then he would be off, on another bus just like this one, for Chicago, where he didn't know a soul, to find a girl running from her life, a girl who did not want to be found, least of all by Billy Fox.

The bus made its last awkward turn, entering the terminal. In his favorite imaginings of this moment, he came back to the old town, having seen the world and ready to settle with his girl. The Billy Fox in this version was a smart kid, streetwise and good with his hands and full of—what the older guy had just said, prospects. The girl in this scenario, in every scenario, was Rita. She would be waiting for him, waiting breathlessly for the first glimpse of him as he climbed down from the bus.

The Greyhound slid into its slot in the terminal, and Billy shook hands with the gray-haired man.

"Good luck," he said. "You'll do good there in Chicago."

• • •

Aunt Jo was waiting, despite the rain and the hour. She was the only person in the waiting area. She seemed to scrunch down, as if trying to make herself smaller, striving to give the world as little offense as possible.

"Hello, Billy," she said and flinched as he grabbed her. He planted a kiss on her cheek and she giggled, smelling of cigarette smoke and coffee. A fine rain had begun to fall. Josephine led him out onto the street and opened her umbrella over him, and he saw that the rain came through a large hole in one side.

"Nice umbrella, Jo," he said, and she laughed and shrugged.

At her house she fixed him a ham and Swiss sandwich, and as he ate she watched him the way his mother used to.

Halfway through the second sandwich she nodded. "You still got a good appetite, Bill." The hopeful note in her voice invited him to confirm that all was right in his world. She wanted, of course, to hear the reassuring lies.

"If Army food didn't kill it, nothing will."

Still, she watched him with her owlish eyes, looking for the dark signs.

"I'm fine, Jo," he said. "I'm not gonna throw myself in front of a train."

Later, over bottles of Stroh's and a shared pack of Marlboros, they filled the room with smoke and unspoken thought and touched on every subject except the ones that needed to be out in the open. Josephine was about his mother's age, fifty or fifty-two, and no blood of his, but she'd been his mother's best friend for years, so that she became, early on, Aunt Jo. For a brief time between his mother's passing and his enlistment, Billy had lived here in Jo's spare room. They spoke of the weather and the Tigers and the Army and why Stroh's was better in bottles than in cans and whether the Oldsmobile plant was hiring—it wasn't, but that might change soon—and the running back from MSU who was going to sign with the Lions.

Billy watched Josephine as she blew smoke out into the room. She looked around her cluttered living room, and he could see her trying to picture it as a visitor might. Plaster had come down from a corner near the windows, and he could see where she'd wrapped electrical tape around a frayed cord. On the way in he'd noticed a broken stair and a cracked window.

Your house is coming down around your ears, my girl.

She read his thoughts. "I've got to fix the place up."

Billy nodded. His gaze rested on her television, a tiny black-and-white that she'd had as long as he'd known her. The antenna had a ball of aluminum foil taped to one branch.

Tin foil and electrical tape hold her life together. Jesus. Poor Josephine.

"I think I'll give you a hand, Jo."

"Oh, you got plenty on your mind. You don't have to be worrying about me."

He shrugged. A new look came onto Josephine's face. She was working up her nerve.

"So you got all my letters, right?"

"I know I got some because I even answered a couple."

"Oh, sure. You're a good letter writer, Billy. So you know about, you know, everything. You know she's gone now."

"I know the whole story, Jo, I know she lost her mind and married Kenny Coyne of all the people on God's earth to marry. Kenny Coyne. And I know she's got a kid and now she's gone."

"She's gone, yeah. Chicago. She needed a new place, you know?"

"Whatever you want to call it."

She's on the run. That's what I want to call it.

"I won't be in town long, Jo." Her face fell, and he finished the thought. "But I was wondering if I could stay here for a week or so?"

Now she smiled. "Oh, you know you can always stay here, Bill. I'll get it cleaned up for you."

"No need for that. Just let me have your couch or something."

"I got the bed in the back room—you can have that room again. It'll be nice to have somebody here."

"Well, thanks, Jo." He looked around the place again. "I'll give you a hand while I'm here."

"You don't have to, Billy."

"I like using my hands. I learned some things in the Army."

"Then what, Billy? You got plans? A young guy needs a plan."

He saw the wary look in her eye, but there was no point in lying to her.

"I'll get something, I always do. First I want to find Rita. I want to find her."

"Oh, you won't find her there, Billy. In Chicago? You could drop all of Lansing in Chicago and you'd lose it. That's a place that will swallow you up. I know, Billy, I used to live there. I grew up there."

"I know that."

"I think she just wanted a new place to start. You know, get away from—"

"Get away from her old life, from Kenny, I understand that, Jo. I just want to see her, see if she's all right."

He met her eyes briefly and saw that she wasn't buying it.

"But it's been so long, Billy."

Five years, yes, five years since he'd even seen her face. But Billy believed he was quite different from the naïve kid in the photograph. He had seen some of the world, acquired some experience in life. He thought he was altogether another Billy Fox, and this one might have a chance with Rita. It was worth a shot.

"You know, she wrote me when I was in Germany."

One letter Rita had written, a letter out of the blue. By then she had been married more than two years, long enough to regret most of her choices. There was no complaint in the letter, simply a feeling that the writer had embarked on a life far different from the one she'd hoped for. She spoke of her child, a daughter named Annie, expressed her gladness that the Vietnam War was coming to an end before Billy had to see any of it.

But for that letter, for the manifest sadness of it, Billy thought he might have been able to forget about Rita.

Jo puffed at her cigarette and shook her head. Then she shrugged, resigned.

"You can't blame her for getting involved with that one, or for leaving him, Bill."

"I don't. We were finished by the time I went into the service. We were done. I just never figured her for Kenny Coyne."

"He was an older guy, he had clothes and a nice car and money—those people, they always have money."

Billy smiled. *Those people—drug dealers.*

"A girl wants security sometimes. It's, you know, interesting. Glamorous. It's really fun when you have money for the first time. For a while you don't think about any of your other issues."

Josephine looked down at her threadbare rug, lost in thought, and Billy wondered if there had been a time in Jo's life when she'd had money, clothes, nice things. It struck him that he'd never seen a picture of Josephine as a young woman. She gave a shake of her head.

"And when you have a few bucks, honey, you think it's gonna last forever."

"Anytime you have something good, you think it'll last forever, Jo."

She nodded. "But Rita lived with her mistake."

Billy nodded. He had trouble imagining the child. If things had gone another way, that would have been his child. He couldn't imagine himself with a kid. But he understood that the existence of this child changed everything for Rita, and for them. It meant that a time in his life was gone, with no chance of returning to that time. An image came to him then of himself and Rita, a couple of teenagers wandering along the old section of the MSU campus, daydreaming aloud about their lives—Rita would go to college, she'd attend Michigan State while Billy put together his own business, auto repairs, he thought. Five years later, she was on the run with a kid, and he was an aimless veteran who had no idea where his next paycheck was coming from.

Billy forced himself to listen to Jo talk about the old neighborhood, who had died, who had moved away, how things had changed. He listened and understood that just having someone to listen to was something out of the ordinary for Josephine. That much he could give her, at least. He looked around at her place. He could listen to her and he could do a few things around the place.

He would spend his time in Lansing wisely. He would tend to things. Then he would head to Chicago, for whatever it was worth. He forced himself to acknowledge that this young woman on the run had no interest in Billy, had long ago lost any feeling for him.

He recalled the Old Man once saying that he'd done a kindness, lent money to an acquaintance he hadn't seen in ten or fifteen years.

"For old times' sake," his father had said. *"For old times."*

This thing, Billy told himself, this fool's errand, would be like that. It was for old times' sake.

• • •

In the morning he spent an hour just assessing Josephine's swayback mule of a house, a place that hadn't seen plaster or paint since the fifties. Then he went to a hardware store and bought plaster, Spackle, paint, duct tape, screws, nails, caulking, a pane of glass, a tape measure, and a handsaw. At a lumber yard, he bought wood for the staircase. For the next four days, he threw himself into the work—he fixed cracks in the walls, replaced the front window and the broken stair. He painted two rooms, reinforced bannisters, caulked around the edges of the windows, put a new piece of screen in the back door. In the bathroom he put on a new toilet seat, replaced the handles on the faucets and her ancient shower head, put new filters in the taps, put new grout between some of the tiles. He moved relentlessly from room to room, carting with him his smokes and a cup of coffee and Jo's old clock radio, and he listened to old Motown music as he worked, music he'd danced to with Rita. When he was done with the house, he fixed the legs on broken chairs, repaired a dresser drawer whose bottom had come out, mowed her lawns front and back.

Josephine knew enough to stay out of his way, but he would see her from time to time, peering into a room where he was working, shaking her head in a combination of wonderment and embarrassment. He shrugged. "I don't have much to show for bumming around all that time, but I did pick up a few things here and there. I can actually do things."

Jo set about her own tasks, cleaning her aging house from ceiling to floor. She washed floors and walls, lined shelves and cupboards with new contact paper. She took down curtains and drapes and washed years of dust and smoke from them, and spent hours at her ironing board, singing to herself in a tuneless voice.

At night Billy wandered, visiting old haunts and meandering all the way into East Lansing and onto the campus of Michigan State. He walked fast through the campus, half-convinced that the kids could tell he was an outsider who had no business there, in someone else's world.

In a gas station he bought himself a street map of Chicago and a small pamphlet highlighting the city's sights, and late at night he tried to commit as much of all this to memory as possible— the names of the main streets, the location of the museums and shopping centers. An inset made it seem that the whole of the thing emptied down into the enormous lake that made up the right side of the map. He memorized and took notes and tried to ignore the voice in his head that told him this was all a long shot. There was no telling where in this vast place a woman running from her life would end up, no real way to know she would even stay there. Billy looked at the vastness of Chicago, a city bigger than any place he'd ever been to, and told himself that if it were Billy trying to find a place there, he wouldn't last a week. Still, you had to try. He remembered his mother sitting at the edge of his bed one night, attempting to summarize for him why she'd stayed with his father.

"You have to try. You can't just give up, you have to try."

Just before dinner on the third night of his stay, a man came to the door. He knocked, and before Billy or Jo could go to the door, the visitor stepped inside and said, "Jo? Josie?"

Josie? Billy thought.

He stepped into the living room to intercept. The stranger was about sixty, tall and thin and newly shaven, and he wore his dark shirt buttoned up to the neck. Billy extended his hand and said, "Billy Fox. I'm a friend of Jo's."

The man nodded and smiled. He smelled of Vitalis and Old Spice. "Oh, I heard all about you, son. I'm Fred Hicks. I come to see Jo."

"Me and Fred are very old friends," Jo said.

"Second time around," Fred added, and Billy wondered about the backstory there.

After dinner, Billy excused himself and let the two lovebirds have the place to themselves. For an hour or more he roamed his old neighborhood, noting the things that hadn't changed but many more that had. On Ottawa Street, he found a diner he'd known in the old days and stopped in for coffee. A guy sat on a stool at the far end of the counter, staring at the wall and blowing smoke into the air. He sensed Billy watching him, turned, and after a moment waved. Ray Wills.

Billy moved his cup down the counter.

"Hello, Ray."

"Billy." Ray Wills put an arm around Billy's shoulder.

They made small talk about the Army and Ray's life—divorced now and working at a dead-end job in his old man's TV repair shop.

"So you're set?" Billy asked, knowing the answer.

"No. I'm gonna quit, the old man already knows. I'm going out West. See the country."

"Then what?"

Ray shook his head, puffed at the cigarette, blew out smoke. "Start over. Square one, start over. Find a job, stay clean, get my head straight. Find a girl. Start over—it's what guys like us have to do, Billy. Start over until we get it right. And you?"

"I have to do a few things here in town, then I'm gone. I'm going to Chicago."

Ray watched him, saying nothing.

"Yeah, you know why. I'm looking for Rita."

"That town'll swallow you up, man."

"Maybe so. I can't worry about that."

"Think she wants to see you?"

"Me? No, probably not. But I want to see her, see if she's okay. She don't want anything to do with me, okay. Right now, though, I need to find Kenny Coyne."

Ray gave him a stricken look. "You, Billy?"

Ray's face fell and Billy laughed.

"I'm not using."

"Then what for?"

Billy raised his eyebrows.

"Ah. Think that'll help?"

"Don't know if anything will help."

"He runs with some bad guys. You need to pick your spot."

"Right."

"I've seen him at DeLuca's. Patricio's. The KoKo Bar."

"The KoKo Bar. I always liked the KoKo Bar. Thanks, Ray."

"Be careful."

"Yeah—hey, Ray? You got used TVs there, at the shop?"

"Sure. You need a set? I'll give you a deal."

. . .

Handsome Kenny Coyne, it seemed, had gone to ground, though Billy twice spotted Kenny's "known associates." He stopped for a beer in the KoKo Bar, the closest thing he'd had to a hangout in the old days, a rundown roadhouse on the very edge of Lansing. He knew the bartender, a pouchy-eyed white man named Marvin, and spotted a black kid named Eddie, a Golden Gloves boxer who worked at the Oldsmobile plant.

"Foxy Bill," Eddie said. "No more soldier?"

"Nah. Thought I'd take up boxing." He clapped Eddie on the back. They talked, and Billy fed quarters into the juke box and listened to Otis Redding, Marvin and Tammi, and Junior Walker, and he was trying to decide whether to have one more beer when Kenny Coyne came in.

Billy had to admit that Kenny Coyne knew how to make theater of entering a room. He paused just inside the door as though he might change his mind, looked around the room, nodded to the bartender, and strutted to a place at the far end from which he could watch the door, like an old gunfighter. As always, he was dressed entirely in black: sport coat, slacks, shirt, tie. Kenny was tall, thin, and pale—"Kenny the Count," some people called him—and Billy thought he looked like a vampire fallen on hard times.

"Hello, Kenny," he said.

Kenny made an almost imperceptible nod and said, "Hey. Fox. Yeah. I heard you were back." He ordered a beer and drank in silence for a time. Eddie the Boxer made small talk about his chances in the next Golden Gloves competition and Billy bought him a beer, and Kenny Coyne drank as though there was no one else in the room. As Billy finished his beer, he looked down the bar and caught Kenny's quick look.

You oughtta be nervous. He looked at Kenny now and held the stare until the other man met his eyes.

"You trying to grow a mustache, Kenny?"

Kenny's hand moved to the sparse growth on his upper lip. Then he caught himself.

"So when did you get back, Fox?"

"Couple weeks ago. I heard you had a busy life while I was gone. You got married, I heard. And then she left you."

"That what you heard? Well, good riddance to that bitch. But that's none of your business, Fox. None of that's got anything to do with you."

"Is that a fact?"

Kenny tried on a smile. "She married me, Fox, not you."

"Yeah, talk about stupid choices people make, huh?"

Kenny's color changed, a high patch of red came into his cheeks. "Oh, yeah? Well, she must not have thought so."

"Bet she thinks so now. I heard you beat the shit out of her."

From behind him, Billy heard Eddie the Boxer say, "Uh-oh. Hide the children."

Kenny shrugged. "Whatever I did, she had coming. But like I said, Fox, it's got nothing to do with you. She's my wife. Until I say she's not."

Billy said nothing, just held his stare. He turned slightly to face Kenny.

Kenny made a show of sipping his drink, glancing at his massive watch, pulling out a pack of smokes and tapping them on the bar. He started to take one out, then paused.

You don't want to take that out because your hand might shake.

"I like your outfit, though. I thought dealers were supposed to be subtle. Me, I think all dealers should dress in black. It would give 'em—what? Dignity. That's it. So this is your uniform, you know? Like a car mechanic has those coveralls. You got a black cowboy hat to go with that? And a six-gun, you got a six-gun, Kenny? Then you'd look like—what was the guy's name, the cowboy with the whip? Lash LaRue."

"Don't start with me, Fox. You don't want to fuck with me. This is not soldiers in the Army."

Billy almost laughed. *No*, he thought, *it's not like the Army—it's a small-time pusher in Lansing, Michigan, who's seen too much television.*

He pushed away from the bar and moved toward Kenny.

"Billy—" Marvin said, backing away behind the bar.

Don't do this, the voice in his head said. It might have been Jo's voice, it might have been his guardian angel, but all he knew was that he was not going to pay any attention to it.

"I want to hear again how she had it coming, you beating the fuck out of her. Tell me about that one more time. People always said I'm kinda slow-witted."

Kenny turned to face him. One hand went to his back pocket, and he was flicking open the knife when Billy decked him. Kenny went down hard and hit the base of the bar with his forehead. He grunted and tried to get up, but his foot was caught in the legs of the barstool.

"Now, Billy—not in here, Billy," Marvin said, and sounded worried.

"Dude had it comin'," Eddie offered. "Nasty dude."

Billy bent over and picked up the knife. He tossed it on the bar. "There you go, Marvin. Put that in your collection, with all the marbles and yo-yos and whatnot."

Kenny had extricated his leg, but seemed in no hurry to get up.

"See you around, Kenny. Sorry, Marvin. I'm going now."

He waited outside the KoKo Bar, leaning against a light pole, and when he heard the door open, he knew it would be Kenny. He waited with his back to the tavern until Kenny made his final dash toward him, and then spun round and met him. They traded punches, and Billy caught one on the side of his face but he'd been waiting for this time, this moment, and he laid into Kenny with urgency, driving his right into Kenny's ribs and midsection, his left to the head. In close, he drove an uppercut to Kenny's chin and Kenny wobbled. A straight right put him down.

Kenny rolled over and got to his knees but no further.

Billy stood over him and thought his chest would burst with the urge to finish Kenny. He moved around in front of Kenny and cocked his right hand back.

One punch in the proper place would cave in Kenny's face. He heard his own ragged breathing and Kenny sucking in air through a damaged mouth. His chest throbbed with the urge to ruin this man, to ruin something. He listened to his breathing and to his heart.

"Ah, what the fuck," he said. Then he swung his open hand and caught Kenny with a loud flat slap that nearly knocked him back onto the pavement.

"Guys that beat the shit out of women, bad things happen to them."

"Bad things—" Kenny panted. "Bad things gonna happen to you, Fox."

A few feet away Eddie the Boxer leaned against a tree, arms folded across his chest. He nodded.

"Not bad, Billy Fox. Nice combinations. You got no speed, though. You easy to hit."

Billy smiled and nodded and tried to catch his breath.

"That boy usually runs with a posse, some bad people. You want to lay low now."

"I was just leaving. You take it easy, Eddie."

In the morning Billy went to see Ray Wills. On one last frivolous impulse, he bought a small color TV for Josephine and deposited it without ceremony on her living room table.

Josephine was speechless. She kept saying "a color TV" as though Billy had invented it.

• • •

Billy Fox waited for the doors to open on the bus for Chicago. Josephine stood at his side like a watchful mother and managed to make him feel twelve years old. She watched him earnestly, holding the bag of food she'd prepared. Grease stains spreading across the bottom told him there was fried chicken inside.

The door to the bus opened with a sound like gas escaping, and the short line of passengers began getting on. Josephine watched him with moist eyes. She tried to smile.

"You did a good job on the house, Billy. You did so much in just a few days. I'm so grateful."

"And you put me up and fed me. Seems like as far back as I can remember, you were always putting somebody up and taking care of them. I know you took care of me and my Ma when the Old Man left, before she got back on her feet. I never forgot that."

He leaned over and kissed her on the forehead. She gave him the bag and stole a quick kiss on the cheek.

"You be careful. That Chicago's a big place. You don't know what can happen to you."

"Maybe something good. It's possible. Give my regards to Fred," he said. Josephine blushed and turned away.

"He's—we're real good friends."

"Yeah, I saw that."

He got onto the bus, and he waved to her as it pulled out of the bus station. When he turned away she was still waving, and he knew she'd stand there watching the bus disappear into the night until she could no longer see it.

A long-ago image came to him then of the two of them—Billy and Rita—sitting on a bench in a park. A couple of Lansing kids, a pretty, dark-haired girl and a tall, skinny boy with a mop of bushy brown hair, both of them forever young. It could have been any of a dozen or more such occasions, but one in particular always came back to him, a time when they'd stayed in the park long after dark, long after the park's closing, and talked well into the night of their plans and the many choices open to them. In the end, they decided they would marry at twenty and move to Los Angeles— Rita's idea because she thought she might become an actress, or work in make up.

Hollywood, Billy thought, and shook his head.

Now it was a whole different reality for both of them. That time and those dreams were lost to him.

Still, she'd left her husband, she wanted to start over, and Billy might be able to find her. After that, anything was possible.

ONE

Lost Soul in the Big Town

Later, Billy would remember that the first thing he'd seen in Chicago was a man dancing by himself in the bus terminal. This one image would stand out amidst the general chaos that was his first impression. Chaos and darkness and a crazy guy dancing. People were shoving to get off the Greyhound, and the cavernous depot had eaten the daylight, and this guy along the far wall of the depot was dancing. Billy followed his rumpled, sour-smelling fellow passengers off the bus and stood for a moment to get his bearings.

He fetched his duffel from the storage compartment and walked toward the end of the depot. There he found more chaos, and noise to match it—a crowd of people jostling, one group leaving the area and another hurrying to a bus on its way out of the city. The music was louder now. A radio was somewhere close by playing something Billy recognized—Smokey Robinson and the Miracles. If you lived in Michigan, anywhere in Michigan, you knew all this music. You knew the Soul stuff out of Detroit and all the people on those labels, the Motown people, and before them the Gordy label and the Tamla label. Here was Detroit music pounding in the dark tunnel of a Chicago bus depot, and the dancer was boogying to it, a small man sliding and shuffling and clapping to the music and drawing a crowd all his own. A small, white man in a belted sweater, this boogie-artist was, wearing a red bandanna and dark glasses despite the dense gloom of the depot. He was sure-footed, nimble, and he stayed on the balls of his feet, spun and came back to the same spot, and clapped his hands. People slowed to watch him, and Billy found himself drawn to the entire scene, the smiling people, the slick moves of this nutcase in sunglasses.

There was a bar just inside the station, a windowless dive with half a dozen men sitting around it. He needed a cold beer and a plan. Across from him, a dapper black man was attempting to pick up a young white guy in coveralls. Billy watched them for a moment, slightly surprised—he'd always somehow believed homosexuality to be the province of white people. The bartender took his eyes from a ballgame long enough to pour Billy a beer. He sipped absently from his beer as he unfolded one of his maps. The lake, he knew, was east, and if he could find that, he would have the basic directions. He'd studied this map and others, and now that he was here, he wondered if you could learn anything from a map. An old white man on the stool a few feet from him watched a Cub player hit a ball into the seats and cackled. He wore a sweat-stained, red baseball cap and a sport coat made for a man with shorter arms. His gray hair stuck out from under the hat in a dozen directions, and he'd cut himself shaving in several places, so that he looked as if he'd been in a fight.

"It's their year," the man called out to no one in particular. Sensing that he'd gotten Billy's ear, he turned and fixed him with a dark-eyed stare.

"This year," he tapped the bar with a bony finger. "This year, 1977, is the year they'll do it."

Billy nodded and looked around for a less exposed place to sit. The old man leaned into his line of sight and nodded.

"It's all gonna happen this year. 1977. And if that happens, I know the world's gonna end. Maybe Carter'll bomb the Russians. Which will piss *them* off, and then we'll have the End Times."

Billy shrugged and looked away.

The old man went on, implacable. "It's in the Bible. The End Times. You read the Bible, son? Me neither, but they tell me the End Times are coming. 'Course, somebody tells me that every couple years. But I suppose this time it's true."

Now Billy caught something in his voice, the change in tone that said the old man was having fun with him. He looked at the old man and saw the glint of humor in his eyes. Billy smiled.

"So what is it that's going to cause all this?"

"I think the Cubs, those dingbats, are gonna win the World Series. Then I'll know it's the End Times. The Apocalypse. You know about the Apocalypse?"

"No."

"Me neither, but it's supposed to be bad. I think it'll shut down all the saloons." The old man cackled now, and Billy laughed and decided to pay for this amusement.

"How about a beer?" Billy asked.

The old man shrugged. "Why not?"

Billy ordered the old man a beer. He watched the old guy drain half his beer, saw the old man studying him. His eyes took in the duffle on the floor.

"You come in on the bus?"

"Yeah."

"Where from?"

Billy started to say *Lansing*, thought better of it, and said "Kalamazoo."

The old man caught the hesitation and said, "You sure, son?" and Billy laughed.

"More or less. I've been knocking around."

"I did that too, when I was a young fella. No good can come of it," he said, and slurped his beer. "What brings you to the Big Town? Probably not family, or you wouldn't be sitting here talking to old crazies in dark saloons."

"I'm looking for somebody," Billy said.

The old man squinted. "You sound like a character in a movie."

"I know. That sounds a little, what do you call it? Melodramatic. But I am looking for somebody."

The man gave him an amused look. Then Billy said, "So which way is the lake?"

"Why? You gonna throw yourself in it?"

"No. Not yet, anyways."

"Go left when you leave this joint."

"So that's east. Good."

The old man nodded. For a while they drank in silence, and then the old man surprised him.

"You need a room, there's a YMCA on Wabash, south of here. And there's one up on Chicago Avenue, north of here."

"Is that where you stay? The Y?"

The old man laughed. "Oh, my current lodgings are more suited to my current financial status. Which is to say, I live on the cheap, son."

Billy didn't know what to say to that. He finished his beer, pushed change toward the bar rail for the bartender, and patted the old man on the back.

"I got to go," he said, and nearly added, *but I have no idea where.*

"Okay, well, good luck, son, hope you find him, or her, or it. And thanks for the beer."

• • •

He found himself in the heart of downtown Chicago, where word of the Apocalypse had clearly not arrived. There was still daylight, but the sun was setting fast. The air was dense with a smell he'd come to think of as street-grit, the smell of late nights, exhaust hanging in the air, food smells, and tobacco smoke. Street-grit. This, at least, was reassuring to him—he'd experienced this before. Lansing smelled like this, and Detroit smelled like this, and Flint. Someone had once told him that New Orleans had the smell of coffee and pecans, but Billy doubted this. A city couldn't smell like coffee and pecans, not all of it. Somewhere, if it was an actual city, there would be a part of it that had this peculiar after-smell of all the things people did to get by in the daytime.

But this was a place with its own smells—he could smell water on the air. He hadn't realized you would be able to smell the lake. Onions, he smelled onions, and somewhere nearby someone was making popcorn and roasting nuts. And there was noise, traffic and the gush of air as a bus hit its brakes and the raucous noise of a cabbie leaning on his horn, and at the corner three small black boys pounded on identical plastic buckets. They filled the air with untamed percussion, the three of them grinning at one another as they drummed. They searched faces as they pounded away, hoping to coerce donations. Billy walked over and watched them drum for a minute, then dropped a buck in an upturned fourth bucket, earning a grin from the kid closest to him.

First a beer for an old man in a bar and now a dollar in a kid's bucket. At this rate, he wondered if his money would last the week.

A street sign told him he was on Randolph Street. For a moment he stood there, resting the heavy duffel bag on the sidewalk, the sole human being on that street without purpose or destination, bouncing up and down on the balls of his feet until he grew self conscious.

Every time, every time in a new place, Billy experienced a moment of light-headedness, a quick disorientation that came with a flash of panic. He had been in many new places in the past year, all over the western half of the States. And now he was standing on a corner in Chicago, just standing, aware that he had embarked on a farfetched course and wondering how he'd manage to keep himself alive.

He stepped out onto the sidewalk, swinging his duffel bag over his shoulder, and people made paths around him on both sides. He wouldn't have been surprised if someone had called out, "Hey, Rube." He had enough cash to last perhaps two weeks, and no clear idea what was to come next. He realized how he must look, with all these Chicago people striding purposefully past him.

It struck him that in a life brief but nonetheless filled with missteps and miscalculations, this was as stupid as anything he'd ever done.

He began to walk up and down Randolph to get some sort of bearing. His initial impression was immensity, walls of concrete, walls of glass and steel. And movie houses, big ones—the Bismarck to the west, the United Artists to the east. Just a block away, he could make out a huge block of granite that showed on his city map as the combination of City Hall and the County Building, and just beyond that, the dark scaffolding of the elevated train.

He'd memorized some of these streets, all the major arterial streets, but he'd tried and failed to memorize all of them from the numbered streets on the south to Howard on the north. He knew that this was a vast place unlike any he'd ever lived in. Jo was right, you could drop Lansing and Kalamazoo in this place and they'd be swallowed. Jesus, you could lose Detroit in this place. He knew, as well, that he had no idea how to find a girl who'd come to such a place quite literally to prevent anyone from finding her.

He had a few bucks in his pocket, his life's belongings stuffed into a canvas bag, a pool cue, and very little of what anyone might call *prospects*.

Talk about traveling light through life.

Thus, Billy told himself that his first order of business in Chicago would be to manage not to starve or die homeless on the streets.

A cop car moved slowly in the westbound traffic, and the cop in the passenger seat gave him the look. Billy looked away, pretended to be looking for something, and caught his reflection in the dark glass front of the bus station—a washed-out looking boy, slightly underfed, bushy hair uncombed, jeans and a jean jacket. Clearly out of place.

He hefted his duffel bag and slung it over one shoulder to show it.

See? I've been in the Army protecting our shores. I'm not a hobo.

Okay, he thought. A plan—first order of business was not to starve here or die homeless on the streets or get busted. Tall enough order, he told himself. Tall enough.

Now, to look for things—for a place to stay, for work, for a cheap meal. Though Billy knew all of those things were of critical importance, he did precisely what he knew he'd do as soon as he hit Chicago—he went to a phone booth and dug into the phone books. The voice of reason that lived in the back of his head told him she wouldn't be under her own name, but he rifled through the White Pages quickly, hungrily. He tried her actual name, Rita Bellavia, then her mother's maiden name, Linderman. The voice told Billy he was goofy, that she wouldn't be under her mother's name either, that she was smarter than that. For that matter, she wouldn't be in a phone book.

He walked. Head down and leaning to counterbalance the weight of the duffel, he walked, aimlessly at first, taking it all in. Eventually he told himself just to march in one direction until he found a room.

The room was in a YMCA. He paid for two weeks. The room was small and clean. More importantly, there was a cafeteria with decent food.

That night, he lay for a time on his bed, listening to the street sounds outside his window and summing up his situation—a room for a week, maybe two, food money for about that long if he stretched it. Time enough to look for something to get him by.

So. So I'm not gonna die on the street my first week here. It's a start.

TWO

Signs from the Heavens

"The road don't give nobody a thing except blisters," Billy had once heard his father say. If asked to verify this wanderer's wisdom, Billy would have agreed that the road had given him little—except perhaps a sense of irony. He had developed a dark sense of humor about his situation. Signs frequently amused him—the sign on the bus stop bench, for example, asked, *"Earn money in your spare time?"* and promised *"Three hundred a week from your own home!"*

Billy imagined himself asking the sign's owner if the deal still held for a guy who might be living in an alley soon.

A bus rolled to the corner and Billy saw another sign: *"Start your own business. Send for our brochure."* The subway stations were full of these promises, as were the trains themselves—*"Make $250 per week in your spare time," "Earn a degree in just fifteen weeks!" "Start a New Career in the Exciting Field of Sales," "Join the Management Institute of Northern Illinois."*

If the signs were all true, you could get rich in your own house, get a college degree over the summer, become an engineer in a year or an electrician in six months, direct your own enterprises, and build an empire without getting off the couch. The skies would rain money. What all of them had in common, it seemed to Billy, was that you ponied up your cash first and they did their business on you. This called to mind another saying of the Old Man's—*"Everybody's got an angle."*

And that, Billy believed with unshakable conviction, was the gospel truth.

He watched the bus roll away with its promise of money in his spare time and asked himself, "So, what's my angle?"

For, clearly, a guy standing on a corner in a town where he knew no one, a guy down to his last few bucks, this was a fellow without an angle.

Yeah, Billy would have added, *and without a clue.*

He bought a twenty-nine cent notebook and wrote down everything that seemed to have any significance. For two weeks he walked endlessly, first through what a guy at the YMCA desk called "The Loop," on the premise that the busiest part of the city was the most likely place to start looking for someone. He'd never seen a place so dense with people, nor a town where the tallest buildings made a wall that blocked out the sun. At one point, he walked east as far as he could, past a park and a huge fountain, and found himself staring at the lake for the first time.

"Jesus H." he said aloud. It might as well have been an ocean, for there seemed to be no end to it, no far side. He stood staring at it for a time, mesmerized. From here, he made a long circuit of exploration that took him past beaches already populated by kids, sunning, chasing dogs, throwing Frisbees, playing volleyball, being beautiful. It seemed they were all beautiful—the boys were tanned and muscular and went to great lengths to show off their bodies and their athleticism, and the girls all looked like starlets, in brightly-colored bikinis, long hair flying in the breeze. He noted that almost none of them ventured into the water and wondered when it was possible to swim in the huge lake. He cut across the sand and tried on an air of self-possession, a streetwise guy who knew where he was heading, but five yards into the beach his boots slipped so badly he might have been on ice, and he turned back quickly to avoid falling.

He became self-conscious of his pale skin, his clothes. At one point, a guy chasing a ball ran into him and they both nearly fell onto the walkway.

"Hey! Watch where you're going," the guy said. Then he added, "Fucking hillbilly," but he was moving away as he said it.

Hillbilly?

He looked down at his clothes—tight jeans over scuffed boots, a white t-shirt with his smokes tucked up in one sleeve.

I look like James Dean's ghost, he thought, and quickly left the beach, lest they all start pointing him out.

By his third day in Chicago, the boots had grown heavy and the jeans were hot, and he told himself he had no idea how a person searched an entire city, a strange city, for one human being in three million. He walked endlessly and showed the wrinkled picture everywhere—grocery stores and gas stations, bars and diners, to vendors on the corner selling papers. The more people who frowned or squinted at the photo and shook their heads, the more stupid he felt.

He walked and asked his questions and tried to get a fix on the city's streets and landmarks, and wore out the soles of his boots, as well as his own fervor. He was beset by the frequent sense of the ridiculous nature of his search. If there was one thing Billy feared, it was appearing ridiculous.

• • •

At the end of his second endless week in Chicago, he stood on the corner of Division and Clark, waiting for a sign. Not from God, necessarily, for he was not yet convinced there was one. Just a sign that this was where he was supposed to be. And if not here, then where? He was beginning to believe the answer to that question might be *nowhere*. More than once in the past year he'd woken in a strange place, unable to remember for a moment where he was—just one more hot, dark room on a street he didn't know. Different rooms, but the same smells of sweaty sheets and cigarettes, the same panic squeezing his heart in a cold fist.

A cop car went by, and the red-faced one riding shotgun gave him the look.

Yeah, you made me for a drifter.

What was the word now? A *transient*. The cop squinted his way and Billy met his eyes. If they spoke, Billy knew exactly how the conversation would play out.

I'm looking for work, Officer, he'd say.

But the cop lost interest, bored and hot, and they drove on.

Up the street he saw a hot dog joint. He'd told himself he wouldn't eat until he knew where his next buck was going to come from—he was down to just a few dollars—but here was food, hot food, and he could smell the onions and the dogs and the Polish sausages sweating on the grill, and he shook his head. Almost time to stand on corners again. Hardest thing of all, you were either cut out for it or not, the ability to buttonhole strangers and feed them a line of crap—*Hey, buddy, help a guy get back on his feet? Hey, man, I'm trying to get to* (fill in the blank here but first you needed to know the names of places a guy on foot might be trying to get to). *Hey, Miss, I just need to get a sandwich.*

No, I don't want to do that again, Billy thought. I'll shovel shit somewhere in this place first.

Billy looked at the hot dog stand and began moving that way. He was just a few feet from the doorway of the hot dog stand when he saw the man in the suit—a white suit, an *ice cream suit*, his mother would have said, rumpled but a white suit nonetheless. And then the hat, a porkpie with the brim turned up all the way around, like something out of a gangster movie. A small man, but this man in the white suit moved up Division Street toward Billy in a rolling walk, in what might have been his tough-guy strut, deep in thought. So deep, Billy thought, that he was nearly talking to himself. He could see the man's jaw moving. The man looked up, seemed for the first time to notice the hot dog stand, and stopped, jingling his change in his pockets in that way that Billy's father had, as though reminding himself he wasn't broke yet.

The man in the suit never saw the two kids step out from a doorway behind him. Two of them, one white and one black, and Billy knew the look and what was about to go down. The white kid bumped the man off balance, and the black one gave him a push, and he went down. The white kid reached down with a practiced move and came up with a wallet. Then they were off. They'd gone only a few steps when a cab driver in a turban came running toward them, a big, brown-skinned man with a black beard. The kids took one look, stopped on a dime, and went back the other way. The man in the suit was still on the sidewalk—he seemed stunned or injured. Then, as the kids ran past him, Billy saw a bony leg shoot out, and the white kid went down, dropping the wallet as he hit the pavement. He scrambled for the wallet, but the man in the white suit was on him like a cat. For a moment they were both reaching for it, even as they grappled with each other, and then Billy saw the wallet go flying off the curb. A passing pickup truck rolled over it. Billy walked over and picked it up. He turned in time to see the kid get to his feet.

They faced each other, a wiry middle-aged man in a white suit and a tall, thin street kid in a sleeveless t-shirt. If asked, Billy would have said the kid had already made his second mistake—there was no reason to turn this into a fight with witnesses—no, an audience. A few yards up the street, the second thief had stopped at the corner, started to come back, and then had second thoughts. The small street action had drawn a crowd—four or five passersby, three of the cab drivers parked beside the hot dog stand, a woman with a dog. The second kid shook his head in irritation and took off.

Billy hefted the wallet in his hand and told himself he was probably quick enough to take off without fear of pursuit. He'd have money. As though he'd heard the thought, the man in the white suit looked his way for the briefest moment in time, then turned his attention to the problem at hand.

The fighters circled in that old minuet of the street, the kid with his hands hung low, they all fought that way now—Muhammad Ali had ruined an entire generation of street fighters who all thought they could box with their hands down around their waists while they bounced and boogied. As Billy watched, the kid began dancing and bobbing and moving his head, and looked startled when the man in the suit cracked him in the mouth with a stiff left. The kid licked his lip, glared, and waded in throwing wild punches. One grazed the small man along the side of his face, but the others caught nothing but the air. The man in the suit moved steadily to his left, and just when the kid adjusted his stance to this movement, the man shifted his feet and began circling to the right. He threw the jab again, and another one, and then the right hand, which caught the kid on the cheek. The kid threw another roundhouse and took a punch in his eye, a perfect straight right, and the eye started swelling immediately. The kid shook his head as though this might make the swelling go away. The man came inside then, moved inside the kid's reach. The kid threw a half-hearted punch at the air, took a fist in the mouth, and then bolted. A heavy-set bystander gave chase but stopped after a few paces, panting and grinning.

Billy waited as the short man patted and smoothed his now-abused costume, put the hat back on, and gave it a little pat. He straightened his tie, tucked at his shirt cuffs, brushed dirt from his white trousers. He missed the place where his knee had hit the pavement.

The turbaned cab driver said, "Are you all right, sir?" and the man in the suit held up a hand and nodded.

"No problem. And thanks."

"You did good," the cab driver said, and the man shrugged.

The man in the suit looked around for the wallet—no, he knew exactly where the wallet was. He looked for Billy. Billy held up the wallet and stepped forward.

"Here you go."

The man glanced at his wallet and then looked Billy in the eye. He grinned, but Billy had caught the look that preceded the grin. It had passed in the merest fragment of a second, but Billy knew this one, a measuring look, as though by looking Billy in the eye this man in the unlikely suit could tell if he'd taken anything out of the wallet.

"Thanks." He took the wallet and made a show of wiping it off.

"A truck rolled over it. If you got credit cards in there…"

"Nah, no plastic for me. I'm a guy that pays cash." Now he looked in the wallet, held it up. "Doesn't look like they got anything."

"Good," Billy said and turned to leave.

"Hey," the man called to him. "Thanks."

He was holding out his hand. Billy shook it, and the man came up with a small vinyl packet from which he extracted a business card.

"Here, take this. I'm just around the corner on Wells. My, ah, place of business, I mean. I'm Harry Strummer. If I can do anything for you—" He squinted as though to get a better look at Billy. "You looking for work? If you're looking for work I could make some calls."

For the first time Billy Fox was embarrassed.

To hide his embarrassment he looked at the card. It said "H.A. Strummer, President." Below this was the name "Peerless Detective Services," and just below that, as though it explained the name of the firm, the card promised "Discretion, Professionalism, Persistence. Licensed in three states."

Billy bit back a sudden impulse to ask which three states. Instead he just nodded and said, "Okay. Thanks. I've got a couple things going right now—"

"Oh, sure, sure. Maybe sometime down the road, you're looking for something, give me a jingle, I'll get on the horn. Smart guy like you, there's a lot out there."

Billy heard that note in the voice, that Good-time-Charlie salesman's note that said he was bullshitting and they both knew it, and the question came out as if of its own volition, "How do you know I'm smart?"

"Your eyes," Harry Strummer said, as though this was obvious, and Harry Strummer's own eyes said he was serious.

Billy stopped himself from asking what else Harry Strummer could see there.

"Okay, thanks," he said, and left. At the next corner, he stopped to wait for the light and shot a quick glance over his shoulder. The short fellow in the ice cream suit was walking toward Wells Street, hands in his pockets, looking at the traffic. But he hadn't gone very far. He'd stood for a while and watched Billy.

• • •

For the next four days, Billy pushed himself as hard as possible to turn a fast buck, and he wasn't fussy how he did it. He made long, aimless circuits, asked questions in diners and gas stations, found places where work might be available with no questions asked, then walked back and forth like a street-walker showing her wares until someone asked him some variation of, "Hey, you looking for work?"

And always Billy remembered his time in Denver and the answer was, "Hell, yes."

On Jackson, in front of a rooming house, he watched a couple of tired, thin men wrestle with the contents of a moving van until the guy in charge asked him if he wanted to make a couple bucks. He spent the morning unloading and carrying boxes and furniture that might have killed both the winos on the man's "crew." The guy gave him twenty bucks. He spent an hour pacing a stretch of Halsted that seemed to be an unending line of Greek restaurants until a harried-looking guy came out of a doorway and asked him if he wanted to earn some money. Billy followed the man into the paved-over yard behind a tavern and helped him carry out a succession of old beer coolers, piles of pipe, hard-used tables, and a rusted-out ice machine. He spent the next day helping the man and his brother gut the old tavern. They paid him cash.

He found a cheaper room on Wilson Avenue. A sardonic-looking man took his money and said "Welcome to Uptown. New in town?"

"Uh, yeah. Just got in."

"Watch yourself."

Here again, in this new part of a strange town, he sought out work—and work there was—day labor, hiring men out of a storefront. He took a forty-five minute trip out to an abandoned warehouse with a dozen other men on a bus that stank of sweat and muscatel-breath, carried out old equipment, and ripped out drywall and rotting wood. For this work, the day labor outfit took a chunk out of Billy's modest earnings. He kept little money on him and hid the rest in his room, rolled up in an empty Vaseline jar. Another day at this warehouse, then two more days riding the wine-stinking bus out to another place where he and the rest of "the crew" unloaded trucks in the heat. The first day on this job, one of the older men fainted. Billy fetched water for him, then helped the man to a sitting position. The man waved off the idea of an ambulance and the foreman walked away. Billy watched the old guy gulp down water.

"Help me up. If I can get on my pins, I'll be fine."

Billy held him up, startled at how little the old man weighed. He put an arm around the old man to steady him and could feel his ribs, his spine. He wondered how a man got to this place in life, and he thought of his father. Billy thought it more than likely that the Old Man had ended up like this, living on the far final edge of life. He looked around and was reminded that he was the only member of the crew under fifty. After a couple of days, the old man did not show up for work with the crew. A day or so later the foreman said he heard the old man had died.

The Wilson Avenue rooming house was a dead-end place just up the street from a school. He told himself this was temporary. It was smelly and crowded and at night the halls were filled with radio noise and snoring, but no one bothered him. One or two of the older men on his floor nodded when they saw him, and the wizened little man at the far end always spoke, said something about the heat, cackled about the street noise. Gradually he came to understand that for some of the men in the building—there were few women—this was probably their last move. They'd stay in this dank, musty place with its ripe-smelling hallways until they died. The first time this thought struck him, it was followed immediately by its logical conclusion—that if he was already staying in a place like this, there might be no future.

I won't stay here, he told himself. I won't die in a place like this, and I won't sleep on the street again.

But for the time being he was here, and he learned to make do with the limitations of the building. The toilets and showers were in a long, narrow room at the end of each floor, and it was here that he frequently passed the other men on the floor. Some of the men had nothing to say to him, while others were friendly. One of them, a tall black man with a shaved head, pointed out that the showers made the difference.

"A man can't stay clean, he's gonna lose his self-respect. You got to be able to shower."

The hallway smells told him about his neighbors—they smoked, all of them, and filled the hall with a bluish-gray cloud that seemed to grow denser late at night and in the early morning. One of them—perhaps the guy two rooms down, a young white man with a goatee and tattoos, was a pot-smoker, and added that earthy aroma to the blue cloud. They cooked in their rooms, on hot plates, and a certain burnt-bread odor told him at least one had a toaster. He smelled eggs, bacon, fried onions, and once in a while a very special rancid odor that he recalled from his youth, when his father would fry bologna on a skillet and make rank-smelling sandwiches.

When he entered the rooming house from the rear stairs, he saw the back windows of the rooms on his side of the floor. The windowsills were crowded with the small pleasures of a solitary life in a rented room. His neighbors lined their windowsills with mustard and catsup bottles and squat jars of mayonnaise and pickles. It seemed the longer a man had lived on his own, the greater his collection of window condiments.

On his own windowsill Billy kept a mustard jar and a couple of bottles of soda. On the unsteady dresser in his room he kept a loaf of bread, a jar of instant coffee, and a plug-in plastic coffee pot that another old-timer sold him for a dollar.

He tried not to focus on his room. He understood this was no way to live. And it seemed he wore his worry on his face. A black man whom he'd merely said hello to once or twice looked at him in the hall one morning and said, "Cheer up, babe, you ain't gonna be here long."

The plan was simple—he would establish himself in this town so that he could act and think like a native, make sense of his search, be systematic. Logical. And so he worked and put away his cash and pounded the streets and stood on corners and eyed the crowds. In the back of his head he understood the improbability of finding her like this, yet he was unable to stop.

When he wasn't working, Billy walked endlessly, covered half the length and breadth of the vast city, so huge it was beyond his imagining. The lake alone taxed his credulity. There seemed no farther shore to it, and he thought he might someday try to walk all the long way around it, just for the chance to see what lay at the far side, but the beaches stopped him. Sometime in the colder weather, when the beaches were empty, he would try to see what lay across the big lake.

And the city itself was like nothing he'd yet seen. Several times he lost his bearings, got himself turned around so completely he had to find the sun to determine where the lake was, the lake that anchored all of it to the east. The big diagonal streets trashed the logic of the orderly street grid and confused him greatly. Once, he managed to lose his way so completely that he found himself laughing at the folly of it all, on a corner where all the signs were in Spanish. A cab driver saw his lost look and picked him up, taking him back to the rooming house. In the cab Billy made small-talk. The cabbie was from Ethiopia.

"I've never met anybody from Ethiopia," Billy said.

"I never see nobody so lost, boss," the cabbie said. He grinned into the rearview mirror and showed Billy a mouthful of perfect teeth. They both laughed.

At the rooming house the cabbie waved off Billy's offer of money. He frowned at the rooming house.

"You be careful here, boss. This neighborhood no good. I know. I live here."

But he began to learn the streets, figured out the places to avoid, kept pushing, convinced that if he learned enough, got his bearings, he would be able to make hard sense of the place, ask the right questions in the right places, find what he'd come for.

I can do this, he told himself again and again. If I spend enough time here, I can figure the place out and I'll find her.

And then what?

A recurring scene—he would find her on a packed street and

she'd look at him as though he'd grown horns, then she'd turn her back and walk away.

Those first few nights in Uptown he strolled around, stopped on corners for a smoke, quickly learned which ones were already occupied by men with darker business. Twice he made mistakes, twice people followed him late at night down streets where he shouldn't have been—first a pair of white guys in t-shirts and bandanas, then three black boys who couldn't have been sixteen. Both times Billy thought of making a fight of it, but he'd been on the wrong end of enough street fights, and so he ran.

On his night walks through the neighborhood he saw fights, fender-benders, fast kids being pursued by slow cops. He watched a woman in an African dress loudly berating a dark-haired man who tried unsuccessfully to look menacing in the face of her anger. Once he watched two men rolling around at the edge of the sidewalk. He thought of breaking up the fight but a man nearby shook his head.

"They're brothers," he explained.

A block from his rooming house was a school called Truman College. Several times he sat outside and smoked and watched the students coming and going, a wondrous mix of Asians, Latinos, whites, blacks, men in dashikis, women in saris, and Muslim girls with faces covered. Billy wondered if there was another place anywhere with such a dazzling mixture of humanity.

Uptown had its smells, as well. On cooler nights the wind blew in from the lake and he could smell it, a mixture of fish and water plants, the air was heavy with it. Most times the streets smelled of fried food—peppers, grilled onions, meat seared over an open flame or stir-fried in a wok. He found an A&W with two menus—the traditional burgers-and-hot dogs menu and a second one of Persian food. Just up the street there was a storefront grill serving Ethiopian food. He tried it all, the Persian sandwiches with a spicy green sauce and Greek gyros, and he loved it all, though the Ethiopians nearly killed him with the hottest food he'd ever eaten—a wonderful plate of sliced beef and vegetables that went down like ground glass and made him gulp his water and ask for more from a laughing waitress who brought him a pitcher.

And it seemed that Uptown was never quiet. Billy thought he'd never experienced so much noise—traffic, people shouting, laughing, a drunk haranguing the moon in a voice like a foghorn. Just outside the rooming house a sax player practiced a couple nights a week, occasionally joined by a guitarist and a bass player, and people tossed coins in a hat on the sidewalk for them.

Just south of the rooming house was the great gray monolith of the ballpark, Wrigley Field. Several times, his walks took him past the ballpark. One of his few childhood memories of his father was a ballgame, a day trip to Detroit to watch the Tigers and the Yankees. Now he stopped outside the park and listened to the crowd noises, the players' names announced over the loudspeakers.

Just outside the ballpark, he again encountered young street drummers beating the life out of their plastic buckets. The air shook with the noise. The one in the middle winked at him—the same kids from his first day in town.

Billy looked from the manic young drummers to a cop nearby.

"Can they hear this inside the ballpark?"

"Sure, you can hear it for a mile." He nodded toward the park. "But the fans don't mind. The Cubs have lost six in a row, so I think they're all happy for the diversion."

Billy dropped a buck in the kids' collection bucket and winked back.

One evening, ranging far from his rented room, he found a pool hall. It bore the unlikely name of St. Paul Billiards, promised pool and sandwiches. A sign on the wall said some famous player had shot pool there in the '60s. And though every bell and warning told him the pool hall was a mistake, a pool hall in a strange town for that matter, he went in, found a decent stick, got a table, and started playing just badly enough to draw mild attention. He swore at missed shots, scratched a couple of times, and sent the cue ball flying off the table. A balding man who smelled of wine offered him a game for a quarter a ball. Billy took him on, stepped back when the man belched wine at him, then beat him easily. He looked around, grinning as though he'd done a great thing, and spotted the guy he was looking for. He was a well-dressed man in his twenties, thin, homely, and making up for his looks with his perfect hair and meticulous dress—dark blue shirt, light blue summerweight sport coat, perfectly shined shoes. A careful man of precise movements.

"Nice game," the man said.

"Thanks. Wanna play?"

"Sure. Five bucks?"

Billy forced a look of discomfort, hesitated.

"C'mon, a fin, I'm not that good," the other man said. "Gentleman's game."

"Okay."

They played, and for a time Billy paced himself so that he stayed with his opponent, who forced poor shots until the last couple of balls, then won handily. They played again double or nothing, then a third game, and the blond let him win this one.

"So we're even, huh?"

Billy nodded, played Farmboy, and said, "Takes me a while to get goin' sometimes."

"Hey, you're not bad. Better than a lot of guys."

"Thanks," Billy said, shuffling from one foot to the other.

"Make it interesting? Twenty bucks?"

Billy wet his lips, shrugged, nodded, and tried to look reluctant. They played three more games, two at double or nothing, and he won them all. Eighty bucks the dapper man owed him.

He paused to get a Coke, looked around. Their game had drawn half a dozen onlookers, and he might have been worried except that the other hustler didn't seem to know any of them. Billy was mildly concerned about a small man in a baseball cap and sunglasses watching them from across the room, head tilted and looking amused. But no one said anything. They played one more game, and Billy came from three balls down to win this one.

"You're better than you make out."

"I go on hot streaks sometimes when I'm pretty good, and then other times—" He shrugged as if it was all a mystery. "This where you play?" He held out his hand, and the pool shark put a wad of twenties in it.

"I play wherever there's a game."

"Well, I like this place fine," Billy said. "Tomorrow? Give you a chance to win your money back?"

"What time?"

"I gotta be someplace in the afternoon. How about five?"

The man in the summer suit nodded, barely able to conceal his anger.

"Five. I'll be here. You be here, too."

Billy let the mask fall. "Why would I miss it?"

He stuffed the money in his pocket, replaced the cue, and walked out, with no intention of ever seeing the St. Paul Billiards Hall or the guy in the summerweight suit again.

At night he drank, and this led him to his first serious misstep. He'd spent two hours in a dark, tough-looking Indian bar with a picture of Geronimo over the register where he could feel the patrons, Indians all, looking at him and wondering what this white boy was doing in a tavern where he didn't belong. But to his surprise, no one bothered him. There was a pool game going here, too, but he knew better.

When he left, he found another tavern, cheap drinks but noisy white guys yelling at the Cubs on the TV set. He stayed until he'd lost sense of the time, and when he left they were waiting for him. He had no idea whether they were guys from the tavern or just kids lurking outside, but they caught him unawares, hit him in mid-stagger, and though he threw a couple of punches it was no fight. He took a few blows but the worst of it was the sidewalk, which he hit with a thunk that he both felt and heard. They went through his pockets and were gone.

The clerk was there when he got back to the Wilson Avenue rooming house. He looked at Billy and shook his head, then went back to his racing form.

You're making a great impression on the Big Town, Billy.

The face Billy found in the mirror made him curse—a dark

cut at the edge of his left eyebrow, a pink swelling under the right. The old break in the bridge of his nose was red and swollen again, and the side of his face was dark with street grit where he'd lain on the pavement. His hand was bleeding as well—he'd landed on his knuckles when he'd fallen.

"Goddammit. Nice face, asshole," he told himself.

It was, he had to admit, a sort of face he'd seen before, on the Old Man, on the drunks in the old neighborhood. A face he'd seen in pictures in his father's fight magazines—Lou Nova after Tony Galento worked him over or Carmen Basilio against just about anybody. He tilted his head to this angle and that and decided Basilio'd never taken this much punishment without giving some back. He poured himself a shot of vodka from a half-pint and fell onto the bed with his clothes on.

The next morning, Sunday, he stood under the shower for a long time, then did his best to fix his face. He gingerly mopped at the cut, first with warm water, then with a handkerchief dabbed in vodka. The swelling had gone down under the other eye and on his nose, so that the cut was the worst of it, and the rest of his face simply looked discolored in places. He shaved and put on clean clothes.

Then he sat on the bed and assessed the other damage. They'd gotten some of his cash but he still had some money in the Vaseline jar. When he was rooting through his wallet he found the card:

HARRY A. STRUMMER, President
PEERLESS DETECTIVE AGENCY
Discretion, Professionalism, Persistence. Licensed in three states.
1154 N. Wells Street, Room 431

Billy mused for a moment over the loopy title of this man's "business." Then he reminded himself that he was in no position to be fussy. If he was going to stay here for any length of time he needed to stabilize things. This Harry Strummer was his first actual "contact." His only contact in the city. On Monday morning, he would check out the Peerless Detective Agency.

To celebrate his decision, Billy Fox decided to buy himself breakfast. He walked until he found a place with empty stools at the counter, a Steak 'n' Egger. He took the stool at the farthest end of the counter. A young waitress came with a glass of water. She was small and thin, with large gray eyes that missed nothing. But she'd been a waitress in a diner long enough to know what to ask and what not to ask.

"Morning. You okay, Hon?" He heard a Southern accent, Tennessee or Kentucky, he would have said. She scanned his bruised face, then looked down at her pad.

"Sure. Fell down the stairs. Clumsy, I guess."

She nodded and glanced at his bruised knuckles, but said nothing. She slid a menu in front of him and asked, "Coffee?"

He nodded. While she was getting the pot, Billy took out the business card again and stared at it, rubbing his fingers across the raised lettering as though it was a talisman and might bring him his first luck in this town. The waitress poured coffee for him, and he was looking her over when she met his eyes. She took in the damage to his face and he looked away.

The waitress brought glasses of water to a pair of newcomers and shot him a sympathetic look. He tried to hide his embarrassment in the menu. Her nametag said "Millie."

As she walked back toward the other customers, he watched her. He was staring at the tight skirt stretched across her hips when she caught him, a practiced look over her shoulder. She frowned, and Billy looked down at his coffee.

Well played, Champ, he told himself. Jesus.

He bought himself bacon and eggs and left the waitress a generous tip. As he left, he glanced her way. She raised her hand in a small wave.

THREE

Career Opportunities

The office of the Peerless Detective Agency was on the fourth floor, and there was no elevator. Room 431 was the first office in a narrow corridor of perhaps ten similar offices. From what Billy could see, only three were occupied, and the building's owners had chosen to save money by keeping the far end of the hall unlit. Billy wondered what a client would think of a business that literally hovered at the edge of darkness.

A pebbled glass door proclaimed "PEERLESS DETECTIVE" in gold and black letters. Below the name, the sign said, "Please Come In."

Even so, Billy knocked. A voice inside said, "It's open," and he turned the knob and pushed, then ducked just his head in.

At a desk along the far wall, Harry Strummer was watching him, eyebrows raised, and Billy would have said from something in Harry Strummer's face that he'd been expecting Billy.

"Hello, uh, I'm—"

"Hey, kid. Yeah, yeah, I remember you. Billy, right? Billy Fox."

"That's right."

Harry Strummer took in the bruised face, missed nothing, but he just smiled.

"So come on in and close the door behind you. We got the air going."

Billy closed the door behind him and stood just inside the office, taking it in. "The air" was on—he could hear the death rattle of a window unit in its last days—but the air in the room was humid.

Somewhere he heard jazz playing low. His first impression was of clutter. There were papers and files and folders on nearly every surface and two phonebooks open side-by-side on a desk. Near the window was a water cooler with paper cups, and, in a space that might have comfortably fit two people at desks, there were three people and four desks. Closest to the door, a woman was typing at a boxy-looking computer with a tiny screen. To one side of her desk was an enormous typewriter. The music was coming from a radio on a corner of her desk. She looked at him, gave Harry Strummer a quick look, and went back to her work. At the far side of the office, a tall bald man sat on the edge of a desk, looking at some sort of gun-shaped tool. This man paused from his work and gave Billy a long, slow look.

Ex-cop, Billy told himself. There was, Billy's old man had once said, a face they all get, cops, a face they learn, so when they stop being cops they've still got it.

Yeah, you made me for the kind of guy you've busted a hundred times, and I made you for a cop.

Billy gave him a short nod and the man nodded back. Blue eyes, long stare, unblinking.

"You been boxing," the tall man said.

"Yeah, badly."

Harry Strummer was grinning at him. He waved Billy over to his desk.

"So...you come by to see about work?"

"Yeah. You said you might be able to, you know—I thought maybe you'd know about something."

"Yeah. I looked around, made some inquiries."

Billy looked away at the word "inquiries."

"Here's what I can tell you—restaurant up the street here on Wells, the Old Jerusalem, they need a busboy. Liquor store downstairs from us, you probably saw it when you came in, they need a guy to do stock. They pay okay, I think. You'll earn your money, though."

"I don't mind work," Billy said, but he heard the flat sound of his own voice.

Harry Strummer seemed to be studying him. "Here's the other thing...I could use somebody here."

From the corner of his eye Billy saw the bald man look up at this, but he kept his eyes on Harry Strummer.

"Here? In the office?"

"Well, from time to time, yeah, we'll teach you how to handle the phones, most of our business comes in over the phone, but I can tell you're not an office guy. There's stuff that comes up where I need somebody, another body, able-bodied guy. Right now, for instance, we got four things going, four jobs, and there's just me and Leo here, most of the time." He indicated the bald man.

Billy shot a quick glance at the woman in the room, and Harry shook his head.

"Doris there don't go out in the field. She's in charge here." The woman looked up for the first time, giving Harry an ironic glance. She had a hard face that might have been pretty once, and tired eyes—he'd seen the look, the face of a harried mother, or somebody married to a drinker. Forties, maybe forty-five, bushy red hair slightly out of control, nice skin. Polite, too—she met his eyes and refused to give him and his unimpressive clothes the once-over, didn't stare at his banged-up face.

"Doris, Hon, this is Billy. He might be doing some work for us."

She nodded and said, "Hello, Billy," then smiled and took ten or twelve years off her face.

"And that's Leo, who I already mentioned. He's my chief investigator."

Billy thought he heard the woman called Doris snort at this.

The tall man saluted with the gun-like thing he was playing with. Billy waved a hand and said, "Hey, Leo."

Now that they'd shared that first look, Leo smiled, a happy kid's grin.

Billy glanced around the office. It was a dog-eared sort of place, cluttered with furniture that didn't match, a torn window shade, a wet spot high on one wall where the plaster looked to have sprouted mold—the Old Man would have been at it with his scraper and his trowel, a smoke hanging from his mouth.

"So what do you think, Bill?"

Billy looked back at Harry Strummer and was a split second from "Thanks but no thanks." Instead, he said, "I don't know anything about this kind of work."

"We'll show you what you need to know. It's like anything else, you start at a place, they train you. They train bank tellers and guys that flip burgers." He watched Billy for a moment, and it seemed to Billy that this man did that a lot, just watched you between the sentences.

"You don't like it, you can quit and you're no worse off than you were. But it'll be interesting for you, I think. We do some interesting work here. You'll see the city, meet people—all kinds of people. You'll learn things." Harry nodded in agreement with himself. "When I was your age, I did odds and ends for an old-timer, a real detective. Guy had a gift, a great gift. Smartest man I ever knew."

From the other side of the room Leo said, "Wayne Ziegler," and nodded.

"Wayne Ziegler. That's right. And I learned a lot."

Billy looked around the room, nodding. Time to back out of this, he thought. Then he heard himself ask, "So what happens here? What do you do? Follow people?"

Harry Strummer shrugged and tilted his head to one side.

"Well, if the case requires it, yeah, but we do a lot more than that. Although following people without being seen is a lost art. A lot of the stuff we do is a lost art."

"There's a reason for that," Doris muttered, but Harry seemed not to have heard her.

"Mostly, people come to us with a problem and we try to do something for them. We help people here, all kinds of people, in all different situations. But we help people with their, you know, issues."

Now he shot a look at Doris, as though challenging her to dispute this. She went on typing. He looked back at Billy.

"I'll pay you a hundred and a half a week—minimum wage would be about one-twenty-five. A hundred and a half and the occasional cash bonus. Stay six months and we'll talk about, you know, benefits. Interested?"

"Maybe. I'm not in any position to be fussy."

"Want to start now?"

"Why not?"

"Good. You're hired. When we're done, you give your information to Doris so she can put you on payroll. Now come here."

Harry led him over to a desk and told him to pull up the visitor's chair. Billy took a seat facing him. Harry spread four manila folders on the desk, like a dealer showing card tricks.

"Here's four cases. Four people come to us because they need our services." He tapped one with a finger. "This guy wants us to follow his wife." He tapped the next folder. "This guy don't know where his wife *is*. He wants us to find his wife. This lady," he said, tapping the third folder, "is looking for her son." Harry Strummer's gaze rested on Billy for a moment before he went on. "And this last one, this lady here is looking for an item of great value."

"Great value, huh?"

"A precious artifact."

"So you've got all four things going at once."

"Oh, no," Harry said. "We've got four going on already that I referred to before. These are new. If we take them on—and we probably won't take all of them—we'll have eight. I'm telling you, there's always something coming through that door or over that phone."

"So detective agencies are always kind of hopping."

"Except for the times they're not," Doris said without turning.

Harry glanced her way and dismissed her with a shake of his head.

"I'll tell you, Bill. When there's nothing going on, just keep watching that door. It'll swing open and somebody will come stomping in with a worried look in their eyes, and we'll have a case. You got a city of three million people. Thousands of them have troubles requiring somebody to help them out. And they don't know who to turn to. Some of them find us."

"How? How do they know?"

"Word of mouth, Bill. The world runs on word of mouth. You take care of somebody, provide a professional service at a fair rate, and word spreads. People hear about you. I have an ad in the phone book, too. People just find us."

Billy looked at the four folders. "So you're good at finding people, huh?"

Harry gave him an odd little smile, a man reflecting on a private joke. "Yeah, you might say that. That's one of our areas of expertise. We can find people. We can find things. And other services as required." He shot a sly look over at Doris, who looked up from her work and shook her head.

Billy looked from one to the other and then glanced at the folders on the desk.

So, he thought, *you know how to find people. I'm in the right place, then.*

"We're gonna start you out with a couple of lessons. Leo will give you your first one, and then I have a task for you. An assignment."

"Already?"

"No time like the present. Leo, can you show Billy what you've got over there?" He looked at Billy. "Leo's going to show you how to pick a lock."

Billy felt himself grinning. "Really?"

"Comes in handy."

"Isn't it—I mean—illegal?"

Harry gave him a blank look. "Picking a lock? Why, no, I don't think so. It's just a thing. There's all kinds of occasions when you might need access to a place and don't have a key. Everybody loses his keys, right? Go ahead, pull up a chair with Leo. We'll talk later."

Billy did as instructed and Leo gave him the cop look again, but only for a moment. The look was replaced with a pleased expression, a man and his hobbies, Billy would have said. Spread out on the desk were half a dozen locks of various design, and beside them a row of odds and ends that included a pair of paper clips, screwdrivers large and small, and several slender steel rods. At the far end of the row were two of the gun-like objects Leo had been playing with earlier.

"You ever pick a lock?" Leo asked.

"Can't say I have."

"You never needed to get into a place back there wherever home is and didn't have a key?"

"No. Well, once or twice I had to get in through a window."

Leo shook his head. "You attract too much attention going through windows. Hard to look, you know, dignified, crawling through a window. It's hard to look natural. But if you can get in the front way, you can look like you belong there, like there's nothing going on. So here's the deal—your typical dead-bolt lock has tumbler pins in it, and the key pushes some of them in, so what you want to do with a pick is figure out how to push the right pins in. Watch."

Leo picked up a lock and inserted two of the thin steel rods. He kept one still while working at the lock with the other. In a few seconds the lock popped open. He then repeated the process with the two paper clips, opening another lock with a single steel rod and an Allen wrench, and then a third with a tiny flathead screwdriver and a long needle. Finally, he demonstrated each of the gun-things on a standard door lock. He put down the lock and held up the heavy screwdriver.

"And you can use a big one of these to turn out the entire cylinder. You try."

For several minutes Billy fumbled with two picks and a Yale lock, then gave up.

"Nah, try again. Nothing's easy the first time you do it."

Billy tried again and finally snapped open the lock. He nodded and picked up a second lock, and worked on this for some time with the picks. Eventually it opened. He felt himself grinning, like a kid who's just learned to tie his shoes.

"Good work," Leo said. "Now you can pick a lock. In your free time here, sit down with these other locks and try the different tools, to prepare yourself for any emergency."

Billy had to wonder what sort of emergency would require him to pick a lock. Still, it was something new. A new skill.

He shrugged. "So there's no such thing as a good lock?"

"They're all good for what they're supposed to do. The average person can't pick locks, the average burglar can't. He's hoping he'll find an open window or something. But there's no lock that can't be picked, in my opinion. You want to make your door foolproof, put on a couple of heavy brackets and lay a two-by-four across them. Like they did in the old days. You got a big cross-beam across your door, nobody's picking that. Try a couple more."

Billy fumbled and worked the picks and the paperclips and the knitting needle, at one point getting one sharp end of a paper clip under his nail.

Leo smiled. "You drew blood your first day. That's gotta be a good sign."

In the end, Billy was able to open three different locks with Leo's makeshift range of lock picks.

Leo looked at him. "See? You been here, what? An hour and a half? And you already learned how to pick a lock. Learning something new, that's what you want to keep doing in life. You stop learning, you turn into a vegetable."

From across the room Harry called out, "Leo's the company philosopher."

Leo nodded. "You'll learn something new every day here, Bill."

That's just what I need.

In his room, he sat on the bed and began making notes, random notes without any plan to them, but his notes on what he'd learned thus far. He'd begun to learn the neighborhoods, understood there were particular communities where a woman with a small child might choose to live if she were relatively new to the Big Town. He remembered something Rita had once told him, about visiting an uncle and aunt and being taken to a ballgame—a Cub game at Wrigley Field. That meant her people were north siders—south siders would have taken her to a Sox game at Comiskey Park. He would look north. For now, that was as far as his thinking could take him, but it was a start.

FOUR

Street School

The man in the chair was enormous, a heavy-limbed giant with a gut and a crew-cut and a face dark with anger. As he told Harry Strummer his tale, he smoldered and shook with his rage, leaning so far over the desk that it seemed any moment he would fall upon Harry and smother him with his huge body.

At one point he pointed a fat finger in Harry's face, close to his eyes, and Harry gently pushed the finger aside.

When the big man was finished, Harry leaned back and said, "Can't help, Mr. Dobrowski."

"Why not?"

"We don't usually take on this type of case. You need one of the big agencies for this."

"Oh, sure, the ones that'll charge me my left nut for their services."

"Not necessarily. But we can't take this one. Besides, we've got a few things going on right now."

The big man looked around the office as if to question whether they had anything at all going on.

"We're a small agency, sir. We can't take on everything. And we don't do this kind of work." A faint edge had come into Harry's voice, and Mr. Dobrowski was taken by surprise. He glared for a moment, then got up, said "Fuck it!" and stormed out the door, making sure he banged it against the wall on his way out.

They listened to him pounding down the stairs, cursing as he went and muttering threats against his wife and her boyfriend.

Billy smiled. "You didn't want to take his case because he'll do somebody some damage. Am I right?"

"There's that consideration. We never want to lead a client to somebody if there's a chance he'll do harm. But basically, Bill, we don't have to work for assholes, or madmen. Never get involved with anybody driven by rage like that. They're unpredictable, and there's always the chance they'll turn on you if it doesn't work out the way they want. So, no, I've got no interest in helping this walking time bomb find his wife and her lover."

For a moment Harry seemed to lose his train of thought. He stared across the room, and a slight look of distress seemed to cross his face. Then he looked at Billy.

"We get to pick who we'll work for, that's the thing." He clapped his hands together.

"So these first couple of weeks, we're going to teach you the ropes, the basics of the detective business."

"*The ropes*," Billy soon decided, meant running him ragged. For his first two weeks as an "operative" it seemed that he never stopped running, never stopped moving for more than an hour at a time. Billy made deliveries and drop-offs, he picked up packages and envelopes, he made phone calls to the various utilities and credit agencies. He wrote down information and gave it to Harry. When Harry wasn't sending him out, he gave Billy old case files to study—"To give you the flavor of the thing," he said. In his free time, he watched Doris show him how to type up client forms on the massive IBM Selectric.

"Sit down, Hon," Doris said. "Let me show you this dinosaur."

"My Ma was a typist," Billy said.

Doris just looked at him, and he understood he'd missed a point.

"When I was a girl, I visited my grandma in the projects over there by Roosevelt Road, not far from the produce markets, and there was a man we used to see driving a wagon, a horse-drawn wagon, on his way to get a load of fruit and vegetables. My grandma used to go to the window and say, 'Right down there is the last wagon in Chicago, pulled by the last workhorse.' I always wondered how he felt, that man driving the last wagon in Chicago, and you know what, Billy? Now I know, 'cause I'm working on the last typewriter in Chicago."

"It's a good typewriter, top of the line," Harry said absently, rummaging through a drawer in his desk.

"If you have a good computer, you don't need a typewriter."

"You have a computer."

"*This?*" Doris said, and pointed at it with her hand limp, as if contaminated by the computer. "This thing has already died several deaths. It freezes up, it crashes, it wants to die."

Harry shrugged. "It's a rebuilt computer," he said to Billy. "It was the best we could do at the current time." He shook his head. "She thinks a new computer is the answer to everything, it's a panacea."

"A what?"

"A cure for everything."

"For somebody like us," Doris said, "it *is* a cure for everything. Every respectable business in Chicago has computers, they keep their records on them, and their inventory, and their files and whatnot." She gave Harry a long look. "Every business in town. Except this one."

"I don't like them. That printer thing sounds like somebody shooting BBs at the window."

Doris looked at Billy again.

"It's the age of the computer, Billy. It'll change the world. The Army has computers that talk to one another, from one part of the country to another." She looked around at the office, her eyes coming to rest on a gray file cabinet. She sighed, shook her head, and began showing Billy the various forms used in the office.

Later, Harry showed Billy the case files on former clients, cabinets filled with manila folders, hundreds of them. A small smile crossed Harry Strummer's face as he displayed the contents of the cabinet.

"I been in this business a long time."

"I can see that."

"I've kept records of every case I ever had, even some of the ones I decided not to take on. You never know when you're going to need information about somebody. But you keep files, meticulous files, you got everything you need right here. She wants to keep it all in that box where a lightning strike could wipe it all out. I want things where I can grab 'em, spread the file out across the desk, compare one piece of the file with another, or put two files out and compare two people, see if they have any point of connection. How am I going to do that on a computer? A business lives and dies with its records, Bill."

Harry walked over to his file cabinet. "Yeah, I still have files from those early days, all my files from my days in Kansas City and Milwaukee. They're all there," he said. He pointed to each drawer. "This top one is Ongoing, that one is Closed, and the third one is Incomplete."

"What about that box in the corner?"

"That's dormant."

"*Dormant*," Doris repeated with annoyance. Harry laughed. "I considered *comatose* but that sounded too dramatic." After a moment he added, "I've got 'em all, from my first agency in Kansas City to now."

"So you had an agency before this."

"For a while. It wasn't like this. I didn't have my network there. I was mostly using other people's contacts and advice, I didn't have—" Harry waved in the air for a word. "I didn't feel independent there. Nice town, though, I liked Kansas City." Then in a musing voice, he added, "It didn't like me."

Billy sensed that he'd reached a dead end. A distant look had come into Harry's eyes. Billy watched Doris for a moment then asked, "Did you like Kansas City, Doris?"

"I wasn't there," she said without looking up from her work. "I actually have a life of my own." Then she added, "Which I was busy screwing up at the time in question."

"Weren't we all," Harry added.

. . .

At the beginning of his third week at Peerless Detective, Harry called him over to his desk. He spread four folders out.

"These are the cases we already had going. Each one of these is somebody that we're supposed to look for. That one," he said, nodding at the folder on the left, "I think I've found this person. Now I have to decide what to do about it. This one," he pushed a second folder out with his finger. "we're not gonna find."

"Why not?"

"Later. I'll explain later. To the client first, of course. These two here, they're both kids on the run. We're gonna look for them. One of the things I'm going to give you, you're going to help us find one of them. But that's later. So this week, here is your first actual field assignment."

He handed Billy a white business envelope.

"Tomorrow you'll deliver this to a Mr. Hans Anger, at the address on the envelope."

"*Anger?*"

"Doesn't mean he's pissed off. It's German."

"In German it means '*angel*,'" Doris said without turning.

"There you go. Just deliver this. No need to chat with him afterwards. Then Thursday morning you will spend some time—in my car, no less—performing routine surveillance on this gentleman, Mr. James McCaffrey, and you'll note what you see in that notebook of yours. Thursday afternoon you'll do another thing for me. Surveillance again. And I think Friday I'll let you make a delivery for me."

Doris suppressed a laugh here. Billy shrugged.

"Simple stuff," Harry said.

. . .

For the first fifty yards or so, the big man with the mop of brown hair was gaining on him. Billy could even hear him breathing. He kept on running, down an alley and up a street and then down another street, and Hans Anger, all two-hundred-seventy pounds of him, stayed with Billy. He was huge, bent on violence, and clearly not an angel. Billy cut across an intersection against the traffic, and over the horns and the cursing he could still hear the big man's feet pounding hard and getting close. At Western Avenue, Billy dashed back out into traffic, slipped in front of a bus, and made it to the far side. He stood leaning against a street sign and gasping. On the far side of the street, the big man was bent over, panting, spent.

"God almighty," Billy said.

Hans Anger sucked in air and stared black death at him, and then he walked away.

• • •

Billy watched as Harry entered the hallway of an apartment building on Damen. Harry rang the bell several times, finally leaning on it in a way calculated to irritate the resident. Then Harry went out on the sidewalk and made a show of staring up at the windows and shaking his head. He went around to the back of the building, emerging a few minutes later and making another display of peering up at the windows, this time with a folded document in his hands. A moment later he left, and Billy stayed in Harry's parked car across the street. Five minutes later James McCaffrey emerged from the apartment building and looked up and down his street. He got into his car and drove off, and Billy pulled out behind him and followed him. He watched and noted James McCaffrey's itinerary, the same itinerary McCaffrey had gone through the day before: a diner on Elston, a hardware store on Diversey, his place of business—a small construction company—then lunch at a tavern down the street. But on this second day, McCaffrey made a trip back up Elston to a padlocked building off an alley. Billy watched as McCaffrey got out of his car and looked around. He opened the lock, looked around again and went in, emerging a moment later with a bundle wrapped in some sort of canvas. He locked the building, tugged a couple of times on the lock. He took a furtive look up the alley, then walked back to his car, watching the street. Billy followed him to his hardware store again and watched him go behind the store and move a pile of crates to get at a small shed. McCaffrey opened the shed, reached inside and seemed to move things around. Billy saw him set the bundle down inside. Then he closed the shed and put the crates back in place. When he was finished, the shed was completely buried.

• • •

"Let 'em see you," Harry had said. "Don't be afraid to let 'em see you after a while."

The first two times, the dozen or more kids outside the Dunkin' Donuts took no notice of Billy. A colorful bunch, Billy had to admit—hats, braids, and beards, as well as a couple of Fu Manchu moustaches, a Mohawk, a girl with orange hair, and one with what appeared to be a rainbow. The third time there, he stood across the street in a doorway. A smaller group was by the Dunkin' Donuts this time. Billy stepped out of the doorway, and two of the boys saw him. The one with the Mohawk said something, a third kid looked his way, and Billy left. Later that night he returned and stood on a different corner, still facing the Dunkin' Donuts. He walked away, came back, stood in a doorway, walked around the block, came up behind the Dunkin' Donuts, and this time went in. He bought a coffee and a donut and went across the street, eating, sipping his coffee, and looking everywhere on the street but in the direction of the Dunkin' Donuts. From the corner of his eye he saw the attention he drew.

Just as he finished the coffee, he saw a kid nod in his direction. Billy began to move off, slowly. A short, red-haired boy started walking away from the Dunkin' Donuts, moving fast on Belmont. Billy waited a moment, then left the corner, walking slowly up Clark Street. When he was out of sight he broke into a run, cut down an alley, and ran the length of the block. When he emerged he made his way back to Belmont. In the distance, a block or so away and moving fast, he saw the kid who had left the Dunkin' Donuts. He kept to the far side of the street and followed the kid until he turned up a side street a half mile from the donut place. When he made the turn onto the side street, he saw the kid up ahead. Billy slipped behind a parked car and watched the boy stop at a frame building. The kid looked up and down the street and then went down a short flight of stairs to a basement apartment. Billy moved closer, wrote down the address and the name of the street.

The next morning Billy delivered a manila envelope to the alderman and one to the local watch commander. Later, he took an envelope, soft with cash, to a man named Jerry Singer.

"Give him this, then sit and watch his operation. Ever watched a bookmaker at work?"

"No."

"Might be educational for you. Watch Jerry, watch the people in his place. Then we'll talk later."

Jerry Singer's place of business was behind a TV repair shop on Clybourn, past a long row of housing project buildings. Singer's "office" was busy—half a dozen men in conversation or just reading the racing form or the sports pages. Billy stayed for an hour after delivering Harry's envelope.

That night, Billy wandered and watched the faces of strangers and told himself he would get better at this, he would become skilled at finding people in the big town.

His room was stifling, and the whole place smelled of cigarette smoke. Someone down the hall was blowing softly on a harmonica, and the old man at the far end had his radio on, the oddly reassuring sounds of a ballgame. After a while, Billy decided to go back out.

He walked for a time, thought about going to a movie, and then realized he didn't know where the nearest theater was, though he knew he'd passed several. Instead, he found himself once more at the Steak 'n' Egger, where he was served by the same young waitress named Millie.

When she gave him his food she said, "Your face looks much

better now."

"What? Oh, yeah. Thanks."

"You got to be careful. It's a big town."

"I know my way around it."

She nodded and walked away, and he heard her say, "If you say so, Hon."

A few feet away, a tiny old woman had spread hundreds of pennies on the counter and was painstakingly attempting to count them out. The young waitress watched her without expression. The lady looked up at her, blinked, said, "Oh, dear," and shook her head.

The waitress sighed and made a sympathetic face. "You lost count, right?"

The tiny woman nodded and seemed to shrink back on her stool, as though expecting disciplinary measures.

"Here, sweetheart," the waitress said, and patted the old woman on her birdlike wrist. She moved the pennies to one side and shoved the woman's plate of toast and her cup of tea in front of her. She said, "Eat your toast while it's hot," then started counting the pennies. Billy watched her—she hummed as she counted, and she was halfway through the pile of coins when she looked up and met his eyes.

"More coffee?"

"Uh, sure."

"Here, sweetie. I have to wait on this gentleman and I'll be back, okay?"

The lady blinked and looked around, unsettled. "Should I count some more?"

"No, no, I'll do it when I get back. You eat your food. Drink your tea, it'll get cold."

She gave Billy an amused look as she came over. He noticed for the first time that she had a faint wash of freckles across her nose and cheeks. He wouldn't have called her pretty, not quite, but he'd seen her smile, and it gave her a dimple on one cheek. And the uniform, this universal uniform of the waitress in every diner on earth, tight and shiny and black, made it all interesting.

He nodded. "Lot of pennies."

"It's all she's got, poor thing."

"You're nice to her."

"She lives alone. I think she comes out just to be around people. It doesn't cost me anything to be nice to her. So—our town treating you any better? It can be tough on somebody new in town."

"How do you know I'm new here?"

She shrugged. She wasn't smiling but her eyes showed her amusement. "You've just got a look about you, that's all. You seem like you're, I don't know, looking for something."

An old man down the counter lifted his coffee mug and she went down to fill it, then leaned on the counter as he told her something that made her laugh. Two men got up from a booth and waved to her, and she called them by their names. Eventually, she made her way back to the pennies lady and finished counting. She shoved most of the pennies into her hand and dumped them in the register.

"Here," she said. "This is what you got left. So let's get rid of these annoying pennies, all right?"

Billy watched her dump the rest of the pennies into the register. From a pocket in her apron she produced a dollar and gave it to the old woman.

"Oh. I didn't know there was so much."

"They add up."

When she came over to give Billy his check, he said, "I saw that."

"You saw what?" She gave him an innocent look.

"What you did for the old lady."

She shrugged and said, "I didn't do anything, just made change, is all." She walked away.

"Well. Goodnight."

"You take care now, hear?" she said over her shoulder.

When he left the diner he walked up the street. A few yards away a group of women were waiting for a bus. He glanced their way and then stopped. He felt as though a fist had grabbed his heart. In the middle was Rita. He saw her black hair and the blue dress, her favorite dress. He began moving faster, he started to wave, he opened his mouth to call her name. One of the women gave him a wary look. The black-haired girl in the middle turned his way and frowned, just a stranger in a blue dress. He stopped and turned around, looking back up the street to hide his embarrassment. He walked back the way he had come, his heart still banging against his breastbone.

• • •

On Friday morning, Billy was asked to deliver a bag of groceries to a Mrs. Anna Ricci.

"Mrs. Ricci," Doris said, shaking her head.

"Just deliver them?"

"That's it. Give her my regards," Harry said. "Tell her I was tied up with something."

"Okay."

"And ask her how she's doing—but if she starts to give you a speech, tell her you're on a schedule."

Mrs. Ricci lived in a yellow-brick apartment building with a yard full of weeds. A small dog sat in the middle of the yard, nearly hidden by the shrubbery, and barked at Billy, but his heart wasn't in it.

Billy rang the bell. There was no answer. He rang a second time and was ready to leave when a tentative voice said "Who's there?"

"I'm from Harry Strummer's office," Billy said into the speaker.

A minute later, a small stout woman with her gray hair in a tight bun appeared at the glass door. She stared at him for a long time until Billy held Harry Strummer's card up to the glass.

Mrs. Ricci nodded and pushed the door open.

"Hello, young man."

"Hi. Harry sent over some stuff for you." Billy held up the bag and handed it to her.

Mrs. Ricci peered in and said, "Oh, he's such a nice man. You know, young man, he's always been—"

"I've got to run, Ma'am. I'm late for my next, you know, errand."

"Oh."

"But he sends his regards. Oh, and how are you doing, he wants to know."   .

"Oh, you know." She shrugged lopsidedly, one shoulder weighed down by the shopping bag. "I'm feeling okay but—" She nodded toward the wall. "The voices, you know."

"The voices?"

She nodded. "On my phone and through the walls. You know who it is, don't you?"

Billy shook his head.

She leaned forward. "Harry knows. Ask Harry," she whispered.

Billy nodded. "I have to go, Ma'am."

Late that morning, Harry got up from his desk and said, "Come on, Bill. Let's walk. Like Mr. Rogers says on TV, 'It's a beautiful day in the neighborhood.'"

He grabbed a fedora—Billy had already learned that Harry loved hats—and led the way. They strolled up Wells Street, and Harry pointed out things of interest and mused about the golden days of Old Town.

"Old Town? That's what this is?"

"Yeah. It's one of the old neighborhoods. Used to be, this was a wild place. It's still got a lot of things going on, but not like it used to. There was a time, back in the '60s, when this street was jumping, more than just shops and restaurants, there were clubs here, big ones and small ones. Jazz, rock-and-roll, you name it. 'The Hungry Eye,' 'The Butcher Block,' 'The Purple Pickle.'" He paused in front of a restaurant.

"Right here there was a jazz club. I saw Jimmy Smith here—you know jazz players?"

"Little bit. He plays the B-3."

A cabbie honked his horn and waved, and Harry waved back. "You're a musician."

"I didn't say that."

"Most people, they'd say 'Jimmy Smith plays jazz organ,' or

'Jimmy Smith plays keyboard.' You said 'he plays the B-3.' So you're a musician?"

Billy shrugged, annoyed. "I fooled around with it. That's all. I'm no musician."

"Okay," Harry said, and he looked amused. "Anyhow, Wes Montgomery played here, like two weeks before he died. I was gonna go see him but I was a little short that week, thought I'd catch Wes later in the year." He stared at the front of the restaurant, then turned to Billy.

"I guess you know Wes Montgomery."

"Yeah. Guitar players I know. Played with his thumb." He made an air guitar and pretended to play. "Used the ball of his thumb. He had a callous there, gave him a sound nobody else had."

Harry nodded as though reaffirmed in something. They walked on another half block and he indicated a small building, a house converted into a club.

"And that same time, one Friday night I'm walking by here and there's a little Xerox of a story from the *Sun-Times*, says this kid is gonna be playing here, blind kid from Mexico. I watched him for a set, incredible talent."

"Jose Feliciano."

"You got it."

Harry stopped at the corner and did a little turn on one heel, hands in his pockets. He looked around at the street and smiled, jingling the change in his pockets.

"Oh, this was a great place. A place for a young guy. Clubs, places to eat, great music, girls down here, lotta girls, you'd see half a dozen of 'em together, every one of 'em good-looking."

"When you don't have one, they all look good."

Harry was about to say something more when he stopped and smiled at Billy.

"Hey, so you're a philosopher. Pretty smart for a young guy."

"I know that much. Probably not much more."

"And that's smart, too. Let's go further your education."

A waitress came out of a restaurant and called out, "Hi,

Mr. Strummer."

Harry tipped his hat to her. "Hey, Ruthie."

At the corner of North Avenue and Wells, Harry stopped and said, "Just stop and watch everybody coming and going."

"What am I looking for?"

Harry laughed and said, "Life. No, just look around and we'll chat in a few minutes."

And so Billy stood next to Harry and listened to him jingling his pocket change, and watched the street. He noted the new facades on old buildings, noted the businesses, the restaurants and shops up and down Wells Street. In the week before he'd met Harry Strummer, Billy had covered this street looking for a way to make a buck, but had spent much of his time looking on the sidewalk and off the curb for dropped change, and so hadn't noticed much else.

Confused as to what he was supposed to be seeing, he shot a covert glance at Harry Strummer, who seemed to be watching people. To a bystander, Harry might have seemed aimless, or a man at his leisure, but Billy already knew to watch the man's eyes, and saw that he studied the people going by with well-disguised interest. From time to time, he broke up his scrutiny of the street and occupied himself with an endless series of small actions. He squinted up at the sun, peered up at the street signs and consulted a tattered piece of paper, hummed a few bars of "It was a very good year," and broke into his own humming with a line or two from the song. He put on and removed his sunglasses, wiped the lenses on his tie, put the glasses back on, took them off and put them inside his suit coat, looked in his wallet, counted his pocket change, removed his hat and pulled a thread from the label, compared the nails on both his hands, lit a cigarette, inhaled, blew out smoke, and looked at Billy with a look of mild interest.

Billy laughed. "You're like a little kid that can't sit still."

"When you're doing any kinda surveillance, when you're tailing somebody, you want to look like you're the last guy on the street that would be interested, like you're the last guy that might notice anything. But I notice things."

"Like what?"

"No, you first. You're the one in training."

"I don't know. Just a lot of people going back and forth. Like on their lunch hour. Whatever."

"Don't say 'whatever.' It means 'I don't give a shit.'"

"I didn't mean anything by it."

"It's okay. What else? What kind of people. Think—you saw it, so it's in there."

Harry pointed to Billy's forehead.

Billy looked around to buy a minute, then began to remember people he'd noticed.

"I saw one guy, he was lost, I think. Black guy, real thin, piece of paper in his hand that he kept looking at. I saw this foxy chick—a girl, I mean, orange dress, like a summer dress—"

Harry grinned. "She doesn't count. Anybody would have noticed her."

"I saw a couple of businessmen in ties, I saw some kids running across the street against the light, thought they were gonna get killed. Let's see, I saw a guy carrying some kinda gas can." He looked at Harry to see if he'd recalled enough. No reaction—Harry just watched him behind those sunglasses.

"Okay, let's see, what else? Oh, yeah, I saw a couple of old people, the woman looked nervous, like she's not used to the big city. She was hanging onto the man's arm."

Harry thrust out his lower lip and nodded. "Not bad, that's not bad. The last part, I mean. Those were tourists, German tourists, I think, and the lady was a little unnerved by all of it so, yeah, she was clinging to her husband."

"How could you tell they were German?"

"Couple things. I watched their mouths as they talked, and it didn't look like English. And the man was wearing those little braided leather sandal shoes, with socks. Americans don't do that. German, I think, maybe Swiss or Austrian. But tourists. Okay, here's what else I saw. The guy that was lost is a cab driver. I saw him get out of his cab about a half a block up the street, and he went up to each address and stared at that paper. So yeah, he's lost, which makes him a fairly typical cab driver. African, I think."

"African?" Billy smiled. "How could you tell—oh, his clothes. His shirt."

"Okay, the shirt, yeah, good. Some kind of tunic thing. But any guy can wear a tunic, and half the brothers dig this African stuff, so he could have been homegrown. No, I made him African from his face, his facial expression—Americans got a way they look, we look a certain way. If you went to Poland, or Ireland, say, a local guy would pick you out on the street as an American by your facial expressions. So this guy looked African to me. And he had scars."

"Yeah, I saw that. Knife fight, you think?"

Harry turned to him, amused. "You watch too many movies. Those were tribal scars. I think he's Nigerian. Remember Dick Tiger, the fighter? He had those scars on his face and his body, tribal scars, initiation stuff with a spear, a young man's, you know, rite of passage. We think we've got it bad with puberty! And speaking of puberty, those kids running through traffic, they were running from somebody but they didn't think they were gonna get caught."

"Because they were laughing."

"Right. But they weren't entirely sure, so they kept looking over their shoulders. Now, that guy with the gas can?"

"Ran out of gas and he's trying to scrape up money."

"Yeah. But here's where I've got an unfair advantage over you, Bill. This is more or less my neighborhood. I work here, I eat and drink in most of these places, I go in the shops, I know people, and I'm on this street, this corner, a lot. And I can tell you the guy with the gas can is a con man. The gas can's his prop. Come back here in a couple days, maybe a week, and you'll see him again. He's smart enough not to be here every day, but every few days he works this neighborhood. When he's not here, he might be up there by DePaul University, or farther north by Cubs Park, and it's always the same story—'Hey, can you help a guy out? I broke down on Lake Shore Drive and I need to get to Arlington Heights and I just need a buck for gas, just a buck and I can get home.' And he holds up his prop and people give him money."

"Okay. I'm impressed. What else did you see that I missed?"

"A lady that was having trouble in her life. Looked near tears."

"I didn't see her."

"Not a pretty woman, and dressed plain. Sometime in her life people told her she was plain, so she's gonna spend her whole life dressing the part." Harry shook his head.

"Anyhow, she's got trouble in her life, new trouble, because she was going somewhere fast, like maybe trying to get to a hospital. I saw her watching the street for a cab that didn't have a fare."

"One other person I noticed. A young guy, about your age, standing on the corner across the street. If I had to bet money on it, I'd say he was looking to grab a purse or pick a pocket. Purse, I think, this guy didn't look skilled, and it takes skill to pick somebody's pocket."

"Maybe he was waiting for a bus."

"Nah. He was watching people, looking at women's bags. Like that. And if you caught his eye he looked away."

Billy looked around.

"No, he's gone now. I think he finally saw me watching him. If you were a purse-snatcher and two guys on the corner seemed to be doing nothing else but watching you, you'd take off, too. But you did pretty good. When you've been at it a little longer, you'll notice more. C'mon, let's walk, and you can tell me about your week's worth of assignments."

Eventually they stopped at a park bench on Clark Street near the Historical Society.

"Okay. Let's go over your assignments. First, Hans Anger."

"I thought I was gonna get killed. I never saw a big man who could move like that. I didn't know which would happen first—he'd catch me and kill me, or he'd have a heart attack."

Harry laughed. "You find big men that are quick and it's a shock. But you served him his papers?"

"So, what's the big deal with serving a guy these papers?"

"It's a game with some of them. They tie themselves in knots figuring out ways to avoid getting served. As long as they don't get the papers, they can say they haven't had any legal notice that they're supposed to come to court. And Hans Anger thinks he's a pretty smart player. But you just found our boy and gave him his papers, so now he has to go to court and face his formidable ex-wife. You ruined his game and his day. Is it any surprise he wants to cream you?"

"Dangerous work," Billy said.

"I know guys that do nothing but serve people with summonses. They get good at it, they like it. There's, you know, a competitive element to it, one guy trying to outsmart the other."

Harry looked at Billy's notes.

"And you found our kid, our missing kid."

"That was him? The one I followed to the basement place?"

Harry shook his head. "Nah. That guy led you to the kid we're looking for. He went to tell the kid somebody was watching them all at the Dunkin' Donuts. This kid, the one we're looking for, he's become a creature of the night. That's when he comes out. You told me where he was, and I had Leo sit out there in his car and wait, and sure enough, around midnight the kid comes out to breathe. Leo had his picture. So we found him."

"Now what happens?"

"We told his old man already. That was the little thing you dropped off at the alderman's office. It's his kid."

"Oh. The alderman's kid—"

"All families have trouble, Bill. How was Mrs. Ricci?"

"She was—well, she said she was okay except for the voices. She said you knew about the voices." Billy shrugged. "What voices?"

"Ah, she hears things and gets confused. She's old and she lives alone. Someday you might be there, Bill. You're old, you live alone, you start talking to the squirrels outside your window. You'll be seeing Mrs. Ricci again, Bill," Harry said, chuckling.

Billy looked around at the street.

"Go ahead. I think you have something you want to ask."

"Couple things. First of all—kids on the run. That's a regular thing we do?"

Harry nodded slowly. "A specialty of the house. You already know we look for people. But we've had good success finding kids. I don't mean we can find them all, but if the client gives us good enough information, we have a shot. A good shot. And actually, we have another case that just came in—guy wants us to find his daughter. Yeah, we're pretty good at tracking down people." After a moment he added, "All kinds of people."

Harry looked him in the eye and smiled, and Billy wondered if he was imagining a little extra glimmer of amusement there.

"Yeah," Harry said, breaking off his gaze. "We do all of that. What else did you want to ask me?"

"That thing I dropped off at the police station—we do work for the police?"

"This was personal. We did something for this man, Lieutenant Joe Jerome. Sometime he'll do something for us. At least, that's how I hope it comes out. You never know about people. But in general, you do favors for people, for decent people, they remember you. It's all about being a reliable individual, and it's what builds your cadre."

"Your what?"

"Your *cadre*. The people in your, you know, in your sphere of life, the ones you can look to for information or count on for a little help. So I've done favors for local politicians and cops and other detective agencies. I've even done a favor or two for a connected guy."

"Connected? Like, a gangster?"

Harry shrugged. "I don't know him in that capacity. I know him as a guy with some business enterprises here and on the south side, as a guy with a kid who he had some concerns about. The kid ran away once. I found him. The guy owes me."

"A gangster," Billy said, and shook his head.

"Just because you're a gangster doesn't mean you're free of life's problems. This one's got a kid he doesn't know what to do with and health issues and a wife with a terminal illness. He just happens to be a hood."

"So who else is in your cadre?"

"Well, Leo. And Doris, of course. And an old street cop named Dutch—you'll meet him eventually. An old street guy named Babe, old Babe that nobody takes seriously because he lives in alleys, and that's funny because there's nobody that notices more on the street than he does."

"Not even you?"

"Not even me. And let's see…there's a couple of tavern owners, Joe Danno and a lady named Marie—well, bartenders and you know, publicans, they don't even count because they're a source of information for the whole community, you see. A good bartender listens to people, he remembers their names and what they've told him. It's part of his job. And let's see, a certain short-order cook I know, and a guy who runs a junk shop on Clark Street. And there are others." He grinned. "Too numerous to mention. It's what you have to do to get by, you need a little help, a boost. If you live by your wits, you come to understand your wits aren't enough unless you've got somebody else in your corner. Difference between your mature, streetwise guy and a young fellow."

"Oh, yeah? Billy said, sensing just who the *young guy* in question was.

Harry nodded. "Your young guy thinks he can do everything alone, thinks he's Sergeant York."

"Some guys prefer to do what they have to do by themselves, without somebody else's help. It's better that way."

"Yeah? See how far that gets you in life. This is something I know about, Billy," Harry said, the smile gone. "I know about this, I was a guy like you. Thought I could do everything by myself, and I'll tell you what's worse, I thought I didn't need advice from anybody. You should always listen to advice."

"From everybody? Half the people on the street wouldn't know—"

"That's not the point. It don't cost you anything to listen. Just listen…you can sort it out later, but listen to what people say. Listen to what they say about themselves, listen to what they tell you about yourself, learn to listen. And then think about what you hear. Think about it. It's how you'll get by."

Billy wondered what had prompted this small sermon. He changed the subject.

"So what about McCaffrey?"

"We will resolve that tonight. If I can borrow you for a couple hours."

"Sure."

Harry eyed him, squinted. "There's something else. Go ahead."

"That envelope I dropped off for Jerry? I'll tell you what I think—I think you were testing me. You were trying to see if I would pocket the cash, or just some of it. I could have taken, like, a twenty." Billy shrugged. "If it got back to me, I could say, 'why would I just take twenty bucks from an envelope full of cash?'"

Harry nodded. "Good. Yeah, of course, every time you let an employee handle cash, especially the first time, it's a test. We're getting to know each other here. You're testing me, you're still worried you're gonna be some kind of glorified errand boy." Harry gave him a sidelong look. "You're trying to figure out if you're going to want to work for me."

Billy thought for a moment. "No, I know I want to work for you. I think I can learn things. I think I can pick up things that will be useful."

"Good," Harry said, and patted him on the shoulder.

I'll learn how to find someone, and that will change everything for me.

FIVE

The Case of the Blonde Venus

That night Harry picked him up in front of his hotel. Leo was in the passenger seat and Billy saw the doubtful look in Leo's eyes as he surveyed the rooming house. But Leo said nothing. As Billy got in, Leo nodded.

They drove to the spot behind McCaffrey's hardware store where Billy had watched McCaffrey stash the bundle. The store itself was closed, and that stretch of Elston, in an area of factories bisected by the railroad tracks and the river, was nearly devoid of traffic. They moved the crates, and Harry nodded at the lock on the small shed.

"Go ahead, kid, use your newfound skills."

Leo grinned and handed him a pair of lock picks, and the two older men stood between Billy and the street and let him pick the lock. It took him less than twenty seconds.

"Nice work," Harry said.

"Not much of a lock," Billy said.

Leo laughed. "Got that professional cockiness already."

Inside, hidden beneath a pyramid of paint thinner cans and cardboard boxes, they found the bundle. Billy picked it up and hefted it—solid and heavy and bound in canvas and duct tape. He shrugged.

"Feels like a statue. Is that what we're looking for?"

"I'll show you back at the office."

. . .

It was, indeed, a statue, perhaps eighteen inches tall. Harry unwrapped it and dusted it off and they stood back and admired it. A Greek or Roman thing, Billy would have said. A woman draped tastefully in a robe that clung to her in all the appropriate places, a blonde woman looking distractedly to one side, like a preoccupied goddess.

"I like it," Leo said.

"Yeah, it's nice."

Billy gazed at the beautiful Greek lady. "So it's worth a lot of money?"

Harry shrugged. "I don't know about statues. I know I like this one, but we're looking for what's inside."

"We gonna bust it open?" Leo asked.

"That would not be helpful."

"There's something inside?" Billy asked.

"I believe so."

Harry moved the statue around to get a better look at it, then tipped it over and examined the bottom. He tapped it, nodded, and showed it to Billy and Leo.

"See? It's been plugged. Under this felt, there's a plug."

With that, he worried the edge of the felt until it came up, then pulled it slowly away to reveal a circle of wood inserted into the base of the statue. Harry patted his pockets.

"I don't have my knife, Leo."

Leo produced a Swiss Army knife that appeared to have thirty blades.

Harry looked up at Billy, the blade poised over the statue. "You carry a knife?"

"Used to. Lost it."

"You should always carry a knife. And I don't mean for swordfights. There's no end of things you can do with a knife." He winked at Leo. "A knife, duct tape, WD-40. You can do just about anything if you've got those three things. You can fix anything, take most things apart."

As Billy watched, Harry dug at the edges of the wooden plug until it came loose. He pulled it out and peered into Mr. McCaffrey's statue. He dug around with his long slender fingers until he found something.

"Oho! What have we got here?"

He withdrew a slender roll of papers wrapped in a layer of flannel. He removed the flannel and flattened the papers out.

Billy and Leo leaned in.

"Okay, so what do we have?" Billy asked.

Harry tapped the papers. "We have the malfeasance, the miscreancy, of Mr. McCaffrey."

"What's that in English?"

"This is the secret financial life of Jimmy McCaffrey, who has kept his actual net worth a treasured secret from his hapless wife, who actually trusted the sonofabitch."

"This a divorce case?"

"More or less. This is something we're doing for an attorney. Mr. V. C. Carter."

"Sunny Carter," Leo said and laughed.

Billy looked from him to Harry.

"Private joke. Anyhow, Mrs. McCaffrey is divorcing Mr. McCaffrey, and on the face of things he's broke, he's on the verge of bankruptcy. But in the course of our work, we found that Mr. McCaffrey has a very large yacht in Florida and a house there that his wife is unaware of. That is to say, he's top-heavy with cash, he's made of money. And what he's done is to create two sets of records, the one his wife knows about, and this one that he's kept hidden from her. He's got wall safes and safety-deposit boxes and every other thing you can imagine, and his wife knows about all of them—she even swiped the combination to a second safe—but he's a trickster, our Jimmy McCaffrey. In our conversations with Mrs. McCaffrey, she told us he's got certain prized possessions…a gold watch from his grandfather, an autographed baseball from Babe Ruth, a couple baseball cards worth tens of thousands of dollars. So those are things they're negotiating over. And this statue. You see, Billy, it's a reproduction. It's nice but it's not worth a hundred bucks. So we started thinking about the statue. If it was actually worth a real lot of money, he'd have had it in a case, but he didn't. It was out in the open. Then one day, she says it's gone. He's moved it. Told her he got rid of it."

Harry shrugged. "Seemed obvious to me, the statue was worth something somehow. One day it's his prized possession, next day he gets rid of it. Hmmm. So we started to follow him. We figured he had it somewhere he thought was safe. So what we did was spook him a little. Leo broke in to his office—or made it look like he was in there. He never actually went in. But McCaffrey didn't know that, so he panicked a little. Then we did that little charade by his apartment, when I rang his bell and knocked on his back door."

"He thought you were carrying a summons."

"Right. He also thought it was time to move this old girl here." Harry spread the documents out on his table, then smiled at Leo and Billy. "A man of substance, our Jimmy. Hidden bank accounts, deeds, stock account information. All of which we will give to Mr. V. C. Carter, attorney-at-law and bird of prey. He can smell money that's hidden away. I'd rather have the CIA after me than Sunny Carter. And he will give all of this information to the aggrieved Mrs. McCaffrey."

"He'll see what we've done."

"Nah. He won't know till it's too late. Where's the glue?"

For the next ten minutes, Billy watched as Harry made a small dense roll of typing paper, wrapped it in the piece of flannel and stuck it back inside the statue. He then applied the merest trace of glue to the plug and carefully slipped it into place in the statue's base. He applied a thin layer of the glue to the felt covering and put it once more onto the statue's bottom. Then he sat back.

The blonde goddess still looked distracted, but she was otherwise perfect.

Harry shook his head. "You know, when this is over, I might ask Mr. McCaffrey if I can have this statue. Put her on a windowsill with a couple of plants. Dress up a whole room, this lady."

"You want me to put it back?"

Harry nodded. "Leo will drive you. Wrap it up again in this

cloth and put it back exactly the way you found it."

They pulled once more into the alley behind McCaffrey's place of business, and Billy once more picked the simple lock while Leo kept watch. When they were done, Leo patted him on the back.

"Nice work. You did good."

• • •

On Saturday, Billy went to the zoo. He paid little attention to the animals, but scanned the crowd, looking for a single woman with dark hair showing the zoo to her small child. It seemed that every mother with a small child in Chicago was here, and that he was the only unattached male. Eventually, he grew self-conscious and left.

Early the next week, he rode shotgun as Leo "repossessed" a car.

"Basically," Leo said, "this guy stole his ex-wife's car just to piss her off. The things people do after a divorce," he said, shaking his head. "Nobody behaves properly."

Billy watched as Leo approached the vehicle in question carrying the device doctors use to check blood pressure.

"What are you going to do with the blood pressure thing? Is that in case the owner has a stroke?"

"It's a sphygmomanometer, for your information and edification. Watch."

Billy stood aside and watched as Leo slipped the corner of the device inside the door and began to pump. When the door was squeezed open several inches, he took a long metal rod and poked inside the car door. It opened with a pop.

"Wow. That's pretty cool."

"Your top-of-the-line cars like this Imperial are all coming out with these power doors. I can open any power-door car with these two items." He grinned. "You see how much you're learning in just a couple weeks? Sky's the limit here, kid."

That night, he used the phone in the lobby of his rooming house to call Josephine, to tell her he'd found work.

"Oh, I knew you would, Billy. But you be careful in that place."

"I haven't gotten myself killed yet, Jo," he said with a laugh.

• • •

During the nights, he grew accustomed to the sounds of the rooming house—the muffled harmonica, the old man's radio tuned to the Sox game, the faint sound of a jazz station. The rustling of a dozen men lying or sitting on small beds. And coughing—it seemed that half of them coughed. Billy read magazines left out in the hall or pored over his growing collection of street maps. On some level, he understood that much of this was to reassure himself that he was doing something to find a lost girl in a huge town. More and more he understood Harry Strummer's dictum that sometimes you had to get lucky.

SIX

The Case of the TV Star

The glass door swung open and brought a gust of street air and perfume, and a client. Billy said "wow" to himself. This client had stopped traffic in her day. And though her day was long gone, you could still see it. Dark hair gone nearly all silver, a nice face, but lined, high cheekbones gone sharper with age. She looked at Billy as she came in, hard green eyes, not a lady to mess around with.

"Taking them young, Harry?"

"Yeah, the world's passing me by, so I need new blood." Harry rose from his seat and embraced her, and her perfume filled the office. His mother had used a perfume like this, but Billy didn't believe his mother had ever looked like this woman.

Harry introduced her as Beverly Morse. She winked at Leo, whom she obviously knew, said "Hi, Hon," to Doris, and asked her, "Does this guy still think he runs the office?"

"Hey, Bev. How's tricks?" Doris asked. "Cute blouse."

Beverly Morse took the seat Harry offered her, and he had barely gotten back behind his desk before the guest leaned forward and hissed, "I need you to get me a gun. Sell me one, find me one, lend me one, whatever. Hire me an assassin. I need a gun."

"What? A gun? Whoa!"

She looked over at Billy, and he realized he was staring. He forced himself to stare at a client file.

"What for?"

"For use in the assassination of an asshole."

"Want to clarify that for me?"

"My kid is living with this, this mook, this animal, who beats the shit out of her."

"Is this Betsy? Little Betsy?"

"She's not little anymore. She's big enough to make her own mistakes now, and she's making them like she's afraid she'll run out of time."

"And she doesn't want to hear from you about it."

"That's not it. She's the one who told me he hits her. He drinks, he gets into fights, he's just an idiot and a big bully who likes to belt women around." She sank back in the chair, and her face fell. "All the guys in the world, and my kid winds up with a creep." She looked at Harry, and a certain slyness came into her face. "As I recall, you used to be a guy who didn't like to see that in the street, a man hitting a woman."

"I still don't like to see it. But I don't have a gun, I don't use 'em, I don't believe in them. And I wouldn't give you one. That's not the way, Bev."

"So what is the way? And don't tell me to go to the cops. I already did that, and they said if she comes forward and files a complaint—and you know what will happen to her then."

"Peace bond, order of protection. Maybe it works, maybe not. I know."

Beverly took out a cigarette and Harry lit it for her. She puffed at it, and then began talking about how she'd hoped to get her daughter back in school, into college, and insisting that Betsy was a good kid who had shown little judgment about men.

Harry was nodding before she was finished, and at one point Billy could see that he was no longer actually listening. He was thinking. Finally, she seemed to understand that she'd lost him, but she did not seem irritated.

When he looked at her, he had an odd smile on his face. "I have an idea here. Give me the particulars on this gentleman."

An odd small thing happened—Beverly seemed about to snap at him, perhaps that this was no gentleman, and then she caught the look in Harry's eyes. Billy watched her face change, relax. He looked from the woman to Harry, and he saw that they'd played out this scene before, this one or something like it, and this woman knew enough to leave him alone at such a moment.

She leaned forward and began speaking in a low voice, giving Harry information that he wrote down on his little notepad.

At several points Harry interrupted her to ask questions. "Does he gamble?"

"Yeah, he plays the parlay cards, bets on baseball."

"Police involvement in his life?"

"He was dealing, copped a plea to do a couple of months for possession."

"And he's obsessed with Betsy?"

"No, he just won't let her go. He'll leave her someday, Harry. The assholes are all like that. But he won't let her leave him. No, the only thing he's obsessed about is his goddam car."

Harry brightened. "His car? What kind of car?"

"Thunderbird convertible, bright blue."

When he'd asked all his questions, Harry sat for several minutes looking at his notepad and occasionally making a small sideways nod. Once or twice he appeared to be in a silent debate with himself. Then he made a loud sniff, put down his pen, and said, "Okay."

"Okay what?"

"So here's what I can tell you—we, that is my associates and I, Leo and Billy here, we will make a formal call on this gentleman, this Jeffrey Peck, and speak to him. We will lay the situation out for him."

"And then?"

"We will remonstrate with him."

Beverly made an exasperated shake of her head. "Harry, if I wanted somebody to—"

Harry held up a hand for patience. "Work with me here. And let me finish. Be polite, Hon, it's always the best way. Anyway, we will remonstrate with this individual and show him that the path he's taken is a foolhardy path because of Betsy's uncle."

"Her uncle?"

"Her uncle. Her uncle Nick, who lives in Cicero and is a known associate of current and deceased members of a nationally-known organization. Yeah, I know, she doesn't have an Uncle Nick, but for the moment, she does. And if it comes up, if he mentions her Uncle Nick, she should look shocked and then she should say nobody ever calls him 'Nick,' that he prefers 'Nicholas,' and she should then clam up about him. If Mr. Peck pushes it, she should say Uncle Nicholas is just crazy. And a very bad man. I think this will work, Bev."

She gave him a long look and then smiled. "This sounds goofy."

"Goofy, maybe. But unexpected. Offer people the unexpected, and you have an advantage in most situations."

Beverly looked around the office and Harry gave her time. In the end, she shrugged her shoulders. "I wasn't going to shoot anybody anyway."

"I know that."

"And maybe this is just goofy enough to have the element of surprise."

"Oh, he'll be surprised. I promise you."

Billy looked around the room. Leo was watching Harry expectantly. Doris never looked up, but she was nodding.

Beverly pulled a dark red wallet out of her handbag.

"Not yet," Harry said. "Let's see if it works, first. If not, we'll come up with a plan B."

"In my short-lived career as an actress I never got to say this, but Harry, money is no object."

"I'll keep that in mind when determining our fee."

When she had left in a sudden gust of perfume, Harry stared at the flamboyant doodles on his blotter and put the flesh on his plan. "So we're going to do a thing for a client."

He winked at Leo, who clearly needed no further explanation. Then he looked at Billy as though trying to decide something. After a moment he said, "Okay. You'll be in on this with us, Bill. This will be a little different from some of our other, you know, activities on behalf of clients. But you will find it interesting."

From her busy corner of the office, Doris smiled with the look of someone who had seen this movie before.

"I'm going to ask two things of you, Bill," Harry said.

"Okay."

"First, I want you to say nothing, but just to stare at the gentleman we're going to visit. Just stare—without blinking, if you can do that—you think you can?"

Billy froze his face and watched Harry for a ten-count.

"Yeah, like that, exactly like that. Good. Okay, you can blink now. Remember to say nothing, even if this guy starts giving us lip. Your job, your role, is the silent, slightly crazy guy. Leo—" Harry nodded sideways to indicate Leo. "—Leo is going to, you know, interact more with the subject."

Leo wiggled his eyebrows.

"Okay. And you?"

"I make a speech, tell him how things are, the lay of the land."

"Are we gonna pound this guy?"

Harry winced. "No, nothing like that. We don't do that sort of thing. You pound the guy, all you've done is given him a reason to want revenge. And you've also shown him we're not going to hurt him seriously. No, you want to put his imagination in play here. You want his imagination to run wild, you want him thinking about his worst fears. See?" Harry spread his hands wide and said, "So we meet here at seven or so."

He got up and then remembered something. "Oh, yeah, I almost forgot the second thing—you got a tie and a coat?"

"A sport coat? Yeah. A tie, I don't know about."

Doris got up from her screen without looking at them, went to the wall cupboard and came out with a handful of ties.

"Pick one," she said.

"You guys keep ties around the office?"

Harry shrugged. "You never know when you need to observe a certain level of dress—fancy restaurants require a tie and if you don't have one, they show you the door or they stick you with a bad one that has, like, dead escargots on it."

"You'd be surprised what else we keep around the office,"

Doris said under her breath. She held out the ties.

Billy grabbed a solid black one. Doris said, "No," and managed to make one syllable a lecture on dress.

"The blue one with the design. Take that. What color is your coat?"

"Gray. Light gray."

She nodded. "That'll go. You'll look nice."

"She knows about these things," Harry said. "All right, seven, right here, and we go see a fella about his unacceptable behavior."

They convened at seven, and Billy was amused to see that Leo had put on a heavy tweed jacket and a bright yellow tie and managed to look like a guy going to his first dance. But it was Harry who was transformed. He had put on an expensive-looking black suit and a dark blue paisley tie. He wore a crisp white shirt and darker glasses than usual. The straw fedora was gone, and Harry had doused his hair with gel or hair oil and slicked it back. In the corner of his mouth he chewed on what appeared to be a silver toothpick.

"Wow, a new look, huh? Who are you supposed to be?"

"A guy to be taken seriously. So let's go see if it works."

They drove in Leo's long cruiser of a car, a spotless Lincoln kept with loving care in a garage.

"Nice car," Billy said.

Leo said, "Thanks. It's my hobby."

"There's babies that don't get as much tender love as this car," Harry said. "Bill, you and I will sit in the back."

On a narrow side street close to the lake, they cruised at Harry's suggestion to a place just behind a blue Thunderbird, then parked and waited. Leo listened to the Cubs, and Harry occasionally shared an observation about their flaws as a team and a franchise.

At a little before eight, the door to an apartment building opened, and a tall, well-built man emerged. He wore a tight red knit shirt and walked with the slightly rolling gait of a man used to working with weights and, Billy thought, fond of the results.

"See that?" Harry asked.

"Yeah," Billy said. "He looked at his reflection in the door."

"Let's go. On two—one, two."

They got out of the car with drill-team precision, and Harry took point, walking directly toward the man.

"Mr. Peck? Mr. Jeffrey Peck?"

The big man slowed down and frowned. He took in Leo and Billy with a quick glance.

"Excuse me, I want to get by," he said. He spoke with easy confidence, but Billy had seen the quick look of alarm.

The man moved to his right, and Harry sidestepped to cut him off.

"You are Jeffrey Peck?"

"Who are you?"

"My name is not relevant here. But I've been asked to speak with you on certain matters."

"Such as?" Peck said. He forced himself to look at Harry directly, but Billy could see how badly he wanted to watch Leo, who had moved just to Peck's left.

"It has been brought to our attention, and to the attention of other concerned individuals, that you have shown a tendency to do physical harm to a certain young woman. This would be Elizabeth Duggan."

"Betsy," Peck said and took an unconscious step back.

"Indeed. You've taken a hand to her, I believe."

"Yeah? If I have, that's none of your—"

Harry shook his head from side to side. "Oh, sir, that is not quite the case. You've done violence to the young woman, and her family is concerned."

"I give a shit about her family—" Peck said.

"You need to listen to this gentleman," Leo said, moving closer to Peck's side.

"And her family—" Harry went on as though he had not been interrupted.

"—includes individuals that you would be wise not to offend."

"Oh?"

Jeffrey Peck frowned, struggling not to let this mysterious

new information break his focus on the three men confronting him. In the glass of the doorway behind Peck, Billy caught their reflection—three men in sport coats, each with his hands clasped low in front of him. They might have been three men at a funeral or the bodyguards of a dignitary, and Billy wondered if this was part of the desired effect. Billy watched Peck's eyes—he could see the man trying to keep his gaze on Harry, but more than once the eyes flicked Billy's way, and now and then Peck was powerless to keep from watching Leo. Indeed, Billy would have been watching Leo as well. The transformation from easygoing operative to hired thug was startling—he'd managed to make his eyes look wider, crazier, and he was breathing audibly through his mouth.

Peck reviewed his possibilities, tried on bravado. "So I offended her family, huh? And I'm supposed to be worried about this?"

"If you have any sense at all." Harry kept his hands folded in front of him, but tilted his head slightly as though trying to get a better look at Peck.

"Is that right? So what'd she tell you? Betsy. She probably—"

"Excuse me, sir, there's some misunderstanding here. We don't know this young lady. We represent her uncle. He is concerned about a family member, as anyone would be, as you yourself would be. You have a sister, am I right? Well, you understand then. A gentleman must look after the members of his family."

Peck shook his head. "I don't know her family, I don't know her uncle."

Harry showed the faintest of smiles. "Oh, but he knows you, sir. You play the parlay cards, right? Well, they're our cards. You make a bet of any kind anywhere in the city of Chicago, you're betting with us."

Peck blinked, the earth was tilting beneath him.

"And you had a little brush with law enforcement, selling a certain controlled substance, am I right? Well, the gentleman I represent looked the other way that time. You might have seen me and my associates on that occasion but Nick—my employer— looked the other way. You're a young guy, you made a misstep.

But that was our enterprise you were interfering with, the sale of that particular product. You were lucky not to see us, or even a less reasonable member of our organization. And believe me, Mr. Peck, this visit may seem intrusive to you, but a visit from this other gentleman would be unforgettable."

Peck blanched. His eyes widened and took on the look of a cornered animal.

"So what are you saying?"

"Come on, Mr. Peck, you're an intelligent man, anyone can see that. Do I have to draw you a picture? We've come to tell you to cease laying hands on this young lady. Or suffer the consequences."

Billy watched Peck's eyes and saw what was coming. After all, Peck had been a tough guy all his life, getting his way by bullying people with his size and the threat of violence, so he tried on one last hard-guy pose.

"Consequences, huh? I don't know what you're talking about, but I do know that this chick is—"

"Mr. Peck, if you take a hand to the young lady in question, there's a lot of things could happen—the police might find bags of cocaine in your apartment, marked bills could show up in the trunk of your car, a lot of things. But this is the man's niece, this is family, sir, and my guess is you will receive another visit, this time from the gentleman I spoke of, a fellow named Wally. A crude man, I will be the first to admit, but effective in his way. And then this matter will be resolved. This matter will be—" Harry paused for two beats and said, "—finished. Do you understand what I'm saying to you?"

Billy could see Peck trying to decide whether the tough guy persona would work one more time. In the end, he gave up.

"I'm not looking for any trouble," he began.

"You've had your only warning, Mr. Peck."

With that, Harry turned on his heel and headed back to the car, Leo moved out front, and Billy followed. After a moment, Leo stopped and stared at the blue T-bird. After a long pause, he pointed.

"Is that your, uh, vehicle?"

Peck looked suddenly from Leo to his Thunderbird.

"Yeah," he said, and there was a faint trembling in his voice.

Leo stared at it as though he'd never seen a blue T-bird. Then he gave Peck a long look from under his brows, and he couldn't have looked more malevolent. He held the look for perhaps five seconds and then said, "Nice car." Then he reached out and touched it, just grazing the finish with his long finger.

Inside Leo's Lincoln, Harry turned to Billy and said, "What did you think?"

"I thought some kind of evil spirits took over you and Leo. I couldn't even recognize you."

Leo laughed and turned up the radio, and soon was crooning about a heat wave along with Martha and the Vandellas.

"Ah, you got to be able to play different parts in life," Harry said. "When you're in a fine restaurant and the waiter is a snotty kid, you have to act like you've seen a thousand like him and you've been in better restaurants. And when you're stopped by a cop and he's had a bad day, you have to be a guy that's never been stopped before. This guy here, he's been giving people shit all his life, he's not used to people telling him how things are going to go down."

"You scared him."

"We put the fear of God into that guy," Leo said, momentarily leaving the Vandellas.

"And that was the point of our visit. That was a nice touch, there, Leo. The T-bird."

"Guy like that, he loves his car. I understand this."

"What if he'd just started throwing punches as soon as we got close?"

Leo shook his head. "He wouldn't."

"How do you know that?"

"It was in his eyes. And his shoulders," Harry said. "His shoulders slumped, right from the start. He wasn't going to fight anybody."

"So do we visit him again?"

"No, I don't expect we will. I think he'll split, that's what I think. If he stays with the young lady, he'll keep his hands off her. But a guy like that, he won't be comfortable in this thing, he'll take off and find somebody new to screw around with. So either way, I think Betsy won't get beat up anymore, at least not by this guy. I don't like the fact that she's stayed with this animal this long, but that's not our problem."

"Kids," Leo said from the front seat.

"Yeah," Harry said.

"So you've done this before?"

"Oh, once or twice," Harry said, and for the rest of the drive he was quiet, pleased with himself, but quiet.

For the better part of the next week, Billy heard nothing more about Jeffrey Peck, and Harry had made it clear that this was a case without a follow-up component. Then, on a Friday, Beverly Morse blew in on the summer wind. This time, she wore a pale yellow summer dress. He had to tell himself not to stare. She paused for a heartbeat at the door, scanned the room, and then came in, no expression on her face.

She said nothing, ignored Harry's greeting and Doris's smile, just walked over to Harry, bent him back over his chair and planted a kiss on his mouth. She winked at Doris. Then she opened her purse, pulled out a blue-tinted business envelope and dropped it on Harry's blotter.

"I believe that will compensate you and your people for your time."

With that, Beverly Morse made her exit, leaving behind her a mist of elegance, expensive perfume, and sex. Billy watched her go and found himself wishing he'd been the recipient of the kiss she'd planted on Harry.

"She's something, isn't she?" Doris said, with just the faintest trace of amusement.

"Still dangerous after all these years," she added, and Billy pretended not to hear.

Harry hefted the envelope, peeked inside, chuckled softly, and said "I think we can make rent this month."

Just before closing, Harry gave him a folder.

"Before you leave, look this over. This is a kid you're going to help me find."

Billy looked at the clock, decided he had no place better to go, shrugged. "Okay."

There wasn't much to the file, just a few pages and an old photo of an angelic-looking kid in an altar boy outfit. At the end of the file was a fifty-dollar bill.

"Whoa."

Billy held up the bill.

"Bonus. Enjoy yourself."

"Thanks."

"Sometimes I can do it, sometimes I can't. And lock up when you're through." With that, Harry tossed him a key. "Don't lose it," he said.

Money and a key, Billy thought to himself. It seemed to him that the key was the important thing, a matter of trust. But the money didn't hurt.

Billy walked down the street and remembered an old song about a guy who has money in his pocket but nowhere to spend it because he's new in town.

He stopped in a bar and had a beer while watching a ballgame. It struck him that he was the only person in the bar who wasn't talking to someone. He left and headed back to his room, then stopped, reluctant to go back to the rooming house with an entire evening stretching out before him.

What did people do when they had a few bucks in their pockets? He thought of going downtown, taking in a movie, but he did not want to sit alone in a darkened theater. Up ahead, he saw the diner and decided to stop for coffee.

She was there, the thin girl with the Southern drawl, and he was pleased when she smiled at him and said, "How you doing today, Hon?"

"Got paid."

"No day like payday," she said. He ordered coffee and she poured him a cup, then stood a few feet away and stared out at the window. It struck him that if he could come up with something to talk about he might have his first conversation with a girl in a long time. He was about to comment on the hot weather when a customer came in and sat at the far end of the counter, and the waitress was gone.

He drank his coffee in silence and listened to one old song after another. The girl named Millie swung by and refilled his cup, then made her way to the far end of the diner. She leaned against the doorway into the back room. An old Bo Diddley song came on—he remembered dancing to this with Rita. The waitress slipped back a bit further where she thought her customers couldn't see her and broke into a little dance. He watched her bounce and bop in the doorway.

A small girl. And skinny. Skinny but cute.

She caught his eye and burst out laughing, her pale skin flushing pink. She put a hand to her face and shook her head and went out to give an old man one more cup of coffee.

When she brought him his check, she gave him a sheepish look but said nothing.

As she turned away, he blurted out, "My name's Billy. Or Bill."

She gave him a mischievous smile. "Well, do you know which one it is?"

"Most people call me Billy."

She touched her plastic name plate. "This is who I am."

"You don't look like a Millie."

"I was named for my mama and my grandma. I hope to grow into it. Where you from, Billy or Bill?"

"Michigan."

She was about to say something when the cook called out that an order was ready. When she had served the customer, two more orders were ready, and then another man asked for more water. Billy waited to see if she would come back his way and then grew self-conscious. Finally he left money on the counter and started toward the door, frustrated and surprised at himself. As he pushed open the door, he heard her call out to him.

"Bye, Billy."

Billy said, "See you around," and hoped he'd made it sound casual.

She nodded and walked away. "Hope so," she said quietly.

For the next three weeks Harry Strummer kept Billy busy, tired, off-balance, and frequently either confused or amused. He ran more errands that took him far and wide into the city and checked out a series of recent addresses for a man who had skipped out on his family and taken most of the money with him. For every step he took in the course of his job, Billy took two steps in his own time, looking for Rita. At times, there seemed no point to his nocturnal wanderings, but on certain nights he felt a change in himself, a certain quiet elation, a conviction that everything he was learning and doing was sure to bring about a result. It seemed he had fallen into the perfect job for a guy trying to learn a city, for that matter, for a guy trying to learn who he was and how he fit in. When this was done, Billy told himself, he would know how he fit into the world.

More than once he thought of mentioning his situation to Harry, but he was reluctant to talk about Rita, about his own life. And Harry never asked him about his private life, had never even really asked him what brought him to Chicago. When he thought about that, it seemed odd, but he was certain that Harry wanted to let him have his privacy.

At times during this period, his growing knowledge of the city made him confident that he would eventually find her, and at these moments he was exuberant, his thoughts filled with the possibilities. He even dared to imagine them together once more. On other days his quest wore him down, and he saw his tireless search for a woman he hadn't seen in years in a colder light. He saw himself as an outsider might—a transient wandering around a city where he had no life of his own.

Three times in that period Billy stopped in to eat at the diner, and each time the young southern girl called Millie was there.

"Hello, Billy from Michigan," she said on his second visit of the week.

"You work all the time?"

"Unless I've got something better to do. Saturday, for instance, I'm going out with a gentleman. Least I hope he's a gentleman." She looked out at the street and frowned briefly.

When she went to serve another customer, Billy watched her. He tried to remember the last time he'd been on a date. It seemed like something that other people did. He considered his own situation and realized there was something about it that wasn't normal, this was not how a young man lived. But he needed to see it through, come what may.

. . .

One night, Billy followed Harry Strummer. If asked, he wouldn't have been able to say why—perhaps to prove to himself that he could follow a veteran detective, perhaps to learn about Harry's habits, perhaps just to get a look at the man outside of the job. Harry Strummer was easy to tail. For one thing, he made slow progress down the street, allowing his off-balance strut to be interrupted by half a dozen things—he stopped to peer into shop windows, stood in the open doorway of a tavern and waved at someone inside, slowed down to watch an old car pass by. At a corner he stopped to talk to an old street guy, and Billy saw him give the old man money with one hand as he patted his back with the other. A cop in a sergeant's white shirt waved from his squad car and called out to him, and Harry made the sergeant laugh with his response. From across the street a middle-aged woman called his name and Harry blew her a kiss. He seemed to know everyone. It was Harry's street. Billy watched him saunter down Wells Street and wondered if he'd ever seen a man as comfortable in his own skin.

On a steamy Saturday, the three of them, Leo, Billy, and Harry, put on sport coats and ties and provided security at a Mexican wedding. When the wedding was invaded by three big drunken Anglos, the bride's ex-boyfriend and his two friends, Harry met them at the door, snapped his fingers theatrically, and Billy and Leo appeared at his side, expressionless. Harry remonstrated with the three drunks and sent them off. As they left, the ex-boyfriend was blubbering about his love for the bride, and his companions did what they could to console him.

Leo looked at Billy, disgusted. "Guy comes to a wedding in a t-shirt. A *t-shirt*." He shook his head.

· · ·

On a Friday in mid-June, Harry had Billy report to a particular address in the projects on Clybourn near the river, there to drive one Wendell Brooks to the bank.

"To the bank?"

"Yes, so he can cash his Social Security check. You will accompany him there and to the grocery store. While doing this you will see two shifty-looking youths. One is white, one is black. Stare at them. Later, when you're through running errands with Wendell, find the two shifty youths and follow them."

"To where?"

"Wherever they go. Follow them. On foot, in the car, whatever works. And let them see you. Make them nervous. Oh, and when you're with Wendell, just listen to him. He lives alone, he's got no one to listen to him."

And so Billy accompanied the seventy-year-old Wendell Brooks, a wiry black man in an elegant panama hat, to his bank, a grocery store, a tavern—where Wendell bought him a beer—and home again. And Wendell indeed had stories. He'd served as a mess attendant on the battleship *Oklahoma* at Pearl Harbor, and they had to cut him out with a blowtorch when the ship capsized. He'd been stabbed in a fight over a woman, he'd been married three times and outlived all his wives, he'd met Admiral Halsey and cooked for Chester Nimitz, he'd played two seasons in the Negro leagues as an infielder. And he'd outlived all the people in his life, but seemingly counted himself fortunate.

"I'm alive and I've got my faculties and my health. You have your health, you're doing fine, Son. Go easy on the bottle, get your rest, you'll live a long time and see life. You're here to see life."

Oh, I'm seeing life, Billy thought.

Billy let Wendell out a few feet from his door. Just up the street he spotted the two kids, and they saw Wendell. Billy got out and walked the old man to his door. Then he began walking in the direction of the two kids, walking very fast, and they took off. Billy drove around the projects until he came across the two punks again. He gave them the look and they moved on, heads down. He got out of the car and began walking after them until they broke into a run. Then he retraced his steps to Harry's car and drove around until he found them again. This time he slowed down as he passed them and tried to look as demented as possible. He said, "Come here, you," and opened the door. They took off and ran down toward the river.

At the next light a police car pulled up beside him.

The cop on the passenger side nodded. His name plate said *Perez*.

"We've been watching you follow those two kids all around the neighborhood. What's your business with them?"

"I'm trying to scare 'em. They bother this old guy named Wendell."

The cop watched Billy without expression. The driver leaned forward and said something.

"My partner says this is Harry Strummer's car. You work for Harry or did you boost it?"

"I work for him. I'm Billy Fox."

The driver said something Billy didn't catch and both cops laughed.

"Okay, Billy Fox. Now we'll follow the young men for a while. Have a nice day."

• • •

Back at the office, Harry laughed when Billy made his report. "Koss and Perez. I know those guys, good people. How'd you like Wendell?"

"He's like a walking history book."

"Yeah. He is that. Good job, Bill. Come on, let's get a sandwich."

After lunch they strolled up Wells Street and eventually wandered over to Lincoln Park. A large group of people in name tags walked up Clark Street toward the history museum and had to step aside for another group moving in the opposite direction. Some of the people frowned at having to move aside. Harry watched the street traffic.

"Dueling tour groups," Billy said.

"Good," Harry said, and laughed. "We all see the same things, Bill, but some of us notice more, remember more."

"I think I'm getting better. But I don't know if I'll ever notice all the things you do. I think it's a thing just certain people can do. Like people who can do memory tricks."

"You can train yourself. Matter of fact, you can train yourself to do those memory tricks. I can introduce you to a guy—"

Harry froze in mid-sentence and his eyes went soft, lost focus— he looked like a man trying to make sense of small print.

"This guy I know," he tried again, then broke off.

Billy followed his gaze, saw people getting off a bus on La Salle Street. One of them was a tall, slender man in a white shirt and dark tie. He wore glasses and looked up and down the street carefully before heading down Lincoln.

"What?"

"Nothing." Harry looked at him and forced a smile, but his eyes strayed once more.

"Something wrong?"

"No, no, nothing like that. I just thought I saw a guy—can't be the same guy, though. This guy is dead." Then, as though speaking to himself, "Long dead."

He took one more glance in the same direction, then changed the subject.

"Now, on Monday we have business with Sunny Carter. You'll enjoy him."

• • •

Later, in the office, Harry took a call from a client who owed him money. When the call was done, Harry sat staring at the notepad on his desk. After a while he began doodling. Doris asked him something and had to repeat herself before he realized she was speaking to him. When he left for the day, Billy glanced at Harry's desk. On the notepad he'd drawn a dark box around a name, gone over the edges until the box nearly went through the paper, then colored in the box and scratched out the name. It could have been "Derrick" or "Dietrich."

SEVEN

The Case of the Dueling Detectives

The cabbie let them off at Randolph and Michigan, and Harry said, "Let's walk. We're early." He gestured up Michigan Avenue with his cigarette and started walking.

At first Billy was reluctant to break the silence. Besides, this was only the second time he'd seen Michigan Avenue, and the earlier time he'd been acutely conscious that he was the only person on the entire street in jeans and a t-shirt. It was easily the most elegant street he had ever seen, the showpiece of the city, bordered on one side by the art museum and a park that seemed to roll on forever. Half the people on the street seemed to be tourists, the other half looked like money. The late morning sun blessed the glass-and-steel buildings and the cars, and the breeze off the lake brushed across the treetops. Here and there, if you peered through the trees in Grant Park you could see the blue water, already dotted with sailboats. A picture postcard for Chicago.

Beside him Harry was nodding, as though Billy had expressed his thought aloud.

"It's not the real world, Bill, but it's something. I never get tired of walking down here. When I got back from Korea I came down here a lot. I'd walk all the way from back there by the Water Tower, Chicago Avenue, to the south end of Grant Park, looking at the buildings and admiring the women and the cars and the fine buildings, and telling myself I was going to make a new start, make something of myself. It's not the real world, kid, but it's like an advertisement for the city, kind of luring you in, inviting you to see yourself with a life here. I been many places in the world, and I'll tell anyone there's no place quite like Michigan Avenue. One time they asked Cary Grant what his favorite place was, from all his many travels. He told them 'Michigan Avenue in Chicago.' Well, I'm with old Cary."

Harry gave Billy a sidelong look. "I've tried to stay out of your business, Bill. I don't know what you've got in mind for yourself, but you could do a lot worse than Chicago. You're a smart kid and you learn fast. And it's an interesting place—this part's beautiful to look at but it's just for show. But the rest of it, the neighborhoods and the people, every kind of people on God's earth. That college up by you, Truman College, they've got, I think, people from seventy different countries in that school. And of course you got Indians up there, too, dozens of kinds."

"Yeah," Billy said. "I found myself in an Indian bar one night. There was a picture of Geronimo looking down at me. I thought about picking a fight but decided not to."

"Yeah, right," Harry said, and laughed.

V. C. "Sunny" Carter proved to be a study in irony. His offices were on Wabash, on the third floor of an aging office building honeycombed with jewelers and small offices, and there seemed to be business transactions going on in all of them. In one office a small, excitable looking man in a vest looked through a jeweler's loupe at a pile of stones spread out before him. He looked from the stones to the man who had presumably brought them in, a tall heavy man in a wrinkled suit. The small man gestured toward the stones and curled his lip, and the big man took an unconscious step backward.

"Business, Bill. Diamonds and money. We're on Jeweler's Row. Good place to come for that wedding ring that's in your future someday."

V.C. Carter's offices themselves were a model of minimal elegance—dark furniture, paneled walls, small prints of the Chicago lakefront at night. The rooms were presided over by a large black woman with a pretty face and the air of a high school principal, who took Harry's name and in a voice that brooked no rebellion told the two of them to be seated.

A moment later she ushered them into the inner sanctum, holding open the door and announcing, "Mr. Strummer and his associate."

"Come in, Harry," said the man at the desk. He was meticulously dressed, handsome, very dark, and glowering, and Billy wondered if the nickname "Sunny" was the gift of an older family member with a sense of humor. The "V.C." Harry had explained to him on the ride over—it stood for "Vivian Cornell."

"Vivian? What kind of name is that for a kid?"

"Parents will do that to a kid, and black people are no different."

"You sure about that?" Billy said.

"Oh, yeah, kid. If I'm not sure of anything else, I'm sure that black people are just like us."

Now "Sunny" Carter stood, introduced himself to Billy, shook hands with them both, and bade them to sit.

"We'll get right to it if you don't mind, Harry. I've got a client who is under surveillance."

"What's the situation?"

"A spiteful divorce and a paranoid but imaginative spouse. She has him under intense scrutiny. He is being followed, his house is watched, and he believes she's had the place bugged. He's losing his mind."

"Is there a great sum of money involved?"

"There's money, yes, but that's not—"

"It's not the issue. She wants to drive him crazy."

"Exactly. You understand the situation."

"Sure. It's what I'd do myself," Harry said, and when Carter frowned, Harry added, "Just a joke, Sunny. Just trying to keep you loose."

"My impression is that the lady in question is deadly earnest. Quite frankly, Harry, my client is outclassed here. It's a one-sided battle. She's smart and serious and furious with him for his infidelity, among other things. Her goal in all of this seems to be to overwhelm him with the weapons at her disposal and her intelligence, and she is wearing him down with her tactics and the accumulated evidence of her vastly superior intellect. This is a massacre."

"So you want to level the playing field. What do you need?"

"I need you to see what she's got going there and see if you can loosen her hold."

"Do we have any idea who she's using?"

"I do. Fornier and Cribb."

Billy saw a certain look pass between the two men, a quick but clear look of something like complicity. These two had a history, and for the first time during the interview Billy thought he saw amusement enter the lawyer's eyes.

"Fornier and Cribb," Harry repeated. He straightened the knot of his tie, gave Carter a small smile, and said, "Well."

"Yes. It might even suffice for us to let it be known that you're working for the husband."

"Maybe, but I'd feel bad if I didn't at least give professional services. So, you want me to take a look into the set-up and see what's to be done?"

"Precisely."

"All right, Sunny. I'll have a look around and report back to you, and present a plan of action."

"Good. You'll be pleased to know that this client is a man of means, so you will be well compensated for any of your work. And since I am aware of your proclivities regarding the sorts of people you represent—I can tell you that Ron Ryan is a very nice guy. Charming, successful, unintelligent. You've met this man, Harry."

"No, I don't think I have—oh, I see." He turned to Billy. "Mr. Carter means the gentleman is an *archetype*."

Harry looked at the lawyer.

"Tell me if I'm close—tall, handsome, year-round tan, drives a big car, plays golf all the time, tells great jokes, perfect teeth. He's sentimental, cries at weddings and old movies, he means well, and when he pisses somebody off, he never knows why."

"That is the gentleman in question. So," Carter said, and leaned back in his chair.

"So set up a meeting for me, at my office, and we'll go from there."

"Tomorrow?"

"Good. Late morning."

They took the long way back to the office, along Lake Shore Drive, and Harry was smiling all the way.

The lakefront was teeming with swimmers and bikers and people on blankets, and for just a moment Billy wondered if he might force his way into this place, into a life like this. He watched the brilliant blue of the water mirroring the sky, then realized Harry was watching him.

"You want to get out of the car and forget about work and just join them, right? Yeah, I understand. When I came back here from—from the service, I walked up and down the lake till I wore out my shoes, looking at the women, trying to figure a way to get into this life." He focused for a moment on his driving, then said, "You ought to give it a chance, Bill. You'd like it here."

"I might," Billy said, wondering what he'd said or done to provoke this suggestion.

You don't know about me, he wanted to say.

Then Harry seemed to shift gears. "See how blue the water is today? That means the wind is coming in across it from the east. It blows the surface water in and the lake gets warm, so you can swim in it. That's why the beaches are so crowded. When the wind blows out, it blows the warm top water out, and the cold water rises up. The whole lake gets this slate-gray color, and it's so cold it feels like your bones will crack, you think your dick will fall off. I love the lake," Harry said. "When there's a storm, sometimes the lake waves come out as far as where we are right now. They come crashing across Lake Shore Drive and they have to shut the road down. Mother Nature."

"You're in a good mood because we got a sweet job, right?"

"That's only part of it." He said nothing further, and when Billy thought he'd dropped the subject entirely, Harry said simply,

"Fornier and Cribb. I'm having a good day, Kid."

"Who are they?"

"I'll tell you later."

. . .

Ron Ryan was as advertised, a man who had just stepped out of a clothing ad. He entered the office like a man running for Senate, hand extended, saying, "Ron Ryan, nice to meet you."

He was a perfect example of a successful middle-aged man, and the smile that went with this success never left his face, but did not quite extend to his pale blue eyes. Wounded eyes, Billy would have said, the look of a small boy whose team had just lost. The eyes never rested, moving from Harry to Billy in a constant apology, a restless seeking of approval. As Harry jotted down his answers, Ron Ryan looked around the office, his eyes flitting quickly from object to object as though trying to recall how he'd gotten there.

Twice Ryan said "I don't know why she's doing all this to me. But I know it's my fault. I screwed up my marriage."

The interview took no time at all. Harry asked a dozen or so questions, received vague or confused answers, rephrased his questions till they elicited what he needed. When he was done, he wrote in his notebook for a few seconds more, and then slapped it shut.

"So here's what's going to happen, Mr. Ryan. My associates and I will be out over the next few days to get the lay of the land. Since there is apparently surveillance already in place, we'll work covertly, one at a time, and do our best not to be noticed."

Billy saw Mr. Ryan mouth the word *covertly* and read the look in his eyes. Happy eyes, now. *Operatives* were coming into the fight on his side. Harry settled a few details, and Mr. Ryan took his leave, repeatedly thanking them for their "support."

When Ryan had gone, Billy asked, "Would we be taking this case if it weren't for Sunny Carter?"

"Maybe. He's not a bad guy. You heard what he said—he knows

it's his fault. Most of them don't. Or they don't admit it. A guy says, 'I was just in the wrong place at the wrong time,' he means he was hanging around where he shouldn't have been, and he got caught in something. Spend a day in court, you'll hear half a dozen guys tell you they got busted in the middle of a strong-arm robbery because they were 'in the wrong place at the wrong time.' A guy says, 'I've done a lot of stupid things in my life,' he's telling you he's a fuckup. Somebody says, 'I never seem to get a break,' he's saying he spent his life looking for breaks. And he thinks other people did well in life because they got the breaks."

"You don't think there are people who didn't get the breaks?"

"Some. Ernie Banks. Imagine if he'd been in St. Louis or with the Yankees, or the Dodgers—my God, those crazy Brooklyn people would have carried him home from Ebbets Field after every game. But mostly I think people get a certain amount in life and they shouldn't go looking for breaks. Except the poor people. They're born into a thing they didn't cause. Those are the people that don't get a break.

"One of my favorite things people say is 'and one thing led to another.' That's code for 'I did stupid things and then I did other stupid things and then the shit hit the fan, but it wasn't really my fault.'"

Billy laughed.

"The long and the short of it, Bill, is that almost all of these are just different versions of 'I'm in the shitter but it's not my fault.' I used to know a guy, an Irish guy, very scholarly, Tom Flanagan, he always liked to say, 'Hell must be empty—everybody has an excuse.' But Mr. Ryan here, I read this guy's face and his body language, and I think 'Here is a fellow hip-deep in trouble that he knows is of his own making, and he would like us to get him out.'"

"So what do we do?"

"First, you go out to the man's house and see who's watching him. Here's the address."

"I'm looking for someone in a doorway reading a paper?"

"Not in this neighborhood. Mr. Ryan lives on the Gold Coast, overlooking the lake. He lives in a building filled with rich people. Top floor of that building, Ray Kroc lives there when he's in town. Anybody that goes in a doorway to watch people is going to be noticed. No, you look for a guy in a car, maybe halfway down the street."

"In a crummy car?"

"No, this is Fornier and Cribb. They drive nice cars. The thing is, this is a neighborhood where guys don't sit in their cars. They have people park them and they go about their business. And there wouldn't be a crummy car around there—the doormen would have you rousted if you sat in a crummy car. So you're looking for somebody in a nice car. And don't be obvious."

"Who are these people?"

"They are a well-heeled detective agency with offices in Wilmette. They have a small fleet of recent-model cars that they lease, and half a dozen 'operatives'—that's you, in case you didn't know—and an office staff and a budget that would give you vertigo. And they are my rivals, my—" Harry fished for the precise word. "—my devoted enemies. That's what they are. My devoted enemies."

"Why? Just the usual reasons, you're the competition?"

Harry smiled and looked pleased with himself.

"I make 'em crazy, Kid. I operate on a shoestring and I'm unorthodox, and my office, wow, they look at my office and wonder how I can even be in business."

"They've been to your office?"

"Yeah, Fornier came once as himself, and Cribb came in disguise."

"Disguise? What kind of disguise?"

"He put on a moustache, kind of a nice one, too, but he kept pushing it down on one side like he was afraid it would come off. It would have been obvious to anybody that it was fake. Anyhow, I piss them off. We've butted heads on a few cases, sort of like the one we're about to *embark* on. They're well-heeled, and they've got technology and resources and people, but I'm just better than they are."

Billy thought for a moment and then pushed. "Why?"

Harry gave him a long, sly look. "You tell me."

Billy wanted to laugh at himself. He'd only wanted to catch Harry in a moment of cockiness, and now it was one more test. The education of Billy Fox.

"You're unpredictable, and you have—you get your information from a lot of places, and you're smart."

"They're smart, well, Fornier is. Speaks five languages, by the way. He's from Quebec. You want to piss him off, tell him Canada should make English the only language for its people. No, Fornier is smart." He watched Billy and waited.

You got to use your imagination, Harry had told him. *This guy's got no imagination*, he'd said of a local politician.

"They don't have your imagination."

Harry clapped his hands together. "There you go! See, I wasn't fishing for compliments. I wanted to see if you knew what's important. It's not just brains. Fornier is book-smart, and with a certain kind of clientele, a certain kind of case, he's a sharp guy, he's top-notch. But where the case invites people to play outside the rules, well, he's on unfamiliar ground then, he can't think that way. And he doesn't know it, that's his real weakness. It's okay to have weaknesses, we all do. But it's really important to know what they are. So we're going to take on Messrs. Fornier and Cribb, and when we're done, if things go the way they've gone in the past, they'll really be pissed off."

"Are they dangerous?"

"Only to themselves and the surrounding community, Bill. If they were kids, somebody would say Fornier and Cribb were accident-prone. I say they're fuck-ups. So go get 'em."

"How should I—?" Billy began, then thought better of it. He shrugged. "I'll work it out."

"And remember—"

"I know…look like I belong there but don't attract too much attention."

Harry winked. The conversation was over.

EIGHT

Surveillance of the Enemy

The Gold Coast was just a short walk due east from Wells Street, but it might as well have been an alternate universe, a long row of swank apartment buildings facing Lake Shore Drive and looking out over the spectacular lakefront. Some of the buildings were new, but a few were old construction and old money, and Ron Ryan's building was one of these—granite, marble, and red brick, twelve stories with a penthouse.

Billy made one pass up the street, looking for obvious surveillance. Nothing. But, as Harry had said, this was not a neighborhood where you parked your car and waited for things to happen.

In the driveway of the glass-and-steel building next to Ron Ryan's, a limo driver sat in a dark blue Lincoln Continental reading the paper. He wore a blue suit, white shirt, and a cap with a brim. In another life he could have been a cop, Billy thought. The limo driver looked up as Billy passed, frowned, then went back to his newspaper.

Don't make it obvious, Harry had told him. And so Billy made a show of going up to the doorman of the building at the south end of Ryan's block and showing him a note that Billy had written himself, with Ryan's address and the name of a nonexistent person. The doorman pointed him in the direction of the correct address, and Billy walked on, doing his best to look both frustrated and confused. He went from one end of the block to the other, the note in his hand. Occasionally, he would stop and stare up at one of the buildings. In front of the building where the limo waited he paused and peered at the address. The limo driver looked up again, squinted, frowned, and went back to his paper.

Billy wanted to laugh. Harry had explained to him the concept of a neighborhood's profile: *"You don't fit the profile of that community, they'll notice, the people, the cops, they'll spot you a block away and wonder why you're there."*

He looked at the limo driver and said to himself, *I know, I don't fit the profile of your community.*

A few blocks south of Ryan's building, Billy went through an underground walkway that led him to the lakefront. He walked back up the lake and found a bench near the beach just across from Ron Ryan's building. He sat sideways so that he could look at the buildings and still not miss the sights on the beach. It occurred to him that this was a most dangerous place for anyone involved in serious surveillance, a place of constant distraction, where it seemed every good-looking girl in Chicago could be found, all of them tan and long-legged. And beautiful, he would have said, even as he understood it was simply his loneliness that made them so.

He turned and studied Ron Ryan's building. Flowers and potted plants lined the patio of the penthouse, and Billy stared up at it and wondered what sort of life went on in a place like that. He drew a blank—nothing in his life told him what such a life might be like. Ryan's building was dwarfed by its neighbors on either side, glass and steel and new money gradually encroaching on the old, but there was no question where the real class lived. He tried again to imagine a life in such surroundings, with Lake Michigan as your front yard. But he'd met Ron Ryan, who certainly was as miserable at the moment as anyone Billy could imagine.

Still, Billy thought. I'd like a shot at a life like that. Or—he turned slightly to watch a group of eight people, four guys around his age and four girls in bathing suits. Or I'd like a shot at this one.

And now, as he watched the street, a car came out of the driveway alongside the building—Ron Ryan's forest green MG. He saw Ryan wave to his doorman and pull out into traffic in front of a bus. The bus driver braked and hit the horn. Ron Ryan waved to him too, a man waving at everyone in his world.

Billy chuckled. Not a clue, Billy told himself. Not a clue.

And then he saw the blue Lincoln emerge from its driveway. The Lincoln pulled out onto Lake Shore Drive and headed south, in Ryan's direction, and Billy could just make out the driver. He'd taken off his fancy hat and was leaning forward, peering ahead of him at the traffic. At Ron Ryan's car.

"Gotcha," Billy said.

• • •

Harry stood by the water cooler with a paper cup. A few feet away, Leo rummaged noisily through his tool box.

"So he saw Ryan and he took off?" Harry asked. "Is that it?"

Billy thought for a moment. "No. That's the thing, he was already rolling, I'd swear he was already moving out onto Lake Shore Drive. He couldn't have seen Ryan's car from where he was. He was back in this driveway, and there's like a big row of hedges or bushes or whatever you call them between that building and Ryan's. I don't think he could have seen him come out. But he was moving as soon as Ryan came out."

Harry watched him and waited. "That it?"

"I think so."

"You're saying this limo driver who obviously is no limo driver somehow knew Ryan was coming out of an indoor parking lot. Is that right?"

"Well, if you put it that way, it sounds—"

"But is that how it seemed? Like he knew Ryan was coming out?"

"Yeah."

Harry gave a short, sharp nod. "Excellent. Did you happen to see the license plate of the Lincoln?"

"Yeah, but I didn't have any reason to write it down. I mean, I can tell you the first letter is D. That's all."

"Excellent again. You're right, there was no reason for you to notice the license plate. But if he was a real limo driver, his license would start with LV for *livery*. So we know he wasn't a limo driver, and he knew Ryan was coming out before he saw him, which tells us Ryan's car has a surveillance device on it. And you know what that means?"

"That he can't go anywhere without his wife eventually being told about it. He's under constant surveillance."

"That's right, but it means something else, too." He looked over at Leo, who grinned, then back at Billy.

"It means we have an opportunity for mischief." Harry smiled, and then got serious. "Leo, Ryan's got three cars, so—"

"Three bugs." He nodded and looked for a moment like a very large, bald child. He winked at Billy. "This gives me something to work with."

"I'd tell you to be creative," Harry said, "but that goes without saying." To Billy he said, "I think we're going to need you to go back out there tomorrow morning. Tomorrow morning, Leo?"

"Right. Excellent."

Harry looked from Leo to Billy and beamed.

"You're having a good time with this," Billy said.

"It's important to have a few laughs in your work, Bill. Find something in life that has the inherent possibility for fun, and then have a good time with it. Most guys dread every day they go to work. That's no way to live."

He looked to Leo for confirmation. Leo nodded. "This job, every day is different."

"Wasn't it like that when you were a cop?"

"Yeah, but nobody's shooting at me now." He looked at Harry. "At least I don't think so."

"I'll make a call to Mr. Ryan," Harry said. "Tell him what I need him to do."

Harry looked away, gazing at something in the distance, and for a moment he lost his persona. The smile faded and he took on the look Billy had seen earlier on the street. Then he snapped out of it. "Okay, we're in business."

At nine the following morning, before most of the tanned

young people in swimsuits had shown up to toss Frisbees and admire one another, Billy was in position at a bus stop just south of Ron Ryan's building. Around the corner through the tall hedge, he could just make out the glistening black top of the Lincoln. At exactly nine-ten, Billy saw Leo's familiar red van pull into the driveway. Leo stepped out, carrying some sort of purchase order and his tool bag. He had a short conversation with the doorman, who examined the purchase order and frowned at the van—a vehicle clearly not meeting the profile of the neighborhood.

The doorman made a call, and whatever he learned, presumably from Ron Ryan, satisfied him that Leo was to be allowed inside the building. The doorman gestured to a side entrance, a driveway around the building, and Leo drove through this.

Gradually the bus stop filled with people heading downtown, and two buses came and went, each with a different route number. Billy hung back, checked his watch and waited. At nine-twenty-five, he left the bus stop and moved up the street toward the Lincoln.

When he was a few feet away, he took out his "prop," a limp, weathered street map of Chicago. He paused before the Lincoln and studied the map long enough to see the limo driver look up. Billy took a few steps back, looked up at the buildings, down at his map, shook his head. He turned around to study Lake Shore Drive, walked a few paces toward Ron Ryan's building, then stopped and retraced his steps. Then he looked around. A gray-haired man in a suit was walking briskly toward the bus shelter and Billy moved into his line of vision.

"Excuse me, sir, where's North Avenue?"

The man made a half turn and pointed behind him. "Back there, the light."

"And what's this here?" Billy asked, pointing down.

"You're on Lake Shore Drive," the man said, and then moved past him.

As Billy turned, the limo driver put his head down and stared at his newspaper, but too late.

Yeah, you caught my whole routine, Man.

He approached the Lincoln, saw the driver look up and grimace. The driver was a fortyish man with an improbable mop of brown curls. He stared through the window until Billy held the map up to the window. Then he rolled down the window, gave Billy an irritated look, and said, "Yeah?"

Billy held out his map.

"I'm not from here. I'm supposed to see a guy about a job, I need to get to North and Ashland. Am I close to that?"

"No," the driver said. "Jesus. I mean, North Avenue is right up here at that first light but Ashland is a mile and a half west of here. You need a bus."

"Oh," Billy said in a crestfallen voice. At the edge of his vision he saw Leo. As he stared at his map, Leo got down first on all fours, then on his stomach until he was crawling like a snake toward the Lincoln, and Billy was afraid he would burst out laughing.

"What bus?"

The driver gave an irritated shake of his head. "What bus? How would I know? I don't take buses, kid. You need to go back that way and ask somebody. Maybe flag down a cop and ask for directions."

"A cop? Oh, I don't think I want to do that."

For the first time the limo driver smiled. "No, huh? You'd rather not let them know you're in town, is that it?"

"It's not like that. I mean, not exactly." Billy stared at his map and tried to buy more time. "I mean, I'm not on the run. Not like you'd think, anyway. I busted a guy up back home."

The driver eyed him with interest, and Billy read the look. The driver was seeing something else now, not a lost hillbilly, but a young guy to be taken more seriously.

"You did, huh?" The driver gave the question just the right tone of sarcasm.

"Yeah." Billy met the driver's eyes directly now.

Yeah, I can throw a punch now and then, especially if somebody jerks my chain just right.

"Yeah, I did, sir. And I don't say I'm proud of it, but there you go." He met the driver's stare, and in the background now saw Leo standing a few feet from the limo and dusting himself off. Time to break it off.

"Anyway, thanks for your time, sir." Billy waved the map at him and walked away.

At the nearest corner he stopped and sat on the fire hydrant. A few minutes later Ron Ryan emerged in his red Porsche, and in a heartbeat the limo pulled out after him. The driver was frowning. A moment later Leo's van emerged from the parking garage, pulled up at the far corner, and waited for Billy.

"Good work, Kid," Leo said.

"How'd it go?"

Leo kept his eyes on the street as he pulled out onto Lake Shore Drive. The question seemed to surprise him.

"How'd it go? It went fine. How'd you think it would go?"

"I didn't mean there was any question, Leo. Just wondering if I gave you enough time."

"Oh, yeah. You did fine. I been doing this a long time, I really don't need a lot of time. I knew the cars I was looking for."

"I don't know exactly what it is that you did."

"I located the client's three vehicles," Leo said, lapsing into his cop-speak. "Then I ascertained that there was indeed a surveillance device on each one and removed it. Then, as our boss had instructed, I took the devices and put each one on another vehicle."

"You mean on somebody else's car?"

Leo regarded him seriously. "Of course. One on a big white Caddy, one on a silver Mercedes convertible, and the one you saw me planting."

Billy stared at the street in confusion. Then it struck him. "You were putting a bug on the limo."

"Sure. You got a better place?"

"So now they'll be following the Caddy, the Mercedes, and their own car?"

"Exactly." Leo nodded happily. "You know," he said in a thoughtful voice, "you feel—accomplished after a good day's work." He glanced at Billy. "You did good, too, kid." Then he grinned, a man happy with his work.

"Let's get hot dogs."

"It's morning."

"A good hot dog you can eat any time of day," Leo said.

• • •

That night, Billy, Leo, and Harry called on Ron Ryan. He ushered them into his spectacular apartment.

"Here, Bill, look at this, look at the man's view." Harry led Billy over to the windows of Ron Ryan's huge living room. The windows were open, and a lake breeze filled the room. The view was the lake, all of it, it seemed to Billy, miles of lake and beach, and a horizon that might have been from someone else's world.

"Jesus," Billy said.

"This is what I'm saying," Harry said. Ron Ryan laughed shyly, and Harry asked him to give Billy a tour of the place.

It seemed to be laid out like a great X, with an enormous bedroom at each of the four ends, and each had not only its own bathroom but a small sitting room with a sofa, dresser, and mirror, and a small stack of magazines. The kitchen was copper and brass and could have fed a regiment, and the dining room held the longest table he'd ever seen.

"I've never seen a place like this," Billy admitted.

"Neither did I, until I moved in here. Sometimes I feel like I don't even belong here." Ron Ryan looked wistfully at his home. Given his circumstances, the place seemed cavernously empty, a home for a great, noisy family. He shook his head. "The people that live in this building—the guy downstairs owns factories in six countries. The guy upstairs owns fourteen companies and part of a baseball team, and he's here like six times a year. It's a vacation place for him when he's in Chicago. Sometimes I look around and wonder what I'm doing here." After a moment, he gave Billy a sheepish smile. "Well, I probably won't be here long."

"Maybe it'll work out in the end."

"Thanks. I doubt it." Ryan looked around and seemed lost. "I never meant to screw this all up. And my wife—never in my life thought I'd end up with somebody like her, and this is what I do. Take it from me, son, you get a good wife, don't fuck around."

Back in the living room, Leo was going through a side compartment in his tool bag, while Harry stood in the middle of the floor with his hands on his hips.

"Okay, Bill. Where do we look for a bug?"

Billy looked around. "In the phone."

Harry nodded. "Okay, you've been watching TV. The man's got six phones in the apartment, so now what?"

"I'd bug all of them."

"Ruthless! Okay, good. As it happens, Leo already took the bugs from three of them. The others were clean."

Harry gave him that look, that expectant look. A lesson was in progress. Other bugs, Billy thought, in less obvious places.

"I get it. The ones in the phones are obvious—we're supposed to find them."

"Right. Here, watch this."

Harry unscrewed the mouthpiece of the living room phone and showed Billy a small, round listening device.

"Do we take it out?"

"No. It's a phony, I know how Fornier works. The bug is not in the phone. It's over there."

Harry pointed with the phone toward the wall.

"It's in the jack?"

"Show him, Leo."

Leo removed the square covering on the jack and Billy saw that the cover itself was the listening device.

"So somebody finds the bug in the phone itself and relaxes because he thinks he's free and clear now."

"That's it."

"There are other ones that aren't so obvious." Billy looked around. "In this room, I think." Then he added, "Where Mr. Ryan might sit and make a call." Billy pointed to a leather armchair.

"There, maybe?"

"Sharp kid," Ron Ryan said.

"Very good, Bill. Yeah, we took a bug out from the base of that lamp, tucked inside where you couldn't see it. And one more."

"The bedroom, the master bedroom," Billy said, and found that he couldn't look Ron Ryan in the eye.

"Come look," Harry said.

They went to the largest of the four bedrooms, and Harry showed Billy where they'd found a bug, on the back of the enormous mahogany headboard.

"One more," Harry said.

Billy walked around the room, then went into the bathroom. In the small sitting room there was an ashtray with half a dozen butts, and beside it, the *Tribune* sports section. He looked from Harry to Ryan.

"Do you use this room a lot, Sir?"

A rueful smile. "Yeah. It's where I make my calls, you know, uh, private calls. And sometimes I just come in here and use it as my, you know, my den. Funny to have a place this big and not have a den."

Harry pointed to the phone on the small dresser. "This one we were more or less supposed to find."

Billy looked around the small room. "Under the dresser."

Harry said nothing.

No, closer to the phone. "Behind the mirror."

Harry clapped his hands together. "Good. Yeah, that one we were supposed to find and this one—" He reached behind the mirror on the dresser, felt around and pried something loose. "—we weren't supposed to look for once we found the one in the phone. See, they're crafty, this outfit."

"What next?" asked Ron Ryan.

"Oh, you know, some of the more technical aspects of our approach. Better if I tell you about them in my report."

Ryan nodded but seemed confused. He looked from Harry to Billy and shrugged.

"Okay, then. Let me know what you need from me next."

"I think we'll get some results. You'll see results, Mr. Ryan."

In the car, Billy asked, "So what is the next step?"

"We visit the offices of Fornier and Cribb."

They drove north along Lake Shore Drive, and from the back seat of Leo's car Billy watched the lights of a long, dark cruise ship on the lake and wondered what the city looked like from out on the water.

"You ought to buy a ticket for one of those boats," Harry said.

"You reading my mind again?"

"Easy enough if you recognize a thought you had yourself. Besides, everybody that sees the lake has some of the same thoughts, and anybody that sees one of the cruise boats, especially at night, wants to be on one of them. I tell you, Bill, you see the city from the deck of one of those boats, see the skyline all lit up, why…you think it's magical. You think to yourself, that's where I want to live—it's got nothing but promise."

"Nothing but promise, huh?"

"Yeah," Harry said, looking straight ahead at the traffic. "For a young man like you, especially. Nothing but promise."

"Unless you screw it up."

Now Harry shot him a quick glance. "Even if you screw it up. Life's short, but it's not so short you don't get second chances. And everybody screws up something. Everybody."

Harry rubbed his chin and looked out across the water. He said nothing for the rest of the drive.

The offices of Fornier and Cribb were in a glorified storefront on Sheridan Road, close to the lake. They drove past it twice to see if there was anyone inside, and then Harry drove around behind it and pulled calmly into a parking space marked "J. Fornier."

At the rear entrance of the office, Harry paused and said, "Oh, they added a lock. But you know what's better than a lock, Bill? A big bar across the door. Because I'm going through these two locks." With that, Harry produced a small set of lock picks and proceeded to work and wiggle a pair of the long picks, grunting and muttering as he did so. In a little over a minute he'd opened both of them.

"Where does somebody get a set of those?" Billy asked.

"Mail order places, or—well, you know the old saying, 'I know a guy?' Well, I know a guy. Sells radios on Maxwell Street on Sundays. And odds and ends. After you," Harry added, then stepped aside.

Inside the offices of Fornier and Cribb, Harry—wearing rubber gloves, Billy saw—wiped down two of the surveillance devices and put one under the desk in the first office—"This is Fornier's office. This will offend his dignity."

Then Harry removed the phone jack cover in the other office and replaced it with the one from Ron Ryan's house. "And this is Cribbs's office. This will wreck his day. He's got no sense of humor, and no sense of perspective. He'll make himself crazy someday."

He led Billy out into the main office and to a side room filled with wires, technology, a pair of control boards, and several headsets.

"Top of the line, this stuff, all of it. They do a nice job, Fornier and Cribb." He smiled at Billy. "Within their limitations. Which they are not aware of."

In the car, Billy asked, "What now?"

Harry made a show of brushing off his hands. "Like Ronald Colman says in *The Prisoner of Zenda*, 'My work here is done.' We're through for the day. Expect a visit from our competitors." Then he laughed. "Be on time tomorrow. We got things to do, and you don't want to miss Fornier and Cribb."

That night Billy stopped in the diner. The young waitress named Millie was not there.

"She's off tonight," the big cook said as he pushed a pile of grilled onions to one side of the grill.

Billy remembered the young woman speaking of her date "with a gentleman" and felt his face redden. "I just stopped in for coffee," he said, but he didn't think he sounded convincing.

NINE

Messrs. Fornier and Cribb

The next morning, Billy showed up half an hour early and was the first one in the office. He turned on the lights and the air conditioner, opened the shades, and walked around the office. For just a moment he tried to imagine himself as Harry Strummer, opening up his office, his place of business. Once, as a boy, he'd worked for a butcher, and he'd arrived each morning as the butcher, a fat Romanian man named Anton, opened up his business and began setting out his tools and trays and the meats from the big cooler in the back. Billy would have said that Anton was, at that moment, the happiest man he had ever seen. And if it was true that the offices of Peerless Detective were less than impressive, still, this was Harry Strummer's small kingdom, his own business, and Billy thought he now had just the faintest taste of what that must feel like.

Doris came in a few minutes later, gave him a surprised smile, and said, "You're early, Hon."

Leo followed soon after. He grinned at Billy. "I don't have a job going today but I don't like to miss it when Harry talks to Fornier and Cribb."

Last into the office was Harry. He pushed open the door and tucked a large bag under his arm, then tugged with both hands at a leash. Whatever was on the far side of the leash was apparently reluctant to enter the office.

"Gimme a hand here, Bill. He doesn't like confined spaces."

He?

Billy got up from his desk and heard Leo chuckling behind him.

The thing pulling at the other end of the leash might have been a dog, or it might have been a creature from a small boy's nightmare. It was big and dark and now that it saw Billy, it made a low growl that under other circumstances would have sent him into a sprint.

"That's Ferdy."

Ferdy did the growl thing again and shook his head as though to dislodge the leash, a prospect that Billy found perfectly terrifying. Ferdy gave a sudden tug and Harry fell forward, laughing.

"If he wants to, he can pull me down the stairs."

"Great. Can he pull both of us down the stairs?"

"I think he can pull the office down the stairs."

Suddenly, Ferdy trotted into the office. Harry brought the dog to the far side of the room and Ferdy dropped onto the floor as though he'd done this drill many times before. Now Billy could see him in the light, and there was much to see. Ferdy was a huge, muscular dog with a heavy snout and drooping ears, and dark, heavy streaks of color in his coat. Billy had seen taller dogs, such as Great Danes, but he doubted he'd ever seen a dog so muscular.

"He's a mastiff, an English mastiff. Strongest dogs in the world—they can pull a car if they want to."

Billy stared at the monster on the floor and it growled at him. Harry laughed.

"He's just doing that because it amuses him."

"So why is he here?"

"He works here sometimes."

Doris looked from Harry to Billy. "You'd have to go far to find a less professional office situation, Billy."

"I like dogs," Leo offered.

"That," Doris said, pointing, "is not a dog for an office. Are you, Ferdy? No, you're not."

Ferdy barked now, a great guttural sound, and Billy forced himself not to jump.

"What's he supposed to be doing?"

"Office decoration," Harry said.

Doris shook her head. "He's here because Fornier thinks dogs are filthy and Cribb is afraid of them."

Leo nodded, grinning.

From somewhere in the closet Doris found two bowls. She filled one with water from the restroom, and into the other she poured the contents of the bag Harry had brought in. Ferdy began eating almost immediately.

A few minutes later, two tall, dark shapes appeared outside the door. A sharp, irritated rap on the door announced Fornier and Cribb.

"Come in, gentlemen."

The door opened and two well-dressed men entered the office. The first one wore a light gray suit and a pale yellow shirt and tie. He was clean-shaven, with curly blond hair and thick sideburns, and a murderous look in his blue eyes. The second man was taller, dark-haired, with a thick moustache. He looked no friendlier than his companion.

The blond one took the opportunity to sweep the office with a long, slow glance, then made a face of distaste.

"Gentlemen. I believe you know Leo and Doris. This is Bill, he works for us now. Bill, Messrs. Fornier and Cribb," Harry said, indicating the blond one as Fornier. Fornier acknowledged him with a blink. Cribb nodded slightly and then patted his hair and shot a quick look at the ceiling fan.

Ah, wearing a toupee, Billy told himself. *And afraid the ceiling fan will blow it off.*

Billy pointed. "You're the limo driver."

Cribb bristled. "I'm nobody's—" Then he caught the friendly malice in Billy's eyes and stopped. Now he recognized Billy Fox, and a frigid look came into his eyes.

Fornier gave Billy an interested look, then scanned the room, noticed the mastiff along the far wall and said, "For Christ's sake. A dog in a professional office?"

Cribb saw Ferdy now and took a half step back. His eyes widened, and he wet his lips.

"Don't worry. He ate already," Harry said. "Won't you sit down?"

Fornier took a seat. Cribb pulled a chair over and remained standing, with the chair between him and the dog.

"You know why we're here," Fornier began.

"To discuss—"

"Breaking and entering," Cribb said. "How about that for openers?" Cribb spoke through his teeth, contrived menace somewhere between Clint Eastwood and a villain in an old movie. He patted the hairpiece again, and Billy thought he'd never seen anyone so interesting.

"You broke into our offices," Fornier said, calm and reasonable, a restrained manner to match his elegance. "Forced entry."

"Was anything missing?"

"You know what we're talking about. Certain surveillance devices that were put into a case location suddenly turned up in our offices."

"Let's see if I follow. Your professional property finds its way to your offices. Your property in your office, and that's a bad thing?"

"Yeah," Cribb said through his teeth. "Breaking and entering is a bad thing."

"And the surveillance devices were put into a person's residence? Am I right?"

"By the woman who lives there. In her own house."

Harry shook his head. He folded his arms across his chest and looked thoughtful.

"Not currently. My information is that she has moved out and has asked for her mail to be sent to another address. So she is not in residence at that address. Therefore, I think what we have here is illegal bugging. And your bugs found their way back to your offices. Maybe they missed you."

Leo laughed and Cribb shot him a quick look. Leo pointed at the dog, and the muscles in Cribb's jaw began working.

"Everything is a joke to you, Strummer."

"Now that's not fair. I've got an irrepressible sense of humor. I'm also good at what I do. As you gentlemen are, in certain ways, at what you do. The hiding of surveillance devices is not among them, by the way."

"Oh, yeah?" Cribb said, and took a step forward.

Harry shook his head. "You're too excitable."

Fornier gave his partner a mildly annoyed look and moved closer to the desk.

"As unprofessional as you are, how do you stay in business, Strummer?"

"I like to think of myself as the guy who thinks outside the box. See, you view this situation as me undoing all your work, and I see it as a man hired to do a specific job that entailed the removal of illegal wire-tapping devices. Electronic surveillance is still illegal in the Land of Lincoln, you know. Or did you and Mr. Cribb here sign on with the FBI?"

"Like you've never put a bug in somebody's place."

"It's not something I'll admit to. But I will admit that I was hired to help a client out and I went through his place and removed surveillance devices that weren't put in place by law enforcement."

"We've been hired to perform a service for a client."

"So do it. Just don't put any more of your gizmos in Mr. Ryan's house or on his car or in his pants, or wherever."

Cribb took this occasion to lean over Harry's desk and point a finger in Harry's face.

"Listen, smartass—"

From the back wall a low, chesty growl shook the room.

Cribb jumped back. "Jesus Christ!"

"He doesn't like it when people point. He was brought up in a house of very strict manners. So, where does that leave us?"

"Well, I hope we've come to some understanding," Fornier said, and managed a condescending smile. "Don't piss us off, Harry."

Harry folded his arms across his chest. "Listen to me. Stay out of this man's house. Watch him with telescopes, fly overhead in a helicopter, crawl under his table in restaurants, go through his laundry, just stay out of his house and off his phone and leave his car alone."

"Don't tell us—" Cribb began, but Fornier held up his hand

and silenced him.

"I'm not accustomed to being told how to do my job."

"How did it all work out for you this time?" Billy heard a new, harder note come into Harry's voice. "Here's the thing. You tell me you were just doing your job, and I'm telling you that's what I was doing. What I was hired to do. You insert more electronic junk in this man's life, I'll find it, and you'll never know where it will show up next."

"You won't find what we put in."

"Yeah, I will," Harry said, looking around his room. He nodded toward Leo. "Or he will. We'll do what we have to do, just like you. We'll find it and we'll do this dance all over again."

"But don't come into our offices again," Fornier said.

Billy heard the *but* and realized Harry had won.

Fornier stood slowly, looked from Billy to Leo to save some face, nodded to Harry, and left. Cribb followed, pausing at the door just long enough to glare at Harry. He looked around and gave the office the same look his partner had on the way in. He sneered, but Billy noticed how hard he tried not to look at the dog one last time.

When the door closed behind them, Harry said, to no one in particular, "I thought that went pretty well."

"What just happened, really? What do you think they just agreed to?"

"I think we've convinced them not to put any more bugs and devices in our guy's house or on his car. That's all I was trying to do. Let them follow him around the old-fashioned way. Do them both good." He looked at Billy. "I was just trying to do what we told old Sunny Carter we'd do."

He watched Billy.

"Even out the odds. Level the playing field."

Harry nodded. "There you go. Sometimes in life, that's the best you can hope for, an even chance."

"That's all you want," Leo added. "You just want a fair chance."

Harry smiled and pointed a finger at Billy. "That was a nice bit there, you pissed Cribb off on two counts, calling him a 'limo driver.'"

"And letting him know you made him," Leo added. "Good work, Kid. He's got real thin skin, that Cribb."

"So these guys are more or less your enemies?"

"No, no, nothing so serious. We've pissed them off, that's all. I can go two years without running into them. We're just rival professionals, that's all. And they're not always top-shelf. Not bad guys, though, when they're not pissed off. We've actually done a couple of things together."

After lunch that day, Billy sat paging through the contents of a folder. Harry was doodling on a pad on his desk.

"What did you want to be when you were a kid?"

Harry looked up, surprised. He shrugged.

"Oh, you know, the usual stuff. I saw G-men in the movies and I wanted to be an FBI agent. For a while I wanted to go out West, live out there in the mountains, see the country. But the thing I wanted to do the longest, Kid, the thing maybe I still want to be, and you're gonna laugh, but I always wished I could be the wise man of the village." As Harry said this, Billy saw Doris mouthing the words with him, the *wise man of the village*, without so much as pausing as she sorted pages in a file.

"The *what?*"

"The wise man of the village. The guy they turn to in trouble, the guy who knows about life, about the world, and can give people answers that will help them out. *Magnificent Seven*—ever see that movie?"

"Sure."

"Remember in the beginning, the Mexican villagers don't know how to stop the bandits from terrorizing their village every year, and so they go and see The Old Man. Somebody says, 'We must ask The Old Man. He will know.' And he does. He's got all the answers. He doesn't have any power, he doesn't have any money, but he's got this other thing—he's got wisdom. He's figured out life. That's who I'd like to be, that old man that's figured out life. And people could come to me with their troubles and I'd be able to help them out."

"That's what you do, isn't it?"

"No, it's what I'd like to do. What I do is fly by the seat of my pants, and things don't always work out the way I'd like 'em to. And how much can I do? How many things can we take care of for people? How can you know what advice to give people? You never know how life will turn out. But if I had that thing, that knowledge about life—I think that would be a great thing."

Doris had paused. She stared straight ahead, her gaze just above the monitor screen. Harry seemed to be lost for the moment in his own thoughts. Billy pictured him sitting in an office somewhere—no, on a bench in a park, with people waiting patiently in a small line to come sit down next to him, tell him their problems, and get his answer, his wisdom. Billy smiled at the image, and Harry, snapping out of his reverie, misunderstood the smile. He reddened and gave Billy a sheepish look.

"I know, it's a crazy idea. Some ambition, huh? What the hell. You've got to have a goal in life, or a couple of 'em."

"Right," Billy said.

I have a goal, for right now, at least.

"But you got things you know about, am I right? Things you feel pretty confident about."

Billy shrugged. "In the service, they taught me to take a rifle apart and put it back together again. Talk about a pointless skill, right? And they taught me to drive a truck. I can do minor repairs on cars. I can do a few carpentry things and replace your windows if they break. Let's see—the cook taught me how to make omelets. I think that's it. Oh, and I play pool."

"Pool, huh? You any good?"

Something changed in Harry's eyes. Billy couldn't be sure, but he thought he'd seen something. Amusement?

"Yeah. I'm not bad. I ran forty once."

"Forty?"

"It was a long time ago, and I was playing a lot more. I'm out of practice now. But I'm still okay. I can still run a table on a good day."

"Maybe that's a good thing, that you're out of practice. That hotshot stick comes under a special heading: *'Skills that can get me hurt.'* You know?"

"I never play for money anymore," Billy said.

Harry gave him a long look but just said, "That's good." Billy Fox looked away and wondered if his ears were turning red.

TEN

War Heroes

The air conditioner died on a Tuesday. Leo stuck a rebuilt industrial fan in the window, which blew like the North Wind and sounded like a jet engine. For the rest of that week, they inhaled the grit of Wells Street and the hot, dense air of July, and the ceiling fan stirred it and made sure it did not escape.

Twice, Harry had him serve a summons. The first man took the document and walked away, muttering about the mountain of troubles in his world. The second one—in a Clark Street tavern—looked at the summons and threw a shot glass at Billy's head, then chased him out of the bar.

"Why do I get to serve all the summonses?"

Harry looked over at Leo. "Tell him."

"Because you're more qualified."

"How?"

"You're faster," Leo said.

"And young guys heal better," Harry added. They both laughed.

Toward the end of the week, Billy found himself overwhelmed by his attempt to compare and make sense of the files on two men who might actually be the same person. He was staring at the files covering his desk when he heard the downstairs door open.

A man came up the stairs with a heavy step, paused on the landing outside the door, and loudly cleared his throat. Billy saw Harry lean back, watching the door. The visitor swung the door open and barked, "Hi. John Sheedy is my name," and advanced across the room like a fighter cutting off the ring, hand extended.

Harry got up and shook, said, "Harry Strummer. Yeah, you called."

"Yes, I did. I've heard good things about you, Mr. Strummer, very good things. That's why I'm here. I'm not a man who wastes his time."

"Al Akers, you said."

"That's right. I guess a veteran street cop would know a good detective, am I right?"

This would-be client looked around the room as he spoke, making certain, Billy thought, that his entrance had been noted. And of course it was, for he was in several ways a loud man—he wore a bright blue and yellow plaid summer sport coat over a bold peacock blue shirt. His shoes and belt were glossy white, and he had spent enough time in the sun or under a lamp to guarantee a tan that would outlast the summer. Several times he said things intended to be amusing and laughed aloud at his own jokes, and when he spoke in that deep bell of a voice he scanned the office to ensure that people were listening.

On the far side of the room, Doris paused in the middle of addressing an envelope and looked at him.

"How you doing, Hon?" Sheedy said, and went back to his tale, unaware of the venomous look Doris gave him.

At one point in his narrative to Harry, he said, "I'm the kind of guy who will pay for what he wants." Then he turned to catch Billy's eye and added, "Hello, son."

He smiled and waited for Billy to acknowledge him, then turned his attention back to Harry. Billy looked back at the files, but found it impossible not to listen in on the exchange between Harry and John Sheedy. At first it wasn't really much of an exchange, but rather Sheedy's narrative, and Billy noted how Harry sat back and let the client say what he needed to say. Sheedy gave a long account of his various possessions and enterprises—*"I've built up three companies from nothing, from nothing, you understand."* He spoke of his need for someone to investigate, follow, watch—*"You hire enough people, one of them will screw you."* And he castigated his competitors—*"They'd like nothing more than to bring me down, especially if they could use one of my own to do it."*

At some point, Billy stopped reading the file information of George Kesselring and Gary Kessel and listened as Harry led Sheedy with questions. From Harry's questions, *"When did you first suspect there was something going on in-house?" "What evidence do you have of people in your organization conspiring against you?" "Tell me who you suspect—or who you don't completely trust,"* Billy thought he saw the emerging pattern, of a man driven by paranoia and little else, for it was clear from Sheedy's answers that he had nothing solid, no real evidence of any kind that anyone in his company was "screwing" him.

Finally, Harry sat back and looked around the room, considering what he'd heard, and then he asked one last question.

"Is there anybody you trust completely?"

Sheedy was answering before the question was fully out.

"I trust my girl Gerry—Geraldine Makowski—she's my right hand. Officially she's the Administrative Assistant to the President, but she's my right hand. I would be lost without her. If there was ever the perfect employee, it's her. And you should see her—well, you'll get a good look if you come work for me, she's flat-out gorgeous. Remember Rita Hayworth, when she was young? She looks like Rita Hayworth."

"I still see Rita Hayworth in my dreams. Listen, Mr. Sheedy, I'm not sure—"

"Hold on, Mr. Strummer. Hear me out. This is a top-shelf company we're talking about, so money is no object. If I haven't made myself clear, I'm a man of substance. And I'm the kind of man who says what he means and means what he says. I don't mean to blow my own horn, but I'm a stand-up kind of man. I'm a decorated veteran. I don't like to talk about it, but—a war hero, in case you're interested."

For a moment, Harry looked as though Sheedy had slapped him. Then he seemed to compose his face.

"What I was going to say, Mr. Sheedy, is that the guy you want for this job is Alex Webb. He's a man with expertise in the area of corporate espionage, fraud, you name it. Me, I'm a guy that does small security jobs and personal investigations. Here—" Harry opened his desk drawer and pulled out a flat box filled with business cards. "Here's Alex Webb's business card. He's good."

John Sheedy held the card and peered at it as though bugs had died on it. "I wanted to hire you. Al Akers said you were the best."

"The best at what I'm experienced at, maybe, and I'm flattered. But there has to be a fit between the client and the investigating agency, and I'm telling you that's the best fit you'll find. He's top-notch, and it's a pretty big firm—he's got nearly three dozen employees. He's more in your league."

Something changed in Sheedy's face, and he gave the card a second look. "Huh," he said. Then he got up, said, "Thanks for your time and your help. I'll give this fellow a call."

"Use my name, Sir," Harry said.

When Sheedy was gone, Billy waited. For a moment Harry stared down at his desk blotter. Then he looked up, but at Doris. He made a little snort and shook his head. Doris nodded and went back to work.

"So what did I miss?"

"You didn't miss anything. You took it all in, you just don't know what to make of it. How you doing with those two guys there?" Harry asked, indicating the two folders.

"I think they're the same guy. I think *you* think they're the same guy and you want to see if I figure it out."

Harry winked. "Good."

"So why aren't you taking Mr. Sheedy's case—it sounds like you could write your own ticket."

"That's true. After all, didn't the guy just tell us he's *a man of substance*? With a *top-shelf* company?"

Here he gave his high-pitched laugh.

"No, this Sheedy, I don't think we have time for."

"Why?"

"Why? Well, first of all, it's his so-called 'case.' You know what the real case is? Doris knows, right?"

Doris put the finished envelope atop a neat stack. "I think his case is a girl named Geraldine. That's what I think."

Harry grinned at Billy and held out his hand toward Doris. "She ought to have her own agency," he said.

"I think so, too," Doris said in a quiet voice.

"Wait, I'm missing something here."

"The case, Bill, is that this guy has the hots for his assistant Geraldine, and he thinks somebody else is putting the moves on her. And maybe even—" Here he turned to Doris.

"Our girl Geraldine likes it. She found a younger guy than old Moneybags."

"Man, I didn't catch any of that."

"He talked in very calm but very vague terms about his suspicions and his workers and his competitors, and his voice showed emotion only when he started talking about her. Maybe I'm reading too much into it, but it sounded to me like he was trying to tell himself what he wanted to hear, that she is the only person he trusts and she's beyond reproach. Sounded like a man whistling in the wind to me."

"Okay, I'll tell you what I did catch. At some point there he pissed you off."

"What pissed me off is Al Akers referring this guy to me. Akers gets a few drinks in him and he wants everybody to know what a connected, street-wise guy he is. You tell him you want an audience with the Pope, he'll tell you he's got a guy to set that up."

"No, this was something about Sheedy that you didn't like."

Harry gave him a frank look. "I didn't like anything about him, Bill. Except the white shoes. I've always wanted to be able to wear white shoes." For a moment Billy thought this was all Harry would say. He held his ground and watched Harry.

"Look, Bill, this wouldn't be the first job I ever took for an asshole, it's not even that. I don't mind if a guy sits in that chair and squirms and tries to find a reason why he isn't a screw-up, but I have no use for the ones that sit there and lie to me. He's a bullshitter, and he's—what's the word? Manipulative, that's it. He's manipulative."

"He seemed like a nice enough guy. A blowhard, maybe."

"Maybe he is a nice guy, but I doubt it. He's in our office twenty minutes and he's bragging about half a dozen things."

"Like what?"

"Like he's 'a man of some substance.' Who says that? Guys that have it, they parade around in their money, they'd wear it around their necks if they could, but they don't walk around saying stupid things like that. And he called himself a war hero."

"Maybe he was."

Harry gave Billy a long look. "You were in the service."

"I wasn't a hero."

"If you were, can you see yourself telling a stranger you were a hero?"

"I guess not." Something in Harry's face caught his attention. A small flash of anger, and then, for the briefest shard of time, a look of sorrow.

Billy saw it as an opening and took a shot.

"So you were in the service?" he asked, and kept his face as immobile as he could.

Harry looked surprised. "Me? Nah, me, I was 4H," he said, and laughed.

"Yeah, very funny."

Harry waved Billy's question off as though it were nonsense, then composed his face once more.

"You see, Bill, the guys who actually saw all this stuff, did things, got the medals, they don't talk about it—"

"They don't want to blow their own horn."

"Yeah, that's part of it, but also they don't want to talk about it or think about it. I once knew a guy, he served in the Pacific, he was in every island fight all the way across, from Guadalcanal to Okinawa. I know this guy was wounded multiple times, and I heard he won medals, but all he ever wanted to talk about was the time him and his squad were stopped in their tracks in the jungle by some kinda giant lizard that stared them all down. A dozen guys with modern weapons faced down by a creature that would die in spring weather in Chicago. All he ever wanted to tell you about was his adventure with the lizard. This guy, this Sheedy that announces he's a man of substance and a war hero, he's also an asshole. And he's a man likely to play fast and loose with the truth in ways that I don't need to deal with. So, no, we're not going to do anything here. Let him tell his war stories to somebody else. And good luck to him with Geraldine."

Harry ran his hand across the back of his neck, looked at the clock, and said, "I'm going out for some of that beautiful fresh air on the street. I'll bring back hot dogs from Sammy's." He asked Doris if she wanted one, and then he left.

When Harry had gone, Billy looked at Doris, but she busied herself with the office mail. He went back to his work, and for a time the only sound in the office was the rocket-like sound of Leo's fan in the window.

"He was in the service, Billy. To answer your question."

Doris spoke quietly, as though fearful that Harry would walk in at that moment.

"I thought so."

"This is between us. You shouldn't let him know you know about this stuff. He served in Korea. He saw action, I know he was wounded, and I know at one point he was afraid they were all going to freeze to death on a hilltop. He actually lost part of a toe to frostbite—watch how he walks sometimes, he's just a little bit lopsided. And there was a fight where he was wounded and the guys on either side of him, both friends of his, were killed. He can't even talk about that. The guys that saw that stuff, they don't want to remember it, how scared they were, what happened to them, to their buddies. Sometimes the ones that come back, they feel guilty that they got out. I think he's like that."

"Okay. Thanks."

"Don't mention it. *Really* don't mention it," she said, and laughed one of her infrequent laughs.

. . .

In the afternoons on his lunch hour, Billy fell into the habit of wandering the neighborhood and trying to see it the way Harry Strummer saw it, trying to notice anything unusual. He found himself trying to tell things about the people he saw from their facial expressions, their body language, their "props"—a street map, a handwritten note on a scrap of paper, a camera. More than once he spotted the con artist with the gas can. Once he caught a young guy watching women go by, but he was interested in the purses rather than the women. Billy stopped across the street from the kid and stared until they made eye contact, and the kid suddenly moved off.

On one of these walks, just a block from the office, a man leaning against a tree on the far side of the street looked up just as Billy passed by. He was a good-looking man with a sunburnt face. He wore a baseball cap and a sport shirt, and he was pretending to read a newspaper. He gave Billy an interested look and then looked away.

I'm not your type, Pal, Billy thought.

That Saturday morning, he took a succession of buses around the north side, walking a few blocks each time he disembarked. He tried to imagine this section of the city as a circle and told himself he was cutting this circle into sections, smaller and smaller sections. From time to time, he stood on a busy corner and watched people coming out of supermarkets or laundromats, and he spent a lot of time looking at women in playgrounds.

Late in the afternoon he stopped in the diner. Millie was just tying her apron, a pencil in her mouth. She walked toward Billy as he sat down at the counter.

"Afternoon," she said through the pencil, then laughed and took it out of her mouth. "Excuse me, Hon."

"How was your date?"

She met his eyes and then looked away, shrugging. "I've had worse. I've had better." She handed him a menu, brought him water, and stood staring out at the street as he pondered his choices.

Billy could smell her—shampoo or soap, a clean smell. He realized he was staring at the menu and she was standing a foot away and waiting for him to order, and he could not remember feeling more off-balance in a girl's presence. He looked up, and she was watching him with those big eyes. In the end he ordered a hamburger, just to be ordering.

When his food came he ate quickly. A woman with two small children hurried by, and Billy reminded himself why he was here in Chicago.

He finished his food, and then on an impulse asked for a cup of coffee. He sat there sipping it slowly, looking around the diner at everything and everyone but Millie. Outside the diner, the street was crowded with people shopping, wandering, many of them young. He noticed the couples. There seemed to be a great number of couples. They didn't all look happy, but they were couples nonetheless.

Billy put money on top of his check and got up to leave. Millie slid down the counter.

"You have a nice day, Billy."

He nodded and was about to say something as simple as "You, too." Instead he said, "You want to grab a cup of coffee sometime, or a Coke? Or something?"

What am I doing?

"Or something?" She smiled, waited a heartbeat, then said, "Sure."

Billy had no idea what to do next. He stood there looking at her, and she held his gaze, clearly amused by his indecision.

"Well—"

"I get off at seven today, I work till seven tomorrow."

He wet his lips and waited for thought. He had nothing. He heard himself say "Well" again and knew he was blushing.

For Christ's sake!

"How about tomorrow? I'll stop by at seven and we can go somewhere."

"That sounds fine," she said, in the tone of an adult being patient with an addled child.

"Okay," he said, and left with a wave. When he hit the street, he was grinning.

She'd put on lipstick and put her hair up, and managed to make herself look a little less like a small town girl far from home. They found a restaurant down the street.

"You hungry, Millie?"

"I don't know. Are you eating?"

"Sure."

And so the date went from coffee to dinner. He asked her questions about herself—she was from Tennessee, just outside of Memphis, and had come up to Chicago "to get a new start on things" but did not say why, and he knew not to press the issue. Billy told her stories of summer in Lansing, looking for garter snakes in the fields, watching shooting stars, roaming far and wide without adult supervision. She laughed easily and made him comfortable. She asked cautious questions, and he told her in as vague terms as possible about the Army and bouncing around the country, and alluded to things in his past that, like the things in hers, had not worked out. As he spoke, she watched him with a slight smile.

She was most interested in his tales of Harry Strummer and Leo and Doris.

"I thought detectives followed people around."

"Sometimes that's what the job calls for. But we do a lot of other things."

"I guess so. It's nice that you work for a man you like."

"He's okay, for a boss," Billy said, and shrugged.

"No, you like him."

He laughed. "Yeah. I do."

Through it all he had the sense of time racing by, told himself he was actually out with a girl, a nice girl. Jesus, he was on a date. He looked around the restaurant and realized that, like Millie, he was smiling.

It's like I'm sixteen or something.

Then they were done. He suggested a walk down to the lake, but she said she had to be going.

"You want to—do this? Again?"

"Sure. And next time we can maybe talk about the other stuff."

"What other stuff?"

"The stuff you'd really like to talk about because it bothers you and it's important to you."

He shook his head. "I don't think there's anything—"

She held up a hand. "There's—there's spaces between your stories, and your eyes go kind of distant. It's okay, Hon, but it's there. I've got to go."

"I'll take you home."

"No. I'll get a cab. Here's one" she said, flagging down a cab.

When the cabbie pulled over, she held out her hand. Surprised, Billy took it, and then she leaned forward and gave him a kiss on the cheek.

At the end of the week, Billy cashed his check and went out to buy clothes. He bought a beige summer-weight sport coat and two shirts and a pair of shoes. He told himself he was just trying to make sure people took him seriously, that there was no significance to it all.

Billy started out the new week doing legwork for Harry. When he returned to the office, Harry was with a new client. As soon as he entered the room, Billy sensed that there was something in play, something going on that everyone else was aware of.

The client was a young white man in a corduroy sport coat and a shirt buttoned up to the neck. His blond hair was clipped close to his scalp. He was speaking with Harry, answering questions rather than asking them, and when Billy crossed his line of vision, the visitor gave him a long look. Billy nodded to him. On the far side of the room, Leo was playing with a long-handled screwdriver and a gargantuan lock, but shooting an occasional glance the young client's way. Doris kept her focus on her work, squinting at some problem on her screen, but there was something straight-backed and alert in her posture that told Billy she was listening.

"Well," the client was saying, "I'm not sure. I'm just not sure. I don't even know for sure if she's here, she might be in, you know,

Detroit. And then I'd just be, like, throwing money away, you see my position?"

"I do, Mr. Harris," Harry said, and never took his eyes off his visitor. Billy saw the client look away.

There was something odd about the way Harris spoke, something unnatural, but Billy could not put his finger on it.

Harris scanned the room, seemed to be interested in Leo for a moment, and then looked away when Leo met his gaze.

"Well," Harris said, getting to his feet. "I'm going to think about what you've told me and I'll get back to you, I really will."

Harry nodded. "Very good. I hope to hear back from you. We're not a big agency, but we're very good at what we do. But if you think you'll feel more comfortable with one of the bigger agencies looking for your sister, I certainly understand."

"Thank you, sir," Harris said, and they shook hands. On his way out, Harris took a last look at the people in the room. He shot a quick final look at Harry and then was gone.

"Did you just talk yourself out of a client?"

Harry stared at the door as though he hadn't heard the question. Then, as Billy was about to repeat the question, Harry turned.

"I don't know." Harry seemed to be looking his way but somehow right through him. "I don't know what that was. Wasn't a client, I'm pretty sure about that."

Now Harry looked around his office. Doris met his gaze and raised her eyebrows. Harry waited.

"That was weird," Doris said. "He sounded like he was reading a script."

Harry nodded, once. "It was almost like he was casing the place."

For a moment Harry seemed lost once more, deep in thought. Then he looked around his office in puzzlement. "As if there's anything here you could sell on the street for more than ten bucks."

"You mean there's something here *worth* ten bucks?" Doris asked.

"Hey, he could get at least that on the street for you, Hon."

Harry shifted in his seat and looked at Leo. "You made him

uncomfortable."

"I got that effect on people."

"So what do you think he wanted?" Billy asked.

Harry gave him a thoughtful look. "I don't know, but I know his name's not Harris."

"You think he gave you a fake name?"

"I do."

From the corner of his eye, Billy saw Doris look up from her work, and some of the air seemed to have gone out of the room.

"Why?"

"When a guy who isn't used to aliases gives you a phony name, you can tell sometimes, there's a little extra emphasis, like they're trying to sound natural with a name they've never used before. I think I heard it with this guy."

"So who do you think he is, then?"

"Some kid getting his jollies at my expense, a thief trying to see if we have anything of value. Who knows?" He stared off into space again. After a while he said, "Maybe we'll see him again. Wouldn't be surprised."

• • •

A few days later, Billy decided to walk all the way home to his rooming house. He was three blocks from the office when he saw Harry Strummer. Harry was standing at the corner of Lincoln and Wells with his face buried in a newspaper, but Billy understood that the paper was a prop. A bus had just pulled up and Harry was watching the people get off. He had an expectant look on his face. When the bus pulled away, Harry peered up the street, and Billy understood he was looking for the next bus.

• • •

Late that night, Billy went out and hit some bars near Wrigley Field. His search took him into places that furthered his education—just south of the ballpark he saw the Cerveza Fria sign too late and found himself alone in a roomful of Puerto Ricans. No one said a thing to him, nor did anyone have to. He left halfway through his beer and had the good sense not to ask the bartender if he'd seen a girl named Rita. On Roscoe, he found himself in a bar full of drunken baseball fans. A half dozen of them were singing the Notre Dame fight song, and the bartender, a tough-looking woman with dyed black hair, frowned irritably when he tried to ask about Rita. She indicated the noisy singers and shook her head.

On Halsted, he walked into a new-looking bar where the pounding bass of the jukebox shook the air. A thin, gray-haired man near the door looked him up and down and said, "Well, look what we've got here." Half a dozen faces turned his way, all of them male. He fought the impulse to turn and run, instead forced himself to go to the bar and ask the bartender if he'd seen a girl of Rita's description.

The bartender, a big man with a ponytail, leaned across the bar and said, "Sweetheart, she wouldn't be coming here."

A man a few feet away said, "But you can stay," and someone laughed. Billy put on his most casual face and walked slowly to the door. Someone whistled. By the time he hit the street he was blushing furiously, and he just barely suppressed the impulse to break into a run.

ELEVEN

Lost Harriet

The client was another cocky-looking man who looked like an aging lady-killer, smelled like money, and grinned as though he were about to make a sale. Ten minutes into his conversation with Harry, the gentleman burst into tears.

"Take it easy, Mr. Witter, it'll work out. She'll come back."

"I just don't know what to do. She's all I've got since I lost my wife. And she hates me. And you know why, don't you?" Witter wiped his eyes with a monogrammed handkerchief. "She hates me for being the one who didn't die."

"She probably hates the world right now, and you're the easiest target."

"Do you think you can find her?"

"I never predict these things. If she's desperate to get out of her life, she'd leave town and keep running."

Amen to that, Billy thought.

"But we have to assume she's still here. And if she is, there's a good chance we'll find her."

"She could be anywhere."

Harry nodded absently and began asking questions about the girl, whose name was Harriet, and her interests. He determined that Harriet's friends in Lincolnwood had no idea where she was. He showed interest when Witter told him that Harriet had a friend who'd moved from Lincolnwood into the city, somewhere near Wrigley Field, near the ballpark, a girl named Tania.

"All right, Mr. Witter. If this angle doesn't work out, maybe we'll come out your way and talk to her friends, see if we can pry something loose. But I think you've given us something to work with."

Witter nodded and shook hands and looked hopeful.

• • •

For the next two days they struck out. Harry sent Billy into donut shops and tattoo parlors and diners in a one mile radius of the ballpark, and no one had any idea who Harriet was. They drove by a comic book shop and Harry pointed to it.

"I want you to come back here tonight and linger. Get into conversations, see what comes up."

"Why not drop me off now?"

"Because you look like a guy who's working. I want you to come back looking like one of them, that way they might talk to you."

And so it was that Billy returned to the comic book shop, this time in jeans with shot knees and a black Led Zeppelin t-shirt. He asked no questions for the better part of a half hour, then got into a long comparison with the guy behind the counter about the cops in Chicago and the cops he'd experienced, in Denver, in Omaha, in Houston, in Lansing. Eventually he dropped Harriet's name here and there.

It made little difference that he could see—a couple of kids talked to him, the tattooed and pierced young folk, and one of the girls gave him the eye, but no one had anything to say about a girl named Harriet.

Just before he left, a guy with a shaved head and an odd pigtail approached him. "You cool?"

"Guess so."

"Family?"

"No, just a friend. I went to school with her brother."

"She's not here. And she's dropped the old name, Man."

"Oh, yeah?"

"Yeah, you're not looking for 'Harriet' anymore. She's

Judy now."

"Know where she went?"

"No. Probably still around. What happens if you find her?"

"Whatever she wants, I guess."

"If she comes back—"

"Here," Billy said, and tore off the top of a matchbook. He wrote the office number down. "If you see her, tell her to call this number and not to talk to anybody but Doris."

"Strange, but all right."

For the better part of the week they looked for Harriet while they pursued other tasks.

"You know, kid, there's no guarantee she's still in town. If she really wants to get away from her family, she won't stay here. So she could be gone. I've got a couple other places to check out, though."

When they returned to the office that afternoon, Doris told them she had taken a call.

"A kid, she sounded nervous, but like she was trying to remain, you know, poised. She asked for me."

"Then what?"

"I said, 'This is Doris. What can I do for you?' Then she hung up."

Harry looked from Doris to Billy. "Hey, Billy gave her your name. That was her. Smart play, Bill."

"Why? We didn't get anything from it?"

"We know she's here. That's something. Now we find her."

That evening, Harry brought him to a bar in a basement just north of Wrigley Field. A small tin sign said, "Marie's."

"So who is Marie?"

"A lady with nearly limitless contacts."

"More than you?"

Harry gave him an amused look. "Oh, I think so. I think she's got more than anybody."

The bar itself was five cracked steps down and dark as a bat's home, and smelled of open liquor and disinfectant—and perfume, for the half dozen or so customers were all women.

Billy hung back momentarily, wondering if they'd just entered the female equivalent of the gay bars he'd already been introduced to. Two of the women in the bar gave him a long look that could have been hostility or interest, but the room was too dark to make out their eyes.

The woman behind the bar was perhaps sixty, but fighting it hard, with a tight blouse and dyed hair and enough eye-shadow for Cleopatra. She gave them a businesslike nod, and said, "Hello, Gentlemen," and then gave out a little squeal of happiness.

"Oh! Is that you, Strummer? Harry Strummer's in my saloon. Hello, Harry, you old shit."

"Hello, Marie. Still living in caves, I see."

"And who's the handsome kid behind you? Your bodyguard?"

"This is Bill. He works for me."

"The Sorcerer's Apprentice, then. Come on in and have a cold one, gents. The girls don't mind."

Indeed, the women at the bar now smiled their way and went back to their conversation.

"Business, Harry?"

"Yes, but a couple of cold ones would go down nicely. What do you have that's good?"

"Tuborg."

"Oh, we're drinking Danish today, Bill."

Marie opened two beers and poured them into a couple of tall glasses. Then she went over to her jukebox, opened it, pressed a button, and told the women at the bar to pick songs.

"Thanks, Marie. A little background noise always helps."

"So what can I do for you, Harry?"

Harry flipped the photograph on the bar. "I'm looking for this young lady."

Marie laughed. "You're kidding me, right?"

"It's the only picture her old man has. She's seventeen."

"Name?"

"Harriet. Not using it, though. We think she's calling herself 'Judy' now. We know she's around. She made contact. Called the office and then hung up."

Marie looked at him for a moment. While she was considering what she'd been told, the door opened and a couple of younger girls entered and called out to her. Billy watched them and sipped his beer.

"You like that?" Marie said. "The Tuborg, I mean."

Billy felt himself blushing. "Yeah, it's good."

She turned her amused attention back to Harry.

"You got anything, Harry? I need something to go on, and then I need the usual."

For Billy's benefit she added, "That's the usual assurances, Bill."

"All I can tell you is that she lived in Lincolnwood, and her old man sells insurance. Her mother died in January."

"Ah. That's what set this off. You know that, right?"

"Maybe. I'll defer to your wider experience."

"What's he like? Did you check him out?"

"Yeah. Drinks, but then who wouldn't in his situation?"

"Lotsa guys, but we'll let that go for now. What else?"

"Shows up for work. Did his best to smile in my office, but he broke down talking about her. I don't think there's any violence. I could be wrong. But I don't think so."

While Marie chewed this over, Harry added, "If I find her, I'll see if she's okay. Then I'll see if she wants to go back."

"He knows that?"

"Yes."

"I'll see what I can do."

With that, Marie patted Harry on the hand and moved off to speak with the women. A moment later they were all singing along with Marvin Gaye and Tammi Terrell. Harry drank his beer in silence.

When they were finished, Harry tucked a twenty under his glass and waved to Marie.

"I'll call if I hear anything, Hon." She smiled at Billy. "And you stop by if I can help you find yours, Bill."

Billy waved and tried not to show his confusion. Outside, Billy turned to Harry.

"What do you think she meant by that?"

"What she said. She'll help you find who you're looking for if you want."

"What makes her think I'm looking for somebody?"

Harry gave him a wry look. "It's pretty plain, kid." He shrugged and said nothing more about it.

Four days later, Doris took a call from Marie, wrote down the particulars, and gave the note to Harry.

"Okay," he said. He looked at Billy. "We're dining at McDonald's."

At one o'clock they entered a McDonald's near a post office on Clark Street and took a booth in the rear.

Within seconds, two young women entered—one was in her twenties, and Billy recognized her as one of Marie's customers. The other was a teenager, an older, more sullen version of the girl in the photo.

"Ladies. Have a seat."

"We're not going to stay," the older one said.

"Marie would be pissed off at me if I didn't buy you lunch. Tell Billy what you want."

Billy took orders and went up to get the food. When he returned, Harry appeared to be making small talk with the older girl. Harriet sat with her arms crossed and looked out at the street.

Billy passed out the food and drinks, and they began eating in silence. Finally, the young girl put down her hamburger and shook her head.

"I'm not going anywhere with you."

"No, you're not," Harry said. "Now eat your food."

"What are you here for, then?"

"To do my job. I'm not the police or the truant officer or the CIA or the Red Chinese Army or whoever else you don't want to talk to. I'm a private detective doing a job. I already told your father I wasn't bringing you back."

"What then?" Harriet asked, clearly confused. She looked

to her companion, who just shrugged and said, "Marie likes him. He's okay."

"I told him I'd look for you, and I did that. We also just accomplished the second part of my job."

"Which was?"

"To be able to tell him you were all right. I see that—although if you don't eat, I might have to tell him you were on some kinda hunger strike."

This brought the faintest of smiles, and she made a little nod and took a bite of her hamburger, then a drink, then a couple of fries.

"Good. Now this brings me to the final part of my assignment, as I see it. I'm to deliver his message. First, if you want to come home, you're welcome there with no questions asked. If you don't want to but you need something, something from your room, maybe, or money, you're to call my office and speak to the lady that you already called once."

"Doris."

"That's her. She manages the office, which means most of the time she's my boss. Anything you need, you tell her, and we'll convey that to your dad."

Harry sat back and munched on a French fry. He looked at Billy. "You going to eat all your fries?"

Billy pushed his fries over to Harry and they waited.

"That's it? That's all?" Harriet said. She looked at her companion, who just shrugged.

"That's it. Unless there's a message for your father."

She shrugged and looked uncomfortable. She shot another look at the older woman, then a quick look at Billy and Harry.

"If I don't come home, is he gonna make you come after me?"

Harry laughed. "Miss, nobody can make me do anything. Except maybe for my girl Doris. And she's not interested in you."

"I don't know about coming home yet. Tell him I'll think about it."

"Okay."

"And I'll call your office. Doris. I think I need money and some of my books."

"Good. That's it then."

The girls got up to go. The older one nodded and tried on a smile. Harriet paused as she left the booth.

"Is he okay? My dad?"

"Ah, you know. He's lonesome. But that's his problem. You just got to keep yourself safe. See what happens."

She gave him a small wave, and then they were gone.

Harry looked at Billy, then at the remains of his lunch. "If we do this again, it's got to be Wendy's. McDonald's is for teenagers."

Outside in the parking lot, Billy said, "That went pretty well, right?"

"As well as could be expected. We can tell him she's safe, she looks okay, she's with decent people, she doesn't hate his guts. We did our job."

"And now?"

"Now he can pay me." Harry clapped his hands together and said, "Come on, take a walk with me."

They strolled up Wells Street and were stopped by a man whom Harry had done work for in the past. They made small talk for a minute, and when the man was gone, Harry pointed to the tavern behind them, the Earl of Old Town.

"This place here? Best place in the city for folk music. All kinds of great people come here. Bob Gibson still plays here." Harry seemed lost in thought for a moment, then snapped out of it.

"So you're wondering why I come up here and watch the people get off the bus."

Billy blinked and felt the blood rushing to his cheeks. Harry raised a hand.

"I know, I know, don't worry. You were curious, or maybe even you think there's a problem."

"You look worried sometimes. Since that first time, when you said you thought you just saw a guy that you knew was dead. 'Long dead,' you said."

"Yeah, I did."

"You've been preoccupied, too. You space out sometimes."

Harry gave him a small smile. "There are people that will tell you I spaced out years ago and never came out of it. All right. Here's the thing. It's him. The guy I thought I saw, it's him. He's from a case I had a long time ago in Kansas City. Not a pleasant case. One of the, ah, principals, got killed by his partner. And that guy I saw, he was involved. My best sources told me he ran, he left town and was killed in a robbery attempt in another city. St. Louis, they told me. He was an accountant, this guy, and he was actually the cause of a lot of it, that trouble. They told me he was dead, and he turns up here. I see him on the street less than a mile from my office, this survivor of a very bad case. So it spooked me a little. But it's nothing for you to worry about. He's not dangerous. It's just not pleasant to see him and be reminded of that time. I don't like to think about that time."

"Well, thanks for telling me."

A sudden worry crossed Harry's face. "You said anything about this to Doris?"

"No, there was no reason to."

"Good. Like I said, it's not a big deal. There's no danger from this guy. Just an accountant. A creepy guy, but no danger. Took me by surprise, seeing him. But it's no big deal."

"Sure. Right," Billy said, unconvinced.

TWELVE

Developments

The weather grew hotter and wetter. It rained for nearly a week, and when it wasn't raining, the humidity was stifling. Billy could not remember ever feeling this hot. He wondered what others made of him, this young guy always walking, constantly walking, alone, through neighborhoods where he didn't know a soul. His search for Rita was beginning to seem pointless, a foolish waste of time based possibly on an unfounded idea. It struck him that there was no actual evidence that she was here.

On a Saturday when the humidity lifted slightly, he went to the lakefront in cut-off jeans and threw himself into the water. On either side of him he saw couples, it seemed the entire beach was couples, all of Chicago was people in couples, who did not return at the end of the day to a small room in a flophouse. Out on the lake, Billy saw a cruise ship of some sort and wondered what it would be like to see the city from out there.

That night he stopped at the Steak 'n' Egger, and Millie was working. She came over to hand him a menu, and he asked her to go out with him after work.

"No, thank you."

He blinked, tried not to show his discomfiture. "Oh. You're busy."

She gave him a small smile. "I'm busy going home and putting my sore feet up and watching television."

He nodded and turned to leave. On an impulse he said, "Are you busy tomorrow?"

She gave him an odd look, part frown, part question. "I have things to do during the day."

"The evening then. We'll go on a boat ride."

"A boat ride?"

"Yeah, you know, those boats downtown that take you along the river and out onto the lake?"

Now she smiled. "All right."

• • •

As the Wendella boat made its way through the locks out onto the great lake, they made small talk at first and then she asked about his job. This time he had stories for her. Billy spoke for a while of his cases, and was about to start telling her about another client when he had a moment of epiphany. He remembered a small talk with his mother when he was just starting to go out with girls.

"A girl likes a gentleman, Billy, you remember that. And I'll tell you something else, Honey. I see all these girls with their boyfriends, and they're just watching the boy jabber away and they nod and show they're paying attention, and all they want is somebody to listen to them. A girl likes a gentleman and a boy who will listen to her sometimes."

"So you know about me—"

"Oh, do I?" Millie asked, looking amused.

"Well, more or less. I walk a lot, I'm still learning about the city. What do you do when you're not waiting on people?"

"I like to read, I like museums and the zoo, I like music—I have a collection of old records—45s and LPs. Mostly girl singers."

"Tell me some good girl singers."

"They're all good."

He laughed. "Tell me some girl singers maybe I don't know about."

She relaxed and gave him names, mostly female singers from the '60s and early '70s that he had never heard of—English girls like Sandy Shaw and Cilla Black and Sandy Denny, and an American girl named Laura Nyro, and R&B singers Carla Thomas and Barbara

Acklin. Millie admitted that when she listened to "her girls" she sang with them, and frequently danced.

"I always dance to Aretha," she said. "You like to dance, Billy?"

"It's been, you know, a long time."

"A girl doesn't care if a fellow is any good at it. Just that he'll dance with her."

She gave him a sly look and he nodded.

The boat made a long, slow turn, and they saw the city now as someone might see it coming from across the lake, with the museums at the south end of the lakefront and the beaches at the north end, and the spectacle of the skyline in the middle of it all.

She leaned back slightly and he put his arm around her. He waited for her reaction, but she just nestled in.

"I've lived here almost three years now," she said, "and I've never been out here. I've never seen the lakefront from a boat."

After a while, Billy said, "It looks like a perfect place, like someplace where life is perfect and everything is possible."

"You're right, it does. But your life doesn't depend on a place, or at least it shouldn't."

"You an expert on life?"

"No," she said, laughing, "I'm still trying to put one together. Like you."

When the ride was over, they wandered up and down Michigan Avenue and looked in shop windows. He bought her an ice cream sundae from a twenty-four hour restaurant on State Street. Then she asked him to flag down a cab for her.

"You don't want me to take you home, huh?"

"I can get home."

"You're not sure about me yet."

"Actually, you're not sure about me."

Billy opened his mouth to protest just as a cab pulled over. Millie leaned over and planted a quick kiss on his lips.

"Thanks for the boat ride and the ice cream," she said, and looked amused.

. . .

Billy woke up early on Monday and went out for a long walk before going to work. In the office, Leo was recounting an adventure he'd had over the weekend involving two drunks, and they were all listening, Billy, Harry, and Doris.

Then Billy heard the noise in the hall—a man coming up the stairs but trying to be quiet. He heard the man hesitate somewhere short of the landing. For a moment there was no sound from the hall. He was still out there, motionless. Why? Losing his nerve, maybe, rethinking his reasoning, his motivation, whatever had brought him to a nickel-and-dime agency at the top of a staircase on life support. Perhaps he was deciding he didn't need the services of an agency in this wreck of a building.

Billy looked at Harry, who was watching the door. For the briefest moment he was struck by the odd thought that Harry had been waiting for this moment, that somehow Harry understood who was out there in the hall. Then the footsteps resumed, and the door opened and brought them a client. The newcomer was a striking man, well-dressed and handsome, with short brown hair and close-set blue eyes and a deep sunburn that darkened his face. Billy studied him, and for just a fleeting moment he had the odd notion that he recognized this man.

The handsome visitor paused just inside the door. He looked at Billy, then at Harry, and a small look of triumph crossed his face. He looked like a man who had found something he lost. He surveyed the office, flashed a smile that was supposed to take in all those in the room, and then more or less marched toward Harry.

"Mr. Strummer? David Moncrief." He thrust a hand at Harry, who rose from his seat and said, "Right, we spoke on the phone last week."

They shook hands and Harry indicated the visitor's chair. Moncrief sat.

"I've got a problem and I think you can help me. I need a detective."

"Yeah, you said something about that on the phone. Okay. And can I ask how you found us?"

The handsome client laughed and seemed embarrassed. "Actually—you're in the book. I looked up detectives and there you were—and you were on Wells, and I don't know the city that well but I knew where Wells Street was. So—"

He shrugged and looked around the room, nodded when he met Billy's gaze.

A showy fellow—a perfect summer suit in a soft blue that matched the blue of his tie. Perfect suit, nice tie, a pale yellow shirt, oxblood loafers, a Michigan Avenue sort of man. A man who looked impervious to the heat and humidity, as if those mundane things could not touch him. Nonetheless, the showy client fidgeted, played with his cuffs, ran a finger around his collar, fussed with the front of his shirt.

At the moment, the Michigan Avenue Man was explaining to Harry what he needed. There was a girl—of course there was. And she needed to be followed, this girl, the man had come all the way here to bring her back.

Here Harry shot him a look—what did that mean? Billy felt himself blushing. Yes, it was his own story, but Harry wouldn't have known about it. He turned away, and just then the phone rang. Doris put the caller on hold, looked at Harry, then beseeched Billy with a look.

"It's Mrs. Ricci. Can you talk to her?"

Billy sighed and took the call, feeling like a boxer attempting to step up in weight class. Mrs. Ricci was beyond him.

"Hi, Mrs. Ricci, this is Billy Fox. Harry is in a meeting with another client."

"Oh, you're that nice, quiet boy. Listen, they're doing it again?"

"The—who?"

"The government. That Nixon—there, did you hear that?"

"What? The clicking sound?"

"Yes, that's it."

Billy listened in for a moment and the clicks came again, but now he heard it for what it was, a crackling sound, some disconnect in the wires, an issue in the old woman's lines, not the workings of a malevolent government.

"I think it's just the wires, Mrs. Ricci. It's the phone company."

"They're listening in, too?"

"No, you've got bad wires. They need to send somebody out. You know what? I'll call them for you. Give me your number and— is it in your name?"

"It's in my Bruno's name."

"Okay, I'll call them and get them to come out."

"You're a nice boy," she said, and hung up before he could say anything more.

Billy looked up to find Doris watching him. "You're learning," she said.

In the center of the office, Harry was concluding his business with the handsome client.

"So I'll hear from you?"

"Sure. I'll have a preliminary look around and get back to you. It might be that I can't help you."

"I'll still pay you for your time."

Harry nodded. "We'll talk about it." He gave Moncrief his card.

The client paused as if to push this further. Billy saw him shake his head slightly, and then he said, "All right," and smiled. "Okay," he said, and hesitated as though reluctant to leave. Harry waved and turned to a pile of bills on the corner of his desk.

The man in the fine blue suit looked at him and then at Billy. He had an odd look in his eye, a look of amusement, as though visiting a detective was a lark for him. Then he was gone.

Harry looked up from the bills and watched the door as if expecting the visitor to pop back in any moment.

"So what are we gonna do for that guy?"

"For that guy? I don't know yet." To himself, Harry said, "Maybe nothing."

"Oh. I didn't hear his problem, so I don't know—"

Harry swiveled around in his chair. He was looking straight at

Billy, but his gaze and his attention were clearly on something else.

"He says he's trying to find his fiancée. He wants us to look for her."

"Nervous guy, I thought."

Harry gave him a long look. "He gave that impression, yes." He picked up a pencil and drummed absently with it. From the corner of his eye, Billy saw Doris shoot a quick look his way.

Billy decided to let the matter drop. He made his call to the phone company and got a young woman who laughed when she heard Mrs. Ricci's name.

"Oh, that's the lady that thinks the government bugs her phone. I'm sorry, she's your relative?"

"No, I'm just a friend. I think her line is bad. There's a crackling sound. But I don't think it's the government."

The young woman promised to send a man out to check the lines. Billy smiled to himself, and when he turned around, found Harry tapping the pencil on his desk. Something told him not to say anything for a time. Finally, Harry dropped the pencil on the blotter and turned to face him.

"So Mrs. Ricci's all taken care of, eh?"

"For the time being."

Harry managed a smile, but seemed preoccupied.

"So what about this client?"

"Moncrief," Harry said. "He said his name was *Moncrief*. Interesting man," Harry said, half to himself.

"Are we going to do something for him?"

"We'll see," Harry said, in precisely the way Billy's mother had once said "We'll see," imparting two words with half a dozen possible interpretations.

THIRTEEN

White Whales

He would not have been able to pinpoint the precise moment when the change occurred, but at some point Billy realized he was looking for a better place to live. In the last week of June he found an old apartment building a mile or so west of Lincoln Park that had been divided into "furnished rooms and efficiency apartments." He took a room on the fourth floor, overlooking a street lined with maples. He had a bed and a small desk and once more shared a bathroom, but this time with just two other men instead of a dozen. On the 4th of July, when it seemed the rest of Chicago had gone somewhere to celebrate, he moved out of the rooming house in Uptown. The older black man in the next room met him in the hallway.

"See? I told you you wouldn't be here long."

That night he bought a window fan and a small radio and settled into his new quarters. Someone in a room on that floor was watching television, but compared to the old room, Billy felt that he was living in a quiet place. He wondered how long it might take him to put enough money together to rent his own apartment, a studio with a small kitchen, perhaps. It struck him that this was the first time he'd allowed himself to think of living in Chicago permanently. He allowed himself to imagine a life with Rita, the two of them setting up a life together. With a start he remembered the child. She had a child. There would, of course, be three of them, and he told himself the child would make no difference at all.

Over the next couple of days he got a haircut, bought a couple more shirts and slacks. In the office that week he caught Doris smiling at him.

"What?"

"New clothes, new haircut. Looks nice. And it's good to see."

"What is?"

"You're settling in, sort of."

"Actually, I don't know what I'm doing."

"You're holding down a job, taking care of yourself, making a couple bucks. You're doing fine. I know you moved around a bit," she said cautiously. "You saw the country, young guys still do that. Now you're learning the detective business—after a fashion." She smiled. "It's not every young guy who does all that."

"Yeah, but—I don't even know where I belong yet, here or back in Michigan or someplace else. Don't have much to show for my life."

"It's not over yet. You're, you know, putting it together." She put her hands together as if molding clay. "And for now, you're here, in Chicago, and this is the newest phase of your life. Maybe you'll find something and stay here."

"I don't even have a bank account here."

"Oh, for God's sake. You don't have a bank account?"

Harry entered at that moment and said, "What? No bank account? What do you do with your money, hide it in the toilet tank? A young guy ought to have a bank account, establish himself in a place."

"It might not be my place."

"Wherever you are at a given time, that's your place, Bill. Until something better shows itself."

"I guess," he said.

He flashed a quick look at Doris, who said, "Put your money in a bank." Then she winked at him.

"I'll think about it," he said, but on his lunch hour that day he opened a checking account, retiring the Vaseline jar forever. Later that night he wrote a short letter to Josephine, the first letter he'd written in a long while. Four days later, he was startled to find a letter from Josephine in his mailbox, the first mail he'd received in Chicago.

He began to change his habits. Harry had him squire old Wendell to the bank and the currency exchange, and on one of these occasions Wendell told him there was a gym at Hamlin Park with a small basketball court and a boxing ring. Billy began going to the park. At first he just shot hoops in the stifling gym with the neighborhood kids. After a few visits, he worked up the nerve to show up at the ring. As a teenager in Lansing he'd done a little boxing for the local CYO program, and he'd fought a few times in Army competitions. Now he began to work out in earnest, headgear and all. He sparred with a half dozen local fighters and held his own. He cut down his smoking first to just a couple of cigarettes a day, and finally stopped entirely.

Several times he went out at night to small music clubs—they seemed to be everywhere. He preferred the jazz clubs, where he could sit at a side table in the darkness and listen to the music unselfconsciously. By day, he began to allow himself to wander without reference to his search for Rita. He walked east to the lakefront, to Michigan Avenue, to Grant Park. On a warm Sunday he put on his new sportcoat and strolled Michigan Avenue. He had no illusions that this was reality, this beautiful stretch of expensive hotels and fine shops, but he understood that, find Rita or not, he would not go back to Lansing. For better or worse, this was home now.

Billy had the sudden fear that this might not work out either, that he'd be back on a bus in six months. He remembered the disaster that had been Denver. He remembered living on the street.

No. I can do this. I should be able to put together some kind of life.

• • •

The office door opened, and a red-faced man with short gray hair and a thick moustache filled it. He was short but built like a block, and there was something practiced in the way he paused in the doorway before entering the room. He scanned the room, hard-faced and challenging and just this side of belligerent. Billy had to admit it was effective—all of them looked up, Harry, Doris, Billy himself, and Leo, who was in the office replacing the casters on Harry's ancient desk. An effective pose, but with limitations. In a room with a hundred people, Billy still would have made him for a cop. This man would fool no one.

"Anybody home?" the newcomer asked.

"No," Harry said. "Go away."

Leo laughed. "Hey, Dutch."

The man broke out in a grin and took years off his face. His smile puffed up his face so that he looked like a happy German butcher.

Billy saw that the cop had picked him out already.

"Who's this, Harry? You taking in strays?"

"That's Bill. I thought we needed new blood."

Billy waved, and the newcomer nodded, then crossed the room stiff-legged and awkward for all his cocky demeanor—an old bullet wound, Billy guessed. Dutch sank heavily onto the seat next to Harry's desk, and both chair and visitor groaned. He smiled at Doris.

"Hey, Sweetheart."

"Hi, Dutch."

Half a minute of small talk and then their voices dropped, and Billy found himself unable to keep from eavesdropping. At one point he looked up and Harry met his eye, then winked, and Billy understood that he was being invited to listen in.

Easier said than done, though, for Dutch was practiced at this, an old hand at the urgent muttered conversation in a room filled with people. As a result, Billy caught very little of their talk, but what he managed to extract was interesting enough. As far as he could tell, the tough cop was relying on Harry for information, and this was not the first time. It was clear from the way they sat—the cop in the visitor's seat, Harry leaning forward in easy authority, roles familiar and comfortable to both.

At one point he heard the cop say, "He'll be back, we both know that," and Harry just nodded.

When they were done, Dutch got stiffly to his feet, pointed his finger at Harry, and said, "I know I'm gonna get him."

"I know," Harry said.

Dutch nodded and left the office with a sweeping wave meant to include all of them.

"So what's his story? Dutch?"

"Took a bullet in his knee which rendered him unfit for active duty. So he's retired on disability with a lot of time on his hands. But he never stopped being a cop."

"What does he do?"

Harry began to say something, then stopped, as though unsure how to continue.

"You see, there are unsolved cases, and there are cases where the department doesn't have the time or manpower to continue to pursue them. They got people to look into the cold cases, but Dutch, he more or less looks into the ones that he was involved in while he was on the force."

"Is he a little bit crazy?"

"Like most of us, yes."

"And he's got a case he can't let go of?"

"Well, he's got a couple. I mean, he's not obsessed with any one case. And once in a while he needs us to track down a lead or help him find somebody. He sometimes comes in to confer about this particular case. Anyhow, that's Dutch's story. Most of the time I've got nothing for him, I can't help him. But we do it because he's my friend. And that means he owes us, too. He was a good cop. A good man to have on your side. A very good man. A prickly guy—what's the saying? *'He does not suffer fools lightly'*? That's our man Dutch. But he's a good man."

"Okay."

Harry gave him a thoughtful look. "A guy gets fixated on something, he can lose focus, he can miss a lot of things in life."

"Yeah, I guess so," Billy said and looked away, aware that Harry was watching his reaction.

He bought a reading lamp, magazines, and a new pair of running shoes. He boxed and worked out in the small gym at Hamlin Park, he ran and added to his distance every night out, always taking pains to run down new streets, always watching for a glimpse of a certain dark-haired girl. He imagined her with a wary look on her face.

A week after Dutch's first visit to the office, a blue Buick pulled in front of Billy at a street corner, and Billy was surprised to see Dutch behind the wheel.

"What's up, Kid? Billy, isn't it?"

"Right."

Dutch got out of his car, blocking off the pedestrian crosswalk and completely unconcerned about it.

"So where you from?"

"Here and there," Billy said, refusing eye contact.

"Never heard of that place. So where you from really?"

Billy shrugged. "Michigan."

Now he looked at Dutch, who squinted up at him as though trying to place his face.

"Forget it, we never met."

"Didn't say we had. You on the run, Billy?"

"Not from the law."

It should have made no difference, Billy knew, but he felt a sudden surge of irritation that this old cop had somehow made him, had figured out in some way that Billy had bounced around, or at least that he did not belong here.

"No. I was just asking. It's how I am. You need to lighten up, boy. Your jaw's too tight. You look like you're ready to fight."

Billy shrugged, almost against his will. This situation was stupid, and it was proceeding as though it had a will of its own.

"If you smart off to me, maybe I'll pop you one in the mouth."

Now Billy gave Dutch a long, slow look, measuring him, wondering if he'd land a good punch before the older man launched one of his own.

"Yeah, I get it, kid, you're not afraid of me. But I'd still deck you, and you'd be on your back in the street, and that would be worse for a young guy like you than just getting hit."

"All right, what do you want from me?"

"I want to know a little about you, that's all. You work for Harry, and Harry and I are involved in things that are kind of important to me, so I just like to know about anybody that's, you know, that's got anything to do with it. Or might."

"I'm from Michigan, I've been out of the service for about a year. Harry gave me a job and he's been showing me things."

"Good guy to have showing you things."

"So let me ask you something."

"All right."

"You were a cop, you know people on the police force...why do you need to come to a detective agency—"

"These are old cases. This one in particular is from years ago. Cold case. It's not closed, but it is not currently being, you know, investigated. But I'm interested in it still."

"They've lost interest. But it means something to you."

"That's right. For them it's on the back burner, but it means something to me." Dutch nodded. "Notice anything, you know, odd or different about your boss lately?"

Billy shrugged. Then he said, "He's got something on his mind. Leo noticed it, too. I don't know what it is, though. He hasn't said. Maybe he wouldn't tell me."

Dutch was nodding. "He won't tell anybody, is what I think. If he says anything, you let me know."

Dutch bent over in the seat and pulled out his wallet, from which he produced a card that simply read "Dutch Lindner" with a phone number.

"You find out anything, you call me. You ever need help with something, you call me."

"I will. Thanks."

"See you around, Kid. Have a nice day."

The next morning when he entered the office, Billy found a small leatherette case on his desk. He looked over to Harry.

"Present for you."

"What is it?"

"Is that what you did on your birthday when you were a kid?

You looked at your presents and said, 'What is it?'"

"Okay, okay."

He opened the small case and found cards, business cards, perhaps fifty of them, and took one out. It was printed on thick cardstock, the lettering embossed in blue and black.

Along the bottom the card gave the address, suite number and phone number of the firm. In the center, in larger letters, the card read:

William Fox
Investigator
Peerless Detective Agency

"Business cards? I never even knew anybody with a business card."

"You do now."

"They're nice."

"You're lucky, Billy," Doris said. "He had those printed. Usually he makes his own with a little machine in his drawer." Doris grinned and pantomimed laboriously working a small hand press.

"Ha-ha. Very funny. I ordered cards for all of us, Doris, even you."

"What does mine say—'office drudge'?"

"It says 'office manager,' which looks a lot better on a resume."

Whatever Doris was about to say froze on her lips. For once Harry had surprised her. She blushed slightly, muttered something like "better than *secretary*," and turned back to her typewriter.

That night, he walked home to his new room, took the long way, familiarized himself with the streets, and told himself that this was now his neighborhood. At the room he showered and put on a fresh shirt and went out again. The evening was overcast, the air dense and close, and he told himself this was no night for riding buses and searching through crowds of strangers.

At the diner, Millie was talking with a young red-haired man and did not see Billy come in. He watched her body language—she leaned against the counter, a half-smile on her face, as the redhead told her a story. When he was done, she laughed and walked to the far end of the counter, and the redhead watched her move in the tight uniform. Millie took another order, and as she turned, she saw Billy. For a moment, she was startled. He saw her glance briefly at the other guy, and then she bore down on him, shaking her head.

"I'm sorry, Hon. How long have I been ignoring you?"

He nodded toward the redhead. "It's okay. You're popular today."

"Yeah, two boys have spoken to me. Some days nobody does, and sometimes late at night a guy who's had a snoot full wants to lean over the counter and grab my rear end."

"I didn't want to interrupt your conversation."

Her smile faded. She looked down at her pad, pencil poised to take his order.

"I don't know him," she said. "Do you want to order?"

He ordered coffee, and when she came back with the pot and the brown mug, he brought out the small card holder.

"I wanted to show you something."

He pulled out a card and placed it on the counter.

"A business card! You have your own business cards. Billy, that's so professional." She gave him a look, her head tilted to one side. "Maybe this means you'll be staying."

For a moment he couldn't answer. He was about to protest that they were just cards, they meant nothing, but he caught himself. It was true that he'd begun telling himself that this was, at least for now, his home. And the cards certainly sent a message, that he was nobody's office boy or runner.

He smiled at her. "When did I ever say I wasn't staying?"

She gave him a shrewd look. "Oh, once or twice, without really meaning to. A girl can tell these things, Billy. Matter of fact, I'm still not sure you're staying. But the cards are nice."

With that, she poured his coffee, gave him a look, and walked away.

Well, after all, I don't know if I'll be staying, he said to himself. *I'm not sure.*

He watched her make small talk with the redheaded newcomer and told himself he was not sure about anything.

The next day in the office, he caught Doris watching him with a look he'd seen from his mother and Josephine.

"You met any kids your own age yet, Bill?"

"Oh, here and there."

Now she narrowed her eyes. "How about a girl?"

"Actually, yeah, I, uh, there's this one girl, we—"

Doris burst out laughing. "You just told me everything I need to know, that you have conflicted feelings, you don't know whether to fish or cut bait. Well, whatever you decide, be nice to her. There's plenty of guys who don't know how to be nice to a woman. Treat her right, even if you don't think it's going to turn into anything serious."

"Right," he said, and didn't understand why he was blushing.

Harry came in at that moment. He looked from Doris to Billy.

"Am I interrupting some serious discussion?"

"No, I was just telling Billy that he needs to find a nice girl and treat her well."

I came here because of a girl, he wanted to say. *I can't start something with a new one.*

"Well, you're right about that." He looked at Billy. "You free Saturday night?"

"I guess so."

Harry dropped a pair of tickets, small and orange, on Billy's desk.

"Fundraiser for an injured fireman we know. It's not far from here. Free food, cheap cash bar, music, nice people." He looked over at Doris. "Doris is going, right, Doris?"

Doris gave a one-armed shrug. "If I can't find anything better to do."

Harry nodded and said, "She'll be there. You'll have a good time. And it'll be over early enough that you can probably find a saloon open afterwards if you're still looking for action."

Billy fingered the tickets. "All right. Thanks."

He read the information on the ticket. "A benefit for Mr. Timothy Rooney. St. Josephat's School Hall. Free buffet. Cash bar. Ten dollars suggested donation."

"They're paid for," Harry said over his shoulder as he left.

FOURTEEN

Slow-Dancing

They stepped inside the old parish hall on Southport.

"Oh, how cute," Millie said. "I remember places like this back home, dances and dinners at the church hall."

"Me, too," Billy said. "Dozens of them. And school parties. When I was little I would run wild in a place like this, getting into all kinds of places with my friends where we weren't supposed to go."

Billy ran a finger around the inside of his collar, adjusted his tie, and took Millie's hand. The venue was indeed identical to the ones Billy recalled from his youth—a polished wood floor and a high stage at the rear, in this case holding a battered upright piano that looked as if it had seen war. A five-piece band was getting set up—two guitars, a sax, drums, and a keyboard—young guys, which was promising. He looked around and wondered if all the halls in America were made by one guy, one traveling architect or builder who moved from city to city and built church halls. In this one they'd set up a bar along one side, and long tables on the far side held the buffet. Predictably, the bar was the most crowded place in the hall.

The older guests had already staked out their tables here and there, and he could tell the ones who wouldn't move again until it was time to eat.

"A *dance*," Millie said, half to herself. She looked at Billy. "We're going to dance, right, Billy?"

"Yeah, sure. Remember, I didn't say I was good."

"A girl doesn't care about that. Girls just want somebody to dance with them."

He took her to the bar, and they were intercepted by Harry Strummer.

"Hey, Bill. For once you're traveling with a higher class of people."

Billy introduced Millie to him and she said, "I've heard a lot about you."

Harry raised his eyebrows and said, "Don't believe everything you hear." But the look in his eye said, *He didn't tell me he actually knew a girl.*

"Let me introduce you two to the guest of honor and then I'll leave you alone. Unless I'm assaulted."

Billy blinked. "Am I working?"

"Ah, not as such. No, you're off duty. I wouldn't want to take you away from this pretty lady. But you never know. So just, you know, keep your eyes open."

He led them to a corner where a number of people were congregated around a dark-haired man in a wheelchair, whom he introduced as Timothy Rooney.

The man winced and jerked his head toward Harry. "You're working with this guy? No good can come of it, Kid. Harry knows kinds of trouble that other people haven't discovered yet."

Billy led Millie away, and they watched Harry work the room. Harry waved to people in the far corners of the hall. A big man in a good grey suit approached Harry. He was perhaps fifty, and, Billy would have said, a type—tall and beefy, muscular but now going to fat. His black hair was combed back straight, and it glistened. As he spoke to Harry, the big man's eye scanned the room, and he waved to one woman after another.

Yeah, Billy thought, in your day you were that guy. You walked into a room and expected all the babes to be watching you.

"Handsome, for his age," Millie said. "And very conceited."

The big guy slapped Harry on the shoulder and went off in search of female admirers.

The band started up and Millie gave him a look. He led her out on the floor and danced to a fast song, then to an old Ventures tune done up as a samba, and Billy laughed at his own ineptitude. Then the sax player gave them a ballad and they slow-danced. She put her hand on the back of his neck, and he felt the blood rushing to his face.

Harry came by their table. "Some interesting possibilities for the night's entertainment. That couple over there, big bald guy, lady with badly-dyed red hair? That's Bud and Sheila Rice. They'll have too much to drink and they'll get into a shouting match and she'll go home and maybe lock him out."

"So then what?"

"Depends how much he's had to drink by then. If he's really pie-eyed he'll sleep in his car. Otherwise he'll go home and bust down the door."

Millie studied the bald man. "Will he beat that lady up?"

"Nah. He'll just start busting up his place. Besides, I don't think he can take her. She's tough. Last time, she had him arrested, then she bailed him out." Harry looked around the room. "Okay, over there, three guys in black sportcoats, they look like pallbearers? Those are the Boylan brothers, and they will get into a beef, usually the two smaller ones against their baby brother—that's him, the beefy one with the long sideburns. He'll deck one or both of them and then he'll start crying." Harry shook his head and said, "Families, huh?"

"Yeah," Billy said, and looked away. He took a pull on his beer and remembered a church hall like this one in Lansing, and a local dance, and his old man getting tanked and bellowing at Billy's mother, and the shoving match and fistfight that followed. He wasn't even sure who his father had been throwing punches at.

Billy bought them drinks and they sat for a time, and he was watching the dancers when new blood entered the room—Doris and a woman approximately her age. Doris was wearing make-up and a lavender dress, loose at the waist but tight in other places, and Billy heard himself say, "Huh." She didn't seem to have done anything with her hair, but from the admiring looks she was getting from the men in the hall, the hair wasn't an issue.

"That's—"

"Doris, right?" Millie finished for him.

"How'd you know?"

"You and Harry both noticed her at the same time, and I saw the look he gave her."

As Billy watched, Doris said something to the dark-haired woman she was with and scanned the room until she found Harry. She gave him a look, no smile, just the look, and Billy wondered what was going on.

A loud argument broke out on the far side of the hall, the Boylan brothers, two of them nose-to-nose. One Boylan pointed a finger in his brother's chest. Billy excused himself and looked for Harry, who was already advancing upon the debaters. He got close enough to hear Harry say, "Everything all right here, fellas?"

Several nods and one of them said, "No problem."

"Help yourself to the food," Harry said.

The younger brother looked at Harry. "Who're you?"

"Just a friend of Mr. Rooney. We don't want anything to mar the evening."

Billy saw the young guy trying to figure out this small man in a dark suit.

The older brother stepped in. "Hello, Harry. Just a little difference of opinion here."

"Okay, Butch. Nice to see you."

The younger brother caught Billy from the corner of his eye. Billy stood with his hands folded in front of him and kept his face expressionless. The Boylan kid looked from one to the other, clearly out of his depth, and shrugged. All three of the Boylans moved off to the buffet table.

"See? Nice guys, nobody really wants to fight."

"Boy, you called that."

"Tell you something else. They're not finished. They'll fight someplace later. Maybe the parking lot." He shrugged. "Now go back to that nice girl."

Billy moved around the room and returned in time to shoo off a guy about to sit down next to Millie. From the far side of the room, Doris caught his eye and waved, then saw Millie. She tilted her head slightly and gave him an approving look and a thumbs-up.

They lowered the lights, and the time for all the talk and the eating was done. Now it was a dance. The guys in the combo hit their groove, and the church hall was transformed. It could have been the eighth grade dance in Billy's neighborhood. The leader of the group took over a tiny electric keyboard no bigger than a box organ, but he might as well have been playing a concert grand for the effect he had on his dancers. The couples out on the floor stayed there, joined by others until there were only a few people who hadn't been drawn into whatever this moment was. Billy saw several couples dancing in a tight clinch who'd been bickering just a moment earlier, and a man and woman who'd been sitting with their backs to each other slow-dancing like teenagers.

"Aha," Millie said, and managed to brush his ear with her lips.

"Aha what?"

"Take a look."

He followed her gaze and then saw them, Harry and Doris. They were slow-dancing and speaking to one another, casually it seemed. Then the song ended and they loosened their grip on each other, but didn't quite let go. The combo started another tune, a bit more upbeat—Billy recognized it as "The Soulful Strut," an old R&B hit, and now some couples retreated and the confident ones put something together.

He watched as Harry and Doris put together a little strut of their own, Harry holding Doris a few inches away from him and leading her through their steps. Doris was smiling, her face slightly flushed. At one point Harry twirled her around and she laughed and nodded, remembering the step, and Harry gave a shrug.

Billy nodded. *You guys have done this before. A lot.* The other dancers began to fall away, some unconscious signal telling them to leave the floor to these two, and soon Harry and Doris were dancing alone in a wide circle. Someone coming into the old hall at that moment might have thought these two were unaware that there was anyone else in the room.

The tune ended and the other dancers clapped, and Harry and Doris looked embarrassed. The musicians saw their moment and built a ballad into it, the sax man taking over for much of it, and all the dancers came back. Doris started to walk away, but Harry caught her hand, pulled her to him, and they danced now, closer. A few bars into the song, they dropped formalities and Harry put both arms around her waist, and Doris clasped her hands behind Harry's neck. She put her face against his and they danced. More or less. Billy wouldn't have been surprised if they'd stopped dancing right there and headed for a dark corner of the hall.

Yeah, he said to himself. *I wondered about you two.*

He looked at Millie. She was nodding.

"So—they're, like, together?" Billy asked.

She laughed. "*Like, together?* Yes, Billy-boy, they are *like together*. I think they're fighting it. But they're together, or they were one time and—"

She stopped and watched Harry and Doris with a distant look in her eyes.

"And what?"

"And they remember it. How it was."

The band went into cruise control and played slow doo-wop songs and ballads—"Beyond the Sea," "My Girl," "Earth Angel." And Billy remembered this, at dances in steamy old halls and the rented back rooms of taverns, the moments near the end of the night when everyone was out on the floor slow dancing. He recalled once or twice when he seemed to be the only one without a partner. He glanced at Millie. She met his eyes, and he took her out on the dance floor.

They danced without speaking, and she pressed herself to him and he felt his face flush.

"I know a nice girl who wants to go home and fool around," she said, brushing his ear with her lips again.

On the way out, Billy introduced her to Doris. As they left, Doris winked. Harry was watching the room, distracted. He snapped out of it and said good-night, told Millie she was hanging out with a dangerous guy. They all laughed. As he left the hall, Billy shot one quick look behind him. Harry was looking around with his hands in his pockets, and Doris was watching him with a look of concern.

. . .

At the door to her apartment, Billy made nervous small talk and shuffled from one foot to the other. Millie watched him with an amused look and then took his hand.

"Come on, Hon," she said, and pulled him inside.

She lived in a studio apartment. A miniature house, he thought—one big room with a little nook for her bed at one side, a narrow bathroom, another nook on the far side where a refrigerator, a tiny stove, and a table with two chairs had been wedged in.

"I know, it's small, right? But there's only one of me."

"I just have a room," he found himself saying. "You know, for now. But this is a lot better than what I've got."

It smelled of her perfume and something else, like tea.

She made them coffee, and they talked about how Chicago seemed to them, a couple of outsiders—"Hayseeds," she said, and it made him laugh in spite of himself.

"Sometimes it seems too big, that I've made a mistake coming up here. But I wanted a new start in a new place, and I'm gonna stay here. I've got a job and this little place, and I'm gonna have a life here."

"Yeah," he said, just to be responding, and she smiled.

"You don't know if you're staying, though. That's where you're at. You're still trying to make up your mind. About all kinds of things." She smiled and gave him a sly look, and he wondered if he looked as stupid as he felt.

"Well," he said, and she pulled him onto the sofa.

Later, when he thought it was time for him to go, she led him over to the small nook where her bed was.

"Stay tonight," Millie said, and began undressing. She sat down on the bed and looked up at him, her head tilted slightly.

"You're not comfortable with this, are you?"

"It's not that—I mean, are you?"

She laughed. "It's my idea."

All his life, during moments when there was something to say, something critical and plain and necessary, Billy Fox had found himself, on almost every such occasion, confused, inarticulate, mute. There was something he needed to say here, several things at once, it seemed—that he wanted to be honest with her, that he was spending most of his free moments obsessively looking for another girl, that he had no intention of getting into anything serious with anybody, not her, not anybody. It seemed to Billy that there was not time enough, nor words enough, in the world for him to make all of this clear. He found himself unable to say anything.

"What do you want to do, Billy?"

Oh, God, where do I start?

He took a long look at Millie. He noted her patience, the way she waited, sitting unapologetic and unashamed in her bra and panties, just waiting for him to say something, anything. He sat on the bed and put his arm around her.

"We don't have to do anything, you know. We can just sleep," she said.

Then she kissed him, and they fell back on the bed.

They made love, tentative at first—Billy felt inept, as though this were his first time. Then he relaxed, and it seemed that Millie lost her inhibitions as well, and soon they had torn the sheets off her bed. At some point Billy hit the back of his head on the wall and smacked his forehead on her headboard.

When they were finished, Billy lay there, spent and heavy-limbed. In the semi-darkness he saw that he was covered with a sheen of sweat.

"I'm soaked," he said. "Your bed is going to—"

She put her fingers to his lips. "We're both soaked. The bed will be okay."

After a while, her breathing grew steadier and he knew she'd fallen asleep. He understood that he should feel guilt over this. It was wrong, but his overriding emotion was exultation.

My God, he told himself. *I'm in bed with a girl. I'm not sleeping alone in a little room.*

He told himself he would sort out his feelings in the morning.

In the morning she was, of course, up long before him, fully dressed and making coffee.

"I don't have eggs," she called out. "How about toast and coffee and then I send you on your way?"

He got up on one elbow, then sat up. He looked around at the small apartment, aware again of the flower smell of the place, of her.

"Okay," he said. "Thanks."

She bustled around the little place, timing the toast to appear when he'd washed up and dressed.

When he came to the table she stopped and put a hand to her mouth.

"Oh, dear."

She pointed to his forehead. "You have a bruise. You look like somebody jumped you."

"I'll make up a story," he said, and they laughed.

She set the plate down with a jar of raspberry jam and a plate of butter, then sipped her coffee as he ate. She let him have breakfast in peace…he was thankful for that. He stole a glance at her. She was looking around at the room, a small smile on her face. He saw her sniff at the aroma of her coffee and then take a sip. He was thinking of the cigarettes he'd just given up when she spoke.

"And Billy?"

"Yeah?"

"If you're gonna give me a little speech about how this was just a mistake and you aren't looking to get serious, just save it."

He looked at her and forced himself not to look away. This was that time, he knew, when all men are shifty, spineless, weightless, cowardly. This was that time when you wanted to leave.

He nodded.

"You have my number, you know where I work. You want to

see me again, you know how to do that."

"Thanks," he said, because that seemed like the logical response. "Nice coffee."

"My favorite thing in the world," she said, and he thought they were past the awkward part.

FIFTEEN

Back Stories

The next day, Billy watched them in the office, Harry and Doris. They might have been two strangers at the public library. Harry paged through the contents of a file, and Doris sang softly to a tune on her radio as she studied the month's bills. Harry handed Billy a couple of files and asked him to look for inconsistencies in either or similarities between the two.

"There's a chance this is the same guy, both of these. What happened to your head?"

"It—I just—I guess I bumped into something."

Harry nodded and gave him an odd look.

"That's a nice girl you were with," Doris said.

"How can you tell?"

"I told you," Harry said. "She's like a wizard. She knows things."

"She has nice eyes. No, I don't mean it that way. They're pretty eyes, yeah, but they're a good person's eyes. Be nice to her."

"I'm nice to her," he said.

Doris held his gaze for a moment and then turned back to her work.

Later, Harry pulled him out of the office for a hot dog and a walk. And, as it transpired, an explanation.

"So you and that young lady had a nice time?"

"Yeah. It was a nice party. Thanks for the ticket."

Harry gave him a slow look. "I know what you're probably thinking."

"No, you don't. You're pretty good but you can't read minds yet."

"Well, I know what I'd be thinking. I'd be thinking there's something going on between Doris and me. Doris and I. No, me. Whatever it is. Something between us."

"No, I'm thinking there used to be something between the both of you. Maybe in the old days."

"And when would that be?"

"I don't know."

"You see, Doris and I, we go way back."

"That much I know already."

"How?"

"She knows about you, about your, you know, your story."

Harry came to a stop. "Which she told you."

"No. She doesn't give away much. She gave me a couple of pieces, that's all. I know you told me you were 4F."

"4H, actually. It was an attempt at humor."

"Okay, but I know you served in Korea, and you were wounded there."

"Lots of guys were wounded there. What else?"

"You had a sister."

"Yeah. She died." Harry looked away, closing off this avenue of discussion.

"And I know you and Doris hung out or something in the old days. But that's all I've got."

"Yeah, we hung out. Come on, let's walk."

Billy hesitated, let Harry go a few paces, and then began walking, making no effort to catch up. Harry turned.

"What?"

"You see, I'm learning. I'm learning from you. I'm getting to know when somebody's bullshitting me. Which is what just happened."

"Hey, I just said what you said. I confirmed what you knew. We hung out, we were in the same group of kids. She was a little younger, but in the same group."

"And all these years later she winds up working for you."

Harry shrugged. He stood with his hands thrust into his pockets and made his metallic jingling and looked puzzled, as though it had all happened without his approval.

"Sometimes a thing comes to pass in life and you can't even see how it happened, you can't see the steps. I knew her when we were kids. Then the world changed, it got more complicated. I went to Korea and when I got back, the world I left was all changed—you know about that, I think. Some people had moved away and some people were gone. Dead, a couple of them. And people had paired up. Some people paired up that you would never have expected to get together."

Harry ran a hand across the back of his neck and shook his head.

"That part I understand," Billy told him. "That part especially. I came back and found out that this—that somebody I knew had gotten married, to the last guy in the neighborhood I would have expected."

"Hard to take, isn't it?"

"Yeah. You want to take it apart, the place you've come back to, you want to put it together again the way it was."

"And it's gone. You've got to accept a new world. And if you can't, well, you'll make yourself crazy. That's how it was for me for a while. After Korea. It was like everything was changed and I'd lost years of my life. For a while I thought I'd lost the best years, but that's not how it is."

Harry was silent for a moment, and Billy thought perhaps this line of conversation had hit a dead end. Then he seemed to snap out of his trance.

"The old romances, kid, some of them stay with you forever. And it's not that they were the greatest times ever, but because they're your past, your youth. A smell of perfume, a little bit of an old song from when you were young, and just like that, you're back there in that moment. We all want to be young again. But the past is past, you have to acknowledge that it's your past and not the reality of your life. I know that as sure as I know tomorrow's Friday, but sometimes we ignore what we know to be true. We kind of lie to ourselves. Everybody does it."

Billy shot him a sudden look to see if Harry knew more about him than was possible.

"Yeah, I know, it's crazy for me to be talking to you. I don't even know your situation. I'm just really thinking out loud, about that time. It was hard for me. Anyhow, I don't even know how I got on this—oh, yeah, how does it happen that Doris works for me? Well, we met on the street one day, and she was going to interview for a job. I didn't have a secretary or anybody to take care of the office—my last one took off with no notice. She ran away with her boyfriend someplace. Anyhow, Doris was looking for work and I needed somebody, so there it is."

Billy nodded and remembered how they looked on the dance floor and said to himself, *I bet.*

"So there's no big story, really," Harry went on with his embroidery. "It's just—"

Harry stopped across the street from the Treasure Island and looked across the street. Billy followed his gaze and saw a half dozen or so people waiting to cross the street, and a man behind them, walking away briskly and carrying two shopping bags. The accountant. Billy watched Harry's face. He watched the man as if he had just brought hard news.

As they headed back to the office, Billy looked straight ahead, but from the corner of his eye he saw Harry look behind him. Billy forced small talk and Harry responded, each time a beat slow, like a horn player out of his depth.

Preoccupied, Billy thought. No, troubled.

Later, in the office, Harry asked Billy to make a couple of calls, one to the alderman for a friend having trouble with an inspector, one to a client who had cancelled an appointment. As he spoke on the phone, Billy watched Harry making his own calls. Twice after completing a call, Harry hung up and just sat there staring in the direction of the street.

Billy shot a quick look at Doris. She had paused in her typing and turned slightly in her seat, pretending to be shuffling through a pile of papers but watching Harry.

...

Later that week, Harry took him out for a drink at a tavern on the northwest side.

Billy watched the streets as they drove through one crowded neighborhood after another and told himself finding someone in this town was an impossibility.

No, I can't think that way.

The tavern was called The Bucket O' Suds and was presided over by a short, chubby man with a high-pitched voice and thick curly hair who called out Harry's name before they'd even cleared the door. It was a tavern of a certain character. Deceased animals hung suspended by wires from the ceiling—a duck, a huge fish, a sea turtle. There were human beings as well—a raucous group sat at a long table, oblivious to the sea turtle swimming overhead, and a dozen or more people lined the long, dark-stained bar. The world's most garish jukebox sat next to the door and throbbed with a big band tune. Smoke hovered over all of it.

Billy stopped just inside the door and looked around, smiling. "It's like I walked into the past. My folks used to take me to a place like this—ours didn't have the, you know, the menagerie."

"This is what taverns used to be," Harry said. He introduced Billy to the owner, Joe Danno, and ordered them beer and shots of a bourbon Billy had never heard of.

He sipped his whiskey and bided his time, and when Harry was gazing at the improbably crowded back bar, Billy caught him unawares.

"That was him, right? This afternoon? That was the accountant."

Harry gave him a slow look. "Now I'm getting obvious."

"I wouldn't say that."

"I've trained you too well. Like I said, seeing that guy depresses me. I wish he would move. You're a smart kid."

"I'm learning."

"Yeah, you are. But you're spending too much time watching your boss. I'm all right, there's no problem here. You're a smart guy…but a genuine smart guy, the first real lesson he learns about life is how much he doesn't know. Young guy like you, you probably think you know a lot about life."

"I've had, you know, experiences. I think I've been around. For my age. For a guy my age."

"And so you have. You've had some hard times, and that teaches you things, too. You probably think you've seen the elephant."

"Yeah, I think I know some things. What I don't know, I'm pretty sure I can figure out."

Harry nodded and puffed at his cigarette, took it out and studied it as though there were messages written on the paper. He raised his eyebrows and looked at Billy.

"Let me show you something, Billy. Hey, Joe, can I see the bottle for a second, yeah, the Ezra Brooks—no, better yet, the Old Weller. No, I'm not gonna pour it in my glass."

Joe set down the fat bourbon bottle in front of Harry. Harry picked it up and looked at the label.

"This, by the way, is a great old house. Stitzel-Weller. They make the whiskey for the Berghoff, and they make this one here and some others. Anyway—" He turned the bottle over slightly so that its bottom was visible. Billy saw that there was a deep indentation, that, in fact, the bottom of the bottle was more or less hollow.

"See that?" Harry said. "That's the punt."

"*The punt,*" Billy repeated, and Joe said, "The what?"

"That's what it's called, the punt. You got one in wine bottles, champagne, cognac, some of the whiskeys, a lot of kinds of booze. They all hold standard amounts, so this thing isn't intended to rip anybody off. What it does is give a different impression of the reality of the thing. The bottle looks bigger than it is, and when you get down to about here," he pointed to the final two inches of the bottle, "then you've got a lot less whiskey left than you think."

Billy looked at it, at Harry, and shrugged. Harry leaned over and grabbed one of the hefty shot glasses from the rail.

"You got one of the old ones, Joe?"

"Yeah, wait a minute." Joe rummaged around in a box under

the bar and came up with a small, delicate looking shot glass.

"Why would you replace this little guy," Harry began, "with this behemoth?" He hefted the first shot glass and then laid it in the palm of Billy's hand.

The weight of the second shot glass was surprising—you could bounce this off someone's head and do damage.

"Well, it's bigger. And it feels, you know, like a nicer quality glass. Holds more, looks better, feels like you've really got something."

Harry looked at Joe, nodded once. Joe filled the small shot glass with tap water and then poured the small glass out into the larger one. The small glass filled the larger one, and then the water overflowed onto the bar. Joe whipped out a bar towel and dried the bar.

"It's presentation," Joe said. "The customer pays his nickel and he wants to hold something in his hand that's worth it. You give him the little shot glass, and he thinks you're short-shotting him."

"There you go. Thanks, Joe."

Joe smiled at Harry. "A *punt* huh? Like in football?"

Harry nodded. "Spelled the same way."

Joe looked at Billy. "The stuff this guy knows."

"I know. I'm learning that."

"Anyhow, Kid, every old guy you meet for the rest of your life is going to try to tell you about the world, everyone—me included. Most of 'em will tell you it's all bullshit, or you can't trust anybody, or God will send angels, or all you need is love. And they're all full of it—although that love thing, that's not so far off the mark. You have somebody to love, somebody that loves you, no questions asked—unconditional love. You got that, kid, you got the makings.

"But here's what I want you to remember. Remember this bottle with its more or less false bottom and that shot glass there that looks like something it's not. The world is not a lie, Billy, and the people in it, they're not all con artists. For everything, though, there's a hollow bottom, there's less than you think you're gonna get. Somebody's always holding something back."

Billy looked at the two shot glasses sitting beside one

another. "Always?"

"Except if you fall in love, and even then you have to understand that the person you love might be holding back something of herself. Or himself, if that's your taste." Harry grinned.

For a moment Billy looked around, nodding, and then he turned to Harry and said, "How about you, Harry? You holding something back?"

As he'd hoped, the question caught Harry in that rarest of moments, off his guard. He smiled and waved Billy off and looked away. He gave himself a moment and then faced Billy once more.

"I'm trying to further your education here, Buddy. I'm not holding anything back."

"Nothing?"

"What would I hold back from you?" Harry shrugged. "Your wages maybe, if you prove to be a slow pupil."

Then Harry called Joe over and asked him to tell Billy about some of the rare whiskeys and odd liquors on his crowded back bar.

SIXTEEN

Self-Fulfilling Prophesies

For much of that week Billy stayed away from the diner. It seemed to him that he was at that place where a relationship was about to form but could still be prevented.

Prevented, he thought. Like it's a sickness.

But it was clear that a relationship with Millie was possible, imminent, and he understood that there was something basically dishonest in all of this. He told himself he had more than enough on his plate that required his attention. There was Rita, and there was the troubled Harry Strummer, more than enough to worry about.

And so he walked. He tried a few side streets he'd never been down, found dead-end streets, took a wrong turn at some point and two guys in berets followed him. A cop car rolled by and the berets disappeared. And he sat. He sat alone in his furnished room and paged through a magazine. Billy had a sudden image of himself, the way an observer might see him—the only young guy in the big wide city chasing illusions while life went on outside his window.

Late in the week Billy stopped by the diner. He told himself he wanted nothing more than a little company, a respite from his rented room and his endless circuit of the streets of the north side.

Millie gave him a questioning look when he entered. He ordered a sandwich and they made small talk. As he ate, she kept to the far end of the counter and did not look his way. When it was time to give him his bill, she laid it down next to his plate and gave him a frank look.

"You're a hard boy to figure out. First, I thought I'd see you before this, and then it seemed you'd be layin' low. That happens, too. But here you are."

"Better late than never," he said, just to be saying something.

"I don't know about that."

He finished the last of his cup of coffee and realized he didn't know how to tip a girl he'd just slept with. He laid money on the counter, then added to it, shook his head. He stole a glance and she was laughing at him, it was that obvious. He held up a finger and she came down the counter.

"Was there something else?" she asked with an arch look.

"Want to go to the beach?"

Jesus, where did that come from?

"The beach?"

"Well, I know a lot of people don't like the beach, all the sand and it's hot, and, you know, crowded—"

He was babbling. He heard how he sounded and felt the blood rushing to his face.

"I love the beach," she said, measuring him with a look. "I just don't like to go by myself."

"All right then."

"All right then," she countered, watching him.

• • •

The lake, Billy knew, was starting to have a narcotic effect on him. Being near it was like being in a foreign place, and it seemed to induce in him an odd state of mind. As Millie rummaged in her bag for sunscreen, he stared out at the water and felt himself relax, ridding his mind temporarily of trouble.

"You're quiet all of a sudden," she said, without looking up from the bag.

"I know. But I'm okay."

"You sure?"

"Yeah. I like it here."

Billy was conscious of the glare of the sun, the shimmering

heat, the sand inside the waistband of his swim trunks. He was thirsty, and he was certain he was getting sunburnt, badly burnt. Without asking, Millie began to rub sunscreen on him.

"I'm afraid this is too late, Billy boy. You're gonna burn."

"It's okay. I'm white as a bedsheet."

"Like me," she said. Her gaze fell on a group of kids a few feet away, darkly tanned guys with their golden girls. "We look like a couple of ghosts."

"You have a little bit of a tan."

"It'll fade." She gave him a coy look. "Things fade." Then she smiled. "It will sort of fade and leave more freckles." She looked at her shoulder. "I hate my freckles."

She lay down beside him and closed her eyes, and he had a sudden urge to put an arm over her, there was nothing romantic or sexual in the impulse. Just to protect her. He lay down and thought of something his mother said.

"My Ma liked the water, whether it was a beach or a person's swimming pool. She always said if you worked at it, you could let your mind go blank, just think about the water and the sky and the heat and the sun. And forget about everything else."

"Can you do that, Billy? Forget about everything else?"

"Sure. Why not?"

"Because I don't think you're a boy who can do that, make his mind go blank. Half the time you're with me, you have other things on your mind."

"Not right now."

"That's good."

He watched Millie emerge from the water. Her hair clung to her face as her swimsuit clung to her slim body. Small and pale, at this distance she could have been twelve. Two of the tanned girls from the nearby group ran past her, their brown skins contrasting with Millie's skin, and with Billy's own.

She shook water from her hair and sprayed him, then sank down on her knees beside him.

"Yeah, you're getting burnt really bad," she said. She touched his shoulder.

He looked at her shoulders and back. The points of her shoulders were red, the freckles fading for the moment.

"Hope you don't lose your freckles. I think they're kind of nice. I like them."

He glanced at the two golden girls coming back from the water.

She gave him a small smile and stroked his shoulder. "No, I know what you like."

She looked over at the group on the blankets. "Those girls there, with their beautiful tanned bodies and their golden hair, that's what you like."

"Those ones there? They all look alike," he said.

This made her laugh. "Yeah, they're all goddesses! No, you like them and you wonder how to get a life like those kids over there, I mean like the one you imagine they have."

Billy wondered if she were psychic.

"What about you? Don't you ever imagine other people's lives? Don't you ever try to imagine what it would be like if your life was different than it is?"

"Of course. All people do that. But I don't do it much, and I know it's just daydreaming. That's the difference between us. We both daydream, but you wish you could make it real."

He was about to deny it but caught himself. Of course he wanted a different life. Who wouldn't?

"If you had my life, you'd want a better one."

"And because you want a better life than you've got, Billy, you won't be needing to be involved with, you know, my life."

She waited for him to meet her eyes.

"You're looking for a girl with a nice life, without problems, without any kind of trouble. I'm not that girl. Trouble is, Billy, there aren't any girls like the one you want. Not even those blonde girls over there. Watch the one in the pink bikini. She likes the dark-haired guy, and he doesn't even look at her. That girl probably doesn't even like her own looks, pretty as she is."

Billy stole a look at the girl in the pink bathing suit. She stared after the others who were now cavorting in the waves, throwing one another into the water. She shook her head and looked away.

He looked at Millie. "You're pretty good. Maybe you should be the detective. You notice everything around you?"

She shrugged her thin shoulders. "I notice a lot. But I can pick out an unhappy lady a block away. Sisters under the skin, I guess."

"Still, you're smart. What else can you do?"

"Predict the future," she said quickly and looked him in the eye. "I can do that."

He looked away. He watched a large dog kick sand on a dozen people as it bounded down to the water. When he looked at her she was watching him. He met her eyes, and it seemed to him that she was willing him to speak.

"It's like I spend my life looking for things, for people, for a new start. I'm always looking for something, ever since I got out of high school. When I was in the Army, and after, I kept waiting to come across a place that would work out for me."

"And now you're here."

"Yeah. Trying to see whether this will be a place for me."

"I think you're looking for a *place* where you belong, a special place. That's how it seems to me. You're looking for *a place*. But the place is the people."

Billy looked away and tried to think of something to make light of the moment, wondering how she could make him blurt out these things.

She tossed a handful of sand at him. "Hey, lighten up, Billy. Something else about me, I'm a girl who knows how to appreciate a nice thing or a nice day, and we're having a nice day. Aren't we? At least I am."

"Sure. But it's hot and I've got a girl throwing sand on me, so I need to get wet."

He got up and, after a moment's hesitation, grabbed her hand and tugged her to her feet, and they went into the bone-splitting cold of the slate-blue lake. He dove under the water and came up spitting. Millie was staring out at the tall wood pilings that marked the deep water. In the distance, a cruise ship moved parallel to the beach and she cupped a hand over her eye to look at it, a smile on her face.

There ought to be somebody that appreciates you, he thought.

Billy told himself that whatever this was would be finished soon, and that it would be his fault.

• • •

Billy would have said that he hadn't heard the door, but when he looked up, a young woman was standing just inside the office in a bright orange dress and a cloud of perfume. She was in her early twenties, pretty but tough-looking, the make-up applied with a trowel. She had large brown eyes—pretty eyes—and a flat nose that long ago had been broken. Beneath the heavy rouge and powder were old acne scars. Tight blouse, tighter skirt. The girl gave Billy a quick, hard glance, and took in the rest of the office, her gaze resting for a moment on Doris. As though she could feel the girl's eyes on her, Doris looked up, smiled after a small pause, then went back to her wizardry. Then the girl looked at Harry. She patted her hair.

"Mr. Harry Strummer?"

"Yes, Ma'am."

"I would like to hire your, uh, services. I need your help on a situation."

Harry seemed to stare for just a heartbeat longer than normal. Then he said, "You can sit, Ma'am."

She took the client chair and leaned forward. When she spoke, she looked around the room to see if Billy and Doris were eavesdropping.

"My name is Susan Johnson," she said, emphasizing each syllable.

"How can we be of service, Miss Johnson?"

She began speaking, and she spoke so low and fast that Billy caught very little of it, except for the times where she had to slow down her recital and correct herself, or where Harry pointed out a problem or contradiction.

"He left you when you were *twenty*?"

"No, no," she laughed, flustered, and brushed an imaginary hair from her face.

"No, he left us when I was *ten*."

"And you believe he's here, your father."

"Yes. Yes, I do. I have his addresses—" She handed him an index card.

"Then why—"

"I mean, his old ones, where I heard he was living. But I don't think he's there now. I'm kind of lost here, I don't know this city."

"Well, people who lived here all their lives get lost, Miss Johnson." Harry frowned at the index card. He said "Huh," then looked at her. "Last known address is on Leland, eh? Not sure where that is."

She flung her left hand out. "Up that way. North."

"Oh. Right."

She wet her lips. "That's what I've been told. It's somewhere north. Up by—is there a Wilson?"

"Yeah, there's a Wilson. Okay," Harry said quietly. "How did you come to us, Miss Johnson?"

She smiled now. "Oh, I looked you up in the phone book."

"I see." Harry looked off toward the far side of the office. After a moment, he said, "We charge a daily rate—"

"Oh, I have money," Susan Johnson said, and produced a thick roll of bills. She gave Billy a quick glance, then looked back at Harry.

Harry laughed and raised both hands, as if fending off the money.

"Hold on, hold on, Miss Johnson. Keep your money till we need to do something like that."

"Don't you want, like, an advance payment?"

"A retainer, you mean. Uh, sometimes, yes, but here, there might not be anything we can do. So just wait and see, okay?"

Harry asked a few questions, took some notes in his tiny notebook, and then said, "Okay. We'll be in touch. And then we'll see what our next step is. If he's here, though, in Chicago, we'll find him."

Susan Johnson hesitated, then said, "Thank you, Mr. Strummer." She seemed unsure of what to do next, and Billy would have said something had not gone the way she'd expected. But she took a final look around the office, glanced at Billy, then left.

When she was gone, Harry waited a moment, listening to her steps on the stairway. Then he looked at Doris. He raised his eyebrows. Doris went on typing for a second, and just when Billy decided she was unaware of Harry, she turned. She met Harry's gaze, gave one short shake of her head, and said, "Uh-uh."

"What I thought. What did you think, Bill?"

"She was nervous. And you kind of confused her by not taking her money. I think she expected you to be more interested in her case."

"I don't think there is a case."

Billy thought for a moment. "She seemed kind of stiff."

"Everything she said was rehearsed," Harry said, "and she still managed to screw some of it up."

"That's 'cause she hasn't had much practice," Doris said.

Harry looked at Doris.

She shrugged. "I could be wrong. She could just be a tough-looking little chickie who gets nervous around strangers, but I saw the look she gave Billy here—twice, if I'm not mistaken."

Billy said "So?"

"When she looked at you, she turned that on. It's something she's learned to do. Like I said, I could be mistaken, but if I had to make a guess, I'd say she was a working girl."

"A what?"

"A hooker," Harry said.

"Which doesn't make her bad," Doris added. "In my opinion."

"But it means she isn't Susan Johnson," Harry said, "and she isn't looking for her lost father. She says she's not from here, but she knows where Leland is. And Wilson."

Billy shrugged. "So what's her game then?"

"Isn't that an interesting question?"

For a long moment Harry stared off in the direction of the street, slapping his notebook against his knee. Then he looked at the page he'd written on.

"I don't like this," Doris said.

"What don't you like?" Billy asked her, but she ignored his question and watched Harry.

"I don't like this," Doris said again.

"I heard you."

Billy shrugged and looked from one to the other for an answer.

Finally Harry looked at him. "Maybe it's nothing, maybe it's something. It's just—a couple of things here and there and you think you see a pattern."

"What pattern?"

"Just things that could mean something. Or they could just be random. Just coincidence. You believe in coincidence, Bill?"

"I guess."

Harry nodded. "Of course there are coincidences. But usually when I see a couple things happening together, I don't assume coincidence. I assume they're happening together for a reason."

"What things this time?"

"A couple of days ago, you and I were walking and I thought I saw somebody I used to know, somebody who shouldn't have been here. And once or twice lately I think somebody's been following me."

"You see him?"

Harry raised his eyebrows. "Of course I saw him. He slipped back into a gangway when I turned in his direction. A kid, I think."

"Nobody you know, then," Doris said.

"No."

"Pickpocket, maybe?" Billy offered.

Harry shook his head. "No. He was watching me. They don't do that, pickpockets."

"So what next?"

"We work with what we've got. And what we've got is Miss

Susan Johnson. We should have tailed her but there didn't seem enough reason for that. But she gave me an address where she thought her father might have been. I guess we're supposed to check out this address on Leland."

"Want me to do it?"

Harry stared as though he were looking right through him.

"No, not just yet. I think we send Leo."

"Why not me?"

"She's seen you. She hasn't seen Leo."

Harry reached over and picked up the phone, and when Leo answered, he told him to check out the Leland address and get back to him.

An hour later, Leo called. Harry listened, nodded, thanked Leo, and hung up.

"What did he find?"

Harry looked at him. He touched a fingertip to the paper with the address.

"There's no such address. Where this is supposed to be, there's a vacant lot right under the El tracks. Kind of a dark place, Leo says, even in the daylight."

"So what do you think?"

"Leave this alone," Doris called out without looking up from her keyboard.

Harry shrugged. "What do I think? I think I'm supposed to go there and I think somebody will be waiting for me. Which means—" Harry got up and went over to the window. He peered out at the street. "—that they've got somebody watching the office so they'll know when I leave." He looked at Billy. He nodded. "I think this is coming together for me."

"What's coming together—"

Harry held up his hand to stop him.

"I don't know yet. But I'm getting some ideas. When I can tell you more, I will."

For a moment Harry looked down at the blotter as though trying to read sense from the chaos of his old scribbling. He looked up and saw Doris watching him.

"What?"

"You be careful."

"About what?" He shrugged and grinned.

SEVENTEEN

The Case of the Brothers Aleksy

Billy surprised Harry and Doris, who were conferring over a file from the red cabinet. Harry smiled and Doris let her face go blank. They both looked at him, a guarded look, assessing how much he'd seen.

How much of what? Billy wondered.

"Hello, Bill," Harry said, and Doris muttered, "Hi, Hon." She swung herself around on her rolling chair to her own desk, hit a key, and began typing into a letter she'd already had on the screen.

Harry tucked the folder back into the open drawer of the cabinet, spun around, and tapped an envelope on his desk.

"Got something for you, Bill," he said, and things were back to normal, but Billy had seen the look that said he'd happened upon something he wasn't supposed to see.

In the late afternoon, after dropping off Harry's envelope to a lawyer in a basement office on Diversey, Billy grabbed a hot dog from a vendor and walked all the way down to the lake. For the last half mile or so he found himself walking just behind a couple of girls dressed for the beach—cut-off jeans, bikini tops, beach bags over one arm—good-looking girls, a redhead and a blonde. At one point they seemed to notice him, both of them at once. The redhead met his eyes, then resumed talking to her companion. He remembered his first days in town, his awkwardness among the self-assured young denizens of the beach. Now he had a job, a buck in his pocket, and a girl—well, he knew a girl.

Now he remembered what had bothered him earlier—Harry

putting away the folder he and Doris had been discussing, quickly and smoothly changing focus and subject, as though the folder had never been there. But Billy had seen it. A manila folder with a green border, an old folder. He was unable to shake the notion that they had been discussing something they were unwilling to share with him.

Once before, when he'd come into the office and found Leo and Harry hunched over the big desk, faces close together, Billy had felt shut out of something, and now he recalled surprising Doris and Harry once as they ate a fast lunch at their desks. That time they actually froze for a heartbeat and then greeted him, leaving him with the odd feeling that they'd been discussing him.

It struck him that perhaps they were not as sure of him as he had thought, and he wondered what that meant. That he could not be trusted?

When he returned to the office, a red-faced man with bristly gray hair sat on the floor peering into the upturned air conditioner. Around him were the innards of a second air conditioner.

Harry watched him with a distracted air.

"That's Hughie," he said as Billy entered. "He's fixing our air conditioner."

Hughie held up a part. He smiled at Billy.

"I'll have it working again in an hour. Tops."

Harry Strummer tapped a business card on his desk and stared off into space. He looked at the card again and then saw Billy looking at him.

"New case. I want you to sit in on a meeting, Bill. I'm a bit stretched right now, so I think I'm going to let you handle the thing. On your own."

Billy felt himself grinning.

So you trust me this far. All right.

"What have we got?"

"A young client, a young gentleman from what we call 'the North Shore.'"

"Where you drove me, up there by that Baha'i temple place.

Those houses that look like palaces."

"That's it. Wilmette, Winnetka, Kenilworth. But to prove that those folks with their wealth and substance are no different from you and me, we have a client from there. He's looking for his younger brother, and he's a kid himself."

Harry looked at his desk clock. "From the way this young fellow talks, I'm expecting him at precisely 9:30, which means he's out there on our stairs right now, looking at his watch."

They both looked at the door, and within thirty seconds it opened. A handsome face thrust itself into the room and said, "Mr. Harry Strummer?"

"That's me. Now you can come all the way into the office."

The young man reddened and came into the room. He was tall and slim, with high cheekbones and brown eyes and dark red hair; but for his flat Slavic nose, he might have been a model.

Dressed like a model, too, Billy thought—gray sportcoat, pale yellow shirt, royal blue tie with some sort of paisley design. His hand went to the knot of his tie but it was a wasted gesture. There was no chance this kid's tie would be crooked.

"I'm David Aleksy."

"Come in and sit down."

David Aleksy sat tentatively, as though the chair might collapse. He nodded at Billy.

"This is Billy Fox, one of my investigators. And I'm Harry Strummer."

They shook hands all around, and David Aleksy did his best to look businesslike.

"So you're interested in finding your brother."

"Right. My younger brother, Karl. He's seventeen."

"What can you tell us about Karl? Why does he need to be found, for instance?"

"Well, he's seventeen. And he's—he's loose. He's here in Chicago by himself and we don't know where he is."

"And by 'we,' you mean you and your parents? Did they send you here?"

"No, they don't—they think I'm in a summer class. College. I go to Michigan State University. I'm a junior. My father doesn't—" The boy looked away for a moment and then spoke in a dead voice. "My parents are divorcing. My mother drinks and cries and wonders what happened to her baby, her younger son. My father just wants to be divorced. He doesn't really care if Karl comes back or walks in front of a bus." He looked from Harry to Billy. "But I do."

For a moment Harry looked down at his notepad. "So," he said. "What makes you think he's in Chicago?"

"He told me that's what he would do someday if he got the chance. He'd go to Chicago. And be a jazz musician." Aleksy shrugged, this was clearly a foolish idea.

"What's he play?" Billy asked.

"Saxophone. And he's good, I have to say that. He's very good. He can play any kind of music, and he likes to just, you know, join in with other musicians."

"He jams whenever he gets the chance," Harry said.

Billy looked at Harry. "So he's got his horn with him."

"Yes."

Billy looked at him and nodded. "What's he look like?"

"Like me. A lot like me, I guess. But he's small, he's only about five-foot-five.

Harry looked at Billy and raised his eyebrows.

"So we're looking for a small guy with a big horn case." Billy said. "And he's got red hair. What else?"

David Aleksy thought for a moment. "He has this hat, it's like a little fedora. He thinks it makes him look like a jazzman."

Harry pointed to his straw porkpie hat on the corner of the desk. "Like that one?"

"Yes, only dark. It's black."

"My associate here will be working on this, and when we have something to tell you—"

"I'd like to help. I don't know if he'd talk to you."

Harry looked to Billy for his reaction. Billy nodded.

"All right then, David. Be here tomorrow around—what? Noon?"

Billy nodded.

"Why noon? Shouldn't we look for him first thing in the morning?"

Harry smiled. "The kind of people he's hanging around with if he's a kid on the loose and an aspiring jazzman to boot, they don't get up *first thing in the morning.*"

David Aleksy nodded and got to his feet. He shook their hands and said, "I'm just afraid he'll die here. Like a homeless person."

"We'll find him," Harry said. "Have no doubt about that."

When young Aleksy had gone, Harry looked at Billy. "Okay, Bill? You got this one?"

"Sure. I'll make a couple of stops tonight, lay some groundwork."

That night, Billy hit the corners where young street kids and runaways might congregate. At a Burger King, a kid told him about some musicians that hung out near the ball park and played in the parking lot. He found the horn players, but no Karl Aleksy. They told him "Little K" hadn't been around in several days.

The oldest of the horn players was a black man with light eyes. "What you want with Little K?"

"Family's looking for him. His brother."

"Who you, then?"

"A friend of his brother. He's worried."

The horn player nodded as though there was good cause to worry.

"Yeah, we all know Little K. He got some boys looking for him, he owe some money. He play a nice sax, but he can't play cards." The man then gave Billy several places to look for Karl.

David Aleksy showed up two hours early the next morning. Billy and Doris exchanged a look.

"We haven't found him yet, David," Billy said. "Usually takes more than twelve hours."

David Aleksy blushed and shrugged.

"I know that. I just—I didn't have anything better to do, Mr. Fox."

"Have a seat."

David Aleksy sat at the edge of the guest chair. His posture suggested that he might dash from the room.

"I looked for him myself for a while, you know."

"Didn't know that."

"I did. Not that I knew what I was doing. But I—" He shrugged.

"You tried. You looked for your brother, you did the right thing."

"You find me kind of—ridiculous, Mr. Fox. You think I'm stupid."

"No, that's not it. And people call me Bill. Of course, you're not stupid, you go to a good school, you're, you know, well-spoken. You were smart enough to come to us for help. Most guys want to do everything themselves."

From across the room Doris looked up and raised her eyebrows.

"I think you're sort of—what Harry, Mr. Strummer, that is, would call an *innocent*. You lack experience on the street. Which is what we have. We have experience."

"Do you think you'll find my brother?"

"Yes. We will. We'll use what you've told us about him and what our experience tells us, and we'll use our, uh, resources." Billy glanced at Doris and saw her suppress a smile.

"I'll try not to get in your way."

For the next two days, Billy squired David Aleksy around the North Side of Chicago—by day they tried the donut shops and hamburger joints, by night they hit the small jazz clubs. At the Dunkin' Donuts at Clark and Belmont they got their first lead. A black girl with dreadlocks heard them asking about Karl Aleksy and approached them with an amused look.

"You looking for a little white boy plays sax?"

"That's right," Billy said.

"He's my brother," David added.

The girl frowned at Billy. "But not *your* brother? You all look like brothers."

David and Billy looked at each other in surprise.

The girl laughed. "Yes, you do, you look alike. You some *pretty* white boys, I'll tell you that. Hey, Leona, don't these boys look like brothers?"

A girl at a table turned to look at them and nodded. "Sure do."

Billy shrugged and shook his head in puzzlement. "So you've seen the kid with the sax?" he asked.

"Sure. He real little, dragging that big old saxophone case around. He play with those old men down in Lincoln Park. But he layin' low right now."

"Has he been here?"

"Nah. Try Mickey D's."

David Aleksy gave Billy a blank look.

"The golden arches, David."

They timed their visit for dusk, ordered food, and then sat sipping a couple of Cokes. David was eager to hear about life in Chicago, and Billy was telling him about the things Harry and Leo seemed to know about, when David stood up suddenly. Billy turned and saw a smaller, bedraggled version of David standing near the counter. His horn case was on the floor a few feet from where he stood staring up at the menu.

"Karl," he called out.

The boy made a sudden move as though he'd bolt, then remembered his sax case. He moved toward it but his brother covered the space between them and stood in front of the sax.

"Come eat with us."

Karl made a half-shrug, and David put an arm around him, shepherding him up to the counter. When they'd obtained food for Karl, they came back to the booth.

Karl Aleksy set down the horn case and stood facing them. The case was nearly as big as he was, and somehow he'd gotten himself a topcoat cut for a taller man, so that he looked like a small boy who's pilfered not only father's horn but his clothing. Billy saw that the Big Town had knocked him around a bit—he had a bruise under one eye, dark circles under both of them, and his skin was the palest green. He tried to give his brother a hard stare, but his eyes kept moving to Billy.

"Who's he?" Karl thrust his chin in Billy's direction.

"This is Billy Fox. Mr. Fox is an investigator for Mr. Harry Strummer, who I hired to find you."

"They paid money to find me?"

"No, I'm paying money to find you. Sit down and eat."

The boy slid into the booth and pulled the horn case in with him. David leaned forward to say something and Billy put a hand on his sleeve. He shook his head.

For several minutes Karl ate, keeping his eyes down. He tore into his food like a child raised by wolves.

"Haven't been eating much," Billy offered.

Karl shook his head, stole a glance at his brother. "I'm a little low on bread right now. I need a gig."

"Come on home, Karl."

"This is where I live now. I want to stay here. I can take care of myself. I can play music here."

David shrugged. "Finish school and come back here. It'll still be here. Come on back with me."

"I don't want to go back to them."

"You'll be going back with your brother," Billy said. "He's the one who's concerned about you. It's a tough town—I think you're finding that out already. You should come back here when you're ready."

The boy studied Billy and frowned. "I thought they were older. Detectives, I mean."

"I just started. I'm still learning. Like you and the sax."

"Come on home, Karl."

The boy's shoulders slumped then, and Billy couldn't remember ever seeing a kid look so defeated.

"Hey, you did good for the first time in the city," Billy said. "You played your horn a couple places here, right?"

"I did."

"Next time, you'll have more experience. Come on, Karl. Come with us."

"I have some stuff at my friend's house. Oh, and I owe a guy money. Like fifty bucks. Which I don't have."

"Don't worry about that."

They drove Karl to his friend's house, a rear apartment in a building that looked ready to collapse of its own weight. He emerged with a plastic bag filled with clothes.

As Billy was loading the kid's stuff in the trunk of the car, he heard Karl say "Uh-oh, they're here."

"Who is?" Billy straightened and saw a black Chevy pulling up behind them. The driver emerged, a fleshy man in his twenties with a shaven head and a snake tattoo along his temple. Two others followed, thinner versions of the driver.

Billy felt a quick moment of nerves and then shook it off.

He gave me this to handle, and I'm going to handle it.

Billy looked them over. The driver was big and cocky, but Billy caught the quick look of uncertainty in his eyes. As for his companions, one was tall and long-armed but had his foot in a cast. The other weighed perhaps a buck-and-a-quarter. Billy glanced at David Aleksy, corn-fed and solid and awaiting instructions, and suddenly liked his chances.

"Hey, faggot," the big one called out. "Where's my money? Come up with the bread, asshole, or I get the horn. And I'll bust your other eye."

He moved toward Karl, and Billy stepped in his path.

"What do you want here?"

"This punk owes me money. A hundred. Get out of my way."

"It was fifty yesterday," Karl whined.

"Yeah? That was yesterday, now it's a yard. And what's this to you?" He squinted at Billy.

"I've been hired by his people to bring him back. And that's what's happening here."

"Oh, yeah? You and Pretty Boy here?"

Billy shook his head. "Pretty predictable—you see a guy in nice clothes and he's 'Pretty Boy.' But yeah, me and Pretty Boy are taking the kid back with us."

"You don't want to fuck with me."

"Kick his ass, Ray-Ray," the tall one said.

"*Ray-Ray?*" Billy said.

The big man looked slightly embarrassed. "That's me, Ray-Ray Buchanan." He moved a couple of steps toward Karl Aleksy.

Billy shrugged. "Back home that would be a little boy's name."

Ray-Ray made a slow, showy turn. "What'd you say?"

His companions moved up until each of them was facing one of Ray-Ray's boys. Billy glanced at them. They were both nervous but awaiting his instructions. Good soldiers. He winked, then faced Ray-Ray Buchanan.

"We're leaving, Ray-Ray."

Billy pretended to turn away, but he thought he knew what was coming. Ray-Ray swore and made a grunting noise and came at him. Billy had seen this in a dozen bar fights—a guy, usually a big guy like Ray-Ray, would come running at his opponent, growling or swearing, flying at the other guy with a clumsy karate kick and a haymaker. It was mostly for show, the other guy was supposed to duck and cover his head. The kick and punch almost never landed. Ray-Ray made his noises and launched himself at Billy, who sidestepped and hit him in the soft gut with a left. Ray-Ray's own momentum provided the power, and he went down hard and loud and smacked the side of his face on the alley floor. He got up, swinging before he was even on his feet, and Billy smacked him in the eye and moved around behind him.

The other two went into action, more or less reluctantly. David traded punches with the tall one in the cast, fought with no art but a lot of heart, and his opponent finally lost his balance with the cast and fell over backward. On the far side of the car, Karl wrestled the thin one to the ground and they grappled and clawed at each other's faces until the skinny kid yelled "I quit, I quit."

Ray-Ray was up on one knee, struggling to regain his feet and gasping and muttering that he was going to kill all of them.

"Stay down or I'll hit you in the mouth."

The fat man glared, but his heart wasn't in it.

"Let's go," Billy said, and the Aleksy brothers climbed into the car. As he slid into the driver's seat, Billy looked at Ray-Ray and his two fallen comrades.

"You need to rethink this, man. You're not cut out for this kind of work."

"Fuck you," Ray-Ray said, but without feeling. "You got lucky."

Billy shrugged and shut the car door.

"That was so cool!" Karl said.

"Sometimes you get the bear," Billy said, quoting his grandfather. "Sometimes the bear gets you. And you guys did good, both of you."

"You had the big guy, though."

"Yeah, but you did all right. And you did a service to the city. Those guys, you taught them a lesson. Life's all about lessons. They'll go home and think, 'Hey, I tried to rough up a couple of regular guys that hadn't done anything to me and I got my ass kicked. What's the lesson to be learned here?'"

They laughed, and after a while, David Aleksy said, "You sound like Mr. Strummer."

Billy laughed and admitted to himself that it was true.

He drove the brothers to a bar-and-grill and sent them both back to the men's room to clean themselves up. David had a small cut at the corner of his eye and a swollen lip. Young Karl had bloody claw marks on his cheek to go with his older bruises, and his face was filthy. His hair stuck up in places. Both of the brothers looked as though they'd been rolling around in a barnyard.

When they came back, Billy sat them down at the bar and ordered Cokes and, for himself, a beer. The brothers Aleksy spoke to each other in subdued tones, and Billy could hear David making an entreaty for Karl to stay at home and in school at least until David finished at Michigan State. Billy let them catch up with each other and watched them eat. From time to time he saw Karl eyeing someone's food.

He's hungry again?

Billy ordered him a burger without asking. David thanked him repeatedly and laughed at everything his brother or Billy said, and Billy understood—he'd accomplished something, he'd come to the big city and found his kid brother, who might be safe for the time being if they could get him to stay home. He'd been in a fight, probably his first fight since grade school. And he'd performed well.

We're sending you back to Michigan State with a fight under your belt and stories to tell, Billy thought.

After a while, they all sat in a calm silence until David looked Billy's way.

"Are you from Chicago, Bill?"

"No. I'm from a couple miles from where you go to school. I'm from Lansing."

"Wow. Small world, as my Mom used to say. So what brought you here?"

Billy fought the urge to sound colorful—*I'm looking for a girl.* Instead he settled on "I just needed a new start."

Both boys nodded at the same time as though this made wonderful sense, their eyes bright with admiration. A man of the world, making a new start. David looked around the bar and smiled.

He nodded, in spite of his cut eye and his swollen lip and the fact that he'd probably ruined the topcoat. "You know, this is a pretty nice town." Little Karl nodded in agreement and Billy laughed.

David looked at him. "I wish I knew your story, Bill."

"It's not much of a story. It's sure not interesting."

"Well, I'm grateful for your help."

"Just be sure and tell Mr. Strummer what a fine job I did."

David nodded and looked around the bar again, a dazed but happy expression on his battered face. Billy watched him and wanted to laugh, the kid's joy was so obvious. He'd found his brother, he'd tested himself in The Big Town, he'd traded punches on the street.

As though he could hear Billy's thoughts, David turned his way. "I really owe you a lot."

Billy clapped him on the shoulder. "That's why they call us 'Peerless,'" he said, and laughed.

The next day, David Aleksy showed up with his brother in tow, both of them cleaned up this time—David had apparently bought his brother new clothes. Harry handed him a bill and he wrote out a check. A day's time had allowed the bruises to darken so that the two Aleksy boys looked even more hard-used than they had the day before.

Harry squinted at the boys. "Got yourself banged up a little, huh? Been running with a tough crowd?"

David smiled and nodded toward Billy. "We had a couple of adventures with Bill."

Harry turned and gave Billy a sardonic look. Then David reached inside his sport coat and took out an envelope. He raised his eyebrows in question and Harry read his mind. He nodded.

David handed the envelope to Billy. "Something for you, Bill." "Well, thanks."

The boys left, with David giving Billy a final wave and a smile. Billy looked in the envelope…a hundred.

"Oh!"

"You got a bonus. Well done, Bill. And you managed to get the shit beat out of the clients."

"Yeah, I was sorry about that, but I think they liked it."

Doris said, "Of course they liked it. They had adventures."

"And now," Harry said, "they have something to tell people about. Nice work. Next time be a little more circumspect. People hear we're endangering all our clients, it'll hurt our reputation. And our bottom line."

That night, he took Millie out for ice cream and told her of his adventures with the Aleksy brothers, embellishing here and there and wondering if he'd inherited just a bit of his Old Man's gift of storytelling. Millie laughed and put her hand across his, locking her eyes onto his.

"Your own case, Billy. This was yours."

"Wasn't much of a case. I just found a guy."

"You did more than that. And Harry knew you would be able to handle it."

"Well, I don't know what that means but—"

"It means Harry trusts you. And he has confidence in you."

He nodded and said, "It means I fit in there. I'm part of it."

And I'm part of this, with you, he thought, but was afraid to give voice to the admission.

In the coming days, he decided he'd left enough of himself on the sidewalks of Chicago—it was time to stop looking for Rita. It occurred to him that he had done all this, spent weeks scouring a town strange to him, without a single piece of evidence that she was even here. He acknowledged that Rita was probably long gone. He felt foolish. He was finished with this.

Billy would not have been able to pinpoint the moment when their relationship changed, but it was clear to him that it had. At some point Millie had slipped into his life, and he into hers. At some unremarked moment it had become natural. He called for her at the diner on a regular basis. The cook and one of the older waitresses greeted him by name, and he learned that they were Hector and Madge. He began to look forward to seeing her, having someone to tell of his adventures in the employ of Harry Strummer.

Once or twice a week he slept at Millie's place—there was still an understanding, for both of them, that this was her space, and that for his part, he needed some separation. But they saw each other several times a week now. Restaurants, small music clubs, movies—a sci-fi epic called *Star Wars* and the new James Bond movie. More than anything else they walked, which Billy found amusing.

All the walking I've done, and I find a girl who just wants to walk.

One night she explained it to him.

"All the time I've been here, I've seen how much people just stay outside in Chicago in the summer. There's just people everywhere, going places, looking at outdoor things. Street fairs where they block off the whole street, and there's music, and art fairs, and parades. And I just felt left out. I mean, I'm a big girl and I can go out by myself if I want to, but it's not the same thing, not if everyone else is with friends or with their, you know, their person. So if you ask me where I want to go, if you give me a choice, I'm gonna say, 'Let's go someplace where we can be outside and do things.'"

He learned that she liked museums and had a weakness for the zoo. Twice on hot Sunday mornings she dragged him to the zoo. They had coffee outside the zoo café and watched people in rowboats on the pond and speculated on the likely wildlife on the small island at its far end.

Billy scoured the neighborhoods for things she might like and discovered the summer carnivals. It seemed that they were all connected to Catholic parishes, and he dragged her to three on consecutive weekends.

In Millie's company he was at ease, and pleased with himself. She—this relationship—was confirmation of his new life, what he'd been able to put together. At the very least, he was carving out an existence for himself in Chicago, and he stopped seeing himself as a transient. He had a job and a place to stay and a girl. And for a time that was enough, actually a thing of no small wonder to him—his first relationship with a girl since Rita. At odd moments he pondered his future, wondered whether this moment, this time with Millie, was that future. At some point it became clear that she thought of them as a couple, that she had settled into this understanding without qualms. And for the time being, he tried not to question what he had.

But not for long. July bled into August and a week of gray skies and oppressive humidity, and Billy began to grow restless. At first he ascribed his feelings to the change in weather. One night he walked through a heavy rain to pick Millie up from work. By the time he arrived he was soaked and irritable. For the rest of the night he said very little, and grew defensive when she asked if anything was wrong. The next evening he felt oddly distracted, preoccupied with what might be going on with Harry Strummer. He spent that night at Millie's, but lay awake long after she'd fallen asleep. He rolled over and looked at her and felt a sudden wash of guilt.

This isn't going to last either, he told himself. *I don't belong here.*

He understood then that he would end up hurting this girl. He was unsure why, just that it was inevitable.

The second week of August, he finally saw her. It took him a moment to realize what he was seeing, but it was Rita. She'd dyed her dark hair blonde. She was riding on the Clark Street bus heading north. She sat in a window seat and looked down at something in her lap—a book, perhaps, or a magazine. She'd always loved to read, occasionally chiding him for not reading more. Now she looked down at what she was reading, and in this unguarded moment she looked lovely, her lips parted slightly. She'd been in the sun, her olive skin a light golden brown. He opened his mouth to call out to her but caught himself.

The bus rolled to a stop and disgorged passengers, took on a few new ones. He realized he was gaping at her. His need for this moment came rushing back to him. Looking at her, he understood why he had done this. She was beautiful and she was here, and he could find her and talk to her and change his life. He raised his hand in a tentative wave, dropping it immediately. The blood was pounding in his ears and he admitted that he was terrified. He took a step back, fearful that she'd see him. The bus moved on when the light changed, and she was gone. He was breathing heavily and the tension clenched his heart like a fist.

For several minutes Billy stood there. He watched the bus until he could no longer make it out, squinting into the distance each time it stopped to see if Rita emerged. Then he told himself to focus on what he could take from this.

She lives up this way, she lives north. She was settled into her seat, so she wasn't getting off soon.

She's up that way, he told himself. *I'll find her now.*

And then what? he asked himself. For the first time Billy understood that he would be terrified when that moment came, that he would face some sort of judgment in Rita's eyes.

Well, then I'll face her and I'll be scared shitless. Won't be the first time.

As he walked home he thought of Millie, and a sudden wave of guilt suffused him. He saw her face, and a dark weight pulled at his heart.

Oh, Jesus, how do I do this?

But the fact was clear that he had come to Chicago to find Rita, to see that she was all right, to help, to do something for her, and it seemed clear to Billy that he was honor-bound to finish this. He allowed himself a glimpse of the old fantasy, of the two of them settling down—here, in Chicago, where he'd begun to put down something like roots. The possibilities made him giddy.

At about the same time on each of the next two nights, he stood on the same corner and tried not to make it too obvious that he was scanning the passengers. He got on one bus but decided this was too risky—he did not want to force a "chance" meeting, not before he was ready and knew how he wanted to approach her.

At night he pored again over his maps, and now it seemed that a new focus came to him. He was no longer staring at streets and landmarks to kill time or go through the motions of his search. He told himself to look at the map the way Harry might. He thought about what he knew and what was likely, and a new strategy came to him.

A woman with a small child. You couldn't keep the child inside in this weather, you'd both go crazy. Even a woman trying to stay underground needed to come out.

Billy looked at his map and noted the green shapes that dotted the north side landscape.

A park. She'd need to take her child and herself to a park.

For the next week he visited the parks and smaller playgrounds north of the place he'd seen her on the bus, eventually settling on a spacious park west of Clark Street. A big park with the odd name of Indian Boundary Park.

• • •

The dog days of August had come to the offices of Peerless Detective. Leo was in Milwaukee repossessing a car and looking for a runaway husband. Billy spent much of the week feeling oddly off-balance. The streets seemed different to him, as though he were seeing everything for the first time. The city gave him odd background noises as well, as jets cruised overhead, a squadron of them rehearsing for the Air and Water Show. He remembered Millie saying she wanted, for the first time since she'd moved here, to go down to the lake and watch the show. He tried not to think about Millie.

Billy was sent out on a half dozen minor errands, including deliveries of food to both Mrs. Ricci, who now believed that aliens were somehow a part of her landscape, and old Wendell. Harry was in and out of the office, busy with small tasks and meetings, poring over files and maps and documents. More than once Billy saw him look at the clock on the far wall, and if asked he would have said Harry was waiting for something to break. Doris studied him, and met Billy's eyes once. She tried to draw Harry into conversation, and when he was on the phone or occupied with some task, she watched him.

Twice that week Billy visited the park in the evening and made himself as unobtrusive a presence as possible, planting himself on a bench with a newspaper. It was a large park, and busy in the evening, with a small zoo and a playground, and he peered at all the women with their children. He had the sudden image of a dozen angry women pointing him out to a cop, and he felt himself blushing.

Finally, on the following Saturday, he had just arrived at the big park when he caught a familiar gesture or movement from the corner of his eye. He turned and saw a woman shaking her hair out the way Rita shook her hair, a woman with a small, dark-haired girl.

"Of course," he heard himself say, for the woman was not Rita but her sister, three years older, tough and protective and exactly the person who would take her in with no questions asked. Peoria, Billy thought. The sister lived in Peoria, he'd always heard. Yet here she was.

Billy forced himself to leave the park. He found a bench at a bus stop up the street from which he could keep an eye on Rita's sister and the little girl. At one point, the child drifted away and came dangerously close to the street, and Rita's sister rushed over and grabbed her. The little girl's face was toward him and he could see the vague resemblance to Rita, and it struck him that if things had gone their projected way all those years ago, this might have been his child. A sudden and surprising pang of disappointment washed over him. Billy had never thought much about having a child, but here was the reality, and the sense of lost possibility was painful.

Eventually they left the park, and Billy followed. They walked, and his heart lifted for it meant they were staying close. Two blocks south of the park the sister went up the stairs of a two-flat, and Billy tried to calm the urgency in his chest.

I've found them. I know where they are. I've found Rita.

Twice he walked around the block, head down each time and trying to keep from grinning like a madman. Eventually his elation turned to fear, and he understood that he was terrified of his first meeting with Rita. But he knew where she was, and that changed everything.

EIGHTEEN

Escalation

The client was an old friend who was clearly embarrassed to be coming to Harry with his case. He spoke in a low murmur so that Harry was forced to lean forward to hear him, and he looked from Leo to Billy to Doris to see if they were listening. When he was gone, Billy looked at Harry.

"He wants us to follow his father? I heard that much. Why?"

"He wants to know if the old man is playing around."

"That sounds like something I wouldn't want to know. There are things you shouldn't know about your parents. Like the fact that they had sex to have you."

Harry laughed. "You're right, but this is a favor for an old friend. Jimmy's done things for me before, so we're doing this for him. I'm going to follow the old man, see where he goes, decide how much to tell Jimmy. And he'll be satisfied. You have to be willing to do favors for people, and they'll repay them. You call in your markers when you need to."

Then Harry shrugged. "It's all connected, kid." Harry watched Billy for a moment. "You're not buying it, huh?"

"I didn't say anything."

"No, but I see it, it's in your eyes. That's the other thing in our business, Bill, people's eyes. You get to where you can read people's eyes. Because you can compose your face, you can control what your face does, but you can't control your eyes. At least most people can't. You watch, you'll see that. Anyhow, you don't have to buy my philosophy. Everybody's got his own."

"I don't think I have a philosophy."

"Sure you do. It's 'I'm going to do things myself, without anybody's help.'"

Billy laughed but felt his face flushing.

The weekend came, and he stayed away from the diner. Twice he went to the park where he'd seen Rita's sister and the child. On Sunday, he saw Rita herself with the little girl. He stayed as far away from them as possible, forced himself to turn the pages of a newspaper, half believing she'd see him anyway, or hear the pounding of his heart.

And what would he say then?

Oh—Rita! Hey. You live around here? I'm just hanging around in this park miles from where I live—in a town where I'm not even supposed to be.

I won't know what to say, he thought. I have no idea what I'll say.

He watched her surreptitiously for nearly an hour, wracked his brain for a way to "accidentally" walk by. At one point he got up and began moving toward Rita and the child, then lost his nerve and parked on another bench. He realized he was sweating heavily and breathing like a man who had run a distance. When they left, he forced himself not to follow them.

• • •

On a Monday morning, Billy ambushed a grim-faced man getting into a Mercedes and served him a summons. The man threw the summons at him and Billy shrugged.

"You've been served, man."

When he returned, he saw Harry sitting in the back seat of a dark Chevy Caprice parked in front of the office building. The two men in the front seat were watching Harry as he explained something. They were both big men, in thick sport coats unsuited to the weather.

You guys might as well be wearing a sign, Billy thought.

He sat down on the front step of the building and sipped

at a cup of coffee. Finally, Harry emerged from the car. He said something to the two detectives and tried on a small smile and waved. He walked toward the office with his head down and didn't notice Billy until he was nearly tripping over him.

"Oh, Bill. Didn't see you." He was oddly pale, and he blinked several times as though trying to focus.

"Something happened. What?"

Harry opened his mouth, shook his head. "Let's go inside and talk."

Doris and Leo stopped themselves in mid-sentence when Harry entered the office. He smiled without mirth.

"I got this guy sitting on the step downstairs watching me, and the two of you—what, at the window?"

"We were just concerned, Harry," Doris said. "You know that."

"They give you a hard time?" Leo asked.

"No, not really. I think they're irritated. But it's not like I anticipated any of this."

"Who was it? Rapp?"

"Yeah, Rapp and that guy Carmody."

Leo shook his head. "Him I don't know. Rapp's okay, though."

Billy looked from one to the other. "*Anticipated any of* what? Want to clue me in?"

"He's dead," Harry said. "The guy. Dietrich."

"The accountant? I never knew his name."

"I know. I thought if I mentioned it, I'd bring bad luck. Well, bad luck has visited Mr. Dietrich."

"And the cops thought you might have something to do with it."

"I called it in. I went there. To his place."

Billy blinked. "Why?"

"I had to talk to him. I wanted to try to put this thing together."

What thing? Billy wanted to ask but decided to let that go for a moment.

"How did he die?"

"Someone beat his face in with a blunt object. A lamp, I'd guess. Then the place was trashed and the door left open, to make it look like somebody was caught in the middle of robbing the place."

"Maybe that's what happened. A burglary gone wrong. It happens."

"It does," Leo agreed. "But this—"

Harry nodded. "Yeah, it's the level of the violence that makes it something else."

"Makes it what?" Billy asked.

"That's what I'm trying to figure out," he said in a hollow voice. He swiveled his chair and looked out the window. "That's what I'm trying to figure out," he repeated.

Billy read the look in his eyes and understood that Harry thought this somehow involved him.

The rest of the week was slow, and Chicago seemed to generate its own heat. On Friday, the handsome client named Moncrief was back in the office, this time in a khaki summer weight suit and a yellow tie.

Billy looked from Moncrief to Harry and saw that whatever was transpiring here was not quite what the client had in mind. Moncrief sat stiffly, bent forward slightly, watching Harry's eyes. He perched on the edge of the chair, and his body language and the dark red of his face gave him an aura of rage. Moncrief held Harry's gaze and there was something else there, a subtext that Billy couldn't quite make out, as though the two of them had shared a confidence or come to a silent understanding.

Then Harry said, "So that's where we're at. I'm just coming up blank, here, sir."

Moncrief nodded slowly. He looked around the room, his gaze resting for a moment on Billy. He got to his feet.

"All right, then, Mr. Strummer. I'll be in and out of town the next few days—business. I'm not really getting to see much of Chicago, which is a shame because it's my first time here. But I'll check back with you when I'm back in town."

"Okay, Mr. Moncrief. Maybe something will turn up for us. If not, I can always refer you to a bigger agency, more resources, et cetera."

Moncrief gave him an odd smile and pointed a finger at him. "I prefer to stick with you, Mr. Strummer," he said, and looked amused.

For several minutes after Moncrief had gone, Harry stared at the door as though expecting the man to come back. Billy waited for Harry to look his way, and finally his silence wore Harry down.

Harry looked at Billy and tilted his head to one side. "What?"

"I don't know. You and him, Moncrief. It's like—I felt like I was watching two guys sharing some kind of private joke."

"Private joke? I can't imagine Moncrief making jokes."

"Well, there's something odd about him. Like there's something else there we should know about and he's keeping it to himself. I don't know, I guess I don't trust him."

"Good, Bill. Neither do I."

"And he's got weird eyes."

Harry laughed. "Yeah. Those eyes. What about that, Doris? You've seen this Moncrief a couple times now, who do those blue eyes remind you of?"

"Paul Newman. If he was mean."

Harry forced a grin and nodded in Doris's direction. "You hear that? The girls, they can tell things sometimes that we miss."

Billy looked over at Doris. "How do you know he's mean?"

"I can tell. I wouldn't want anything to do with him."

"She's good about this," Harry said. "She can size people up."

"Is that right?" Billy was about to ask Doris what her first impression of him had been. Then he saw the "go ahead, try me" look in her eye and decided to leave the field of battle in one piece.

He looked back at Harry. "So you think we'll hear from him again?"

"Oh, yes. I think so. I'd be surprised if we didn't."

• • •

Later that day, Dutch came by the office and Harry took him out for a cup of coffee.

When Harry returned alone, Billy said, "Was that about the

accountant? Dietrich?"

"Oh, it was about this and that, you know."

I know this has got you shook, that's what I know.

Harry rummaged through the morning's mail and Billy watched him. A man he knew had been found beaten to death. And Harry had been on his way to see him.

That night he rode the bus up Clark Street and walked over to the park. The sky was threatening rain and Rita wasn't there. He felt simultaneously frustrated and relieved. To be so close to resolving all of this was maddening, but he still had no stomach for the actual moment, no idea how to approach her, what to say.

Billy told himself he didn't belong here, either, at this park. He thought again of the dead man, a man he had watched getting off a bus, carrying his groceries. A man known to Billy's boss, a man his boss was planning to speak to. In all his life, Billy had never known a person who died by violence. A darkness had come into his life, and he now realized that Harry Strummer was in some danger. Without knowing what was going on, he was unsure what he could do to help.

But I can do what he's trained me to do, Billy thought.

He walked all the long way home to his room and told himself he would stay closer to Harry for the time being.

And so Billy began to tail Harry. The first night he waited outside the office, and when Harry emerged and began walking up Wells Street, Billy followed, this time at a distance where he believed he could not be spotted. Harry walked halfway to the Loop, then turned and went east, toward the lake. When Harry stopped into a restaurant, Billy waited for a time. Then, reassured that no one else was following Harry, he turned home.

The next night Harry got into his car and drove north. Billy flagged down a cab.

"Where to?" the cabbie said in a bored voice.

"Wherever that black Chevy goes. We're following him."

Now he had the cabbie's attention.

"Really?"

"It's my old man. I need to see what he's up to."

"Oh. I got you." The cabbie nodded as though the tailing of wayward fathers was a basic part of his workday.

They followed Harry to his street, and Billy had the cabbie park at the corner. He waited until Harry parked and went inside his building.

Billy paid off the cabbie and walked home.

The following night Harry went to the Sox game with a couple of old friends, and Billy was free to wander. He stopped in a small restaurant for a burger and thought of Millie and he saw the way things were about to happen, that he'd done precisely what he hoped he wouldn't do to her. He thought of Rita and shook his head.

On his way home he bought a paper. He stopped at a street corner to scan the headlines. As he did so, he caught a movement from the corner of his eye. A man was standing just a few feet away, and Billy was sure this man had come to a stop precisely when Billy had. Billy counted to three and turned, just in time to see a figure disappear up the street into a group of people.

He told himself not to let his imagination run away with him. Without actually seeing the man, there was nonetheless something about him, something about the way he held himself, that told Billy the man had been following him. Though he could not have sworn to it in court, he was fairly certain the man had been Moncrief.

Oho, now we're getting to the interesting part.

Billy walked home faster, realizing for the first time that he himself might be in some danger. As he walked he experienced a curious feeling of relief, as though this new sense of peril freed him of other obligations, of the need to make decisions in his life. For now, he had something to concentrate on, something that had a prior claim on his attention.

He said nothing to Harry the next morning. He had, after all, not exactly seen Moncrief, it had just been an impression.

For most of the day Harry was unusually quiet. Doris went home sick after lunch, and Leo was off, so that there were just the two of them in the office. Several times Billy tried to get Harry talking, but Harry gave him short answers. Twice Billy directed comments to him, and Harry did not answer at first, then caught himself and laughed.

"Wool-gathering," Harry said at one point.

Toward the end of the day, Harry gave him an envelope for Sunny Carter and told him to take the rest of the day off.

"How about you?"

Harry indicated the files on the desk.

"I got some things to read through for a case I'm thinking about taking on. It'll take me a while to read through all this stuff."

Billy nodded and said goodnight. But he'd seen the label on one of the files Harry was looking through. It was a manila folder gone brown with age, not a new case. Billy would have said it was one of Harry's Kansas City files.

It was nearly eight when Harry emerged from the office. He went to his car and opened the door, then seemed to think better of it. For a moment he stood with his hands in his pockets, staring up the street. Then he seemed to come to some decision and began walking.

Billy followed on the far side of the street, and when they had gone a couple of blocks he understood where Harry was headed. When Harry was a half block from the accountant's apartment, he stopped and leaned against a car for a couple of minutes and had a smoke. Billy ducked into a doorway and waited him out.

At last, Harry walked down Dietrich's street. The accountant's building was at the far end of a corridor of maples planted so close together that they cast the street in darkness, like a green tunnel. He watched Harry in the distance and was just deciding whether to catch up and announce his presence when he saw the car roll by and pull up a few feet from Harry Strummer. He was already starting to move when the two men got out of the car.

Harry seemed to catch the movement out of the corner of his eye and was turning to face them. One of them had something in his hand, and he swung at Harry. The other tried to get behind him. The one with the weapon kept swinging it, striking Harry's upraised arms and then catching him across the head. Billy saw Harry's fedora fall to the sidewalk, and Harry now gave ground. The man behind him struck him, and as Harry turned to face him, the man landed a blow to Harry's face. He bent down, covering his head with his arms, and the two men both swung at him together.

Billy was running and yelling, and had made it halfway down the block before they saw him. He thought his chest would burst from the need to get at them. Harry was down on the ground now. He tried to sit and fell over. The two men looked at Billy, and for a moment it seemed that the one with the weapon was about to turn on him.

"Yeah, come on, Big Boy," he said, and charged them.

When he was twenty feet from them they turned and ran to their car. The one with the weapon was blond, and Billy had the odd notion that he knew this man. The second man was just slipping into the car when Billy got to him. The man was trying to pull himself into the car, and the other one was already hitting the gas. Billy threw all his weight into the car door and the door caught the passenger in the side of the head.

Billy heard the man groan and say "Oh, shit!" and he grabbed a handful of the man's shirt just as the car pulled away, laying rubber all the way to the next corner.

He went to Harry, who had gotten himself once more into a sitting position. People were now coming to their windows, and a woman was asking if anyone was hurt.

"No, we're okay," Harry said.

"They tried to rob him," Billy called out.

Harry slid back to a fence and pulled himself to his feet.

"You all right?"

"Just get me out of here," Harry said.

Billy put an arm around him and they walked back up toward Lincoln. Harry stopped at one point and struggled to light a cigarette. His fingers were swollen. He managed to get the smoke lit, then took a deep drag. He waved the hand holding the cigarette, peering through the smoke at Billy. He looked like a gargoyle.

"What are you doing here? No, I know what you're doing, you tailed me here."

"Yeah, me and two other guys."

"Nah, nobody tailed me. It's just another mugging in the big city, Kid."

"Right, and they just picked you out at random. 'Cause you look like a man of great wealth."

He surveyed the damage on Harry's face.

"Jesus, look at you, Harry."

Harry bled from both nostrils and a cut lip. There was another cut on his chin where he'd scraped the pavement, and he bled from a badly swollen ear. One eye socket was growing a plum and bore a small cut beneath it, as well.

"This is nothing. I was in Korea. I just need to sit down."

Harry wobbled backward and Billy led him to a staircase.

"Did you look this bad in Korea?"

Harry waved him off and smoked his cigarette and panted as though he'd run a great distance.

"Let's get you to a doctor."

"I don't need a doctor. For Christ's sake, I got into a fight. You never got banged up a little in a fight?"

"The one time I got banged up like you, they took me to a doctor. Come on."

Billy took Harry under one arm and lifted. Harry got up, grinned, made a show of puffing out his cigarette smoke, and then nearly fell over backward.

"Whoa," he said, then added, "I'm okay."

"Sure. C'mon, let's get you to a doctor or something."

"Hey, you don't even know where there is a doctor."

"We'll get a cab."

Harry leaned against him and looked up the street, squinting through the one eye that still worked. "No, listen, I know a—"

"—a guy, right? You know a guy?"

Harry smiled with one side of his face. "Of course I do."

NINETEEN

A Visit to the Vet

It took a few minutes to flag down a cab on Lincoln, and they tried to ignore the attention they were attracting. Several women looked in horror at the damage to Harry's face and frowned at Billy as if he were the villain of the piece. Billy tried to make his role clear by putting his arm around Harry's shoulders, but Harry shook him off with a "C'mon, Bill, cut it out."

A couple of blocks from the alley they reached Harry's "guy."

"This is it, Billy. I'll take it from here."

Billy frowned at the wide glass window filled with tanks of spectacular fish in gaudy colors.

"It's a pet store."

"Fish, actually, he just sells fish."

Billy stared at him, speechless.

"What? Hey, these are not just any fish, these are tropical fish, rare fish, they cost an arm and a leg, some of 'em." He gave Billy an imperious look. "And I know. I used to have a tank full of 'em. Somebody put a brick through it."

With difficulty, Billy told himself not even to try to imagine what manner of conflict entailed a brick into somebody's tank full of exotic fish and tried to focus on the true issue here.

"What are we doing at a pet store?"

Harry managed to fix him with a patient look from the good eye. "He's okay. He's a vet, for God's sake, they're *doctors*. C'mon."

With that, Harry pushed his way through the door and Billy followed. Inside, he found himself in a wide but cramped room filled with fish tanks, some of them huge. A dark-haired young woman was feeding fish, and as she turned she was saying that they were closing soon, but when she saw Harry's face, her voice froze in her throat.

She said "ohmigod" in a tiny voice.

Harry gave her a breezy wave and said, "It's all right, we're here to see Dr. White." Then he added, "We're friends of his."

The dark-haired girl nodded. As they passed her, Billy saw Harry give her a wink that would have frightened small children, and the girl mustered her confidence. She peered into his face.

"Are you all right, sir?"

Harry shrugged and said, "More or less. He back there?"

She nodded, and Harry made his way through the fish tanks to a door in the back of the store. Billy followed.

Harry knocked once on the door and then went in, calling out, "Hey, Les? Lester? You back here?"

A tall, extremely thin man emerged from an inner room with the sports section of the *Tribune*.

"Hello, Harry. How you been? Well," he said, squinting down at Harry's injuries, "I guess I know the answer to that." The thin man nodded at Billy, then ushered them into his inner office and offered them chairs.

"This is Billy, he works for me."

"Lester White. Pleased to meet you, Billy."

Billy shook the thin man's long hand, which managed to be both rough and clammy at the same time and did nothing to reassure him that here was a man to address Harry's injuries.

The two older men exchanged the news of people they knew in common, bitched about the weather, laughed over the Cubs and the Sox, and except for a quick dabbing at the cut eye with a small towel, the man called Lester seemed oblivious to the extent of Harry's trouble. As they spoke, Lester White glanced at Harry's injuries, but seemed intent on ignoring them, as though he feared being impolite. For a time, Billy watched them and kept his silence, suppressed a growing irritation as well, and when Lester looked his way and smiled, Billy saw his opening.

"So you're some kinda veterinarian?"

Lester nodded and smiled. "Yeah, young fella, I'm some kinda veterinarian."

"That works on fish?"

Lester's smile lost a little of its luster, but he nodded. "That's about the size of it, I guess. My patients are fish."

Something in the man's patience ate at Billy, that and this odd lack of concern for Harry's condition. They should be on their way to a hospital now. With an actual doctor.

"Didn't know that was a full-time gig. I mean, I thought when they got sick they just floated sideways and you took 'em out and flushed 'em down the toilet."

"Well, that's one way to deal with a sick fish, I guess. It wouldn't be my first choice, though. There are treatments. Some of the things that kill a fish are very simple: fungus, bacteria, things like that."

Billy shifted in his chair and tried to come at this another way, and Lester White read his look.

"But what you really want to know is whether a guy that makes his living tending to sick fish can help your friend Harry here."

"That's about it. I mean, shouldn't we take him—"

"A worthy question."

"He's good, Billy. He can fix more than a sick fish." Harry tried to wink again. Then he gave it up and sighed. "I've been here before, Bill."

To Harry, the vet said, "Don't wink, you're just pulling at that tissue." Then he turned to Billy and gave him a look of calm appraisal. "But it is a valid question, my friend."

"I wanted to take him to the emergency room."

Harry shook his head, but Lester held up a hand for silence. "Well, that might still be necessary."

"No way," Harry said.

"Your young friend is concerned about you." Lester's look invited Billy to deny this concern. Then he turned back to his patient.

"Well, let's see what we've got here."

Lester came up with a small penlight and leaned over Harry, shining it first in one eye, then the other. He made mumbled sounds to himself, said "uh-huh," and "mmmm," then told Harry to open his shirt. He produced a stethoscope from nowhere, and Billy bit back the impulse to ask if he'd ever used it on a fish.

"And, no, I've never used this on a fish," Lester White said.

"I don't need all this, Les."

"How would you know?" Lester asked calmly.

Lester listened, thought for a moment, and peered again at the cuts. Then he allowed himself to lean back against his desk.

"No concussion, heart sounds normal—that in itself is an achievement, for I am aware of what passes for Harry's habits of sleep and diet. And we won't even bring up his smoking."

"I cut down, way down, just a couple a day."

"You smell like smoke."

"We had a fire in the office."

Lester ignored him, peering into Harry's face as though he'd never seen one quite like it.

"All right. So we'll take care of these other things. Somebody else can take care of your lungs." He shot a sudden look at Billy.

"Do you smoke?"

"Not anymore. I quit. And I never smoked like him."

"Gee, thanks for the support, Bill," Harry muttered.

Lester crossed the room and rummaged in a small chest of drawers, coming back with a box of bandages, alcohol, swabs, and a bottle of iodine. He called out to the girl in the store.

"Tracy? Bring me some ice from the cooler."

Lester pulled his desk chair close to Harry's and took Harry by the chin, turning his face from side to side.

"I'm not even going to ask what you did to get your face to look like this. But I will say you might want to retire from boxing. You're too old for this nonsense, Harry."

"There were two of them."

Lester shrugged and continued to examine Harry's injuries. A moment later the girl came in with a plastic bucket full of chipped ice. Her sense of professionalism had overcome her suspicion, and she gave Harry and Billy a self-assured smile after setting the ice on Lester's desk. She gave Billy a second look, and he resisted the impulse to check out her legs as she left.

With effort, Billy refocused on the "vet" and his work. Now Lester was all business, and silent except for more of his odd murmuring to himself. As Billy watched him, he became aware of the sounds of the clock on the back wall, the Clark Street traffic, his own breathing.

Lester cleaned Harry's cuts with alcohol and the swabs, at one point poking around in the gash on Harry's nose and muttering with quiet exasperation, "You managed to get dirt in there already." Then he painted the cuts with iodine, applied butterfly bandages to hold the cuts together, and held a towel filled with ice up to Harry's bruised eye. As he sat there holding the ice to Harry's face, Lester looked around his office and sang in a surprisingly sweet voice.

"Blue Moon, you saw me standing alone, without a dream in my heart—"

Billy looked around the room and wondered again at Harry Strummer's choice in attending physicians, and when he looked back Lester was still holding the icepack to Harry's face, but he was watching Billy.

"You're right to be nervous about who's taking care of your friends. But I worked with an old fight doctor as a kid, and I paid attention."

"I didn't mean anything. I just never met a vet who worked on, you know, just fish."

"I used to work on them all. Worked on horses in Oklahoma for a time—excellent patients, by the way, very stoic—then I had your basic small animal practice. Got tired of that." He put down the icepack and dabbed at a cut with a cotton swab, then stuck the swab between his teeth. As he peered at Harry's last cut he went on talking through his clenched teeth.

"Hard to take that, sometimes, hard to listen to the pups whine. They're pitiful when they're in pain. Now your tropical fish, he's got lower expectations in life, he asks very little, makes no complaint.

Pretty much the ideal patient, in terms of strain on the practitioner."

Harry grinned through his patches. "His patients keep getting smaller."

Lester nodded and looked at Billy. "Next, I'm going for krill."

"Krill? That's what whales eat, right?"

"Very good. Yeah, that's what I'll work on when I get tired of the sad look in the fishes' eyes."

Lester sank back in the chair and examined his work. "I guess you'll live." He turned to Billy. "You know, Billy, eventually we take on the characteristics of the people we hang around with. You keep tagging along with our friend Harry and you'll look like this someday."

"Wouldn't be the first time."

Lester nodded. "That's exactly what I thought," and Billy had a sudden urge to put his hand over the scar above his eye.

"Speaking of health," Harry said, leaning forward. "You need to eat more, Lester. We've talked about this before. And you got no color, no color at all. You need to get out in the fresh air."

Lester laughed noiselessly. "Harry Strummer, still bleeding, wants to tell me how to be healthy. Harry Strummer who comes into my office with his face bashed in wants me to take better care of myself." He looked at Billy and raised his eyebrows, inviting him to take part in this drollery.

"Aha, yeah, but here's the thing," Harry said. "I don't always look like this. You always look the way you look, like a—whaddya call it, a cadaver. You look like a cadaver. You ought to eat better, get out in the fresh air, chase girls."

"It so happens I'm chasing a girl, Harry. First time in years."

Harry blinked in surprise. "Really, Les?"

"Her name is Betty. You know, the first girl I ever went out with was named Betty. I've come full circle forty years later."

"Well, all right, then, that's a start."

Lester nodded, pleased. He leaned forward to examine his work and nodded again.

"Let me know if things start to hurt, or if those cuts don't close up. I was gonna stitch up that one under your eye but it ought to close."

"What do I owe you?"

Lester grinned. "I ought to pay you just for the entertainment value of your visits. It's interesting to work on a person. I get surprisingly little feedback from the fish. Buy me a drink sometime at Kelly's."

"Thanks, Lester. And good luck with that girl you're chasing."

Lester's face went serious. "She thinks I'm witty. How about that?"

He shook his head at the wonderment of it all and waved them out of his office.

On the street again, Harry hitched up his trousers and regarded the street contentedly, as though his face were unmarked and his prospects were promising. Billy watched him and shook his head.

"I need some of what you have," Billy said.

"Boundless charm?"

"Nah, that's not it. It's something else. It's like you never—I mean, none of this fazes you, right?"

Harry gave him a long look. "Just because I don't cry about it doesn't mean I like it. But there's things you can do something about and things you can't. I don't waste time whining about the ones that are out of my control."

"Like this?" Billy indicated the damage to Harry's face.

"Yes, like this."

Harry looked away and fished in his pockets for a smoke. Billy moved around to get a better look. In an odd way, Lester's repairs called attention to the wounds—Harry's face was a mass of swelling, of darkened cuts and patches and butterfly bandages.

"Jesus Christ," Billy said. And as he thought about the attack, he thought he saw something now that he'd missed.

"I'll tell you what else I think."

"Oh, yeah? What? You're full of opinions tonight."

"This was no mugging."

"No, huh?" Harry turned to face him, irritated or amused,

perhaps a little of both.

"No."

"You're sure? You got it all figured out? Smart guy." A flash of anger came into Harry's eyes, and he pointed the unlit cigarette at Billy as though he were about to launch into something.

I'm sure now, Billy thought.

Then Harry Strummer seemed to catch himself, and he smiled. He paused to make a show of lighting the cigarette and took his pose, a hand in his pocket, the other one ready to wave the cigarette as his prop.

"Okay, so…enlighten me with your theory."

"I saw how they came out of the car at you."

"I'm not even going to ask why you were there in the first place."

"I followed you, all right? I was, you know, concerned."

Harry sighed and shook his head. He started to protest and Billy held up a hand.

"Let me finish. You're walking down the street and they're following you in the car, I know they were. They came scrambling out of the car after you. It was you they were after, I think, not some mark they were hoping to find."

"What for? Why would anybody be after me?"

"You tell me," Billy said.

"No, you're the one making speeches here. Okay, Sam Spade. So what's your conclusion?"

"This was somebody who wanted you hurt. Or this was a message from somebody, one or the other."

Passersby moved quickly, but Billy saw them give Harry a long look. Several shot a quick look at Billy, as though this fight might still be in progress. Harry blew smoke out and looked at him and seemed unaware that he was a street attraction.

"Not bad," he said finally.

"So which is it?"

"Both, maybe."

Harry smoked and touched a finger to one of his cuts, looking for blood. Then he looked around at the street. He had said what he was going to say about this.

It struck Billy then that Harry was holding something back, that he knew exactly what all this was about. Billy saw there was no coincidence that this occurred on the street where the dead accountant had lived. But he was sure Harry would say no more.

He looked up the street, and when he looked back at Harry, the other man was watching him with a half-smile.

"But I know this—I would have gotten hurt a lot worse if you hadn't been there."

"Sorry I didn't get down the block faster."

"You did fine. Did I hear you hit one of them?"

"Caught him with the car door. In the head, I think."

"Good. Too bad it was so dark on that street," Harry said, fishing.

"I didn't see faces."

Harry nodded.

They flagged down a cab and took it back to where Harry's car was parked, then Harry drove him home.

As he went to bed that night, he thought of how close they'd come to doing real damage to Harry. They could have killed him, he told himself, and it was planned, not random, not two kids out getting their kicks. Less than a week ago, a man he had watched on the street had been murdered, and tonight the same might have happened to Harry. Chicago suddenly seemed a darker place. He remembered running toward the fight and hoping desperately that he'd get there in time, remembered his urgent need to land a blow. And it came to him then that in the middle of the fight he'd had the impression that he knew one of Harry's two assailants. Not that he'd seen him clearly, but there had been something else.

In the morning, in that half-awake state just before wakefulness, it came to him.

"Harris" he said aloud. Harris, the awkward client who had seemed to be casing the office.

"Well, now," Billy said.

TWENTY

Kansas City Story

When he was fully awake on Saturday morning, Billy realized that he'd left his paycheck at the office. Harry had once told him that the cleaning crew—two short, stumpy women from Romania—were beyond reproach, but still Billy raced down to Wells Street, a bus ride and a long sprint.

Even before he opened the door he understood that someone was inside the office. He stood to one side, hoping not to be seen through the pebbled glass of the door, and waited, motionless. The person inside the office sighed, cleared his throat, coughed. Billy turned the doorknob and pushed the door open.

Harry Strummer sat at his desk, smoking. The shades were drawn, the lights were off, and the office was nearly dark. Harry hadn't turned on the air conditioner or opened a window yet, so the air was blue with smoke.

"Hello, Bill," he said. "What brings you in on a Saturday? You looking for overtime?"

Billy closed the door behind him. "I left my check here."

Harry peered over at Billy's desk. "I see the envelope sticking out from under the blotter. Those girls take care of us, Bill."

Billy went over and retrieved his check. He stood there, wondering what to do next.

Harry ground out his cigarette and got up to open the shades and one of the windows. He waved fresh air in, then paused for a moment and looked out at the street.

"A cool morning in summer. I like the streets early on a Saturday morning. The whole town is having trouble recovering from Friday. Downtown, you can walk down the middle of State Street or LaSalle without a car hitting you, there's nothing happening yet. I really love it. I love the mornings in the Big Town."

In the raw light through the window, Harry's face looked puffy and oddly discolored, the bruising purple and yellow. He stretched and groaned.

"Still a little sore in places."

"Are you all right?"

"Oh, I'm fine, I'm just a little too old for all this stuff. Your recovery time is longer when you're older. It's why football players and boxers quit before they're forty. Your body can't recover. I'm fine, though."

"That's not what I mean. Why are you here, sitting in the dark on a Saturday morning?"

"It's something I do sometimes. It's a good place to come and, you know, think. If I walk around—like on a beautiful day like this, I'm distracted. But here there's usually nobody to come and bother me, no clients, and the phone might as well be dead."

Billy nodded and said, "Well," and told himself he should leave. He watched Harry plop himself down and put his face in his hands for a moment.

"I don't think you're all right. Not really."

"I can take care of it. I can handle this."

Billy sat on the edge of Harry's desk and looked down at him. "You're sitting here in the dark trying to figure all of this out. Dietrich and what happened to you. I'm thinking you already know what this is all about."

"Well, it's got nothing to do with you, or with the agency, or with—anything. It's just something personal. I've got to deal with it." Harry lit a new cigarette off the old one and blew smoke into the air.

"I've got all morning."

"You need to just forget about this."

"Maybe, but I don't think I'm gonna."

"A man has a right to privacy about some things."

"I don't know anything about that."

Harry gave him a dismissive look and began to shuffle the papers on his desk. Billy noted that one of the items was the discolored folder.

"Is that one of your Kansas City files?"

"What? This? Oh, yeah. Just looking through these things again. Probably not the healthiest thing for me to do, given the demise of the late Mr. Dietrich."

Harry shook his head. After a while he said, "I'm tired. I think I'm gonna have to go home and take a nap. I been here a while. You got a nice weekend planned? How's that girl—Millie?"

"She's fine. I mean—what I really want to talk about is all this other stuff."

Harry looked at him and puffed at his cigarette, and just when it seemed that Harry had dismissed the conversation, he said, "Sit down. I mean on a chair. Get off my desk. If you're sitting up higher than me I feel like I'm talking to the nuns back in school. They hovered, that was always their advantage, they hovered over you and you knew if you smarted off to them, you'd get nailed. Anyway, you're right. I've been trying to make sense of certain things that have happened."

"All of this. And this guy Moncrief."

"Yeah. And other things. Like the fact that I've had people tailing me—well, you know about that. And watching the office, I think."

"And Moncrief is connected with Kansas City."

Harry held out his hands in a gesture of helplessness. "I wish I knew. I never saw him before in my life. If he's connected with that, I don't know how. Besides, that was a long time ago, Jesus, twenty years almost. And this Moncrief is a young guy."

"I didn't tell you this before, but I saw him again. I'm not real sure but I think it was him. Just a few days ago. He was reading a paper over there in the park, but I had a feeling he was watching me."

"Interesting."

"And I've got something else. The two guys who jumped you, I couldn't see them because that street is so dark. I couldn't see faces. But you know how you can recognize somebody from, like, other things—the way they move, their outline, their gestures? I wouldn't swear to this, but I'm pretty sure the guy who worked you over with the club was Harris. Couldn't see his face, but it was him."

"Harris, huh? Our reluctant client who gave us the phony name. Well. That's interesting, Bill." Harry thought for a moment. "That was a month ago. They've been working this out for a long time."

Billy waited for more. Harry shook his head. "And, no, I don't know Harris, either. No idea. Never seen him before."

"So for starters, why don't you tell me about Dietrich, at least. I'm not trying to pry. I mean, they killed the guy and they might have killed you, and I should at least know about that."

"I'm not sure they were supposed to kill me. But all right. You want my biography, huh? Okay. In Kansas City I worked with another guy, Randy Brierly. It was his agency. After a while I went out on my own and he sent me business, and I was doing okay. I thought I was going to have a, you know, a thriving concern. And then I took on this case. A prosperous business owned by two guys who'd known each other since childhood. One of them hires me because he thinks his partner is skimming money. Money's disappearing left and right, and he says he thinks the partner is getting ready to jump ship and disappear. So I got involved and investigated. and what I found was that the partner had something going on with my client's wife. There was money missing, yeah, but the real heart of the matter was the partner and the wife. And so I had to tell all this to the man who hired me and it all went south from there. I mean, I'm pretty sure he knew all along. I think that was part of what he had in mind, I think he really had me out there for that. He just needed to have proof."

Harry took a long, slow look around the room. After a moment, Billy asked, "So what happened?"

"My client confronted his partner. They fought in the office, where they apparently kept a gun. During the fight—well, nobody knows for sure what happened, but the police thought the partner shot my guy, not a life-threatening wound, and my client wrestled the gun away and killed his partner. He then drove home bleeding all over his car and killed his wife, and then he shot himself."

Harry lit a new cigarette, and now had two going at once.

"While all this is happening, Dietrich, the accountant, he splits, he's gone—with the money, that part was true, that the firm was hemorrhaging money, but it wasn't the partner. It was Dietrich. So my case results in three people dead. It made me physically ill. The violence of it. It's still the only case in my life where someone was killed. I left Kansas City right after that."

"And this Dietrich, he got away with the money."

"Yeah, he got away—until now."

"And Moncrief? How would he be connected?"

"Don't know. I'll tell you this—I'm certain I never met this guy."

"Could it be the guy's kid?"

"No, no, the man had no kids. Too bad, too. He was a guy who was good with kids, gregarious, involved in charity things. That kinda guy." He looked at Billy. "Now you know what I know."

"Oh, I doubt that. But it's more than you've been giving me."

Harry laughed. "When I've got nothing, I'm always willing to share."

The smile faded and Harry looked at him, then looked away. Billy sensed that he was trying to decide whether to tell him something. Finally, Harry turned to him and made a small one-handed shrug.

"There's one other thing I didn't tell you. Didn't tell anyone. When I was in Dietrich's place—well, he had my card."

"So?" And then he understood. "Ah. I get it."

"Yeah. I never gave Dietrich my card. But I gave it to Moncrief. And when I saw it there, it was clear to me that the cops were supposed to find it. So I lifted it."

"So this guy was setting you up."

"It would seem so. Now you've really got what I have. That's all of it."

Billy made a little salute with the pay envelope and left. When Harry finally emerged, Billy was across the street in a doorway. He waited and watched until Harry got safely into his car and then left. And late that night when Harry Strummer came out of his apartment building, Billy was there again, standing in a gangway up the street, watching him. He followed Harry to a small restaurant on Clark Street and waited down the block in a tavern while Harry ate. He watched Harry make small talk with the short Mediterranean-looking man at the register. A while later, he saw Harry go into a tavern on the corner. Billy changed his hiding place so that he had a view of Harry at the bar, chatting with the bartender and another man. He hung back in the doorway and waited, moving from one foot to another on tired legs. He looked around at the street traffic and turned back to the tavern just as Harry was waving to the bartender. Just as Harry came out, a bus went by. When the bus had gone, so had Harry.

Shit. He made me.

On Monday morning, Billy was chatting with Doris when a uniformed messenger came into the office with a brown envelope for Harry. They continued their talk, but both of them watched as Harry tipped the messenger and stared eagerly at the return address. Leo put down a lock he had been playing with and watched.

Oblivious to his audience, Harry slit open the envelope with his Swiss Army knife and took out several photocopied pages. Two of them appeared to be newspaper pages. For a while Harry read through the file, frowning, and then stopped. He took out his reading glasses and scanned the page again, then looked off into space.

"Now I got it all," he said to no one in particular.

"So?" Doris said.

"I almost missed it. Because it's buried. But it's there."

"What's there?" Leo asked.

Billy said, "Moncrief. Right?"

Harry nodded and held up the paper. "Yeah, he's here. He's here, he's in a whaddyacallit, a parentheses. Take a look."

Billy moved over and picked up the paper. It was the obituary of Theodore (Ted) Hannah. Written by someone familiar with Mr. Hannah, the obit laid out his long years of hard work and community service, his many favorite projects and local charities. It reviewed the history of his company and spoke of his service in the Pacific with the Navy during World War II. It described his love of fly-fishing, golf, and boating. At the very end of the obituary, Mr. Hannah's family members were listed, among them his mother and two sisters, his late brother Donald, beloved sister-in-law Donna (Moncrief), and Hannah's "loving nieces Terry and Bridget, and loving nephew David."

"Found him yet?"

"Yeah. The—what? Nephew? His nephew. So that's him."

"Yeah." Harry's gaze drifted. "On his wall he had pictures of them, the three kids. Because he didn't have any of his own. And they had no father. So. A boy with no father, but he's got this uncle that's like a father. That's it."

"All these years later?"

"Well, he was a kid. Besides, there's no time limit on revenge. There's no statute of limitations for anger."

"This just doesn't make sense to me."

Harry looked at him for a moment, then said, "Who says it has to? You've seen this guy. You've seen his eyes." He spread the pages on his desk and tilted his head, frowning. He pointed to one of the pages. "And I bet that's it."

He shoved the paper toward Billy. It was an obituary, for Donna Moncrief Hannah, dated a little over six years earlier.

Harry seemed to recall something. "Something I been going over in my head. Might have nothing to do with anything, but a while back—this must have been around five, six years ago, I got a call from Randy Brierly. He said he got a call from a guy, and the guy didn't want to give his name. He wanted to know the whereabouts of Harry Strummer. Said he was an old friend."

"*An old friend,* right. An old friend would have given his name, right?"

"I think so. Anyway, Randy's been around the block a few times, so he tells him I moved West—L.A. That's it, just the one phone call, but every once in a while I think about it. Who was trying to find me back then?"

"So now what?"

"Now we should call the cops, that's what." Doris glared at Harry.

"To tell them what? What have I got that connects him with anything they'd be interested in?"

"He killed Dietrich."

"Maybe. But he's smart enough that maybe he used those two punks. Or maybe he's not in it at all. It's just coincidence."

On the far side of the room Leo shook his head slowly, but said nothing.

"You could have the cops watch him. Put a tail on him."

Harry gave him a sarcastic smile. "Watch him where? We don't even know where he is. And I think this is a smart guy. I think he'll go under for a while if he has to, lay low, you know? Nah. I'll handle this my own way," Harry said, carefully looking at no one in particular.

Harry went to the window. After a few moments he nodded to himself, stepped back, clapped his hands together and said, "All right. That's good."

"There's nothing good about it," Doris said. "You're in danger."

"Maybe so. But I'm on my home turf and I'm not without, you know, resources."

She turned and began folding a page to stuff into an envelope. She sat with her back stiff and her jaw clenched, and Billy would have left her alone. But Harry didn't.

"For instance, I've got you, Hon."

"Do you?" Doris said through gritted teeth. "For how long?"

• • •

In the afternoon, Billy went out in Harry's car looking for another runaway, this time a husband on a bender. He spent two hours in the saloons near the ballpark, crowded now that the Cubs had come back from a disastrous road trip, and finally thought he had a line on the place where the man was holed up. He stopped for a quick lunch and returned to the office. At the landing just below the office he stopped and waited, silent, on the staircase. He heard two voices raised, both of them speaking at once. He heard Harry start to say something and then Doris's voice cut through, sharp and angry.

"Goddam it, don't play around with this, it's not a game."

"Oh, no kidding! A guy is dead. It's not a game, Doris? Really?"

"You're gonna make a game out of it. A contest. I know you."

"What am I supposed to do?" Harry said.

"Leave it alone. Go wait it out. Go somewhere."

"It'll just be waiting when I come back."

"Don't be stupid about this. Let somebody else handle this asshole."

"No. I think I know what I want to do here. I want to settle it."

For a long moment Billy heard nothing. He held his breath on the staircase and waited. Then he heard Doris again, her voice softer, tired. Resigned.

"If I asked you to do this for me—"

"Don't do that. You have to let me do this my way."

Another moment of silence, then the sound of something being slammed down on a desk and Doris muttering "shit" in a tone of utter surrender. Billy counted to ten and then went in.

"Hey, Bill," Harry said. "Did we find this Kearns?"

"Think so. Hey, Doris."

"Hi, Hon," she said without looking up. After a while she made a quick gesture to her face, wiping something from her cheek.

"So what do you have, Bill?"

"I think he has a room at the YMCA by Lincoln and Belmont. And he drinks at a dark old tavern by the El station. I got to meet the owner—an old guy named Johnnie. Says our guy drinks there from around ten to about midnight, at which time he goes to sleep on the bar."

"Nice work. I know that saloon. The old guy's from Bosnia."

"That's Yugoslavia, right?"

"Ah, there's that American educational system at work."

"So what about this thing with Moncrief? What are we going to do?"

"*We?* We nothing. This is my problem, I'll handle it."

Billy opened his mouth to protest but Harry held up his hand to stop him.

"I don't know anything yet. But I'm getting some ideas. When I can tell you more, I will."

For a moment, Harry looked down at the blotter as though trying to read sense from the chaos of his old scribbling. He looked up and saw Doris staring at him.

"I know what you're going to do," she said. "Don't. Let this go."

Harry shrugged. "It might not let me go. I might not be able to let it go."

Billy saw her start to ask another question, then she thought better of it. With a shake of her head, she went back to work, and her anger came off her in waves like heat.

He looked back at Harry just as Harry looked up. "I just have to figure this out, that's all. Now I've got something to work with."

• • •

Sometime after sunset he went to Millie's apartment. He took the longest way possible and rehearsed what he would say, at one point ducking into an alley to say his lines out loud. He wondered if he would sound as foolish to her as he did to himself. He took the rest of the way at a long, slow walk, and by the time he reached her building, he was nauseated.

She met him at the downstairs door, a wary look in her eyes.

"Hello, Billy."

"We need to talk."

She stepped back and led him up the stairs. "I guess so," she said under her breath.

Billy sat on her sofa, and Millie perched at the edge of the chair across from him. He would have sworn she knew what was coming. Twice he tried to start, but stopped, feeling that there were no words to make sense of all of this.

"You want a cup of coffee—while you get yourself together?"

"No, thanks. I'm not—together. And I'm not gonna be. I just have to say these things outright."

She nodded and sat back, and he began, he told her all of it, why he'd come to Chicago, the many nights and days he'd spent looking for Rita. And as he told it, he felt foolish but not nearly as silly as he thought. There was a certain mooncalf logic to it all. Once he looked up and saw that she was shaking her head slowly at him, at his story. Her eyes were wet and he knew his were as well, and he feared he wouldn't be able to finish his story before he started to cry.

When he was finished, he made a gesture of helplessness with both hands.

Millie's cheeks were wet and her nose was red, but she stayed composed. She wiped her cheek and nodded. "That's quite a story, Billy Boy. You poor thing. And nobody knew any of this? Why you're here, or anything else about this girl?"

"No."

She tried on a small smile. "Not even Harry the Wizard who knows so much about people?"

"Not even him."

"That's not good, it's not healthy to have nobody know what's going on in your heart. Somebody should know what's in a person's heart. You're a solitary boy, Billy, and that's not good. But I'll tell you a little secret—I knew all along." She held up a hand. "And I could tell you weren't happy with me. With just me. With, you know, us."

"That wasn't it," Billy began, but didn't know what else he could say to that. He had realized he was in the midst of a familiar moment. All his life he'd suffered these moments, these times in life when there were elemental things to say and he was met once more with this crippling inability to express himself. It was as though his words and ideas were dammed up inside him and he could not force them out. At least he was telling her the truth. That had to count for something.

"I was happy. I was. It's just that—"

Millie made a little shrug. "Sometimes in the middle of a sentence your eyes would kind of lose focus, you'd be watching something behind me or somewhere across the street, and I knew you were looking for somebody at those times. I just didn't know it was a *particular* somebody. I just thought you were looking for somebody more interesting to you."

"No. And I was always happy with you." He met her gaze. "That's true, that part. Maybe I was watching the street because from the time I got here, from the moment I got off the bus downtown, that's what I did, I looked for her. In my sleep, even. I dreamt about looking for her. So it was like second nature. I never stopped looking for her."

"And now you've found her. That's kinda remarkable. What are the chances?"

She gave him a long look that was plain to read—*And she's what you want.*

"I'm sorry. About all of this. I never meant—"

She shook her head and seemed small and frail to him. "It's all right, Hon. It's actually my fault. It's what I do, I attract unhappy men, or I find them, either one. I find unhappy men and I think I'm gonna make them happy, and I don't. I can't. Women do that, we tell ourselves we can make you all happy. I've actually said that to a man, 'I know I could make you happy if you gave me a chance.'"

"You probably could."

"No. You can't make an unhappy man happy. You got to do that your own self, Hon. And right now I think you're pretty far from that."

In the ensuing silence, Billy fought for words. "I feel stupid," he said.

"Makes two of us. You've had another girl on your mind all the time we've been together. A girl with a head on her shoulders has to know when she's with a fella who's not gonna work out for her. Or she ought to. Most of the time you try not to see it, or if you do, you ignore it and tell yourself it's gonna turn into something. But I'm not stupid." She shrugged. "I'm surprised it lasted this long."

He turned away to compose himself. When he looked back, she was watching him, dry-eyed and calm now. In other circumstances, he might have said she looked faintly amused.

"It's just what I expected, Billy. No more, no less. I really don't have a good record with *gentlemen*."

"I just—people get lonely," he began.

And Millie said, "So you do. So you do, Billy boy. I sure do know about that. It's all right, Hon."

Billy sat there for a moment longer, and when she said nothing further, he got up and went to the door. She got there first, opened it for him, and leaned against the doorway as he went out into the hall.

"You take care, Billy. And good luck with your person. This lady."

"Thanks," he said. He began to say "I'm really sorry" and then understood it would be the wrong thing. "You take care, too. Millie."

As he walked away, he realized that this was one of the few moments when he'd said her name.

TWENTY-ONE

Tactics

Billy slept badly and woke before the sun came up, feeling exhausted and light-headed. He recalled feeling this way as a child after his parents had one of their all-night battles. He got up, certain that he would not get back to sleep, and went out for a long run through his neighborhood. As he ran, he thought of Millie and what he'd just done.

On his way in to work, Billy nearly trampled an old man in a ragged Army jacket picking up a dime from the sidewalk just outside the office building.

"Sorry," Billy said.

The old man grinned at him, his face framed by a knit cap.

"Found ten cent," he said holding up the dime.

"Here's a buck to go with it, now you've got enough for a—" He paused, unsure what a dollar and ten cents would buy.

"A hamburg and a beer!" the old man said, and laughed. He held Billy's gaze for just a moment, and Billy would have said there was something there—amusement or recognition. Then the old man nodded and left.

Billy watched as the old guy shuffled away, stopping to rummage through a trash can on the corner. He had the odd feeling that he'd spoken to the old man before.

In the office, Leo was getting ready to go out.

"And take my car," Harry was saying. Leo nodded and left.

"Hey, kid," he said to Billy on his way out.

"What's up?"

"Leo's gonna police the area for us. While we do some other things."

"*We*? As in you and me?"

"And other people."

Harry's gaze moved to Doris's empty desk. He frowned. "She didn't come in today?"

"Nah. Says she's got the flu."

When Billy said nothing, Harry added, "She's pissed at me. I think she'll be in later. But right now we have other things to focus on. We're gonna use some of our—"

"Resources?"

"Ah, you've been listening after all. Yeah." He went to the window and said, "You and I are gonna go for a walk."

Half a mile from the office, near the spot where Lincoln came to an end at Clark Street, there was a museum.

"We going on a field trip?"

"No. We have a business meeting in the vicinity. But you ought to check out this place. That's the Historical Society. You need to know about your city if you're gonna live here."

"Not sure I am."

"No, huh?" Harry said absently. Then he gave Billy the look of a guy with inside information. Billy refused to bite.

They walked for a while along the edge of Lincoln Park, to a place near a horseshoe pit where a couple of gray-haired men were tossing shoes and laughing. Close to the sidewalk was a huge boulder with a bronze plaque. The boulder was badly chipped, as though someone had gone at it with a sledgehammer. Harry pointed to the plaque.

"See that? The last survivor of the Boston Tea Party is buried near here somewhere, but they lost him."

"How?"

"This used to be a cemetery. They had to move it, health concerns. Along the way they lost track of some of the graves."

"So there are dead people in Lincoln Park?"

"More than you'd think. Every time they have to lay pipes or dig up part of the park, they come up with human remains. And there's an actual tomb back there on the other side of the museum. They couldn't move that."

Harry looked around for a moment, wiped off a bench, and said, "Let's have a seat."

"Who are we meeting?"

Harry looked up the street to where a homeless man was peering into the gutter. He nodded toward the man.

"This gentleman here."

As though on cue, the homeless man turned and grinned, and Billy saw that it was the same man he'd given a dollar to.

"This guy? I know him. I gave him a buck this morning."

"Good boy. He's a friend of mine. Hello, Babe."

Harry got up and shook hands with the newcomer, who patted him on the shoulder and then seemed to notice Billy.

"Hey, Kid. I know this kid, Harry. He's got a good heart. Gave me my lunch money."

"Take a load off."

They sat on the bench, and Harry made small talk with the man called Babe. Billy listened and tried to ignore Babe's potent smell, a combustible mix of body odor, old cotton, and smoke. And garlic—for some reason the old guy smelled of garlic. He wore a few weeks' growth of white beard that reached nearly to his eyes, and crumbs of various types had collected there.

After they chatted for a time about the weather, the misfortunes of the baseball teams, Babe's health, and Harry's business, Harry said, "So what do you have for me, Babe?"

Babe said, "Well—" and then seemed to lose his train of thought. Billy shot a quick look at Harry, who just held up one finger for patience.

Babe fumbled for a moment with the various pockets in the Army jacket, fished out the makings of a cigarette, rolled one, and let Harry light it. He puffed on it, blew out smoke, and said, "Here's what I can tell you, Harry."

Babe spoke and Billy listened in wonder. The old man spoke

in a clear voice, as though long accustomed to public speaking or verbal reports, enunciating like an English professor.

"The individual in question is, as you suspected, watching you. Once he watched your office building from a doorway across the street. Another time he sat in a restaurant window and nursed a cup of coffee while he watched for you. Yesterday he sat in a car until a cop told him he was in a no parking zone. This morning—"

"I saw him. Pretended to be reading the paper, leaning on a light post." Harry gave Billy an amused look. "Who does that except in the movies?"

To Babe, he said, "So what can you tell me—"

"This gentleman's current lodgings are a room in a motel. The Motor Lodge up on LaSalle Street."

Harry laughed. "That's a mile and a half from here. How did you—"

"I had a hunch. Not that many places between here and downtown to rent a cheap room. And I've got lots of time on my hands."

"And the car?"

"Is a dark blue Chevy with the license number NX 2063."

"Nice work, Babe." Harry took a couple of bills out of his jacket. Babe held up his hand.

"That's not all, Harry. Couple days ago, he met a couple of guys in that place on North and Wells, cup of coffee, they did business. He gave them money. He didn't look happy, though. They looked like they were explaining something to him, and he wasn't happy. The one guy kept showing him his knuckles." Babe tilted his head slightly and nodded at Harry. "They do that to your face, Harry?"

"Might be. Maybe it was them. What did they look like?"

"Young guys with a strut. Think they're tough. One's got kinda long brown hair, and his partner has taken a different direction—crew cut down to his scalp, like a new Marine. That's the one who kept showing your guy his knuckles."

"When they were finished, your man looked really pissed off, he was talking to himself. The two young guys just kinda looked at each other and shrugged. I'm guessing he hired them to do a certain piece of work and they screwed it up." Babe looked from Harry to Billy. "The English have an expression for when you really screw something up badly. They say you made a Dog's Breakfast of it." Babe laughed and showed yellowed teeth. "I love them, they've taken the English language a lot of new places."

Billy shook his head. "You just watched them through all this and they never noticed?"

Babe shrugged. "Nobody notices street people unless they're asking you for money. We might as well be wallpaper."

Harry pushed the money at Babe again. "Thanks, my friend."

Babe tucked the bills inside his jacket. "The pleasure is mine, Harry. And the money doesn't hurt, either."

Babe gave Billy a small nod, and that look was still in his eyes, the glimmer of a private joke.

They watched the old man shuffle off in his enormous flat shoes. Billy reflected on the old man's amusing turn of phrase, heard once more Babe's reference to Moncrief's *"current lodgings,"* and wondered where he'd heard that phrase before. Harry said nothing. He watched the street traffic, hummed a few tuneless bars of an unrecognizable song. He was smiling.

"What? What is there about all this that you can smile about?"

A bird overhead made a cheerful noise. Harry looked up, squinted, and pointed.

"There, top branch, see him? A cardinal. That's the state bird of Illinois."

"You know about birds? I don't know anything about birds."

Harry shrugged. "Actually, I don't know much, but I like them. I see one I don't know about, I get frustrated, I want to know what it is." He watched the bird for a moment, then turned to Billy.

"We have a situation, Bill. Before, it was complicated, we didn't have that basic thing we need."

"I know, information. Knowledge."

"That's it. And now we do. We know he hired the guys who jumped me, and what's more important by far, we know where he is.

And 'cause we used an agent, old Babe there, Moncrief has no clue that we know about him. Everything just got a lot simpler."

"I don't see how."

Harry nodded. "You will."

In the office, Harry made a quick phone call. He asked two questions, then hung up the phone and sat for a moment staring at it.

"What?" Billy asked.

"There's no Moncrief registered at that motel. Which is what I thought."

Billy spent much of the next hour fussing over his report on the Aleksy brothers.

"Don't forget to put in for your expenses. You took them to lunch."

"It was just McDonald's."

"It was money, wasn't it? Make sure Doris gets it." Harry stared at Doris's desk for a moment, then walked over to the window as he had done half a dozen times in just the last hour. He smoked and leaned on the windowsill and peered down at the street.

Suddenly, he straightened up. He said, "Ah!"

He left the office, saying "I'll be back," over his shoulder.

Billy went to the window and saw Harry cross the street. On the far side, on Wells, a young man with black hair peered into a shop window. Harry stopped a few feet from the shop and waited. The kid seemed to freeze. He turned slowly, and Harry advanced toward him. At first the young man seemed uncomfortable, and from his body language Billy would have said he was making ready to bolt. Harry shook his head and held out his hand. They shook and Harry said something that changed the picture. The kid seemed to relax and a moment later he smiled. He was listening and Harry was talking, and then the dark-haired kid was nodding. Billy saw Harry slip the kid a bill and pat him on the shoulder.

Doris came in looking pale and sullen.

"You feeling better?"

"I'm not sick like that. I'm sick of everything." She came over to the window and looked out at Harry and the dark-haired boy.

"His name's Franco. He's a pickpocket. It figures that our fearless leader would be out talking to a thief."

The kid nodded, and when Harry left, the kid moved off.

When Harry came into the office, he fussed over Doris. She waved him off, saying "Don't irritate me any further, all right?" She turned on her radio and then looked at Harry.

"Franco's going to do something for you?"

"Maybe. We'll see."

"So you know a pickpocket," Billy said.

"A couple, actually."

"Do you know everybody?"

Harry smiled. "No, but that would simplify a lot of things."

"What's the word for that—'*consorting*'?"

"Actually, I'm just calling in a marker. He should do this job for me because he owes me."

Billy nodded. "That's it, consorting with known pickpockets."

Harry shrugged. "It's a complicated world. You know how people always say it's a jungle? Well, it is. And to navigate it, you need people, you need your—"

"I know, your *cadre*."

"There you go. That's right, you need your cadre."

Harry smiled and looked around the room, and the smile died young when he saw the unblinking look Doris was giving him.

TWENTY-TWO

The Private History of Billy Fox

The door opened and the dark-haired boy named Franco entered, shifty-eyed and shuffling his way to Harry's desk.

"Do any good?"

Franco broke into a grin as he produced a thin black wallet. "You could say that, Mr. Strummer."

Harry nodded toward Billy. "Billy Fox, this is Franco. Leo and Doris, you know already."

Franco said "Hey" to Billy, then nodded to Leo. He looked at Doris, who merely waved at him without looking up from her work. Billy suppressed a smile—good, old Doris making it clear that she had no time for common street thieves.

Harry looked inside the wallet. "And you got the cash. Good for you. Okay, Franco, thanks."

"Any time, Mr. Strummer." And then Franco was gone.

"Handy, a guy like that," Billy said. "So if a client doesn't want to pay you—"

He saw Harry's sly smile and didn't have to finish.

"Well, I guess that's one way of getting paid. So—is that whose wallet I think it is?"

"Indeed. Our friend Mr. Moncrief."

Harry spent a moment picking through the cards in Moncrief's wallet.

"So what is the point of this? You pay a pickpocket to lift the guy's wallet—how does that help, that you've got his wallet?"

"Harassment," Leo called out from his side of the office. He pointed a screwdriver at Billy. "Never underestimate the power of harassment."

"He's right," Harry said. "The point is harassment. Trying to distract him, bust up his focus." He held up the wallet. "I've got this Moncrief right here. I've got his IDs and some of his cash, he's out there stalking me and I've got him by the balls. When he stops barking at the moon and cursing the street punks of Chicago, he'll calm down a little and he'll figure it out. He'll know who's got his wallet."

Doris shook her head and pointedly turned on her radio. Harry winked at Billy and broke into a little dance, a couple of quick steps and then a little spin, and Billy started to laugh. Then he stopped. He'd seen this dance before.

An image came to him then of another dancer, a dancer in a dark place, a small strutting guy in the cavernous Greyhound Station, dancing to someone else's radio. Literally his first experience, his first moment in Chicago.

Billy watched Harry bopping in the office and he realized how much more he could recall about that time, the exhaust smells of the buses, the odor of onions frying, the oddly medicinal filtered-air smells. He could even remember what the dancer had looked like, a small man, surprisingly sure-footed but pie-eyed drunk in the middle of the day; dark jacket, glasses, a hat pulled down low over his face. Billy saw now in his mind's eye that the dancer had never really given him a good look at his face, dancing for the most part with his back to the people getting off the bus. The dancing man had gone on strutting his stuff, capering his way out of the Greyhound station and out onto the street. Even as he turned slightly, his face had still been in shadow. Billy thought of the things he'd not noticed at the time and told himself his training with Harry Strummer had changed the way he saw, the way he noticed the world around him. He thought again of the man with the hat pulled down over his face—carefully, Billy would have said now, and his stomach did a sudden flip. He sank back in the chair and the breath went out of him with a small gasp. It seemed beyond the range of possibility, of any possibility even in a wild, strange place like Chicago, but Billy knew who the dancer in the Greyhound tunnel had been.

He thought back to those first days in Chicago, living on the very edge of the place, desperately trying to get his bearings, to start a life. Another scene came back to him—the pool hall where Billy and the local hustler had tried to out-hustle one another. A man sitting along the wall watching them, nodding and smiling, a smallish man in dark glasses and a hat pulled low. He remembered making a fancy shot and the man nodding and smiling, and now, all these weeks later, he recognized the smile, the face, all of it.

"Jesus Christ," he muttered.

He felt the blood rushing to his face and stood up. His anger soon gave way to his utter confusion. Harry turned to face him and froze in mid-step.

Their eyes met, and Billy would have sworn at that moment that Harry was reading his mind.

"What's wrong, Bill?"

Billy glared at him but said only, "I've gotta go out for a minute. Clear my head."

"Sure. You're not coming down with something, I hope."

He turned to Doris, who was watching Billy, and Billy would have said she knew, too.

He walked for more than an hour and noticed nothing. At one point he walked off the curb against the light and was nearly struck by a bus. The driver gave him an angry blast on his horn.

Billy thought he had never been so confused. He grew light-headed, felt slightly faint. Eventually, he found himself at the beach and sank onto a bench to steady himself. He went over all that he could recall of his first days in Chicago, trying to pick Harry Strummer out from the shadows. Odd moments came back to him now—a man in dark glasses and a fedora leaning against a parked car as Billy came out of the Uptown flophouse, a short man ducking quickly into a doorway when Billy turned around. The odd feeling, early on, that he was being watched. He put things together, a moment here and there, and understood that from the very beginning, Harry Strummer had known who he was, where he was. That Harry Strummer had watched him from his first moment—literally—in Chicago. Other moments came back to him, scraps of conversation that seemed at the time to suggest that Harry knew something of Billy's obsessive search for Rita.

"But how?" he said, and the look of a woman passing by told him that he'd spoken aloud.

How and why?

He thought of his many conversations with Harry, his street-school sessions and tavern philosophizing, his adventures with Peerless Detective, and saw that none of it had been what he believed it to be. The whole thing was put on, stage-managed. Stage-managed, that was it. By his good friend and mentor, Harry Strummer.

For what possible reason?

The odd notion came to him that Rita was involved here, that somebody had put the word out that he was coming for her.

That made sense—but who would have dropped the dime on him?

His stomach turned, and he felt more foolish than he'd ever felt in his life.

At that moment he regretted giving up cigarettes, but a cigarette would have made him sicker. He considered his options. The simplest thing would be to march right out of this scenario they'd created for him, without a word, without looking back.

No, he would not do that. He would force Harry to explain it all to him. Then he would be on his way.

● ● ●

Billy paused at the top step as he heard Doris say, "You're going to tell him?"

"Yeah," Harry said.

"Now? With all this? Why now?"

"Why do you think?"

He opened the door to the office, and they both looked up as if he'd caught them making out on the desk.

"Oh, hey, Bill."

Billy remained in the doorway and met their eyes in turn, and he saw that Harry Strummer understood.

Harry glanced over his shoulder at Doris. "I think Bill's got something to say to us."

"Yeah, I do. I saw you. Those times when I first got into town."

Billy could see Harry deciding whether to feign confusion.

"First day here. A guy at the bus station, the dancing guy. And in the pool hall watching me hustle a hustler. That was you, too. And God knows how many other places. And what I need from you right now is no bullshit, just the truth if you think you can manage that. Why?"

Harry held up a hand, it seemed he was always holding up a hand to Billy now.

"I could tell you, Bill, but it would be better for you to read something first."

"Read what?"

Harry and Doris exchanged a quick glance, and she got up and went to the section of the files where the oldest case folders were. Without hesitation, she pulled out a folder and brought it over to Billy's desk.

"Here, Hon. You'll understand after you read this."

"You take your time with that. Doris and I will leave you alone for a little while. When we come back, I'll answer anything you want to ask me."

Billy looked from the folder to Harry and Doris. "How do I know anything you say to me will be the truth?"

"That's for you to decide. After you read that file."

Harry looked at Doris and made for the door. She grabbed her purse and followed, and they left without looking back.

Billy did not open the file at first but sat there staring at it, wondering what this could have to do with him. A file on—who? He shook his head, reached out a tentative hand and touched but did not pick up the folder. He remembered this folder with its green border, he'd surprised them one morning as they conferred over it. An old folder—he could see where the smoke and sunlight had darkened the long outer edge—and he wondered again what this all meant.

He flipped the folder over and saw that the filing tab said "Fox," as he had known it would. Finally, he opened the folder and spread out the documents inside. Most of them were in Harry's handwriting: his notes on a conversation with the client, carbon copies of his reports—carbons, not photocopies, so it went back some years—an unsigned letter from the client, her scrawl on lined paper gone brown with age at the edges. Billy looked at the date of the client's note: 1965.

"Old case," he said aloud, and heard the tension in his voice.

He asked himself why the tension, and answered, *because it's about me. Somehow. The year 1965, I would have been eleven years old. How can this have anything to do with me?*

"This is nuts," he told himself.

He glanced at the client's letter again, put it aside, troubled by it, by something about it.

Then he read Harry's notes:

Male child, b. January 14, 1954. Name: William.

Columbus Hospital, Chicago.

A note on another piece of paper read "St. Anselm's Orphanage, Chicago."

"No. No way." Billy pushed the file away. He told himself to stop reading right here, this had nothing to do with him, there was no point in going any further.

Still he sat there, the tips of his fingers resting on the folder as though drawn there. He felt a chill then, as though a sudden blast of cold air had invaded the room. In the silence he became aware of his breathing, audible, a slight gasping, as though he'd been running. And his heart, he could feel his heart, and a certain pressure behind his eyes. He felt slightly light-headed.

He shook his head, and then his hand flipped the folder open. He began to read, first Harry Strummer's scrawled notes and then his field report, and finally his formal report to the client.

The client.

Her name was Josephine Sadowski.

"Oh, Jesus. Jo."

He sat back and breathed through his mouth to settle himself. Then he straightened up and began paging through the file, his file, quickly at first, then starting with the earliest element, a handwritten letter from Josephine to Harry—addressing him as Harry!—explaining that at the age of forty-six she had begun looking for her grandson, given up years earlier by Josephine's daughter, recently deceased in a car accident. Billy brushed the reports to one side and stared at her letter, the childlike scribbling that in some way he'd recognized as soon as he'd seen it. In the letter, Josephine Sadowski explained that she knew she had no legal rights or hold on this boy, but he was now her only living relative and she wanted to see him, to assure herself that he was all right. She explained that she had no intention of disrupting his life or the life of the parents. She just wanted to know how it had all turned out for the child.

I want to know about his life, she wrote in her familiar scrawl. She apologized to Harry for taking advantage of an old friend, but she didn't know who else she could appeal to.

An old friend. God almighty.

Billy shook his head and felt the world shifting and spinning below him.

Finally, Billy turned to the document he'd avoided as soon as he saw it, Harry Strummer's report to "the client."

In his odd shorthand, an uncomfortable melding of cursive and printing and abbreviation and symbols, Harry had written two social security numbers, several names Billy did not recognize, with phone numbers, the name of a store he'd never heard of, and then one he recognized, Tad's TV Repair. There were three addresses, the first in Grand Rapids, Michigan, the second in Saginaw, the third in Lansing—the address of a printer on Grand River Avenue, where the family of Walter and Adele Fox lived above the storefront business, with their child William. Gus and Adele. Their child Billy Fox.

The final document in the folder was Harry's formal notification to the client that he had "determined the whereabouts of the individual in question." He gave no further information, but encouraged the client to come in so that they could discuss the particulars.

Billy picked up Josephine's note again. *I want to know about his life.* "Aw, Jo."

A heavy dullness had grown in the pit of his stomach, and he wondered if he would be sick. All at once a flood of thoughts and images pressed on him—he saw his childhood, his drunken father, a time in winter when they'd had no heat, he saw Josephine holding his mother's hand.

Images of his mother came to him now, and almost against his will he found himself inspecting, scrutinizing these moments to see if there had been any hints from Josephine that she was more to him than an unofficial aunt.

He thought of his mother again, recalled her painful discomfort, the fear in her eyes as she told him he'd been adopted. A rush of images came back to him now, and he saw them together, his mother and Josephine, he saw them laughing together in the small kitchen over coffee and cigarettes, the two of them turning the air in the room dense with smoke, as though a blue fog had settled on them. He saw them heading up the street on a summer night for a couple of beers at the local saloon, saw them perched at the edges of their chairs in the living room in earnest talk after the Old Man had left. He saw them making potato pancakes together, peeling and grating, forming the patties and dropping them into the Crisco and laughing as the grease crackled.

Billy saw his mother's face, her ease in Jo's company, saw them watching the old black-and-white TV in the kitchen—Jackie Gleason, Lawrence Welk. And now a singular moment came back, his mother listening, nodding, encouraging Jo as the older woman related some story of her past. He saw his mother's face, her eyes as she listened to Jo's tale. And then it came to him.

She hadn't known.

Billy sat there and reexamined his childhood, reviewed many moments of his life, and now it was clear that, hanging back on the periphery for so many years like an awkward guest, was the presence of Josephine. Aunt Jo.

He felt a sudden rage at them all for concealing the truth, *his* truth, *his* life. They'd all known—Josephine, and all of them here, Harry and Doris and probably Leo.

Shit, who else knows more about my life than I do?

He tried to make sense of this new knowledge and thought his head would explode with it.

With one finger he pulled Josephine's letter to him and read it again, this time hearing what lay beneath her words, her desperation, her anguish at the loss of her daughter, her need to find her grandson.

I want to know about his life

"Josephine, for Christ's *sake*."

Billy sank back in the chair. He put both hands to his temples and shut his eyes and wept, for himself and for Josephine and for his mother, for the loss of his youth and for his own confusion. He wept as he had not wept since childhood, and when he was finished, he forced himself to read all of the documents in the folder, carefully this time, missing nothing, for after all, it was his life.

Eventually he composed himself. He put the items back in something close to their original order, pushed the folder away from the center of his desk, and for a time sat there in thought. He wiped his face on his handkerchief, then blew his nose and went over to the cooler for a drink. He sipped from the paper cup and watched the traffic on Wells Street. After a while, he pulled Harry's chair over to the window and just sat there trying to make sense of all of this. His shock over the contents of his file gave way to a fresh rush of anger at the deception, fueled, Billy would have admitted, by his sense of humiliation.

But why would they do this to me?

The door to the office opened and Harry stepped in, closing it quietly behind him. Billy had the sudden thought that Harry had been out there for some time, just waiting for him to be finished.

"I went to get a sandwich," Harry said. "Should have brought you one."

"I'm not hungry."

"I guess not. I wouldn't feel much like eating. My guts would be churning. I know you probably feel a lot of anger right now, like you maybe want to deck somebody."

"I'm all right now. I feel kind of—I don't know, spent. I feel spent."

He looked at Harry and Harry made a "you-first" gesture. "Go ahead."

"Why? Why all this bullshit and, and—tricks? Why all the pretending that you just happened to hire me when all along you knew—"

Billy shook his head in frustration. Once again he faced a moment when it seemed he could not put his thoughts into any order, could not express himself. It seemed there were too many questions to ask all at once, he could not even articulate them all, but he needed them all answered at once.

"I just don't understand why you did all this," he finished.

After a short silence, Harry cleared his throat.

"First, nobody was trying to pull anything here. It was a simple thing. Your—Josie asked me to keep an eye on you."

"*Josie?*"

"That's how I knew her in the old days. We go pretty far back. I knew her whole family from the old neighborhood. Later on, years later, when she decided to find out what happened to her grandson, she hired me. Hard job, by the way. Those orphanages, they don't like to give out that information, they're never sure if it's the right thing, and the nuns—" Harry chuckled. "Toughest bunch on the planet. You keep the Army Rangers and the Green Berets and all those guys. Give me a bunch of nuns."

Billy watched and said nothing.

"So she hired me," Harry continued, "and I did my job. I found you in Lansing, Michigan, and she moved there to be close to you. She wrote me later, said she managed to make friends with your mother, kind of by accident, because she wasn't really trying to intrude there, she wasn't trying to insinuate herself into your life. She was going to watch you grow up, she said. You know, from a distance."

"No, I don't know. Harry, I—right now I don't feel like I know anything for certain."

"Well, that was her plan originally. And when she got to know your Ma, she was pretty happy about it."

"Did she tell you why they gave me up?"

"She didn't know. Her daughter was a runaway. Took up with the wrong guy, got pregnant, didn't tell Josephine anything about it, about you, I mean, for years. She was a tough, hard-nosed kid, she drank and she did some drugs and she decided to give you up. Most sensible thing she could have done, given the life she'd saddled herself with."

Harry paused to give Billy time to absorb this—that his mother had been a teenager on the run with a drinking problem.

"Eventually it came out, she told Josephine. And about a year later, she was dead. Fell down the stairs of the place where she was living—the projects over there by the river, where you go to get Wendell. That's where—that's where she died."

Billy nodded slowly and looked away, unable to trust himself not to cry. The pounding of his heart was almost audible. The shocks vied for his attention—the shock of learning that Josephine was his grandmother, the shock of learning the identity of his mother, the shock of learning that his entire time with Harry Strummer was a charade.

He looked around the office and nodded. "So—you hired me—what?—so you could keep an eye on me?"

"No. I hired you because I liked you. And I thought I could put you to some use. Good use, as it turned out."

"So how much did you tail me when I got here?"

"That first couple weeks, I followed you just enough to see if you were landing on your feet here. I saw you get a room, I saw you go to work for that day labor agency and those junk-haulers. I missed the night you got yourself mugged, I was sorry about that. Welcome to Chicago, huh? But I watched to see that you were going to be all right here. That's what Josie asked me to do. Funny thing is, that day we met, that was an accident. I wasn't following you, didn't have any idea where you were that day, never expected to see you. And there you were, I saw you pick up my wallet, I saw you decide you weren't going to take it. The rest you know about. I hired you, I taught you a few things, maybe it wasn't worth your while, I don't know. Maybe now you'll think you just wasted all this time. I would hope you don't think that way, I'd hope you think you learned a few things. You'd be the one to decide that."

"Of course I learned things. That's not the issue. I feel like I've been lied to. Like I was the only one playing at detective. Billy Fox the amateur detective, and everybody else was in on the joke."

"There was no joke. Yeah, Doris knew about you, and she laughed at me when I hired you because she knew that wasn't part of the deal, part of my responsibility. And Leo just knows I have a history with your people. That's all."

"Now what?"

"That's up to you. But what I'd like you to do right now is take some time off. Just take some time and think. Take a week if you want. When you've done that, I think you'll know what to do next. It's not up to me, not up to anybody but you, Bill."

Harry Strummer sat with his hands clasped and hanging down between his knees. His skin seemed pale despite his tan, and his eyes were puffy. His face still showed the battering he'd taken just days earlier, and he seemed somehow older and smaller. Harry put his head down and looked exhausted. Harry's own troubles, Billy told himself, were far from over. Harry looked down at his hands, and Billy understood the depth of Harry's worry.

As Billy got to his feet, Harry looked up and said, "I'm sorry about all this if it—there was no intent to cause you pain or be deceptive or any of that. So if that happened, I'm sorry. But I'm not sorry I did this thing for Josie and I'm not sorry I took you into the agency."

As Billy moved away, he heard Harry say quietly, "Such as it is."

At the door he nodded. "I have to think about all this," Billy said, and pulled the door shut behind him.

. . .

He headed for the lake, through the park, shuffling through piles of newly fallen leaves, crossed the long bridge over the Outer Drive, and then along the beaches, strangely empty now that September had come. He walked all the way south until he reached the harbor and the museums, and he told himself he'd never marched this far in the Army. Indeed, it seemed to Billy that he'd spent the lion's share of his time in Chicago just walking, pounding pavement and looking for people, both on his own and as a member of the Peerless Detective Agency.

For some reason, as he walked in the fading sunlight, his childhood came back to him, and he remembered times when they had been happy—at least, such moments had passed for happiness in that house when the Old Man was sober and they weren't fighting over money. He recalled later times when to this small household they'd added their friend Josephine, who'd made it clear that she thought he was the most wonderful kid on the planet. Scenes came back to him now, scores of them, in which Josephine's reassuring presence was always a part of the moment, always somewhere in the background, if not arm-in-arm with all of them.

"My *grandmother*," he said aloud, forcing himself to acknowledge fact. He shook his head. "All these years. Jesus. My grandmother."

He thought again of the unfortunate young woman who had given birth to him but been unable to straighten out her life. It was difficult to call this faceless woman his mother, but she was. And now after all these years he knew who Billy Fox was.

Of course he thought of Rita, and after the world-altering revelations of this afternoon, his entire plan to find her and bring her home seemed like the ridiculous notion of a sixteen-year-old who has read too many bad books. More than that, it seemed unimportant now.

He found a bench and sat watching the sailboats and yachts bobbing at anchor, listened to the curious tinkling sound of rigging and tackle against masts. He suddenly had a vision of himself, a young guy sitting alone on a bench as dusk closed on the city and people took themselves to the places where they were welcome. Billy thought of his circumstances and his history and felt perfectly alone. He wished he hadn't come to Chicago, that he hadn't made his way back to the Midwest, that he'd gone on drifting. He wished he had a cigarette, he wished he had a half-pint of Jim Beam.

No, scratch that last one, he thought—he didn't need liquor. On one of the few occasions when the Old Man had made sense, he'd said, "*When you feel like shit, Bill, and you want to drink, that's the one time you shouldn't. If you feel like shit, booze will make you feel worse. It magnifies everything, anger, insults, your troubles, it makes everything worse. Believe me, I know.*"

Yeah, Billy said to himself, he would know, about this one thing, and I do believe him.

He thought of Millie then, imagined himself telling her all of this, and shook his head.

And as for Chicago—he watched the boats and felt the fading sunlight on his back, noted the change in the light and the lengthening shadows. He noticed now a faint note of fall in the air, a hint of cooler air.

No, he thought, it was good that he'd come here.

• • •

Billy washed up and put on a sportcoat, though he could not have explained why. He stopped in a bar and had two quick shots of bourbon, then walked for a while. Dusk had begun to transform Wells Street when he let himself into the darkened offices of Peerless Detective. He sat for a time staring into space and rehearsing what to say. Twice he reached for the phone and quickly lost his nerve. Then he straightened his back, shot his cuffs, picked up the phone.

He coughed, cleared his throat, listened to the drumbeat in his chest. He dialed Josephine's number.

Josephine picked up on the third ring, a tentative "Hello?" as though she might be unleashing new troubles.

You have no idea, Billy thought.

Billy said, "Hello, Jo. This is Billy."

"Oh, Billy, hello," she began.

"Your grandson," he said.

Josephine said, "Oh, Honey," and then she was crying, sobbing as though she might never stop. She tried to talk, to explain herself and justify it all, pouring out the heartbreak of two decades, coughing and choking on the words as Billy tried to stop her. It took him nearly five minutes to calm her, and longer than that to convince her that he was not angry.

"I wanted you to know it's all right, Jo. That's why I called. I don't need an explanation or an apology or anything."

She said "Okay," in a small, fragile voice and then cried, softer now, as though she'd exhausted herself. Billy made small talk about the heat and his job, and agreed with Josephine's assessment that Harry Strummer was "a very smart individual." Then she spoke of her daughter, hesitantly at first, then the words coming out in a torrent, and Billy let her go on about her child. He listened and made small comments to show his interest and waited as she blew her nose and composed herself.

Then she caught him off guard.

"Are you going to stay there, Billy? In Chicago?"

"Oh, I don't know."

"I just thought, you know, you've been there a while and you're doing good there. You're holding down a job. It's better than roaming around the country, which is not good for anybody."

"I guess so," Billy said. Billy told her he would be coming back to visit soon and then they "could talk about things."

"I've got some things to finish here, work, you know."

"You're sure you're not angry?"

"Of course not."

"I always wanted to tell you but I never had the nerve. I wasn't sure how you would react, I mean, to find out I was your, you know, your grandmother."

"You've always been special to me, Jo. And now I've got one more reason. It's better to know. Sometime you can tell me more about you and her."

"You know, Billy, I've never really had anybody I could talk to about her. I was always afraid I'd say too much and spoil everything."

"I know. It'll be okay, Jo," he said.

This one thing, at least this one thing will work out.

TWENTY-THREE

Crime of Opportunity

Billy went home and sat in his room, listening to the radio. So many things had been made clear to him. He revisited all the confusing moments of the past weeks, saw himself going through his many motions blithely unaware of how others might be seeing him. He saw how far his reality had been from the truth. For the first time, he felt genuinely embarrassed about all of it.

A moment from his Lansing days came back to him with odd clarity. He saw himself and Rita walking. In memory, he realized that Rita had been walking a pace or two ahead of him, sullen, smoldering over some argument with her despised father. He had tried to calm her down, asked her to talk it out. Suddenly Rita stopped, and he nearly walked into her. She gave him a hard look.

"You know what the trouble is, Billy? You're eighteen going on nineteen. I'm eighteen going on thirty."

With that, Rita had turned and begun walking faster. He saw himself trying to catch up and wondered if this scene were the true symbol of that relationship. He thought of the young woman he'd watched in the park with her little girl, and his heart sank. He told himself he would go there one more time. Now things were clear to him.

• • •

Billy followed them out of the park, kept back a half block or so. He watched as Rita took her daughter up the street, pausing once to bend over and listen to the child. In profile he could see her smiling. Even from this distance he could see that the child was Rita in miniature. He thanked God for this small kindness, that Rita's little girl didn't look like Kenny the Count.

She crossed the last street before the house that Billy had seen her sister enter, and he slowed down. He kept moving, but stopped at the curb as though he'd struck a wall and understood that he'd go no farther. His heart seemed to be swelling up, filling his chest, he couldn't breathe. The blood rushed to his ears, to his face.

For a moment he saw himself as a passerby might, a young man standing at the edge of a street, looking stiff and uncomfortable in a new shirt with the store creases still visible. He understood now that Rita, just a few yards away, no longer lived in the same world as Billy, this boy standing on a street corner. He wondered why he'd never understood this before, or why he'd refused even to imagine it.

In a thousand daydreams and fantasies, Billy had imagined this moment in endless variation, embellished by his fondest hopes and the stubborn hues of nostalgia. But in all those dreams there was one scenario he had never entertained until the night before in his room, and suddenly all his doubt and confusion had fallen away as he understood what he would do.

Billy waited for Rita to reach her house. He watched with a tightness in his throat as she helped her small child navigate the steps, saw them pause as the child found something to peer at on the stair. He saw Rita laugh at what the child said. Billy waited until they went inside, and then he walked away, feeling gutshot.

That night in his room, Billy lay on his bed and listened to the street noises and told himself there was no further reason for him to stay in Chicago. But where to next?

The fall-scented air came in through his window, the cold-water smells of the lake, the smells of dried vegetation, burning leaves. In those first days in the Uptown flophouse, an old-timer had told him, "You wait, son, wait for the fall, there's no season in Chicago like the fall, no season anywhere, if you ask me."

I see that, Billy Fox said to himself. He wondered what he might do with himself now that what had brought him here was finished. At that moment he felt a sudden surge of anger. He had made a sort of a life here for himself. Why did he have to leave? It seemed that all his life he'd let things decide his life for him, and for once he could make his own choices.

So I don't have a girl and I probably need to find a job, but I put a life together here. There's nobody can tell me I have to move on.

"That's settled," he said aloud. He decided to go for a walk.

As he wandered the streets he thought about his talk with Harry Strummer, and he recalled Harry's words—*Take some time off. Just take some time and think. Take a week if you want.*

And he now remembered coming into the office just as Doris asked, "*Now? With all this? Why now?*"

"*Why do you think?*"

A new idea began to form—He wants me out of the way. He doesn't want to involve me in whatever goes down.

• • •

Billy entered the office, conscious immediately of intruding on a private fight. Harry sat at his desk and looked steadfastly ahead of him. Billy saw the high points of color in Harry's cheeks, the flush across Leo's forehead, and wondered if they'd come close to blows. Leo sat at the edge of the desk and leaned over Harry, and there was an urgency to his entire being.

"So whatever you're planning, I'm in," Leo said. "That's settled."

Harry continued to stare straight ahead and Leo's face grew red. A stranger might have thought an assault was pending. Doris looked from Leo to Harry and let her gaze—an angry gaze, Billy would have said—rest on Harry for a moment.

They all seemed to notice Billy Fox at once.

"Hey, Kid," Harry said, and looked embarrassed. "You came back. I wasn't sure you would."

"Didn't have anything on my calendar. So I'm in, too."

"Now wait a minute, you don't even know what we're—"

Billy waved him off and sat at his desk.

"I like this kid," Leo said, amused.

"Bill, this is not your problem, you could—"

"Humor me for once."

Harry looked from Billy to Leo.

"This is not a game, Bill. It could be *a perilous endeavor.*"

"You mean like when they pounded you on the street that night? No shit."

Harry was shaking his head and then stopped. He raised both hands in a shrug and then said, "All right. You're in. But you gotta listen. This is no time for any cowboy shit."

"No question."

"All right then." Harry looked at him, shot an annoyed glance at Leo, and repeated, "All right."

"So now what?" Billy asked.

"Hot dogs," Leo said. He nodded agreement with himself. "First hot dogs, then we have a council of war."

"Council of war," Harry repeated. "Yeah, that's just what we'll do."

Billy nodded. He happened to notice Doris. She was giving Harry a look that Billy had not seen before, a look, he would have said, of perfect frustration. She gave a long shake of her head and went back to her work.

So it was that they sat around Harry's desk over half a dozen hot dogs and a mound of greasy fries and argued over the way best to handle this.

"Why not the cops?" Billy asked. "What am I missing?"

Doris turned. "You're not missing anything, Billy. He is." She jutted her chin at Harry. "He's bound and determined to do this as stupidly as he can."

Harry stared at a space just in front of her desk. "I want to settle this," he said. "I want to do this my own way."

"Which is stupid."

"It's my life."

Doris was about to argue the point and then seemed to catch

herself. She glared at him, and then she picked up her purse and left the office. Something told Billy she would not be back.

"So what are we going to do?"

"See, this guy is smart," Leo said with a mouthful of hot dog.

"Smart, yes, but an amateur, and that makes him unpredictable. The thing of it is he wants to make this final." Harry met Billy's gaze. "Do you understand? He wants to make this final. I talked to Dutch about this, Bill. If we could find all the people he's used—the girl with the phony address, these two punks that pounded me—maybe we could get him jail time for planning an assault. But it wouldn't be much. He took out the accountant himself, that I'm sure of, with no witnesses. I want this over. I want him out of my life."

Leo put down his hot dog. "Too bad we can't just take this guy out. Just follow him one night and drag him into an alley somewhere—"

"And what?"

"Beat his ass and put him in a cab, give the cabbie a hundred bucks and tell him to drop this guy off somewhere in Indiana."

"You're talking through your hat."

Leo smiled. "I know. It makes me feel better."

"So what are we gonna do?" Billy asked.

"We've got to bring him out in the open."

"How do we do that?"

Harry shrugged. "Give him a shot at what he wants."

"You."

"Sure."

"So you're going to—what? Go to his motel and stand in front of his door until he comes out?"

"Actually, I thought of doing that. But he wouldn't try anything in a place like that, with other people coming and going. Besides, I think I've already got his attention. He's staying close by now."

"You know this?"

"Is that a trick question? Of course I know this. I've tailed hundreds of people. I know what a tail does, I know what a tail looks like, and he's not a pro. He's crazy. It's laughable. It didn't take me long to pick him up, Bill. When he's in a car, it's always the same car—you're gonna tail somebody in a car, it's real helpful if you switch cars now and then. And on foot, he's pretty obvious. Stiff as a board. I turn around suddenly and there he is, staring up at the sky. Another tip, Bill. You're gonna tail a guy, try not to be the only guy on the street looking up at the sky if he turns around. You just look foolish."

Harry doodled on his desk blotter. "I tailed him once. Over in Lincoln Park—he likes the park. He was walking down there by the lagoon—"

"Which is actually a misnomer," Leo pointed out. "That's the pond. The lagoon actually feeds into the lake."

"Thank you, Professor of Geography," Harry said, looking irritated. "Anyhow, I spotted him and I followed him all the way around that lagoon—that *pond* thing, and watched him. It was getting dark, and I could just barely see him after a while, but I could make out that he was talking to himself, and kind of whacking himself with a fist against his thigh. Then he sat down on a bench, and he was having conversations, gesturing and pointing and nodding, and he looked—" Harry shook his head. "It was kinda chilling."

"So what's your plan?"

"I'm going to break a pattern or two for him. I'm going to let him see me the way he wants."

"What does that mean?"

"You heard the term 'crime of opportunity'? Well, we're going to give him a chance at a crime of opportunity."

"Meaning what?"

"You'll see. I don't have it all worked out yet, but I will soon. Then I'll tell you what you need to know."

• • •

Two nights later, Billy waited in the park, down near the water, waited so long that he wondered if the plan had changed.

"Patience," Harry had said. "You're gonna need patience for

this, Bill, you're gonna have to wait. In position."

Well, I'm in position. So where is he?

To the west, Billy could still see the reddish glow of the setting sun, but in the park dusk had already settled. Then Harry Strummer came into view, and Billy sank back behind a clump of bushes. He understood then why Harry had taken so long.

Harry Strummer was drunk. He walked straight down to the pond, a drunk's walk, a little extra stiffness as he tried to muster his balance and control his legs. At one point Billy saw him stumble, then shake his head.

Aw, Harry. This is just going to complicate everything.

The hastening twilight had emptied the park. The sidewalk around the pond was empty. In the distance Billy thought he saw a homeless man sleeping on a bench. He wondered if Harry had called Leo off at the last minute.

Harry stopped at the edge of the pond, leaned on the railing, and stared out at the two small, scraggly islands on the far side of the water. He gripped the railing and appeared to be trying to steady himself. Then he gave up. He found the nearest bench and stumbled onto it, losing his hat in the process. Billy watched as Harry tried twice to retrieve it, finally caught hold of it and put it back on his head. And then he nodded off. His head bobbed once as he tried to wake up, and then his head sank forward. After a moment he slumped to one side.

Billy shook his head and began to creep forward. Then a figure seemed to emerge from the shadows among the trees and moved into view on the far side of the pond. Billy froze. David Moncrief, clad entirely in black, walked to the edge of the water and leaned against the railing as a trio of ducks swam by. For a time Moncrief paid no attention to the sleeping figure on the bench just behind him. Billy moved forward and hunkered down behind a tree ten yards or so from Harry Strummer, and wondered if he could close the distance between them if he had to.

Moncrief frowned in the direction of the sleeping homeless man. Then he turned and looked at Harry and smiled. He said something Billy could not hear, then tilted his head slightly and moved forward a couple of steps. He said Harry's name and then gave a little shake of his head.

"Harry Strummer," he said, louder.

Harry gave a start and his hat slid down one side of his head. As he straightened the hat, Harry sat forward and tried to steady himself, a portrait of perfect confusion.

Moncrief bent over slightly, hands on his knees as though attempting conversation with a shy child.

"Hello, Harry. Wake up."

Harry's head bobbed and the hat slid forward again, and he caught it just before it fell off.

"I've been looking forward—" Moncrief began.

Harry Strummer sat up, straight-backed and alert. Sober. Billy smiled and moved closer.

"I thought you'd never get here, Moncrief. I made you half a mile from here. You'll never learn to tail somebody. Might as well be wearing a sign."

Moncrief stiffened and looked off-balance for a moment, then nodded.

"Ah, a little theater for my sake, huh? Okay, well done. But here we are anyway, Strummer. I've waited a very long—"

Harry held up a hand.

"Save it for somebody who gives a shit. I know all about you, Moncrief. And I know what this is about so save me the speech."

"You don't know anything."

"I know this is about your uncle, and your mother. I know you blame me for his death and I know your mother died about six years ago and you decided to come looking for somebody to take it out on."

"Yeah, the people who caused—all of it, everything."

"Your uncle caused all of this."

"No, you and that prick Dietrich."

"I didn't even know Dietrich."

"Took me almost six years to find him, and lo and behold I find

Harry Strummer half a mile away from Dietrich. I looked for you all the way out to L.A., and then I gave up on you. But I got lucky and found Dietrich, and here you are a couple of blocks away from him. What an amazing coincidence."

"I never even knew he was here. Your uncle set all this up. He had me looking into his partner's embezzlement, when all along he just wanted to know if his wife was having an affair with him. That embezzlement crap was a sideshow."

"No. My mother told me how it was. These people all betrayed him, and his whole life collapsed. And she understood him better than anybody."

From the corner of his eye Billy caught movement. Half a block away a pair of men came into view. Gay men, arm in arm.

Witnesses would be good right now, Billy thought.

"So your mother and Frank Hannah, they—what?"

"They had an understanding. And I knew about it. I used to dream that Uncle Frank would divorce his tramp of a wife and marry my Ma. And he would be my father."

"Some father," Harry said, and Billy understood that Harry was deliberately baiting him.

That old death wish thing, huh, Boss?

Moncrief stiffened. "He was the greatest man I ever knew. I would have been—"

"Oh, save it. He murdered two unarmed people and then shot himself so he wouldn't have to face the music. Don't tell me about his 'greatness.' Cowardly prick."

Something changed in Moncrief's face, and he drew a long slender knife from inside his jacket. Billy looked up the path and saw the gay couple in a passionate embrace, oblivious to anything but each other. No help there.

Moncrief muttered something Billy couldn't hear and moved toward Harry, and then Billy was running, racing as he had not run since boyhood. The breath caught in his chest as he tried to close the distance between them. Harry was on his feet now and backing away, but Moncrief was on him, catlike, and slashed at him. The blade tore through Harry's sleeve and drew blood, and Moncrief nodded.

"This is how it goes, Strummer."

He moved forward with the knife and Harry was moving back awkwardly, holding his bloody arm.

Billy ran and as he ran he saw it all in a blur—Harry bleeding, Moncrief slashing and then turning slightly as he noticed Billy bearing down on him, Harry stumbling back onto the grass, Moncrief tripping momentarily over a tree root, and Billy thought his heart would burst with urgency. He heard himself shouting, screaming Moncrief's name, and as Moncrief faced him, Billy leapt on him. Moncrief swiped at him with the knife and Billy felt the sting as it slashed him through his jacket. But he caught Moncrief high and took him to the ground. They scrambled to their feet and Moncrief faced him.

Moncrief took one step toward Billy, and from the corner of his eye Billy saw the homeless man rouse himself from his bench—rousing himself and pointing a gun and yelling, "Freeze, you cocksucker."

Dutch Lindner. Dutch stood some thirty feet away holding a gun in a shooter's stance. For a second, Billy thought Moncrief would charge the old cop. Then Moncrief began running toward the far side of the pond. Dutch fired a shot that missed and Billy began pursuit, then stopped as Moncrief himself was stopped by new trouble. The gay lovers blocked his way. Then they began walking toward him, faster now, sure of themselves—Fornier and Cribb.

Moncrief ran a few steps away from the pond, and then stopped as a tall figure emerged from behind a tree—Leo.

Billy looked from Leo to Fornier and Cribb, and back to Dutch, and nearly laughed in spite of himself.

They closed on Moncrief then, and Moncrief turned his attention back to Harry, just in time for Harry to smack him in the side of the face with a rock. Moncrief staggered and Harry hit him again, and Moncrief went down, cut at his hairline and over one eye.

Moncrief scrambled to his feet, left eye squinting against the bleeding. He held the knife out before him and seemed to be talking to himself, muttering something under his breath.

Harry stood his ground and Billy and Leo moved up beside him. They advanced to the edge of the pond, the four of them, Dutch, Harry, Leo, and Billy, and Moncrief backed away toward the pond.

For a moment no one spoke. Then Dutch said, "Toss the knife."

Moncrief said, "Fuck you, fuck all of you," and then he turned and leapt into the pond.

"Oh, you don't want to do that," Harry said as Moncrief splashed into the dark water, seemed to bounce, then stumbled to his feet.

Dutch let out a short bark of a laugh.

Moncrief righted himself, one side of his face covered in mud. He stood there in water only to his waist. He stared around him at the water, as though the pond had betrayed him. He said "Shit!" and Billy thought he'd never heard a man impart such feeling into a single syllable.

Leo laughed and looked at Billy. "You see, it's not an actual lagoon. You want to drown yourself, you got to go to the lake and jump off the rocks. But not here."

They stared at Moncrief, who had begun walking off through the shallow water, knife still in hand. A crowd began to gather now, watching Moncrief make his way to the larger of the darkly-wooded islands at the far side of the pond, where no doubt the police would come to take him off. Somewhere in the distance, Billy heard a siren.

Fornier and Cribb approached Harry.

"He got you, huh?" Fornier said.

"I'm all right. I owe you. The both of you."

"That's right," Cribb said, but Fornier just patted Harry on the shoulder and said, "Come on, Dennis. I'm hungry."

Cribb caught Billy's eye, nodded, and was off.

"Not so dramatic, huh, Bill?" Harry said. "Not like the movies."

"In the movies," Dutch said, "There's usually a speech, the villain makes a fine speech."

"I'm thinking Doris was right. You could have gotten killed,"

Billy said. He pointed to the wound in Harry's upper arm.

"Forget it. Looks like he got you, too, Bill. You all right?"

Billy looked down at the bloodied front of his jacket. He pushed away the material—a long cut, bloody but not deep, across his stomach. He shook his head. "I just bought this jacket."

"You cut this a little too fine, Harry," Dutch said, and Harry shrugged and gave a sideways nod, conceding the point.

"You had me convinced you were drunk there, Boss," Billy said.

"You know I never drink when I work."

Dutch looked at Harry's arm. "You need to get that looked at." Then he looked at Billy. "The botha you."

"It's okay," Harry said. "I know a guy."

They waited in the gathering dusk and watched as the police improvised a means to get at Moncrief on the island. They commandeered two of the zoo rowboats and rowed their way to the far end of the pond for a small invasion of Moncrief's island. Predictably, he fought them off like a bloodied animal, swiping with his knife, then coming at them with a rock and finally hurling a bottle he found there. In the end he charged back into the water, where an enterprising cop knocked him flat with an oar.

As they walked toward Clark Street, Billy turned to Harry.

"Fornier and Cribb. I was surprised to see them."

"I called in an old marker. They're all right, Fornier and Cribb."

"And they're good. I thought it was a couple of, you know, gay guys making out."

Harry raised his eyebrows and gave him a long look.

Billy blinked. "Oh. So that part wasn't—"

Harry smiled and patted him on the shoulder. "It's a big world out there, Bill."

Dutch drove Billy and Harry to a nearby hospital for their wounds, and while they were waiting for medical attention, the cops brought in Moncrief. Blood streamed down his face from several scalp wounds, and one eye was closed and swollen like a plum. But he wasn't through, cuffs or no. He swung wildly at the nearest police officer, kicked at an orderly, spat at a nurse, tried to push a gurney into a cop, and he was still wrestling and screaming when they carted him off.

The cut on Billy's chest took eight stitches. He caught a cab, suddenly exhausted. A block from his place he asked the cabbie to turn back to Clark Street. The diner was busy with late-night traffic, and he could see Millie taking orders, laughing at a customer's joke. He caught the driver's eyes in the rear-view mirror and realized how he looked, a guy with a bloody shirt and torn jacket. He shook his head and had the driver take him home. The cabbie did his best to make small talk, but looked clearly relieved when he was able to drop Billy off.

TWENTY-FOUR

Things of Value

The next morning Billy arrived at a darkened office. When he put his hand on the knob he realized that the door was open. Harry Strummer sat inside with the shades drawn and the lights off. His cigarette made a small point of orange light in the center of the dark.

"Hello, Bill. You're here early."

"Do you want the lights on?"

"No. But you can pull up the shades, let the world in."

The bright light of morning flooded the room, making Harry wince. The cool morning air cut through the smoke. Billy set down his coffee and looked over at Doris's desk, strangely tidy, the chair pushed all the way in and the top clear of anything that had a connection to Doris. Her radio was gone.

Billy bit back the impulse to say something. He went to the window and looked out at the morning traffic on Wells Street. Then he glanced at Doris's desk again.

"She's gone, Bill. And by now, long gone."

"She left town?"

Harry took a puff, blew out smoke, pondered the question, shrugged. "Me. She left *me*. She has ended our—whatever word you can apply to this thing we had—she has ended it the only way she knows how, by putting space between us. So, yeah, she left town."

"Do you have any idea where she is?"

"Oh, I have some idea, but I also know she wants me to understand that she is gone, so if I know Doris, and there's nobody in my whole life I ever got to know better than Doris, she will deliberately avoid the very places where it would make the most sense for her to go. She has broken her patterns."

"You know that for sure?"

"More or less."

"You checked out her place, her apartment?"

"Yeah. But I didn't have to, I knew what I'd find. She cleared out, took everything she could carry with her and left the rest. You know, she lived in a rented room, furnished. She told me she was never going to get another apartment until she knew for sure she was going to stay for good. She had too many times in her life when she thought she had something and it turned out to be nothing."

Harry made a little wave. "Like now. Like with me."

"This stuff with Moncrief, it all spooked her."

"Nah. I mean, of course it spooked her a little, but that wouldn't be why she'd leave. This is about me, about how I went about handling all of it."

Harry ground his cigarette into the ashtray.

"She wanted me to show her that she meant something, that it was, you know, more important than handling this asshole with his need for vengeance."

"*If?*" Billy shook his head at the concept of Harry Strummer suddenly gone inarticulate. "You mean, your thing with Doris, that *if?*"

Harry gave a silent laugh. "Yeah. That's what I mean, 'my thing with Doris.' All the different aspects of my life, all the situations I've ever been in, all the relationships and friendships and love affairs, you add them all up and they more or less make up a life. In my case, in the background, through all of those times, there is Doris, always a part of it for what seems like my whole life. Kid, I have trouble remembering a time when she wasn't in my life. Even when I was with somebody else, she was always there, I was always aware of where she was and who she was with and what was happening in her life. And when I look back at those times, I can almost see us watching each other from a distance, and we're both thinking the same thing: *all this other stuff is temporary, and you and I know how this will all end up*. Always, we were both always thinking that."

"So you and Doris, I mean—you love Doris."

Harry gave him a surprised look. "Of course. Sure, I do. I guess I always have. Always."

"And she loves you."

"Used to."

"People don't just stop loving somebody."

Harry gave him a rueful smile. "No, huh? You got it all figured out? Well, maybe they don't. But sometimes they move on. They cut their losses and move on and that's what she's doing."

"So what are you going to do, Harry?"

Harry looked around the office and frowned. He made a dismissive gesture with the cigarette.

"Look at this," he said, as though he hadn't heard Billy's question. "This is what I've got. I've got this little two-by-four room as my 'place of business.' I'm forty-nine years old and I live in a room smaller than this place. I've got a car with a hundred and fifty thousand miles on it. This is all I've got to show for my time on the planet."

"Is that how we do it now? We judge people by the size of the place they live in? Or the mileage on their beater? Because if that's so, then I'm in the shitter, Harry. I live in a, like, a cubicle. My car's a 'Vette, but it exists only in my daydreams."

"You're a kid. You have all kinds of time to accomplish things. You made it in the big city, for starters."

Billy waved him off. "Go out there on that street where you know everybody, just grab the first guy who says hello to you and give them that speech you just gave me. See if that's how they see you."

Harry just shook his head and walked over to the window. He leaned on the windowsill and peered out and puffed at his cigarette. Billy watched him for a moment and then it struck him that a person could be said to live in a wider space, not just wherever he hung his hat at night.

"That's your place in the world, Harry. Right there, where you're looking, that's where Harry Strummer lives. You're like the Mayor of Wells Street. That little room, that's just where you sleep."

Harry turned, still leaning on the windowsill, and smiled over his shoulder. He mouthed *the Mayor of Wells Street* and shook his head.

"So what are you going to do, Harry?" Billy said again.

"Nothing. I can't go after her."

"Why not?"

Harry turned now. "You just went through that. How'd it turn out for you?"

"Different story. Mine was a daydream. I gave up. She didn't love me. I think yours does."

"I shouldn't have said that, I'm sorry."

"It's all right."

Harry returned to his desk and sat down. For a long moment neither one said anything. Then Harry pulled his notepad over to him and began making a list. Without looking, Billy understood what he was doing.

"You ought to be able to do this. It's what you do for other people."

Harry nodded absently. "She'll make it difficult. Maybe impossible."

"Maybe. Maybe she won't. What do I know?"

Harry smiled. "You know a lot, for a rube from Lansing, Michigan."

Harry paused, scratched his forehead with the end of the pen. He looked around the office.

"Leo's in Florida. He won't be back for a while. He's got family down there, and you didn't hear this from me, but I think he's got a woman down there, too. Don't be surprised if he comes back married or something. Anyhow—"

He looked Billy in the eye.

"I don't know what your plans are, Bill."

"I don't have any."

That part was more perfectly true than anything he could say. He had no plans now. He was a free agent once more like the guy who had rolled in on the midnight Greyhound back in May.

"But I thought I'd stick around. I like it here."

"What about—I don't know what your situation is."

"Don't have one."

After a while, Harry had to ask. "That other girl—"

Billy looked away.

"What?"

"That's—" He caught himself about to say *done—it's finished.*
He shrugged.

"Well. I'm sorry. She seemed like a nice girl."

"She's a nice girl, all right."

Harry looked around the office again.

"I could use somebody—"

"Yeah, I'll hold down the fort. While you're, you know, until
you're back."

"Thanks, Bill." He smiled as though a new thought had struck.
"You'll be the entire agency."

"Yeah. I'll be Peerless Detective."

"Might be a while."

"I'm not going anywhere."

. . .

They had a cup of coffee together in a small restaurant up the street.
Harry chain-smoked and drew up a list of business matters to be
tended to, made notes on two cases.

"I'm renting a car. You can use mine. Just don't crack it up."

When they left, Harry patted him on the shoulder.

"I'll be talking to you."

Harry headed up Wells Street to his car and Billy paused to watch
him. He walked head down, clearly tired, the old limp magnified.
For a moment, Billy could imagine Harry Strummer finished, an
old man shuffling through a crowded sidewalk unnoticed by the
people around him. Then a young black guy loading cases of wine
onto a two-wheel dolly called out to him and Harry waved, and

a young waitress rushed out of a restaurant and they greeted one another and Harry said something to make her laugh. A cop car slowed down, and the cop riding shotgun called out to Harry and now it was Harry's turn to laugh. He waved the cops off and went to his car, and now he was walking straight-backed with quick sure steps, a fellow with a purpose. He paused to wipe something from the hood of his car, and Billy saw that he was smiling.

• • •

Billy Fox saw the irony in all of it, that just when he thought he had an idea of who he was, and just when he'd found a place where he thought he belonged, he found himself awash in uncertainty. He spent much of that weekend in endless walking through the warm September days and the cool nights, making great looping circuits of streets and neighborhoods he'd never seen trying to decide what to do. Twice he let his path take him past the diner on Clark Street, and each time he slowed down, hoping for a chance meeting of the eyes, a chance to read her face. On Sunday evening, he went by the diner and saw that she was not working, and without really having a plan, he headed for her street.

An ice cream truck had parked on the corner and drawn a crowd, mostly kids holding their money in sweaty fists and smiling up at the pictures on the truck. On an impulse, Billy slipped into line and when it was his turn, ordered two ice cream bars.

In the airless hallway of Millie's building he stood, paralyzed by indecision, and stared at her mailbox and the buzzer for her bell. The wrappers on the ice cream bars were beginning to sweat.

Now what?

He rang her bell and waited, then rang it again. Something wet ran down his arm. He stepped out onto the street and peered up at her window for signs of life. Moisture ran down his other arm. He looked at the ice cream bars, caught a glimpse of his reflection in the glass of her doorway—an awkward-looking guy holding ice cream bars out at arm's length as though they might explode.

A dark-haired woman emerged from the building and gave him a curious look.

Yeah, I'd look at me too, lady.

Finally with his teeth he tore the wrapper from one of the ice cream bars and took a bite just as a large piece of chocolate began sliding down the bar. He caught the chocolate with his tongue, then licked at the bar quickly to prevent another slide of the chocolate. Ice cream dripped white and wet down over his knuckles and down the back of his hand and wrist. He looked at the second bar and saw that the wrapper was stuck to the bar like a wet shirt, and could only imagine the mess that was taking place inside.

He shook his head and began to eat his bar faster, at one point licking first the bar and then his knuckles and finally his wrist, and it was just then, as he was running his tongue across his wrist in a vain attempt to catch a wayward drop that he realized he was being watched. He turned and saw Millie. His heart was hammering in his chest.

Jesus, a guy tried to kill me with a knife and I'm terrified of this little girl.

She stared at him straight-faced, and at first he thought she might slip past him and enter her building without a word, but then he caught the dancing light in her eyes. He looked at his bar and his hand, now coated with ice cream, and made a sudden lurch to lick at the newest dripping on his fingers. He looked back at her and wondered if there had ever been a moment in his life when he'd felt so foolish. She bit her lip and looked away.

Millie started to laugh, then caught herself. He turned to face her, holding his bar out over the sidewalk, where it began to create a small brown-and-white pool, the flakes of chocolate swimming in the ice cream like tiny boats. Millie shook her head at him, and Billy tried to explain why he was standing there covered with ice cream and why he'd come back at all, but his words made a logjam in his throat. She did nothing to make it easier on him, just fixed the large gray eyes on him and waited. Billy watched her and felt the blood in his cheeks and hoped no one else was watching.

"What are you doing here, Billy?" she said. Before he could

answer she added, "What a mess."

"This one's supposed to be yours," Billy said, holding out the second ice cream bar, now shapeless inside its wrapper.

Millie took it, tore the top of the wrapper open with a deft movement and began licking at the ice cream. She folded the paper halfway down the bar, then made a little twist at the base, where it met the stick, and held it up to Billy.

"See, Hon? It starts coming apart on you, you just wrap it like this and it won't come running down your hand. Oh, look at you, you've got ice cream all the way to your elbow. Don't they have ice cream bars in Michigan?"

"I bought it and then I decided to get you one, and you weren't home so there I was with two ice cream bars and—" It all sounded utterly stupid to him, so he stopped and shrugged, then took a bite of his ice cream.

Her face changed and she said, "Why are you here?"

"I don't know."

She nibbled at her ice cream for a moment, then held out her hand.

"You done with that mess?"

He held out the remains of his ice cream bar and she took both of them to a trash can a few feet away at the corner. She came back and stood a couple of feet away.

"What do you want, Billy?"

"I thought we should talk."

"We talked already, we settled it," she said.

"We talked about it, yeah, but I don't think we settled it."

She frowned. "What didn't we settle? We didn't settle it far as you're concerned, you mean."

She folded her arms around her, as though protecting herself. She looked at his arms and shook her head.

"Look at you, you got it all up and down your arm. There's little tiny kids can eat an ice cream without getting it on theirselves like that." She looked at the street, gazed up at the sky, and sighed. She shook her head.

Billy was about to leave when she said, "Come in and get yourself cleaned up. You can't walk around like that."

She herded Billy into her apartment like a stray pup and then sat on the edge of her chair watching him as he washed his hands and arms.

"Missed a spot. There's chocolate on your elbow." She shook her head.

"Thanks," he said when he was finished.

She nodded toward the sofa. "Sit."

He dropped himself onto it, looked at his hands, and opened his mouth to fill the silence, but she beat him to it.

"What are you doing here, Billy?"

"I was looking for you. I wanted to see you. I went by the diner."

"Why?" She seemed genuinely puzzled.

"Like I said. I wanted, you know, to see you."

"No. I don't know. Trouble is, you don't know what you want."

"Do you?"

"Don't make this about me. You're the one can't make up his mind. So why did you come here?"

He took a moment to compose himself, and understood that what he said to her, how he phrased it, would determine everything. Even if he didn't fully understand what he meant by "everything."

"I wanted to see if you were still here. I had this idea you would be leaving."

"Leaving? Why would I be *leaving?*"

Her eyes flashed in anger, and Billy found himself leaning back.

"Why would I leave? This is where I live now, for better or worse. This is my home. It's not much, but it's what I've got. I have a place to live and a job, and I have some friends here. Leaving would mean I gave up on it here."

Just because of you, her look said.

"I guess I'm the one who probably ought to be leaving."

"Seems to me you've done pretty well here." She tilted her head to one side. "What about your girl from Michigan? That's not gonna work out?"

"No. There was never a chance that was going to work out. And I think I knew it all along. All that time I was looking for her."

Billy looked away. It was the truth, but hard to admit and strange to hear himself pass this judgment aloud. Strange, and embarrassing. None of this was a good idea. He forced himself to look at Millie. She said nothing, but watched him.

"Rita stopped being interested in me five years ago. She came all the way here to leave her old life behind her, and I decided—I just couldn't mess up her life for her. And the funny thing is, after all this time looking for her, I wouldn't even know what to say her." He gave a short laugh at himself.

Millie blinked, shook her head.

"You never even got to talk to her?"

"I could have. I found her, I know where she lives. But I'm not gonna do that. I'm staying out of her life."

"Poor thing," Millie said, and Billy wasn't sure if she meant him or Rita.

"Her life's, you know—" Billy made a waving gesture with one arm. "She's not for me, her life has gone in another direction. She's not for me. Maybe you're not either, Millie. I understand that."

She watched him until he grew uncomfortable in her silence. It struck Billy that no matter how much he had learned, how much he'd changed, there were areas in which he was still without a clue.

Millie had turned slightly so that she was facing the far wall of her apartment. For a moment he had the sense that she'd forgotten him. He got to his feet.

"Sit down, Billy," she said, then frowned. "You in a hurry to leave?"

"No, not at all. I have no place to be." He did as he was told.

"You asked me if I was leaving. What if I was? Would that bother you?"

"Yes."

"Well, I am, actually."

"Oh," he said, and felt his stomach tighten.

She smiled. "That was mean. I'm teasing you. I'm going home

for a week to see Mama. It's been awhile. It's always good for me to see her, help me get my head on straight."

"I'm probably going back up to Lansing sometime soon, too. I have some things to take care of there." She nodded, and he bit back the impulse to tell her about Josephine and his own newly discovered back story. "Things I just learned about."

"Something bad?"

"No, not at all. And I'll tell you all about it when we're both back. I mean, that's if—"

If what? You're really smooth, Billy.

She gave him a long, frank look and then got up and went to her tiny stove to put on coffee.

She came back and sat on her sofa. He shifted in the chair and the stitches across his stomach pulled at him. He grunted.

"You okay?"

"I've been having adventures."

Millie tucked her legs under her and waited for him to begin.

TWENTY-FIVE

Peerless Detective

Billy spent most of that first Monday looking over Harry Strummer's notes and his own notes from two cases Harry had asked him to look into. The phones were dead, almost as though the world knew that Harry was "out of the office."

He took a walk through the park at lunch, and on the way back, he saw Babe peering into a trash can. Billy caught up with him and dragged him to a small Greek diner nearby and bought him lunch. As they chatted, Billy tried to learn more about Babe's life, but Babe showed no inclination to speak of private matters. When Billy asked him where he lived, the old man merely said, "My current lodgings are in a state of flux."

As he made his way back to the office, he smiled at the recollection of Babe's phrasing—"My current lodgings," the same words he'd used in describing Moncrief's hotel room.

And now Billy realized why he'd recognized those words. He had, of course, heard them before, in a Greyhound bus station tavern, from an old man—recently shaved and bleeding from razor cuts.

Babe!

Clean-shaven then, but still the same cackling old crazy. And simply one more cog in Harry Strummer's reception committee for the young and very green Billy Fox.

This time Billy laughed.

• • •

That night he drove Millie to the bus station. When she got out, she leaned over and kissed him.

"I'll miss you," he said.

She paused and looked at him and then smiled. "You hold that thought, Billy-boy."

Billy came into the office of the Peerless Detective Agency and opened the window facing Wells Street. The cool air coming in off the lake smelled of the water, of fall, of change. He took off his sport coat, adjusted his tie, and sat down at his desk.

He popped the top off his coffee and sipped, then read the paper. Two calls came in during that first hour. The first caller was a man named Zivic who wanted to know if the agency could find a runaway boy. Billy told him to come in and talk about it. The second call came ten minutes later.

"Good morning. Peerless Detective," Billy said.

The caller paused. Billy heard the caller's wet breathing, uncertainty.

"Peerless Detective," he repeated. "This is Billy Fox."

The caller said "Hello?" in a tremulous voice.

Billy felt himself grinning. "Hello, Mrs. Ricci," he said.

Soon Whelan is swept up into a whirlwind of old feuds, dark pasts, unlikely romances...and a killer hiding in plain sight.

KILLER ON ARGYLE STREET

Chicago Private Investigator Paul Whelan takes the case when an elderly woman asks him to look into the disappearance of Tony Blanchard, a young man she'd taken in after his parents died. Instead, Whelan discovers a string of murders, all tied to a car-theft ring.

All the evidence suggests that Tony is dead as well, but Whelan keeps digging until he finds himself surrounded by a dangerous maze of silent witnesses, crooked cops, and people willing to kill to keep the truth from surfacing. When a friend from Whelan's past emerges—a friend Whelan thought long dead—his investigation takes a dangerous turn; one that brings him no closer to Tony, and a lot closer to his own demise.

THE RIVERVIEW MURDERS

Margaret O'Mara's brother disappeared thirty years earlier, so when his last known associate is found murdered, O'Mara hires Chicago PI Paul Whelan to investigate.

Whelan makes the rounds through seedy bar and dilapidated apartment buildings where he discovers connections to a long-gone Chicago amusement park where another murder took place forty years prior.

Soon, Whelan finds himself navigating his way through dark pasts, deep secrets, and a mystery that may cost him his life.